MW00471297

The Seven Deadly Simpson Brothers

Adjoa Sarfo-Bonsu

ISBN: 9781520112329

For my family.

ACKNOWLEDGEMENTS

I would like to thank each and every reader who has supported *The Seven Deadly Simpson Brothers* as the first book I ever wrote and shared on Wattpad. It wouldn't be where it is now otherwise.

1

Gun shots from outside my window made me jump, spilling some of my tea.

Usually they didn't startle me as I was so used to them, but every now and again the deafening bangs would catch me off guard.

I used an old napkin to wipe the hot beverage off my now scalded fingers and switched off the kitchen light. I didn't want to peek behind the curtains to see if it had been anything fatal, I didn't have the stomach for that tonight.

Walking into the cramped living room, I sat with my knees drawn up in the tattered sofa I had bought second-hand a few years back when I'd got the place. The one-bedroom apartment had suffocating damp in the tiny bathroom and flaking white paint on the ceiling as well as on most of the window panes. I'd gotten it when I was sixteen and had been renting the place out for the past two years. Even with the poor condition it was in, it took nearly all the money I made from my part-time job to keep up with payments.

I sipped on my hot milky tea and let my mind drift away from those self-pitying thoughts and out of the room. I wondered who had fired the shots I'd heard outside. Had it been one of the Santiagos or one of the Simpsons? The family names belonged to the two rival gangs who played dominant roles in this part of the city I lived, both seeming to consist of only males. I knew that the Santiagos were Venezuelan and the Simpsons were English. I didn't know the details of their upbringings but it was general knowledge that they were both deeply involved with crime, and had been from an early age.

I didn't see any of them often, but when I did I made sure it was just a brief encounter. They could stare me down and make me feel intimidated even without trying. It wouldn't be hard; I was quite a timid character around people I didn't know, especially males. That's just the way it was and I was sure it had quite a lot to do with my upbringing.

By the time my mind was back in the room, my drink had cooled down considerably, so I drank it in gulps before heading to bed. As I slipped between my sheets, I hoped that I wouldn't have any bad dreams about my past which would always creep up on me when I was most vulnerable. I said a little prayer to a God that never seemed to hear me and let my eyes close.

2

School had ended in the early afternoon and I'd gone straight to the pub to work five hours straight. By the time I'd finished serving, my feet ached, my back was sore and all I wanted to do was have a shower and go straight to sleep.

I walked quickly through the chilly autumn night with my coat zipped up all the way to my chin and a worn tartan scarf snaked round my neck. I kept my head down as I made my way home, careful to keep under the street lights and avoid dark areas. The streets weren't really that safe at night, especially for a girl on their own, but I had to make a living and that meant taking risks.

I lived in the west side of the area, which was Simpson territory, and I was reminded of that by the numerous works of graffiti in my vicinity that belonged to that gang. The most common was the seven headed snake, each head for each brother. The Santiagos too had their own symbol, a spike stabbed into the bleeding finger of 'society'. Apparently it represented how much a small gang could cause pain and discomfort to those who were against them. The same way a splinter would do to one's fingertip.

As I walked, my eyes traced the grubby slabs of concrete and I found myself trying to imagine a lifestyle completely different to the one I had. One where I could come home to a big warm house, bubbly and alive, full of family who loved and cared for me as I did in return. Perhaps I had a sister, or more than one, who I could share things with and stay up late at night talking endlessly about crushes with. Or maybe a few brothers who would play rough with me but at the same time look out for me. Would they look like I did? Be brown-eyed and blonde haired like me, or a little different? And what of my parents? The very idea of having two parents, like a lot people had, was alien to me. Would my mother hug me and kiss me when I felt down, teach me how to bake? Would my father tease me about boys and teach me how to do things like play golf or go fishing? Dreaming like this pushed out the truth about my childhood, even if it was only momentary.

I was so lost in my thoughts, I hadn't realised I had walked straight onto a dark stretch of pavement. The lights here had stopped working, they were old pieces of junk that the council disregarded, but I hadn't noticed in time or I would have changed route a while back. Suddenly I felt more alone than I had been previously and I could feel fear rising up my throat. The sound of my heart pounding filled my ears and I couldn't hear anything else. I started walking faster, hoping to get out of the zone sooner, when out of nowhere I hit something solid. I stopped the scream that was about to tear out my throat just in time and I managed a frightened choking sound instead.

"Watch it!" growled an angry male voice.

I was expecting them to just move on, but the shadowy figure stood there, making my knees begin to buckle in fear. I balled my hands into fists inside my pockets, desperately trying to hold myself together. If they were going to grab me they would have done so already...hopefully they were just waiting for an apology?

"Who the hell are you?" his hand shot out and grabbed the front of my coat.

I gasped in fear, my breath hitching up in an instant and I pressed my lips together to try and stop myself from whimpering. My legs were locked and I was afraid I wouldn't be able to even run away - if I got out of his iron strong grip that was.

"I'm sorry," I tried, my voice coming out in a dry whisper.

I didn't know how he'd even heard it, but his grasp on me lessened slightly, only for a second before he stuffed his other hand into his pocket. I couldn't see well but, I could hear him feeling around for something, a knife or a gun.

I wouldn't beg him for my life. I'd learnt many times that begging did nothing for me, however it didn't change the fact that I was terrified. How long would it be until someone found my body? What would they do with me? I had no one. I would just be another unmissed person to add to a record somewhere. Maybe the next life, if there was one, would treat me a lot better.

A blinding light hit my face out of nowhere, making me wince and squint my watering eyes. The figure murmured in what sounded like surprise, then I felt his grip release the front of my coat and he let his arm fall to his side.

"Go home," he grunted, the anger seeming to have melted away.

I stood there dumbly in shock, realising it had been the torch on his phone that he'd shone at me. He turned it off and when I saw the light from the screen reflect off his own face I couldn't have been more astonished.

Walter Simpson.

It had been years since I'd seen him this up close, but there was no way I could mistake his tousled dark hair under the hood he was wearing. I'd only gotten a glimpse of his hazel coloured eyes and I hadn't been able to read them. All I knew was that he wasn't going to hurt me, not tonight anyway.

Managing to get my knees to unlock, I made a hasty escape though the blacked out zone and all the while I could feel his gaze boring into my back. Soon I would dissolve into the gloom and he wouldn't be able to see me at all.

3

"Could you just hold that down for me, Coral?" Hayley asked, adjusting her fabric on the sewing machine.

"Sure," I smiled, securing the polka dot silk for her.

Hayley was one of the very few people who I would consider a friend. We weren't close, but she was someone who was openly friendly to me without caring what people thought. Most people didn't want to know me and that didn't bother me really. They thought I was just a quiet senior girl, not pretty or funny enough to be worth getting to be familiar with.

"Thanks," Hayley beamed after fixing up some of the seams of the dress she was making.

I quite liked my Textiles class. Only a handful of students took it and so the ambience was generally calming and not too stressful. I got to make nice outfits and accessories that I never actually wore. I let the teacher keep them to use as examples for the younger years, nothing that beautiful would suit me anyway.

The both of us stood aside so that another girl could use the sewing machine that was now free.

"How's that handbag coming along?" Hayley asked.

"Just need to work on the inner lining," I replied, tucking a strand of my blonde hair behind my ear. "It's actually almost finished."

"You're so good at bags, you know," Hayley told me. "They always end up great."

"Thanks. I think Miss might like this one a lot more than the previous ones I've done," I said with a small smile, grateful for the compliment. "I used a slightly different technique with the stitching."

"Oh that's nice Coral..." the tone of Hayley's voice had changed, she sounded wary.

There was a communal gasp and the other students started to shuffle back, away from me. I tensed up, feeling a needle of fear shoot up my spine. Hayley's chocolate brown eyes were staring wide above my head and she bit into her bottom lip. I knew I had to turn around, and I held my breath as I did so.

"Hey," Walter scratched the back of his head.

My heart jolted, not really believing what was right before me. Walter, *here,* in the classroom and talking to me? I felt like I was dreaming. It was too soon to see him again just after last night, and not to mention completely unexpected.

"Hi," I croaked back, my breath caught up in my throat.

He stood in the doorway, towering over me. His black leather jacket was unzipped to reveal a fitted white v-neck over his sculpted body. Walter wasn't smiling, but he looked a little uncertain, maybe of my reaction. After all, he wasn't even acknowledging the presence of anyone else.

I was physically shaking and the fear of my fellow classmates made me even more frightened. What did he want? How did he even find me? I didn't want to hang around to find out.

"Excuse me," I said quietly and slid past him and out of the door.

I didn't look back to see what happened behind me and rushed to the toilets to try and calm myself down. I knew I was blushing, rather violently, and I hoped that Walter hadn't noticed before I'd escaped. I couldn't help it, his gaze had been so fixed on me...and his eyes were lovely.

But, I knew not to be swayed. Just because the guy was attractive didn't take away how dangerous he was. He was part of a gang who had no respect for the law, they weren't supposed to be friendly people. That didn't explain what Walter was doing here in the first place though.

I splashed cold water on my face to try and lessen the flush before going back out. I was half expecting for Walter to show up out of nowhere again, but I didn't see him.

I spent most of my day keeping my eyes peeled for any sight of him. Walter had only been in school for a few hours and already the rumours had been circulating. It was common knowledge that out of the Simpson gang, Walter was the most easily angered. Apparently he'd already snapped multiple times at students and teachers, shouting and swearing, nothing out of the blue.

He and his brothers actually used to come to school regularly. Now, it was a much rarer occasion, apart from today. It had actually been almost a year since any of the Simpsons had attended school and it had been a lot calmer whilst they'd been absent. I supposed that the Santiagos had been to, and some probably still went to, a school in their own territory. As for my home and my school, they were both in the Simpson's territory.

I was able to go through the rest of the day only seeing Walter once more from a distance, sitting disengaged in one of his classes as I walked by. I kept my head down, hoping not to make eye contact.

Having an hour break between after school and work today meant that I could quickly eat something to keep me going. I got back to my flat and made myself a bowl of pasta with a handful of salad on the side. After eating, I freshened myself up and got dressed in my uniform of neat black attire. Locking my apartment behind me I tucked my keys into my bag and started my walk to the pub which was in the centre of the London borough.

As I drew closer to the shopping complex, the streets became busier with people strolling about from restaurants and diners, to pubs and the parks. I stayed away from the darker, shaded areas. On my way, I spotted a group of boys near the wall of a building. I immediately recognised the Simpson triplets, three blond fifteen year olds. Rumours had it that they'd been to the youth detention centre plenty of times each, all three clearly following in their older brothers' footsteps.

One triplet was eating a double cheeseburger quite successfully and another was leaning against a wall, his head bowed.

He was so still, he could have been asleep. The last triplet was mingling amongst the people, never straying too far from his two brothers who were leaning against the wall. He seemed suspicious, maybe it was because his hood that was drawn up and obscuring his head, not that it stopped his blond fringe sticking out from underneath. I knew their names were Gomez, Giovanni and Severn, but I couldn't tell who was who, not that I stayed around long enough to try and work it out.

I arrived at work five minutes early and decided to get a head start wiping down tables that had already been used. I found myself thinking about Walter and what exactly he had wanted to say. It kept coming back and I knew the only way to find out was to actually let him confront me.

I scoffed at the thought, easier said than done.

4

"Hi."

I looked up when I heard the voice of someone address me. Hayley smiled down at me and I automatically returned it.

"Do you mind if I join you?" she questioned politely.

"Not at all," I moved the book I was reading aside. "Won't your friends mind?"

Hayley turned to look at the table of her friends that I'd already spotted, watching us and she shrugged.

"Oh don't worry about them," Hayley said, sitting down on the end of a table with me. "I just wanted to know if things were okay with you."

I dropped my gaze for a second, partly wanting to open up to her like I'd never done before...about everything, all my problems. I dismissed the stupid thought quickly and shrugged.

"Things are fine, why wouldn't they be?" I replied.

"Well that whole thing with Walter?" she cocked an eyebrow. "I mean, he hasn't been to the school for at least a year and the first thing he does when he returns, is finds you?"

I was lost for words. It really wasn't a big deal, was it? Was school going to get a whole lot worse just because I bumped into Walter that one night?

"Coral?" I jumped when Hayley touched my hand.

"Sorry," I sighed, catching her deep brown eyes. "Nothing's wrong...I don't know why Walter wants to see me."

"Did something happen?" she looked closely at me. "You don't have to say."

"It's really nothing serious," I shrugged lopsidedly. "I happened to bump into him one night on the way home from work, that's it. Next day, he was at school. I know as much as everyone else."

"Fair enough," Hayley creased her brows. "I do wonder why he's back though. You should try and talk to him."

I couldn't help but laugh, surprising myself because I rarely did, "No way, that's asking for trouble."

Hayley laughed too, "Well yeah, I get where you're coming from. He scares me shitless."

I nodded in agreement and Hayley drank some of her juice.

"So, do you want to go and sit with the others?" she gestured behind her.

I glanced past her shoulder to the table of her giggling friends. Girls also intimidated me a little, if I had to be honest. They could be so genuine but completely fake beneath it all.

"Thanks for the offer," I said. "But I'm going soon anyway."

I could tell Hayley didn't wholly buy it, however she didn't push me.

"Anytime okay?" she smiled as we both got up. "It would be nice to get to know you more."

"You're too nice," I smiled and tucked my book under my arm.

"See you around," she said and went to go back to join her friends.

I was still smiling at how fond Hayley had really become when I left the cafeteria. The smile was swiped off my face instantly when I walked face to face with someone all too familiar.

Walter opened his mouth and reached into his pocket at the same time and I couldn't help but panic. I practically ran past him a second time and ended up veering off into the library instead. If there was one place Walter Simpson wouldn't go, I assumed, it was the library.

I felt my heart rate begin to recede as I walked further into the library and down aisles of bookshelves piled high with hundreds of books. I strolled slowly, looking at the books in the biology section. I read a few blurbs and flicked through a few pages before I felt calm again. One picture book of photos taken in the Amazon Rainforest took my interest and I leant against a wall, admiring the excellent shots of green tree frogs.

"Hey. Don't run," the low voice made my blood chill.

I looked up to meet the hazel eyes gaze of the Simpson boy. My knees had locked up; I wouldn't *be able* to run.

Walter rubbed his black hair and reached into his pocket with his other hand. He was wearing denim jeans with a black top and a leather jacket.

"I just wanted to return this," he said, pulling out a small pink cloth and I immediately recognised my handkerchief.

I flushed red with embarrassment and stared at him, frozen and burning with shame. All this time, that was all he wanted? Simply to return something I must have dropped in my haste? I felt quite bad for judging Walter so harshly, but at the same time I was so relieved the hanky was a clean one.

"Isn't it yours?" he frowned slightly, pushing the handkerchief out towards me.

"Y-yes it is," I swallowed, my voice drying up to a whisper. "Thank   you."

"It's okay," he gave me a half smile and I just about kept my jaw from dropping open, just about. "It would have been easier if you weren't avoiding me."

If it was even possible, I blushed harder. There was no way I could successfully deny it, but it didn't stop me trying.

"I-I wasn't avoiding you," I dug my nails into my palms, hoping I wasn't making things worse.

Walter's smile broadened and I felt my insides giving me a weird fluttering feeling.

"You're cute when you're shit scared," he said, and then he turned and headed out the library.

I was still 'shit scared' even as I watched him go. He wasn't so mean, after all, a cold-blooded gang member wouldn't bother coming to school just to return a handkerchief to a girl he didn't even know.

As Walter went on, another guy who wasn't looking where he was going happened to barge right past him.

"Are you blind?" the boy growled rudely, not even bothering to look to *who* exactly he was talking to.

Walter turned round and grabbed the back of the guy's jacket with a forceful grip and then yanked him back roughly. He twisted his arm viscously and even I winced for him.

"I think you'll find the question is," Walter hissed loudly into his ear and he held him firmly in place. "Are *you* the one who's damn blind?"

The guy managed to turn his face and glance at Walter before his eyes widened in fear.

"I'm sorry," he pleaded. "I didn't see it was you, I swear."

"You mean you weren't aware I was back, huh?" Walter chuckled darkly, releasing the boy and shoving him back roughly before holding his arms to the sides.

"Well guess what bitch? Here I am in the flesh."

Walter ignored the cautious warnings of the school librarian who had come to try and break things up. The small number of students there peeked from behind the bookshelves warily, but at the same time they marvelled at the opportunity to spread the gossip, no doubt.

I took back what I'd thought. Walter was still a mean guy; maybe he just had a few soft spots. One that I gladly fell into.

5

It had been a few days since the short conversation with Walter in the library that had ended so memorably and I'd seen him and some of his brothers around. If I managed to catch his attention, he would always keep his gaze on me, making me so nervous. At school sometimes I would get the feeling that he wanted to talk to me, but I would move on so quickly he wouldn't have the chance.

I'd also been getting to know Hayley. She'd invited me to go to the cinema with her and her friends on the Friday after school and I had declined. I didn't tell her it was because I didn't want to step out of my comfort zone, I'd given her a measly excuse of feeling a bit under the weather and she had given me space. On the Saturday however, I'd walked into her on my way to the pub for my afternoon shift and we'd talked for a little bit, like friends would, I supposed. She'd suggested that we give each other our numbers and that we should arrange something later. I'd actually meant it when I agreed with her that time. Hayley was very easy to talk to and I could tell she wasn't being fake towards me at all.

It was Sunday and I had the whole day off. I woke up late, feeling refreshed when I opened my eyes to a brightly lit room. The sunlight was shining through my closed curtains and when I opened them, it almost blinded me. I smiled to myself despite the pain, sunny weather made me happy, it took away the bad thoughts and memories.

After a shower and some breakfast, I wrote a quick shopping list, put on my coat and was off to do some food shopping. The supermarket was central, neutral territory, so it was no surprise that I saw a few of the Santiagos around on my way back. Four of them had gathered by the railings of the playground and I had to walk past without catching anyone's eye.

I dropped my gaze and fixed it onto the pavement as I got closer, keeping my shopping bags close to my sides. I wished that the plastic wouldn't make so much of a rustling sound, but it still had them turning to face me. The oldest Santiago everyone knew as Carlos, was in his early twenties and the others in the gang were a mixture of his brothers and his cousins.

"Hey, you okay?" one, I remotely recognised as Diego, took hold of my arm as I tried to pass.

"Get off," I grunted, giving my arm a pull.

"Calm down little lady," he didn't let go.

"Diego leave her," Carlos, his older brother, called after him with an uninterested expression.

"But she's cute," he played with my ponytail, ignoring Carlos and then lowering his voice to my ear. "You're looking quite tanned for this time of the year, girl."

"Stop it," I looked up at him with a frown, my heart hammering.

Diego was a lot bronzer than I was, him being Venezuelan, and to be honest I didn't think my skin tone was a single bit tanned for the month of October.

The other two Santiagos, Carlos and Diego's cousins, watched apathetically and didn't try to stop Diego bothering me. He continued to follow me even when I'd passed the playground and I started to grow even more uneasy, wondering if he would stop or not.

"You wanna have some fun sometime?" he purred into my ear.

"Leave me alone," I pushed at him as hard as I could, my bags of shopping bashing about.

"But I don't want to," he tried to kiss my neck, barely budging.

He gripped the both of my hands and forced me to drop my shopping, causing food to spill across the pavement.

21

"Don't be scared," he murmured, holding my arms in a very tight grasp, pulling me roughly against the bricks of a wall that was covered in both the Simpsons and the Santiagos graffiti.

Memories I didn't want back, started to arise and I swallowed, trying to squash down the fear but without much avail. I clenched my eyes shut but I couldn't block out the dark images of a man, a man who was pushing his hands down my top. I was young, too young to even have breasts. His smell was overpowering, something I couldn't quite describe, but something I couldn't ever forget. It would linger on my body every time he'd finished with me...

"Stop!" I screamed, finding my voice. "Stop it!"

Diego jumped; startled by my volume, but if anything, it urged him on. He was unzipping my coat and kissing my neck, pushing harder against the wall. His nails scratched painfully at my skin as he ran his hands along my neck and down to my shoulders. I was crying and fighting back but it didn't stop him, nothing I wasn't used to.

All of a sudden I felt a whoosh of air and then Diego's touches were gone. I opened my eyes and saw Walter pulling Diego off me and shoving him away.

"What the hell were you doing?" Walter demanded.

"What's it to you?" Diego scowled back. "You don't even know this girl."

Walter was trying to hold it together, I could tell by his trembling fists and clenched jaw.

"Try it Walter," a smug smirk slipped onto Diego's face. "Fight me. Carlos and the boys are right around the corner."

Walter wouldn't be able to beat four Santiagos at once, and they both knew it. Diego was trying to rile him up enough for him to attempt it anyway, but thankfully Walter was withstanding.

"Move on, Diego," Walter growled, stiffly stepping backwards, away from him and towards me.

Diego scoffed, "Whatever man, if you're into basic blonde bitches."

Walter's nostrils flared as he inhaled sharply and he was seconds from striking out at the rival gang member when I reached out to grasp the fabric of the back of his hoodie on impulse.

Walter froze, his body tensing up, and then I felt him relax. Once I was sure he wasn't going to blow up, I let go and Walter stayed still for a moment. Sighing, he then turned around and faced his back to Diego, who walked off to join the others with a grunt of dissatisfaction.

Walter said nothing and dropped down to pick up my shopping. I hadn't caught my breath back and so it took me a few seconds to process what was going on before I bent down to collect some of the food stuff as well. Walter placed a packet of spaghetti and a few bags of salad into one bag whilst I finished gathering boxes of tea and cereal.

"Thank you," I said to him, making sure my eyes were on the bags on shopping and not on him as he handed them back over to me.

"No problem," Walter said, still sounding immensely pissed off.

I risked a glance at him at the same time that he lifted his own gaze from the ground to look at me. His hazel eyes widened in shock.

"That cut needs to be cleaned up," he held his hand out to my neck but I flinched back.

I hadn't even noticed I had been cut to be honest, but as soon as he said it I could feel the sting.

"It's not too bad," I mumbled, trying not to get him angry again.

"No," Walter shook his head. "I don't like the look of it."

Somewhere deep within me, I felt a swell of emotion over what he had said.

"I can clean it up for you," Walter offered, his eyebrows furrowed in concern. "I don't live very far from here."

He was about to raise his hand to my skin a second time before he stopped himself, wanting to check it out but not wanting to make me flinch again. I was too busy thinking about how Walter Simpson could honestly feel concerned for me, than to realise what he was suggesting.

"No," I blurted.

"What?" he frowned in confusion.

"I'm fine, I'll go home," I answered and went to walk past him. "It's a tiny cut, I'll live."

"But," Walter walked by my side. "I insist."

I regarded him closely. If he had cruel intentions, maybe he wouldn't have been so good to me these few times. His dark brows were still creased and I wanted to assure him there was nothing to worry about.

"I'm really fine," I said more calmly.

"Okay then," Walter said, and then cracked an unexpected smile. "I was just trying to be nice after all."

His smile made me almost lose my grip on the bags, making them rustle loudly.

"Shit, I'll take that," Walter pulled them off of me, not giving me a chance to object.

"Thank you," I said, unsure what to do next.

"Don't worry about it, isn't it obvious that I don't want to hurt you?" Walter asked, sounding serious.

I risked another glance at him and saw that he looked almost disappointed.

"Okay," I said, surprising myself with what I said next. "Let's go then."

He smiled at me again and I smiled back, ignoring the stinging from my neck.

We walked for about ten minutes west, which was Simpson territory, until we arrived at a peculiar looking house. It was aged, thin in width and very tall, about four floors high and including a basement I guessed. I had to admit, after all these years living in this area, I'd never seen where they lived, and after hearing so much about the gang, their home was a bit of an anticlimax.

Walter put a bag down and got out his key to unlock the front door whilst I stood silently by his side. As soon as it was unlocked, I stepped in after him and gasped quietly at the sight of the interior of the house. It looked the complete opposite to what the outside had seemed like.

The floors were a dark wooden laminate, sparkling clean, and the ceiling was also made of dark brown panels of wood that had little spotlight-like beams that lit the place up. There was a lustrous wooden staircase immediately to the right as we walked in and right ahead lead to the living room I presumed, where I could hear deep male voices.

Walter took me to the kitchen and yet again, I was taken aback. Although it wasn't huge, it was bigger that it looked from the outside and so modern and sleek. The counters were made of dark granite that glittered as it was so clean and there was a large black fridge-freezer and a dining table that seated eight.

"Take a seat," he said and bent down to go through a cupboard.

I sat down and subconsciously watched his rear as he fiddled with things in the cupboard. If I had to confess, he was shaped up very well.

"Right," Walter straightened up, and I almost blushed in fear of being caught staring at him. "I found wipes and a plaster."

Walter looked like he was about to take a seat right next to me and sort out the cut on my neck himself. The last thing I wanted was for him to be so close to me, touching my skin and with all of his concentration aimed at me. I wouldn't be able to take it, I didn't have the guts.

"Thanks," I jumped in, changing my mind. "I'll just go to the bathroom?"

Confusion flittered across his face for a second before he nodded and handed the items over to me.

"There's one downstairs," Walter led me to a door that revealed a toilet and sink behind it.

"Thanks again," I smiled briefly before closing and locking myself inside.

It took a few seconds to calm myself down and try not to over-think things. I couldn't believe that I was actually in the Simpsons' household. It felt unreal and not to mention still a bit unsafe, but what was puzzling was that Walter was being so kind to me. However that didn't extend to all his brothers who were probably at home at this moment.

I used the mirror above the sink to wipe at the cut on my neck where Diego's nails had actually drawn blood.. It stung a bit, but it wasn't terribly painful and I decided it didn't even need a plaster. Opening the door again, I found Walter standing with his back to me in the doorway to the living room, where the voices were coming from. I didn't quite know what to do, so I stood by the stairs for a second, trying to figure that out.

"Did you let someone in?" I heard one of the boys say, making my eyes widen.

Walter shrugged, "Yeah, and?"

"Who is it?" another asked, sounding slightly hostile.

Walter ignored his question and he turned around with an annoyed look on his face, only to find me standing by the staircase.

"Oh, you're done," he seemed surprised, his eyebrows arching.

"Yeah..." I trailed off, unsure what to say or do.

"Come and say hello," I heard one voice call loudly from behind him.

My heart started to race, "Oh no I shouldn't – "

"Yeah, you should," the voice replied and I realised in horror that the owner of it was walking towards the door where Walter was standing facing me.

That owner was Walter's older brother Landon who I recognised because of his lip piercing. I didn't know too much about the guy, but I did know that he slept around a lot and that he was one year older than Walter and me. There were also, without a doubt, all the dangerous and illegal activities he got up to.

"There you are," Landon grinned when his brown eyes fell on me and I immediately saw why no one turned him down for anything.

His black v-neck top was fitted and I tried not to stare at his tall, muscled frame that stood by Walter's similar physique. Landon's hair was even darker than Walter's and was styled naturally. His smile was charming, appearing so friendly, but was it genuine?

"You're freaking her out," Walter elbowed Landon with a frown, pushing him back. "Stop smiling at her like that."

"There's nothing to be scared about," Landon said, automatically making me even more afraid. "You wanna come meet the others?"

Although it was only a suggestion, I found I couldn't exactly say no.

"Okay," I said in a hushed voice and forced my legs to move forwards.

Walter gave me a reassuring smile and I felt a little bit of warmth inside me. The living room was a lot more spacious than I would have thought. The sofas were low and rectangular shaped, complimenting the modern themed interior the house had adopted, as opposed to the ancient looking exterior. There was a thick brown carpet, and more of the spotlights on the panelled ceiling, as well as a huge flat screened TV and what seemed like a study area in the back corner, by the back door.

Once I'd checked out my surroundings, I swallowed nervously before looking at who was actually in the room. Phoenix, the oldest Simpson brother, didn't look happy. His dark stubble was impressive and his green-brown eyes (quite like Walter's) seemed to show how much the guy had been through. I only knew what other people said about him, how he was some kind of top guy in a drug network and how he was apparently responsible for the murders of people involved in that kind of crime.

I caught the emerald eyed gaze of another Simpson brother, a younger one. I recognised him, but didn't know his name. I remembered seeing him occasionally at school several months back, but he'd long since stopped coming. It was his dark blond hair and his striking green eyes that allured me. The boy also seemed to stare back at me for a second before his face turned into a glare and I shifted my view away.

"Who is this?" Phoenix muttered at Walter.

"This is...well..." Walter looked down at me apologetically.

"Coral," I filled in, feeling a little exposed but also sensing that there wasn't an immediate threat to worry about.

"Nice," Landon nodded with another smile, going and spreading himself out in one of the sofas.

"Thanks," I tried a smile back.

"What are you here for?" the blond one snapped at me.

"I..uh.." I stammered, startled by his outburst.

"Eli," Landon said in a warning tone.

Walter scowled at him. "What's your problem?"

"What's yours?" Eli glowered back at Walter. "Why are you bringing sluts to our home?"

Sluts?

I frowned in shock. Was that was I really looked like? I felt wounded and offended. What had I done to make this boy hate me so much, in the matter of a few minutes?

"Watch your mouth," Walter balled up his fists tightly, he was physically shaking with anger.

"Why should I?" Eli challenged him.

"Hey cut that out," Landon looked over at him, all traces of his previous smile, gone.

Eli smiled mockingly at Walter, but his word was aimed at me.

"Slut."

Things moved very fast then.

Walter lunged forwards in an attack and Eli shot up to receive it. Walter forced Eli up against the wall behind them and was about to throw a punch when Phoenix grabbed hold of Walter's withdrawn arm.

"Take it easy," Phoenix said, holding Walter's force back.

"Did you hear what he just said?" Walter hissed with all his fury aimed right at his younger brother, who he had pinned in place.

"Eli," Phoenix turned to look at him. "You don't have to wind people up all the time."

Eli rolled his eyes, "Tell him not to bring slu – "

"Enough," Phoenix cut him off. "Stop pissing about."

"And apologise," Walter growled.

"No," Eli scoffed.

"It's fine," I slipped in before things could get worse, the last thing I wanted was for Walter to lose his temper so much that they had a full scale fight.

"It's not a problem," I said. "I think I'll go home now."

I stepped back and closed the door before they could see the hurt in my eyes. I was trembling and I hadn't even been involved in the physical side of things. It went to show how effective words could be.

I was in the kitchen taking my tattered bags of shopping, which had been through a lot today, when I heard the door reopen and get slammed shut. I winced at the sound and turned round to face Walter who was standing in the hallway.

"Thanks for the help," I said to him, avoiding his eye.

"Look, I'm sorry about him," Walter said, forcing himself to adopt a calmer tone of voice. "He's just so..."

"It's okay," I smiled to ease his displeasure. "It's not your fault."

He still didn't look satisfied and heaved a sigh, "Okay well, I can walk you home."

"I'll be fine," I said quickly. "There's no need at all."

He took my firm refusal with a nod and went to the door to show me out.

"I guess I'll see you at school then," Walter rubbed the back of his neck.

I wanted to know why he'd even started coming to school again at all, but it wasn't my place to ask.

"Yeah, see you," I said uncertainly, stepping out the house.

Did this mean that I could no longer try and avoid the guy? I guess so, and I didn't know whether that was good or bad.

"Bye," Walter said and he waited until I had walked out the driveway before I heard him close the door.

6

I woke up on Monday morning with a text from Hayley asking if I wanted a ride to school.

At first, when I heard my phone ping, I thought it was just spam because I didn't receive messages from anyone very often, but then I remembered that we had exchanged numbers and I had saved hers onto my phone. I was about to automatically reply a 'no thank you' but then I stopped to actually think about it.

Yeah that would be nice thanks, I sent back.

Hayley replied instantly, **Great! Send me your address. I'll be there hopefully in half an hour.**

I didn't want her to know where I lived, so I told her I would meet her at a destination a few minutes from the degraded block of flats that I called my home, in a more 'presentable' area. Getting out of my bumpy bed, I stretched my aching body and went to the mouldy bathroom for a shower. Coming out, and feeling a lot fresher, I changed into a pair of blue jeans and a jumper before walking the tiny distance to the cramped kitchen. I poured myself some cereal that I'd bought just the day before. Seeing the slightly crushed box of cereal made me remember the vile touches Diego Santiago had given me. I squeezed my eyes shut, trying to block out the childhood memories that no doubt followed.

Walter Simpson made his way into my head and I opened my eyes again, feeling a small sense of security. Silly, considering that I wasn't even with him, *and* that he belonged to a gang just as dangerous as the Santiagos. I poured myself a bowl, ate it and washed up in less than five minutes.

I put on my shoes and wrapped my scarf around my neck before pulling on my coat. Grabbing my schoolbag, I let myself out of my flat and locked the door behind me. I walked to the spot I'd asked Hayley to pick me up at, all the while thinking about how kind she was, going out of her way to help me and get to know me better.

Five minutes later Hayley herself pulled up in a small red car and rolled down her window, grinning at me.

"Good morning," she said to me.

"Morning," I smiled back, still standing on the curb.

"Get in then," Hayley gestured.

I blushed slightly at my hesitation and walked round to get into the passenger's side. Hayley's car was old, but cosy. It smelt of the pine freshener she had hanging up on the rear-view mirror and she had the radio playing quietly in the background.

"Thanks Hayley," I said to her as I buckled my seatbelt. "I really   appreciate   this."

"No need to thank me," she replied, putting the car into gear once I'd finished with my seatbelt. "Sorry I was late, were you standing there long?"

"No," I said, enjoying the warmth of the vehicle. "I was just a couple minutes early."

"Oh okay," she said. "So how was your weekend?"

I instantly remembered going to the Simpson household, something I doubt many 'ordinary' people did, and meeting three of Walter's attractive brothers. It also brought back the cutting remarks Eli Simpson had made about me. I didn't know why he had been so horrible, it made me feel like I had done something wrong.

"Coral?" Hayley's voice made me snap back.

"Sorry," I blinked and smiled apologetically. "It was...eventful."

I didn't even know why I wanted to tell Hayley about what had happened, perhaps it was because I didn't have any real friends to talk to. Either way, it was best to not go into details.

"Eventful how?" she raised her eyebrows as she kept her eyes on the road.

"Well," I paused. "I didn't do much."

Hayley creased her brows in confusion, before catching the 'sarcasm'.

She laughed, "Lazy days in?"

"Yep," I smiled. "Well I had work on the Saturday, but was completely free on Sunday. What about you?"

"I was stuck babysitting," she pulled an upset face. "They may be my cousins but they sure do love to get on my nerves."

I grinned, "Do you have a lot of family then?"

"I don't have any siblings, but I've got plenty of cousins," Hayley replied. "Most of them live on the other side of London, others live further out."

We spent time talking about her relatives and it was nice to know more about her. I liked hearing the funny stories about her family gatherings; it took my mind off my own background. When Hayley asked me about my family, I surprised myself by telling her the truth, well as much of it as I could.

"My mother died when I was three," I said. "I don't really remember her."

"I'm sorry to hear that," she said sympathetically.

I didn't mention my father and Hayley thankfully didn't ask. She was so considerate.

"It's nothing," I said, realising we had arrived at school. "Thanks again for the ride."

"Stop saying thanks," she grinned, turning the engine off.

When she didn't immediately get out of the car, I too remained seated, wanting to ask her something.

"Hayley," I started quietly.

"Yeah?" she turned to look at me with a small frown on her face. "What is it?"

"Why are you being so nice to me?" I asked her, looking down at my lap, unable to hold her eye contact for more than a second.

I saw her face relax into a smile out of the corner of my eye, "Coral, do you really have to ask?"

I didn't answer because I wasn't quite sure what to say.

"Okay," she turned halfway in her seat to face me. "Honestly, I think you're a very nice person who needs to be more confident in herself, you know? I don't like seeing you on your own all the time and so you could do with a friend."

I looked at her as a smile slowly started to spread on my face, "You're such a good person Hayley, thanks."

"*Stop saying thanks*," she groaned again, leaning forwards to hug me. "It's no problem. You're a sweet girl and I'd love to get to know you better."

I hugged her back, feeling so happy that I'd finally made a friend after all these years.

"Come on," Hayley said after we'd pulled away. "Let's get to class."

***

I was sitting alone in the lunch hall, still feeling good about this morning. Having someone to talk to could do much to relieve pressure off me, but it would be a while until I opened up to Hayley about a lot of things. *And* she also had her other group of friends to whom she wanted to introduce me to. I had declined, but I had also promised I'd give it a shot another day.

I jumped when someone in dark clothing pulled back the chair opposite me and sat themselves down. Walter was wearing his black leather jacket again and his greeny-brown eyes took in my state.

"You look better today," he said.

I wanted to ask him who gave him the permission to sit down, but I could never speak to him like that. Besides, I didn't mind *that* much.

"How are *you* today?" I asked him, trying to squeeze down the rising nerves. Everyone, and I mean *everyone*, was staring.

Hayley had gone home as she only had a half day; otherwise I would have sat with her or even forced myself to sit with her table of friends. Being alone with Walter made me an even bigger focus of attention, and attention was the last thing I wanted.

"Do you wanna go outside?" he asked me in his deep voice. "You look uncomfortable."

I swallowed. Was it that obvious?

"Yep," he grinned a heart-stopping grin at me.

I dropped my jaw, mortified that I'd said that out loud. Walter wasn't angry in the slightest; he looked amused more than anything.

"Okay sure," I said, standing up on shaking legs.

We walked out of the lunch hall together and I hoped Walter didn't notice how nervous I was by my trembling. He led me out to the athletics track and he sat down on one of the benches that over looked it. I sat next to him before he could tell me to, and made sure that there was almost half a meter between us. If Walter noticed, he didn't say anything.

He leant forwards with his elbows on his knees and his hands running though his thick black hair, "I wanted to say sorry again about yesterd – "

"You don't have to apologise," I interrupted him, gaining a sudden surge of confidence. "It wasn't your fault, it was your brother's."

I didn't know where it had come from, but once I was saying how I truly felt and not holding back...I couldn't stop.

"I have nothing against him really," I muttered. "It's not like I'm going to see him ever again, so what's the point riling myself up about it? He's just a rude person, what else can I say?"

Walter had sat up and was looking at me with a mixture of admiration and surprise on his face.

"So you *do* have a voice," he said afterwards, making me blush. "No, don't be shy. I like it."

He liked it? Wow, just a couple of days ago I would have never imagined Walter Simpson telling me that he liked anything about me, a girl he still barely knew. Well, it gave me a little more confidence, just like Hayley had said I needed, which made being myself a lot easier.

"You never answered the question," I said to him, smiling at my lap.

"What question?" Walter sounded confused.

"How are you today?" I said, my smile widening.

"Oh," Walter chuckled and I had to stop myself from widening my eyes. His laughter was so sexy. "I'm fine, but all this school stuff...I forgot how much it sucked."

34

"Well, it *has* been a while," I stretched my legs out, looking at my shoes.

"How do you do it? The work, I mean," he asked me. "It's damn hard and the teachers move on so fast."

"I have nothing else to do," I let slip before realising how lame that sounded. "Apart from work, that is."

Walter seemed to be thinking, probably about all the things that he had to do in his daily life.

"Where do you work?" he asked me.

"A pub," I replied.

"Which one?" he looked down at me with a half-smile. "Or do you not want me to know?"

My cheeks warmed slightly and I looked away, "It's called The Dartfish."

"The dead fish?"

"No!" I couldn't help but laugh a little. "The Dart-fish. Not *dead* fish. Walter, they don't even sound similar."

He chuckled again and I smiled widely to myself. This was easier than I'd ever initially anticipated. He wasn't as bad-tempered and violent as I'd thought, well not all the time anyway. Not towards me.

"Lunch is over," I checked my watch. "What do you have next?"

"I don't even know," Walter rubbed the back of his neck. "I lost my timetable on the first day. I've been rolling up to class after class until I find the right one...usually when the period is almost over."

I shook my head at him, "Ask for a new one."

"Or, I could just go to class with you," Walter said. "I mean, I'm sure we have at least one class together."

"I take Textiles, Maths and English," I told him. "Do you take any of those?"

"Maths and English," he said.

"Oh?" I raised my eyebrows. "I have Maths now, so I guess we could go together."

Walter nodded, standing up. We walked in a comfortable silence back to the main school building, and I couldn't stop thinking about how strange these past few days had been.

"Help me," Walter blurted all of a sudden.

35

"With what?" I frowned, looking up at him in concern.

"Maths and English," Walter ducked his head, almost out of shyness. "I'm really behind."

He didn't strike me as a person who actually gave a damn about that, but it wouldn't hurt. If it wasn't too early to say, I thought Walter was kind of a nice guy.

"Yeah," I said, trying to think of time to fit that into my schedule of work and school. "I could give you some tutoring, to help you catch up and all."

Walter smiled widely at me, making my stomach flip.

"Thanks Coral," he said as we walked slowly back to school. "Could we meet up tonight?"

"I have work tonight," I declined. "I'm free on Tuesdays, Thursdays, Fridays and Sundays."

"Tomorrow then," he suggested.

"That's fine," I said back. "I can't do my place though."

"How come?" He murmured casually.

"Visitors," I lied.

"My place then," he shrugged and I nodded in agreement.

We had reached the school and continued walking down the hallways to class. It turned out that Walter didn't even have the same Maths teacher as me anyway, and he went to a different class. Maybe in English we'd have more luck.

It was only after school had ended, and in my haste straight to the pub, that I realised what I had agreed to. To my dismay, I would be going back to the Simpson residence, and back to where his all too intimidating brothers were.

7

W ork at The Dartfish was tiring.

I was normally on my feet for five hours, with a fifteen minute break somewhere in the middle, faced with rowdy football fans and messy drunkards. My colleagues were a mixture of ages and gender. I liked and got on well with most of them, but it wasn't as if we would meet up outside of hours for a coffee or something. There was one girl Tiffany who I detested, and the feeling - I'm sure - was very mutual. She was a rude, bitchy thing who loved nothing better than to flirt with all the men who came in. I didn't usually stay late enough, but on Saturdays when my shift *did* go on until closing time in the early hours of the morning, I would see her even go home with guys she'd flirted with that evening.

It was pitch black as I walked home that night. I was pretty hungry, not having eaten anything since lunchtime. When I got to the flat, I was too exhausted to wait around for anything to cook so ate a bowl of cereal and went to wash off the sweaty, grimy feeling from working my shift.

I got into bed, shivering from the cold. The heating was very poor and my small heater that was plugged in would take time to warm up the bedroom. I tucked my legs up and wrapped my arms around my chest, trying to keep in as much heat as I could. I slipped into sleep soon enough and was plunged back into my shadowy past.

I was a kid, not older than seven years old. The first thing I sensed was the all too familiar smell. It was both dirty and heavy with alcohol. There was a hint of something he used as aftershave, a horrible scent that I couldn't describe. He had me cornered in my bedroom; there was no one else there to help me. We were completely alone. His rough, callused hands gripped the tops of my small shaking shoulders and I started to weep, knowing what was coming.

"Please don't," I pleaded with him.

He ignored me, even let out a low chuckle. Begging was pointless, it made no difference. He shoved a hand down the front of my top and felt around, making me bite my bottom lip as the tears started to stream faster.

"Cry all you want," he muttered as he used a hand to unbuckle his belt. "There's no one to hear you."

I woke up with a gasp as a bang sounded a few blocks down from the block of flats I lived in. It was followed by another and another and another. Each one rang out loudly, echoing down the quiet streets and my heart thumped just as loud in my chest.

I lay frozen in my bed for ages, even though the gunshots had long stopped and my room was no longer cold. It was early morning and I knew I wasn't going to be able to sleep again. Sleep would mean rejoining the old Coral and reliving the abuse.

Getting out of my bed, I turned on my bedroom light. I made myself a cup of tea, then turned on all the lights in the small flat to make sure no one was lurking in the shadows. Getting out my books from my school bag, I sat down at my bedroom desk with my hot mug, and started with my homework. I hadn't told Walter that I often did all my work in the middle of the night, at times like this.

It was around 7:30am when I got a text from Hayley. **Pick up in thirty minutes?**

I let out a weak smile; I supposed this was going to become a new thing between us now. I replied back with a yes and got up to shower again, hoping it would make me feel more awake than I currently did. I came out, taking a look in the mirror, and saw the bags and dark shadows under my brown eyes. *Great.* I looked terrible.

I was waiting at the arranged spot five minutes early again and Hayley pulled up, looking all smiley. I tried to smile back and got into the passenger seat.

"Morning," I said to her, turning away to buckle my belt.

"Morning," she replied, waiting for me. "You sleep well?"

I sighed internally and went for a lie, "Yeah thanks, you?"

"Good thanks," Hayley winked back and started driving.

We didn't talk that much today, Hayley must have noticed I wasn't really in the talkative mood, and we rode in silence except from the radio playing quietly. Hayley hummed along to the songs cheerily and I looked out of the window, thinking about Walter Simpson of all people. I had English today and perhaps he would be in my class.

I was amongst some of the first students to arrive in my English class and I sat in the middle row, near the wall. I liked sitting at the edge of any room because it meant that I wasn't in the centre where I could be viewed from all angles. I was gazing at my desk, waiting for the rest of the students to come in. It wasn't long until the class was filled and the teacher started the lesson. I guess Walter and I didn't share any classes then.

The teacher started with a recap of the novel we were currently studying, *The Picture of Dorian Gray*. I had gotten out my notes and started flicking through them to find the right pages when Walter showed up. I hid a smile. Of course he would be twenty minutes late.

"Take a seat Walter," I heard the teacher sigh, not bothering to scold him and probably preferring it if he hadn't showed up at all.

Walter was standing at the front, looking around the classroom and everyone else was trying not to catch his eye. Our class wasn't big and so most people bagged both seats at the two-man desks. No one wanted him to sit next to them. There were no fully empty desks left and I didn't think he'd seen me or the space on my desk yet as he started walking down, glaring at each and every student that he passed.

"Oh hey," he said warmly when he saw me.

Nearly the whole class turned around in their seats to take a look at exactly *who* Walter was talking to, and I ducked my head. Walter didn't care, he pulled out the empty chair next to me and dumped his bag on the desk.

"Did you change your mind about the tutoring?" he asked quietly, cocking a dark eyebrow.

I swallowed, "No – I just....I'm a bit tired today."

I wished I hadn't said that because Walter started looking at me too closely, his eyes searching my entire face. He had such lovely hazel eyes.

"But I can still...you know, help," I coughed into my hand and turned to face the front, sitting stiffly in my seat. Was he involved with any of the shooting I'd heard last night? I *did* live in Simpson territory.

"Alright," he said in his low voice.

We continued with the class and Walter didn't say anything else to me again. Maybe I had made it obvious, again, how uncomfortable his deep gaze had made me. "I can go through my notes with you later on," I said to Walter after the class had ended.

"That would be helpful," Walter smiled back. "I have Philosophy next. What about you?"

"Study period," I said.

"Cool," Walter replied. "See you then."

I nodded back and he stepped out of my way so that I could move past him and out of the class. I could feel his eyes on me the whole time.

I went with Hayley to lunch, and she introduced me to her bunch of friends. I forgot all their names immediately and stood awkwardly by the table, wanting to get away from their judgmental looks. I was Coral, the quiet girl they barely knew, usually there in the background but never worth enough to get to know.

"Shall we go and get lunch then?" Hayley asked me.

Her friends already had their food and I was glad we didn't have ours yet because then I would actually have to sit down and eat with them.

"I gotta go to the library," I mumbled back. "I have an English essay that I should have handed in earlier today. I said I would have it finished by the end of the day."

"But you should at least eat first," Hayley frowned faintly in concern.

"I've got some snacks," I smiled. "I'm okay."

"Okay then," she said, sounding unconvinced. "Well, see you in Textiles I guess."

"Yep, see you later," I said with forced enthusiasm and turned away after a quick wave at the other girls.

I went to the library again, going over my homework that I was bound to have made mistakes in last night. I would have eaten an apple but no food was allowed in there, so I didn't bother.

***

I got to my Textiles class half an hour later and continued working on my bag. Hayley came in moments after and she looked like she was bursting to tell me something. She had an eager expression on her pretty face and I couldn't help but want to know what it was she had to say. But what she *did* say, had the back of my neck prickling with discomfort.

"Have you heard some of the stuff people are saying about you?" Hayley asked in a hushed voice.

"No," I shook my head, gazing around at the class. Some of them were actually looking at me at that moment. "What's going on?"

"Rumours of course," Hayley shook her head with an excited look in her eyes. "Stuff about you and Walter."

"Like what?" I widened my eyes.

"Crazy shit Coral, you wouldn't believe," she raised her perfect brown eyebrows.

"Just tell me," I insisted, not sure whether to be angry or amused about it all.

"Where to start?" she took my arm and pulled me away to go and sit down at a table. "Okay so there's one about Walter actually paying you to give him 'services', which is why he and you seem to always be talking in private apparently."

"We spoke in private once," I rolled my eyes. "And that's so stupid. Do people actually believe that?"

Hayley raised her eyebrows at me, "Ooh Coral, I like this side of you."

You mean the me with no walls put up, I smiled to myself. I liked Hayley, and we were getting closer.

"There's another about how you're the newest member of Walter's gang or something like that," Hayley said. "But everyone knows that their gang is family only, so that one's pretty far-fetched."

"As if the first one wasn't?" I cried in amusement.

41

She laughed, "Yeah, I know. But it *is* the quiet ones you have to watch out for. They're the real freaks when it comes to *stuff like that.*"

"What are you suggesting?" I raised my eyebrows at her.

"Nothing at all," Hayley buttoned her lips with a teasing smile. She was joking of course. "But Coral, can I ask...what is really going on between you two?"

I glanced around at the classroom and yes, indeed, people were still watching me and mumbling between themselves. If only they knew the truth was a lot less interesting.

"I agreed to tutor him," I told her. "To help him catch up."

Hayley still seemed shocked and hissed at me with wide eyes, "*You* are tutoring *Walter Simpson*? The guy who blows his top, at the tiniest things?"

I nodded, giving her a small smile.

Hayley shook her head in disbelief, "Wow Coral you've got some guts, he must like you or something because I swear he glares at *everyone.*"

I only shrugged, "I don't know about *that*, Hayley. But he's not that bad once you get to..."

I trailed off because I barely knew him at all.

"Exactly," a grin spread onto her face. "He clearly has a soft spot for you."

Hearing that said out loud from someone other than myself sounded a little less crazy, but still very unlikely.

"Well I'll tell you how it goes after school today," I said to her, getting up to keep going with my bag. "But Hayley...just don't go around telling every – "

"I wouldn't do that," Hayley assured me. "Trust."

"Thanks," I nodded at her. "Best to see what else the school can come up with, huh?"

"Definitely," she agreed with another laugh.

***

I couldn't find Walter when school ended and the exhaustion had caught up with me fast. All I wanted to do was crawl into my bed and sleep for days, but I couldn't do that.

After spending what seemed like ages within the moving mass of bodies, I made it out onto the street and my vision tilted violently all of a sudden. I balanced myself quickly, trying to calm my racing heart. Was I really that tired? No one around me had noticed, everyone was either on their phones or talking to their friends as they made their way home. I was invisible, as always. Walter was still nowhere to be seen, and I didn't know how much longer I wanted to wait around for him.

I had just given up and had started walking home when he caught up with me.

"You remember the way?" Walter had his hands shoved deep in his pockets.

His black hair looked so smooth and was styled effortlessly but managing to look flawless. He was still looking at me, waiting for a reply.

"I was actually going home," I said sheepishly. "I couldn't find you."

"Well then you live in the same direction as I do," he said with a half-smile. "But look Coral, if you changed your mind about it...its fine."

"No," I said, and I meant it. "I haven't."

"Good," he licked his lips, probably out of habit. "We turn left here."

As we walked to Walter's home together, the worn-out feeling was still there, but I also started to feel restless and on edge.

The house was a lot quieter when we got in this time. I knew it wasn't empty because I could hear footsteps from the floors above and the sound of a shower running somewhere. It automatically had me imagining one of Walter's brothers with steam and water sliding down all over them.

So there I was, standing in the beautifully polished interior, with a pink blush staining my cheeks. Walter kicked off his shoes and dropped his bag on the floor, thankfully not noticing as he was too busy kicking his bag into a small corner by the basement door.

"We'll need that," I said to him with a small smile, glad that the blush had faded. I felt a lot more relaxed already, probably because Eli and his other brothers weren't present right at that moment.

Walter picked up his battered bag again and put it over his shoulder, "Do you want a drink?"

"Some water would be good," I replied, I was very dehydrated, not having eaten or drank anything nearly the whole day.

I followed him to their sparkling kitchen and Walter grabbed a bottle from the fridge, handing it to me.

"Thanks," I unscrewed the cap and took a sip, it was very refreshing.

He leant against one of the black granite surfaces, arms folded across his broad chest as he watched me.

"So where is everyone?" I had to ask him to take some of his attention away.

Walter shrugged and scratched his jaw, "Dunno. They could be anywhere."

"Having so many siblings must be...fun, right?" I refrained from wincing as I remembered my short encounter with Eli Simpson. He didn't seem like fun at all.

Walter smirked, "Sometimes, yeah. But they piss me off a lot too."

"It's to be expected," I smiled down at the ground.

"Do you have any siblings?" he asked me after a pause.

"Nope," I answered. "I'm an only child."

"Man, I would *love* to try that," Walter laughed darkly and I shook my head at him.

"Don't be mean," I grinned.

"Haven't you heard, Coral?" he smirked sexily. "Mean is my middle name."

I *had* heard that of course, but I didn't say anything. My throat had dried up just from the look he was giving me alone. I drank some more water.

"You wanna go upstairs?" Walter raised his eyebrows at me.

I knew he didn't mean it like *that*, but I couldn't help thinking about it that way too. I nodded at him, avoiding his gaze.

Walter chuckled lightly under his breath and my stomach tightened either from the sound of it, or from my hunger. Probably both. He led the way up the stairs and to the landing. There were various doors, all dark in colour which matched the shade of the panelled ceilings. Walter went to one door and walked in without a word, so I followed him.

I looked around his room. It was bigger than I thought it would be. The walls were painted a wine colour, and most of the room was filled with the huge four poster bed, which was draped with black sheets and cloths. There was nothing on the walls apart from a couple dents here and there, and I winced mentally. Had Walter really punched each and every one of them into the plaster? Either he was very strong, or it must have hurt him very badly. There was a big black desk in one corner and a small sofa in the other. Everything was black and dark red; even the light had a wine coloured shade on it, which dimmed the room a little.

Walter and I sat at his desk and I got out my English notes.

"We only had English today, so it seems right to start with that," I said as I put my copy of the book down between us.

"Good," he muttered. "Because I don't know what half of the words mean in that damn thing."

"Yeah it's *Oscar Wilde*, the old English can be confusing."

We got onto a good start with me fully explaining the storyline of *The Picture of Dorian Gray* and Walter listening intently, asking good questions. Before I knew it, forty five minutes had already passed.

"So do you get it now?" I sat back in my seat, tired of talking so much.

"Yep," he nodded. "You're good at explaining things."

"Thanks," I replied.

The door was swung open all of a sudden, and Walter's older brother Landon walked right in.

"Knock first," Walter growled at him, balling his hands into fists.

"Yeah, yeah," Landon was rolling his eyes and then he raised his eyebrows in surprise when he saw me, "Hey again."

He smiled widely and I would have smiled back if Walter wasn't so angry. He got up out of his chair and walked to Landon, pushing him out.

"Nah, I came to borrow something," Landon chewed on his lip piercing, standing his ground.

Walter stopped and the two of them glanced at me.

"Should I...urm...go?" I asked, uncomfortably pulling on my sleeve.

"No," the two of them said together. They looked more alike than I had first perceived. Landon was wearing a loose fitting grey t-shirt, capturing the laid-back look perfectly, and his hair was just a few shades lighter than Walter's.

They spoke in low voices and I turned away to look at the desk, reading over my notes. I didn't hear what they were saying, and I didn't want to. Walter walked to his bedside and I heard him pull open the drawer in his small bedside cabinet. He handed something to Landon who thanked him, but instead of leaving like I expected him to, Landon put whatever it was in his pocket and came to sit his butt on the edge on the desk next to me.

"So Carol, is it?" He pulled a face.

"Coral," I corrected with a shy smile.

"Coral," Landon nodded. "Are you and my brother...you know - ?"

"Get out," Walter interrupted.

He was standing behind me, facing Landon, so I couldn't see his expression but I pictured it wasn't a very happy one.

"One second man," Landon was completely unfazed and held a finger at him. "You don't need to be scared of me Coral, and just ignore him."

I could feel my face burning crazily and I looked away.

"Landon, seriously," Walter stepped past me and grabbed the front of his shirt, yanking him off the desk. "Get out."

"I was leaving anyway," Landon smirked at him and winked down at me. "Give you two some *alone* time."

Walter looked like he wanted to murder his brother and I wasn't surprised. I would want to do the same if I was him. Walter practically shoved Landon out and he turned to face me with a mixture of misery and embarrassment on his face.

"Apologies," Walter sighed, unable to look me in the eye. "He's just obsessed."

I didn't need to ask exactly *what* he was obsessed with, and Walter didn't need to explain.

46

"Do you want something to eat?" Walter changed the subject. "I don't know about you, but I'm pretty hungry."

I was beyond hungry, but I wasn't planning on staying long enough to eat dinner so I shrugged, "I'll have some fruit, if you have any."

He thought about it, "Might have, let's go see."

I got up and we went down the stairs to the kitchen again. I was wary of seeing Eli again, but he still wasn't around thankfully. Walter opened various cabinets of food. There were only pears, which I neither liked nor disliked.

"Take whatever you want," he said to me as he grabbed a roll of bread and some cheese from the fridge.

I settled with a pear in the end and Walter started ripping open his bread roll and stuffing chunks of cheese into it. I heard the sound of the front door being opened and voices were carried down the hallway.

"That went well," one voice was saying.

"Not really, look at the state of *him*. Next time, that sucker Miguel is mine," another muttered back.

The triplets walked into view moments later and I noted that one of them was bleeding from their nose. The three of them looked grim faced and a little dirty, after being in a scuffle most likely. I was aware that Miguel was a member of the Santiago gang. One of the younger ones, I thought.

"You okay, Severn?" Walter asked him.

Severn grunted, then walked past me and grabbed some kitchen roll. His jogging bottoms were a bit muddy, as were his brothers' jeans. Now that I thought about it, one of the triplets always wore jogging bottoms and now that I knew it was Severn, I decided that they must have been his favourite choice of clothing.

"He's not a kid, he'll be fine," one of the triplets, either Gomez or Giovanni, muttered to Walter.

"Okay, shoot me for asking," Walter scowled at him.

"Gio is just being pessimistic," the last triplet, Gomez, muttered. "He thinks we lost the fight, but it wasn't that bad."

Giovanni said nothing and sighed deeply, clenching his jaw. I noted the streak of brown Gomez had in his ruffled blond fringe.

47

Apart from that adjustment, his two brothers had identical blond hair.

Giovanni was suddenly standing right in front of me, still hard-faced.

"Who are you?" he demanded.

"Don't talk to her like that," Walter snapped at him, his body language becoming hostile in an instant.

"Well who is she then?" Giovanni softened his voice, just a little.

"I'm Coral," I said, my voice catching in my throat slightly.

"Well excuse me Coral, but you're kind of in the way," he said to me.

I realised he was talking about getting to the fridge and I quickly stepped to the side. Giovanni reached in and took out two cans of *Sprite* with some grubby hands. It never struck me how tall the fifteen year olds were. I was eye level with their chins and I was two, maybe three years older.

"You live around here?" Gomez asked me, while he leant against the kitchen counter watching me, just like Walter had done earlier today.

"Not too far," I said vaguely.

"Ah right," he scratched his jaw, another similar movement Walter had done once before. "Well I'm Gomez, if you didn't already know."

"I do now," I attempted a smile and he half returned it.

Meanwhile, Giovanni had opened his second can of *Sprite* and gulped down half of it before gathering more food items and heading for the stairs. Gomez picked off some dried mud off of his leather jacket.

"So what are you doing here Coral?" He asked, not looking up.

I finished the rest of my pear, "Helping Walter catch up on the stuff he's missed at school."

Gomez's eyed widened at Walter, who was standing silently by the fridge still, eating his cheese roll.

"You went to school?" He asked incredulously.

"Yeah," Walter shrugged. "What about it?"

Gomez was speechless, "But, why?"

"'Cause I wanted to," Walter ran a hand through his dark brown hair.

"...How was it?" Gomez asked hesitantly.

"Fine. What's with all the questions?" Walter sighed, leaning back on the counter behind him.

"Erm, we haven't gone to school for a whole year," Gomez threw his hands up in the air. "Of course I would have questions."

"Yeah well I'm done answering them," Walter muttered.

Gomez rolled his eyes, "Whatever, help me with him."

I had forgotten that Severn was even there. He was crouched into a corner between the kitchen cupboards, his chin resting on his knees and a soaked ball of tissue stuffed in his nose. The blood had stopped flowing, but Severn had fallen asleep. I heard his quiet snores, and his blond hair looked rather soft, even though it was pretty dirty.

"Fine," Walter said.

Gomez grabbed his identical brother's wrists and pulled him up. I couldn't help but laugh quietly when Gomez almost fell back after hooking his arms around Severn's chest, the bloodied tissue dropping to the floor.

"Don't tell me he's dribbling on my shirt," Gomez groaned, Severn's head resting on his shoulder.

Walter ignored him and picked up Severn from behind quite easily. Severn's head was now resting on Walter's shoulder facing up towards the ceiling.

"Take his legs," Walter instructed.

Together Walter and Gomez carried their brother up the stairs and into his bedroom I guessed.

"Sorry about that," Walter smiled apologetically once he had returned.

"Its fine," I said back. "I should go home now anyway, I'm glad I could help."

"Let me walk you home," Walter offered.

"Oh no, you don't need to do that," I hurried. I didn't want him to see where I lived, at any costs.

"It's dark out now," Walter said, looking at me.

I tried not to look away from his gaze. I did that too much, and I actually I quite liked hazel eyes. His were a golden brown ringed with dark green.

"I'll be fine," I replied with a half-shrug. "I walk home from work later than this all the time."

"Okay, but let me drop you at least half way," he made a deal.

"Okay," I agreed, just because he was insisting so much. It had nothing to do with how I wouldn't mind spending another ten or so minutes with him.

We put on our coats and Walter went up to get my school bag. For a brief moment I felt my surroundings moving around me and I reached out to hold the wall for balance. Not that again. Walter came back down, patting his pockets as if he was feeling for something, which he probably was. Seeming satisfied, and guaranteeing my thoughts that Walter had been carrying *at least* a knife all day, he walked to the front door and opened it for me.

"Are you okay?" Walter asked me once we were walking out the in the gloom.

"Yeah, I'm fine," I lied.

I was actually finding it hard to breathe, as if something was squeezing my chest. My heart was beating too fast and I was out of breath from walking just about twenty paces. I'm sure once I got home and ate something more and also caught up on the sleep I'd been deprived of, I'd be fine. We walked in a comfortable silence which I was glad for, because it meant that I didn't have to try and speak whilst my heart felt like it was pounding in my head.

We got to roughly halfway when I stopped.

"Thanks for walking me," I looked up at Walter.

"No problem," he rubbed his hands together.

I noticed how his gaze searched all over the place, as if there was something to be aware of. I was certain no one was around, but Walter had been in a gang for how many years? It was in his instincts.

"You sure you don't want me to drop you home?" he added.

"I'm sure," I replied. "Goodnight."

He smiled, "Okay, night."

The rest of the journey home felt like it took forever and my headache got gradually worse. I guess that's what happened when you overworked yourself, both physically and mentally. I had no choice; otherwise I would have no home.

I felt like singing praises when my dilapidated block of flats finally came into view, and I might have, if I didn't feel so cold and weak. I got to the main door where I had to put in the pin code to get inside, but the numbers kept coming in and out of focus until they slid down the wall completely. I wasn't aware that I was falling until I hit the ground hard.

I scrunched up my face in pain, unable to even cry out. Gritting my teeth, I tried to move my body but it wouldn't listen. My vision was slowly darkening, and it scared me. It was only when I felt hands grab me, that I managed to shout out.

"Shh, it's okay. It's me, Walter. I followed you home to make sure you were okay," he explained in his deep voice. "I'm glad I did."

He picked me up easily, making me feel even more frail and fragile.

"Tell me what the code is," Walter said, holding me so that I could bury my face in his chest.

"2-6-0-9-8-1," I said in a muffled voice and I heard him key it in.

The door buzzed as it was unlocked and Walter pushed it open with his shoulder.

"Which way?" he asked me.

"Up the stairs," I replied, holding onto the front of his jacket when he started to climb. The sensation was making my head bang. "Just one flight."

"Door number?" Walter had to ask again as I was too out of it to register that he had finished climbing the first flight of stairs.

"Seventeen," I answered, trying to get my keys out of my pocket.

Walter saw what I was doing and he pushed his hand into my coat pocket, causing it to brush mine for a moment. It was a small unintentional touch, but it had felt strangely comforting, which was never the case when it came to men and touching.

Once he had unlocked the door to my flat, Walter walked in and I felt the shame and embarrassment wash over me as he, no doubt, took in his surroundings with distaste prominent in his mind. I didn't have to check his expression to see if it was true, I just knew it.

Walter took me into the first room to the left, which happened to be my bedroom. He lay me down on the bed and walked out without a word. I sat up slowly and leant against the peeling wallpaper.

"Walter?" I called feebly.

He came back in with a glass of water, handing it over to me.

I drank it so swiftly; I surprised myself, "Thank you."

"Stop saying thank you," he said, sounding just like Hayley for a second. "You should take more care of yourself. I knew there was something wrong."

"I do take care of myself," I mumbled as my headache started to ease just a little. "It's just today...I...didn't have time to eat."

"I'm sure it's more than food," Walter looked at me closely. "You look very tired, you've been looking like that all day. You even told me so this morning."

"Okay, fine," I admitted. "I didn't sleep much last night."

"How much?" he wanted to know.

"Maximum was about three hours," I guessed. "The gunshots woke me."

Walter looked almost guilty for a second, "Well...you should eat something now. What should I get you?"

"No need," I gave him a faint smile. "I can get something myself."

"You're not going anywhere Coral," he said, allowing a small smile onto his face, which had been so serious all this time.

"Fine," I gave in to him easily. "There's some fruit in the fridge."

"Proper food."

"Cereal?"

"Doesn't count, to me," he said, folding his arms

"Pasta, or anything else for that matter, takes longer to make," I complained. "I'm sure you have other things to do."

"I don't," Walter denied.

"Okay," I said. "You'll find pasta in the cupboard above the cooker and pesto in the fridge."

"Got it," Walter nodded and then left my bedroom.

52

I heard him rummaging around the in the kitchen and I let my mind wander. I wondered if Walter cooked for himself often, somehow I didn't think so, but he was doing it for me. He was being such a gentlemen, a side to him I'm sure not many people ever saw. Walter returned in fifteen minutes max with a huge bowl of steaming pesto pasta in his hand.

"Thanks so much," I smiled up at him in gratitude. No one had done something like this for me in a very long time.

"Eat it all," Walter sat down on the edge of the bed.

"I can't with you watching me like that," I said, looking at the food.

"I still make you uncomfortable?" Walter cracked a grin.

"No, it's not you, it's just weird in general with anyone doing that," I said quickly.

"Okay sure," Walter tipped his head back and looked up at the ceiling.

I ate quickly as the impending feeling of sleep threatened to swamp me completely. Walter didn't say anything to me, he seemed to be lost in thought. I didn't mind, it meant that I could finish it with no interruptions.

"Done?" Walter turned to look at me once I put my fork into my bowl.

"Yep," I said to him. "Tha – "

"Shhh," Walter cut me off by putting a finger to my lips. "Stop that."

His sudden movement had made me jump and he smirked, his face so close to mine. He took his finger away and left with the empty bowl. I heard him washing up in the sink and I smiled to myself as I imagined him doing it. I got in between my sheets and closed my eyes, drifting off to sleep swiftly. I couldn't help it, I was so exhausted. I heard Walter creeping back into my room moments later. He paused for a few seconds and I could tell his gaze was on me.

"Goodnight," Walter murmured, not sure if I was awake or not, and he turned off the light without waiting for an answer.

"Goodnight Walter," I said, and his receding footsteps stopped. "I don't know what I would have done tonight without you."

"It was nothing," Walter replied and then he left.

8

The next day there was shock horror in the school.

No one could have ever foreseen not just Walter Simpson, but Eli, Gomez, Giovanni and Severn Simpson *too*, entering the premises. I watched from a window in the hallway which faced the car park, where I saw Walter with his hands stuffed deep into the pockets of his black jeans, talking to Eli who was looking down with his brown hair covering his face. The triplets were messing around, pushing each other and laughing. It was just unbelievable that they were back, and for what reason?

Gossip travelled at the speed of light and the school was in uproar by lunchtime. I'd heard a lot of things, everyone was talking. Apparently Gomez had been caught stealing from teachers twice already and Eli had threatened a guy with a knife. I didn't catch much about the other triplets Severn or Giovanni, but I did hear that Walter had thrown someone's scissors at a teacher in a rage. It was very likely that a lot (if not all) of it was false, but it did still make me wary of the other Simpson boys.

"Hey Coral, how was Maths?" Hayley asked as she joined me outside the lunch hall.

"Not bad," I shrugged indifferently.

I had been waiting for her so that we could go and have lunch together. Earlier today, I'd awkwardly explained to her that I didn't feel ready to go and sit with all her friends and she'd told me that it was no problem for us to just sit alone together for the meantime.

"Coral have you spoken to Walter today? You must have some idea for this turn of events. School hasn't been this interesting for ages!" Hayley was quick to get to the hot topic.

"No I haven't," I replied in a low voice as people nearby were listening in.

I took Hayley's arm and walked into the lunch hall to get our lunch to get away from any gossips. It made no difference because we just ended up in a queue where everyone was still talking about the Simpson brothers in hushed, excited and even worried voices.

"I have no idea why Walter's brothers are here," I said to Hayley quietly as we waited in the queue. "I really didn't expect it."

Hayley didn't have a chance to reply because there was a sudden commotion ahead of us in the queue. Stepping up onto my tip-toes I was able to see that the fuss was being caused by one of the triplets. I wasn't sure which one, but I guessed it was Giovanni Simpson, solely because the dispute was over food, and from the little I'd seen so far, Giovanni liked his food.

The fifteen year old wanted a bigger portion but the dinner lady, who had only given him a measly amount, was putting up a fight. I couldn't actually hear the words being said, but Giovanni was angrily pointing at the ladle and the dinner lady fought back defiantly, motioning for his to take his plate and move on. She clearly didn't know that that boy wasn't someone to have on your bad side, whether she was an adult or not.

"I didn't even notice they were already here," Hayley whispered to me. "Wow the triplets are so identical, I never knew."

"Yeah, it's crazy," I murmured in agreement.

I hadn't noticed before but Severn and Gomez were also present. Severn, I guessed, was standing behind Giovanni yawning as

Giovanni attempted to snatch the ladle out of the woman's hand. This wasn't going to end well if nobody stepped in.

"What's taking so long up there?" A guy asked from behind us in the line.

"It's the Simpsons," some other person muttered.

Then I saw the last triplet, Gomez, put an arm round his irritated brother and say something into his ear. Giovanni stopped what he was doing, snatched his plate and walked on still muttering hatefully. The queue began to move again.

"So how did the tutoring go?" Hayley asked me once we'd finally gotten our food and taken a seat.

"Where do I begin?" I rounded my eyes and then smiled. "I mean, I met Landon and – "

"He's the nineteen year old, right?" Hayley checked.

"Yeah," I nodded. "He's actually quite nice, from how he's treated me so far anyway. The triplets are *okay*, but Eli and Phoenix – the oldest one – are the scariest."

"And *not* Walter?" Hayley looked at me sceptically.

I recalled how good Walter had been to me yesterday night when I'd collapsed outside of the block of flats. Anything could have happened to me if he hadn't followed me to make sure I had gotten home okay. On top of that, he'd insisted I eat a proper meal and even went through the trouble of cooking and washing up the pasta for me. That was probably the nicest anyone had been to me, and it was so crazy that it had come from *him* of all people.

"What happened between you two?" Hayley was smirking at me. "Look at that smile on your face."

I automatically blushed, not having realised that I was being so open with my expression, "Nothing happened, I just went through my English notes with him."

"And?" Hayley started to grin.

"Well, he kind of walked me home," I said, skipping out the dramatic stuff.

"That's –" Hayley blinked in surprise. "That's really nice of him. I can't believe this is the same cold-hearted, extremely hot-headed, *gang member* we're talking about."

"Yeah," I shrugged. "He's –"

"Coming right now," Hayley was looking to the left.

I followed her gaze and saw Walter walking between the packed tables with his lunch and a straight, reserved face. He was so good-looking.

"He's sitting with his little brothers," Hayley cooed. "Cute."

"The triplets are cute?" I raised an eyebrow at her.

"Well I was talking about the brotherly bond, but yeah the triplets are cute," she admitted.

"I guess I agree," I said honestly.

"How old are they?"

"Fifteen, I think," I started eating my apple. "They look older, I know."

Hayley nodded in agreement, "Did Walter see you?"

"Don't think so," I said.

"Give him a wave?" she grinned suddenly.

"Is that a challenge?" I grinned back, surprising myself. Talking to Hayley was so easy.

"Yep," she leaned back in her chair, tossing her orange in the air and catching it.

"It would have been awkward if you'd dropped that, wouldn't it?" I gave her a knowing smile, making her laugh.

"Don't change the subject," Hayley said after she'd recollected herself.

"Fine," I said, looking over at the table where the four Simpson brothers were sitting.

They were seated two round tables to our left and Walter was sitting in a chair that faced in my direction. He was eating his sandwich, muttering to his brothers as they smirked about something. I'd read somewhere that if you stared at someone long enough, they would eventually notice you were staring, no matter the situation.

So I stared at him.

And a second later Water's hazel eyes caught mine.

It actually made me jump and I forced myself not to look away instinctively. Walter didn't look away either and his lips formed a warm smile. I wondered if he was thinking about last night, because now I was.

Hayley was looking too and she grinned, pinching my hand that was lying on the table. I winced then raised my other hand to give Walter a small wave. His brothers looked at him with frowns when he waved back, and followed his look towards me. I waved at them too, just on the spur of the moment, which was very unlike my usual self when it came to new people.

The identical looking boys watched me for a second with straight faces, making me want to shrink back into nothingness, but then they all raised their right hands and waved back. Their movements were so in sync I almost couldn't handle it.

"Your turn," I grinned at Hayley.

"Me?" Her grin disappeared instantly.

"Yep."

"What should I do?" she panicked.

"Anything," I shrugged.

We looked at their table again, and the boys were still looking back. The triplets were talking amongst themselves and I knew it was about us, but they seemed curious more than anything.

Hayley swallowed and gave them a very stiff, quite abrupt and pretty twitchy nod which had me biting my lip to stifle my laughter. She was so nervous! Gomez, with the brown streak in his hair, said something to his brothers and then, to our amusement, the triplets smirked and all gave her a purposely slow and flirtatious wink. Walter rolled his eyes at them, but he was half-smiling and probably found the whole thing just as amusing.

The day finished soon enough and I hadn't had the chance to speak to Walter at all. We hadn't had English today and as it was a Wednesday, I had work after school so I wouldn't be going over to his place. I wondered if he remembered that or not, I didn't want him waiting around or looking for me.

I felt someone tap me on my shoulder, interrupting my thoughts. I turned around to face Eli Simpson, the last person I was expecting, especially in a mass of other students. The noise quieted down a bit when people noticed that Eli was there and that he was talking to me of all people.

"Can I talk to you, in private?" Eli asked, not quite looking me in the eye, his eyes were all over the place, and he glared at anyone who's gaze faltered for too long.

What could this guy possibly want to talk to me about? He had been very rude to be for no apparent reason, and what more was that he actually scared me a little.

Eli fixed his green eyed gaze on me again once he noticed my hesitation.

"It's nothing...bad," he mumbled, dropping his gaze and hardening his jaw.

"Okay," I said, scrunching my toes up in my shoes nervously.

He immediately started walking and I guessed he expected me to follow him as he didn't say another word to me, nor did he look back. I followed his tall, slender frame outside where it was much quieter.

"I just wanted to say sorry...about the other day," Eli muttered, turning to face me but still looking down.

While his gaze was down, I took that opportunity to stare at him. His hair wasn't really brown, like I'd initially thought, it was a dark blond instead. He looked quite like the triplets, and his eyes were really the greenest eyes I'd ever seen.

"It's okay," I answered before he looked up and caught me ogling at him.

I wanted to ask him why he had called me a slut in the first place, but I decided not to push it.

"Oh," Eli looked up finally, with a glint in his eyes. "If Walter asks you if I said anything to you, say no."

I smiled amusement, "Why?"

"Just because," Eli smiled back, then he walked away.

Instead of following suit and leaving to get to my shift, I just stood there a bit longer and continued to smile to myself.

Eli Simpson had dimples.

9

"You look nervous," Walter teased me as we stood outside his front door.

I shrugged, pulling on the sleeves of my jumper, waiting for him to stop staring at me and open the door.

"I'm not gonna let any of them hurt you, you know," Walter still gazed down at me. "They wouldn't anyway."

"I know," I said, but it didn't ease the butterflies in my stomach.

Walter chuckled under his breath and unlocked the front door. It was Thursday and the third time Walter was letting me into his home in just a couple weeks. We were greeted by the pounding bass coming from upstairs that ran through the walls and made my heart jump in my chest in time to the beat of the song playing.

"The triplets," Walter said over the noise.

"They got back that fast?" I had to raise my voice.

"They use their bikes," he explained. "I'm gonna tell them to turn that shit down. There's no way we can work in that."

"Sure," I nodded.

"Help yourself to anything in the kitchen," Walter said to me. "I'll be right back."

I crept into the kitchen, even though it was empty, and took a bottle of water that I found in the fridge. Deciding to go and wait for

Walter in the living room, I opened the door and jumped when I saw that it wasn't vacant. To my luck, only two brothers were in there. Gomez, the triplet I remembered with the streak of brown in his blond fringe, was showing his older brother Landon an expensive looking watch. They stopped talking when they saw me, and Gomez slipped the watch into his pocket.

"Hey..." I stood by the door.

Was that something I shouldn't have seen? They probably didn't even hear me over the music which was still blaring and practically shaking the whole house.

Landon cracked a smile at me, immediately making my shoulders sink in relief.

"Come sit! Feel at home, we don't bite," he said loudly in a smooth voice, which sounded a bit like Walter's.

I smiled back and sat down in an unoccupied leather sofa. Gomez got up and walked past me, slamming the door shut.

"That's better," he said, his voice ten times clearer already.

To my surprise, he sat on the end of the same sofa as me and I forced myself to hold his eye contact, he was a kid, he shouldn't have been intimidating at all. It was only yesterday when he and his triplets had jokingly winked at me and Hayley at lunch.

Gomez grinned, "So who was your friend the other day at the canteen?"

I shook my head, smiling at the memory, "Her name is Hayley."

Gomez nodded to himself, digesting my information.

"So you're here with Walter again I'm guessing?" Landon asked me.

"Yeah," I rubbed my face, hiding a smile.

"Why do you like Walter so much anyway?" Landon questioned, stretching out in the sofa and filling Gomez's empty space with his legs.

"I don't," I tried to deny, taken aback by his bluntness.

"You do," Landon and Gomez said in unison.

"I don't," I was smiling openly now.

"Okay fine, why are you *so fond* of Walter?" Landon asked smirking, his lip ring glinting in the light.

I shrugged giving up, "He seems like a nice guy."

"Nice?" Gomez burst out.

"What?" I asked.

The two brothers shared a look.

"Do you wanna know what he's like when he's mad? Which, if I may add, can happen any time?" Landon cocked an eyebrow.

"Okay," I was curious.

Gomez leaned forwards eagerly, "Well one time he got so mad, he passed out. It wasn't pretty."

I raised my eyebrows, "Seriously? How?"

"He couldn't breathe and his asthma made it worse. Plus, he never carried his inhaler with him," Gomez told me.

I was even more surprised, "Walter has asthma?"

Landon shook his head, "Not any more, he grew out of it."

I tried to imagine Walter puffing on a pump, and it almost made me laugh.

"How old was he?" I asked.

"About, twelve, or maybe thirteen." Landon frowned, trying to remember.

"I've never seen him extremely mad before," I thought aloud.

"Do you want to?" Landon grinned excitedly. "Because if I were to sleep with you, he'd go all *King Kong* on me."

My face fired up. I was shocked that he could even speak about something like that so casually. I tried to keep it cool by drinking some of my water and Landon and Gomez laughed at me.

"May I ask why?" I had to ask after I had recomposed myself. "We aren't together or anything like that."

"But you're friends aren't you?" he asked, confused.

I hesitated, were we friends? We didn't really know each other...but we were getting there slowly.

The door was opened and Severn, another triplet I now recognised by his choice of comfy clothes, walked in. The music had stopped, but Walter hadn't returned. He had probably gotten preoccupied with something else.

"I'm joining the conversation," Severn announced, moving Landon's legs aside so he could sit down.

I smiled. These guys were so much more relaxed than I'd initially thought.

"So fill me in," Severn said, gesturing with his hand.

His voice was so calm, but a little forceful too. I liked it.

Landon gave his brother a roll of his eyes, "We were just asking...um Coral? Yeah Coral here if she and Walter were friends."

"Of course they are friends!" Severn said as if it were the most obvious thing in the world. "If they weren't friends, Walter wouldn't have even started going back to school again. It's his final year, remember? He's going to achieve nada."

"Wait what do you mean?" I cut in, wanting him to elaborate more on that.

Severn gave me a chilled look, "I mean Walter's not smart enough to pass anything with the year almost half gone already?"

"No, what did you mean about him going back to school?" I half-smiled.

"Oh right," Severn said. "What I meant by that, is that if he hadn't liked what he saw that night, he wouldn't have gone to school the following day."

"He told you about that?" I raised my brows in surprise.

"He mentioned it," Landon shrugged.

"He was only returning a handkerchief I had dropped," I said.

"Yeah, and you continued to drop that hanky every night so that he would have to come to school and return it to you?" Gomez said sarcastically earning a reluctant smile from me.

"Exactly," Severn smirked. "And if you weren't friends, Walter wouldn't have even invited you to our house, for any reason at all. What do you think about that one?"

I was about to think of a reasonable answer when Walter himself walked in. He looked at us, somewhat suspiciously with those hazel eyes of his, then he brought his hand to his chin and rubbed it absent-mindedly.

"What's going on down here?" he asked.

"Nothing," Gomez and Severn replied in unison.

Walter shook his head at them, and turned to Landon.

"We were just talking," he shrugged coolly.

"Then why did you stop?" Walter asked, unamused.

There was silence, and the boys shared childish grins.

"So how did you get Giovanni to turn the music down?" I asked innocently, changing the subject.

Out of the corner of my eye I saw Severn and Gomez nod gratefully.

"With pain," Walter said bluntly, making me wince.

Walter smiled at me, "I was kidding."

I felt Severn nudged me slightly. He was probably trying to say *If you weren't friends Walter wouldn't even smile at you.* And I was sort of pleased, because Walter smiled at me a lot. I was too busy smiling at my lap that I almost didn't catch Walter mutter to his brothers that he wasn't, in fact, kidding.

Landon stood up suddenly, checking his watch, "Damn, I'm late!"

"Better not keep Cindy waiting," Gomez smirked.

"I swear Cindy was last week," Walter frowned.

"Nah, that was Vanessa!" Severn exclaimed, "Their names sound nothing alike!"

Landon rolled his eyes, walking towards the door, "It's Kirsty this week actually."

It seemed Landon really was a player at heart.

"Well Coral, I'll see you around next time," Landon said winking at me, then he was gone.

Walter stared at the front door that his brother had just left from a little longer, then he looked down, shaking his head slightly in what looked like anger. I took my eyes off him reluctantly, only to catch the eyes of both Gomez and Severn. They grinned at me and I tried not to grin back.

"What's so funny?" Walter asked through gritted teeth, glaring at his two younger brothers.

Severn and Gomez only smiled at him and Walter looked away, sighing deeply before turning his attention to me.

"Shall we go and do some work now?" he questioned.

"Okay," I nodded, starting to get up out of my seat.

"We might as well go up too," Gomez said to his triplet.

"Yeah," Severn replied.

Walter glared even harder at them. I was starting to think that that common expression of his was actually a little sexy.

"What?" Gomez asked, feigning innocence.

Walter decided to ignore him and he left, heading for the stairs. We all followed. Upstairs, Walter and I were about to go into his room when Gomez called out to me.

"Coral, can you help us for a second?"

I shrugged, "Are you sure it'll only be a second? Walter and I have to get on with some school work."

"I swear," Gomez insisted.

"Walter do you mind?" I gave him an apologetic look.

"No," he said, looking down and rubbing the back of his head.

I was stood there, staring at his bicep that flexed just inches from my face and then I shifted my gaze quickly when I realised that Severn and Gomez were waiting for my response.

"Let's go then," I said to the two of them, still feeling a bit warm in the face.

I walked into the triplets' room and I could sense that Walter had also come in behind me. Their room was bigger than Walter's room. The walls were painted a simple blue and there were three single beds all on one side, headboards facing the wall. On the other side of the room there was a desk on which sat a computer and a few chairs where Giovanni was sitting. There was also a corner sofa which was covered in the boys' laundry.

"So what do you need help with?" I asked them.

Gomez went to a chest of drawers and gathered some items in his hands. He came back, showing me...some lipsticks, eyeliners and mascaras amongst other cosmetics

"What's going on?" I gave him a perplexed look.

Gomez put up his hands, "I can explain. I...obtained these items -"

"Stole," Severn coughed.

Gomez gave him a sour look and continued, "...and I wanna see which brand is the best so that I can try to get the same type next time."

"Why don't you just search it up online?" I asked.

"They're designer, you see?" he pushed the make-up towards my eye and surely enough I saw *Urban Decay* and a few other brands. "People are going to say they're all as good as each other, all high quality. So I need to test them out. But the problem is, I'm a guy and I don't know shit about make-up, so can we have your advice?" Gomez widened his eyes absent-mindedly.

I didn't know a lot about makeup either, the most I ever wore was occasional mascara or discrete lipstick.

"I'll try?" I said. "I hope you're not implying that you're going to test them out on me though."

"Oh no, don't worry about that," Gomez flashed a dark smirk. "I got better ideas."

He and Severn shared a sneaky look and then glanced at Giovanni who was still on the computer with his back to us. The two of them silently crept up behind their third triplet who was oblivious, and before he knew it he was grabbed on both sides and dragged across the floor to a chair.

"Get off!" he yelled, not seeming to be mad or anything.

Giovanni tried ripping himself out of their grip, twisting and turning, but Gomez and Severn held on tight to his arms. I found myself laughing, it was comical. They slammed him down onto a chair and held his arms behind it.

"Come here," Gomez waved at me, then he handed me a *Mac* eye liner. "Do your best."

"You want me to use it on him?" I raised my eyebrows.

"Yep. Draw on him."

"Wait, take off his shirt first," Severn instructed, still holding his brother's arms behind him.

"Good idea," Gomez nodded.

They ripped off Giovanni's shirt with such force that it stretched at the seams and despite his age, Giovanni had a decent body. The boys were watching me, I could tell, and Giovanni himself had the audacity to wink. I looked back at Walter who was still standing by the door, looking away, with his jaw now clenched. Giovanni tried to say something but Severn simply picked up a dirty sock from the floor and shoved it into his mouth.

"We need some tape or something."

After they secured the sock and tied Giovanni's wrists, they again handed me the eye liner.

"Go crazy," they grinned at me.

I allowed myself a smile and apologised to Giovanni before leaning down to do my worst with the eye pencil. When I un-capped it, I saw that it had been well used and probably well loved by its former owner. It became clearer to me that Gomez was really a thief and I didn't know how to really feel about that. I hated stealing, but being with the boys like this made them seem so harmless and carefree.

I leaned in close, about to draw a simple line across Giovanni's chest when he thrust his hips up knocking my elbow. I had to say, his sudden movement had scared me, but then I realised how funny it was and burst out into hysterical laughter. I didn't even need to be embarrassed because the three of them joined in with their deep voices, tears rolling out of Giovanni's eyes and his muffled laughter making his body shake. I turned to look back at Walter, but he had gone.

A while later Gomez, Severn and I stood back admiring our work. We had all had a go, and now Giovanni's chest, abdomen and face was covered in different brands of designer eye-liner, lipstick and even smears of mascara. Many different colours too, and I'm sure (as the majority was water-proof) he'd have a hard time getting it off. Of course I didn't tell him that. Gomez had noted down the ones that I guessed were better, and they had thanked me. Well Giovanni had said something incomprehensible, but I took it as a 'thanks'.

I hurried out of the triplets' room, aware of the large amount of time I had ended up spending in there. On entering Walter's room, I already had my apology started when I cut myself off abruptly.

Walter was lying on his bed asleep.

He was on his back, his head turned to the side and his chest rose and fell slowly. He looked so peaceful, I couldn't bear to wake him up. So I curled up in the black leather sofa in the corner of his room, and closed my eyes. Forget the English work, sleep was much better.

I woke up when my stomach grumbled loudly. Raising my head, I glanced at the bed where Walter was still asleep. Checking my phone I saw that it was now twenty past seven in the evening, a lot later than I'd wanted to stay.

Phoenix, the oldest brother, suddenly entered the room, pushing the door open and knocking he did so. He stopped when he saw me and I had to say, my heart stopped too. You could tell he'd been to jail before, I saw it in his eyes. This guy was complicated and he reminded me about how he and all of his brothers, including Walter, weren't as good and law-abiding as they seemed. Phoenix was the definition of dangerous, and here I was in his house.

"What are you doing?" he asked, still looking me right in the eye.

"Me and Walter, we were going to do school work together," I found myself rambling. "He invited me over and well, I said yes, I'd help him with – "

Phoenix cut me off with an uninterested wave of his hand and I zipped up instantly, despite how rude I thought he was being. He was the *leader* of the Simpson gang, he was invincible.

Phoenix walked up to the bed and looked down at Walter's sleeping form. Without warning, he slapped the side of Walter's face, pretty hard. I mean, what a way to wake someone up.

Walter moaned and stretched, making his top ride up his torso a little, to reveal some rather appealing muscles and a glimpse of a tattoo on his hip. To my disbelief, the sudden violence inflicted on him didn't even wake him up. Instead, Walter rolled over to his front his face buried in the pillow.

Phoenix scratched his stubble and then he whacked the back of Walter's head.

I wanted to tell him to stop, but who was I? This guy could probably make me 'disappear' in an instant and nobody would ever notice.

Walter stirred again and groaned, swearing into the pillow.

"What's your problem?" he lifted his head and glared at Phoenix.

"If you want food, go and get it now before it's gone," Phoenix grunted and he left without another word.

Walter ran a hand down his face and sat up, "Sorry I fell asleep."

"It's okay," I replied with a smile. "I fell asleep too."

"Oh, you did?" Walter looked surprised.

"Yeah," I said and then added quickly, "on that sofa over there."

"Are you hungry?" Walter got up off his bed, and stretched again.

"I was actually going to head home," I tried, rubbing my arm sheepishly.

"That's not answering the question though," Walter walked up to me, a faint smirk on his lips.

"Okay," I folded my arms and smirked back up at him. "Yes, I'm hungry."

"Good," Walter grinned. "Let's go eat."

Downstairs on the kitchen counter sat three large steaming boxes of pizza. Two had already been finished but the empty containers were still hot. Gomez, Giovanni, Severn and Eli sat on high stools, eating away at the cheesy goodness.

"Yeah...sorry this isn't so healthy," Walter said while grimacing at his brother Giovanni's eating habits. "We don't really cook that much."

"I totally understand," I said truthfully. "I'm in the same boat as you. My speciality is pasta and pesto."

"Gotta love pesto," Giovanni said, spraying sweetcorn out of his mouth at us.

Walter gave him a blank look and Giovanni turned his face away quickly, making me stifle a laugh. His face was still completely covered in designer makeup and although it was slightly faded, it would take a lot more scrubbing to get rid of it. His mouth was stuffed with food, and his jaw was working in overdrive and he wolfed the pizza down.

My phone vibrated in my pocket and I checked to see what it could be. It was most likely Hayley, as I didn't receive messages from anyone else, but what would she want to talk to me about right now? Like most people, she was probably busy with her family, having dinner.

It turned out it *was* Hayley.

Hey Coral, just seeing how you're doing. If you wanna come round mine anytime for tea, you're very welcome.

I raised my brows in surprise. This was so unexpected, yet so like something she would do.

Hi Hayley, thanks that's really nice of you. Maybe we can arrange a day for that at school?

I hit send and then looked up to see only one slice of pizza left. Walter glanced at it and then looked at me, swallowing a mouthful of his own slice.

"I told you it went fast," he said.

"I don't think you did say that," I murmured and just as I did, Giovanni, who I'm sure had eaten more than anyone there, reached for it.

Walter slapped his hand and snagged the piece himself.

"Ladies first Gio," Walter scowled at him.

He offered me the slice and I smiled gratefully, "Thanks."

"We can order more if you like," he said, looking a bit guilty.

"No, no," I said quickly. "It's a big slice; I'll have a hot drink when I get home."

I could feel the brothers' eyes on me and it made me feel a little uneasy. Well, Eli's gaze did anyway. I looked down as I ate the pizza and when I felt Hayley reply to me, I checked what she had said.

Yep, sure. I'll take it you're tutoring Walter so you're at his tonight? Say hi to him and the triplets for me ;D

I laughed quietly, remembering that lunch time yesterday.

"Hayley says hi," I said, looking up and grinning at the boys.

"Nice," Gomez smirked. "Tell her I said hi back, or better yet, give me her number."

"Wait, who's Hayley?" Severn frowned, looking at his brother.

"Ditto what he said," Giovanni, the final triplet spoke after gulping down almost a whole can of fizzy drink.

"She's a friend, the one sitting with me at lunch yesterday," I replied.

The three of them started talking among themselves with Gomez making obscene gestures with his hands. Walter rolled his eyes, and Eli raised his eyebrows.

"I want her number," they all said at once when they finished.

They frowned at each other and said, again in unison, "I said it first."

It was so weird.

"I'm not giving you her number guys," I said. "When you see her, ask her yourself."

"Okay," Gomez said. "At least, let me reply to her. She said hi to us after all."

I cocked an eyebrow at him, trying to suss him out, and Gomez smiled back innocently at me. He was probably just going to text Hayley his number himself, but there wasn't really any harm in that. It was better than him having hers without her knowledge.

"Here," I went to hand him my phone.

"Don't," Eli said suddenly. "Don't give it to them."

"Why not?" I asked, surprised he was even talking to me at all.

"Because they won't leave her alone. They do it to all the older girls," Eli muttered.

"And you care because...?" Walter asked sarcastically, glaring at him.

"We don't even do that," Gomez said, holding his hand out for the phone.

"Eli's *lying*!" Severn yelled, it seemed to be just for the fun of it.

"You don't care Eli, you never do," Walter answered his own question viciously.

I had a feeling this was about something more than just a phone number.

"What do you know about caring yourself, Mr Anger management?" Eli snapped back.

"More than you do."

"Fair enough," Gomez commented, interrupting their little standoff. "Now can I have her number?"

I tried to answer but Walter and Eli were both talking really loudly and I was afraid it would escalate into a fight or something...which it kind of did.

Half an hour later I stood in front of my block of flats, facing Walter who had just walked me home.

In the end, I had decided not to give my phone to anyone, I had just wanted the boys to stop arguing. And when I meant arguing, it wasn't your everyday shouting and yelling abuse. The Simpsons brought 'arguing' to a whole new level, which included throwing cutlery and punches. They acted as if the flying pieces of metal didn't even hurt, which surprised me because they were, in fact, bleeding.

Thankfully the triplets had pulled me out of it and left Walter and Eli to argue alone. They didn't even call it fighting, and so I didn't want to know what 'fighting' looked like.

"You okay?" Walter asked, his hood drawn over his head. "I hope we didn't ruin your evening or anything."

Even though Eli was less muscled than Walter, the guy had managed one good hit. Walter's cheekbone was cut and although it had stopped bleeding, it was red and looked sore.

"No, I'm fine and I had fun for the most part," I replied with a gentle smile. "I'm the one who should be asking *you* if you're okay."

A smile spread across the eighteen year old's face, and I couldn't help wincing for him.

"Yeah, I'm fine. Believe me when I say it looks worse than it feels."

"Sure, I believe you," I said, giving him a small smile.

We stood in silence for a couple seconds and I looked away from Walter's strong gaze.

"I guess I'll see you at school tomorrow," I said eventually. "We can catch up on that work we never got round to next time."

"Yeah, course," Walter nodded.

There was another pause and I was about to just wish him a goodnight when Walter spoke first.

"So, could we...swap numbers, or something?" he made a pain filled face as he looked at the ground.

I refrained from widening my eyes in shock as he was now looking at me. Instead, I tried to play it cool and I nodded, giving him another smile.

Walter grinned and he fished out his phone from one of his pockets. The action brought back memories of that very first night that had set all of this into motion. He handed me his black Smartphone and I took it, typing my number into it.

"I'll text you," Walter tried not to smile.

"Yeah sure," I was unsuccessful at doing the same. "Well, goodnight."

"Night," he said, taking a few steps back as I keyed myself into the building.

When I reached my flat, I peeked out of the kitchen window which overlooked the street and saw Walter's dark figure walking away into the night. It was after I'd gotten changed, had a cup of tea and gotten into my bed when my phone buzzed.

Glancing at it I was ecstatic to see that Walter had texted me already.

Sleep well x It read.

I don't know why it made me so happy, but it did.

After today I could definitely call Walter Simpson a friend.

10

It was lunchtime and the canteen was crowded. I sat on the end of a table with Hayley and we were talking about last night at the Simpsons house. No one ever got to know the Simpson gang (as most people referred to them as) and so Hayley was interested in anything I had to tell her about the brothers, although she didn't really believe me when I said they were like normal teenage guys for the most part.

"So are you free to come to dinner tonight?" Hayley asked me. "My parents are totally fine with it."

"Today I have work after school and I finish late," I said with an apologetic smile. "But tomorrow, Thursday, I'll be free."

"Okay, tomorrow it is," Hayley agreed.

Finalising it suddenly made me feel anxious about meeting Hayley's parents. It sounded so childish, but what if they didn't like me?

Commotion in the canteen caught our attention and Hayley and I turned to look at the source of it. People had made a circle and in the middle of it, were Walter and Eli Simpson who were facing another guy. Walter had food all over his chest, most likely the lunch of the guy the Simpson brothers were now facing off to. Both boys were still bruised from the 'argument' they'd had the night before.

"Come on," Hayley said, getting up from her seat once our view had been blocked by other bystanders.

I followed her and we joined the crowd. I was just able to see Walter and Eli who were both glaring at the other boy, although Eli seemed to be in the clear when it came to being covered in lunch.

"It was an accident," the guy said, raising his hands in the air and glancing around at everyone. "I don't want a fight."

Walter looked round at the crowd too, "You've already got one."

"I'll buy you a new jacket," stammered the other boy who I now recognised was on the school's rugby team.

Eli laughed. It was surprising to hear such a...nice sound, at a time like this.

"Do you think we need your money?" Eli stepped towards the rugby player who was more built than Eli himself.

"Fight, fight, fight," people started chanting, quietly at first and then louder and louder. Soon the teachers would be coming.

The terrified boy swung at Eli who dodged and narrowed his green eyes at his opponent. Before Eli had the chance to hit back Walter, who had been growing madder by the second, slammed into the rugby player with an unbelievable force and they both crashed to the floor.

Walter started hitting the boy, and when I said hitting, I really meant hitting. Hearing the sounds of his bare fist repetitively smash into his bloodying face, while the boy pleaded with Walter to stop, was horrific. With Walter on top of the guy, Eli kicked at his ribs, neither of them showing mercy for something so small.

Some other rugby players stormed into the middle of the circle and fought back. One kicked Walter in the side, causing him to fall off this opponent and a couple others shoved Eli away from their friend. Soon a full-scale fight was blowing and a lot of boys were throwing punches and kicks. A handful of teachers, including the headmaster, split through the circle and started pulling Walter and Eli away from the beaten boy. Instead of turning on the teachers too, the two boys let them pull them back a few steps before tearing themselves free from their grips.

"You never said you were sorry," Walter growled at the boy who'd spilt his lunch over him.

"Come with me. All of you," the headmaster said in a tight voice whilst a couple of the other teachers went to the aid of the injured boy with first aid bags.

I watched Walter, Eli and the other rugby players follow the headmaster out of the canteen and I released my clenched fists. My heart as hammering and I drew air in through my nose deeply. I didn't like violence at all. Hayley took hold of my shaking hand and squeezed it.

"Sorry I made you see that," she said. "I didn't think it would progress so much."

"Neither did I," I replied.

But I shouldn't have been surprised.

***

"Class," my Textiles teacher addressed us. "Now I'm sure you're all aware of the dog show coming up. We need as many hands as we can get."

Of course, we were aware. The school was calling volunteers to help prepare for an upcoming dog show we were hosting in order to raise money for the charities we were supporting over the course of the academic year.

"For the duration of today's class, I've arranged for you to go and help with the decorations," she said. "It shouldn't take longer than the usual double period and then you can get back to business in the next lesson."

There were a few sighs but I didn't really mind. Making decorations was as creative as what we'd be doing normally. It was probably less work too, to be honest.

Hayley smiled at me, "Let's go down to the art department."

"You'd think our lessons would be held in the art department, wouldn't you?" I murmured as we made our way. "Textiles is still art, in a way."

"Yeah," Hayley agreed, flicking her shiny dark hair over her shoulder. "Making clothes is way cooler than painting naked men anyway."

I half-smiled, "Yeah."

We later arrived in the large art department which had two floors and plenty of space. Other students were already there, most of them art students, but a few who seemed very out of place. I recognised a couple of bruised rugby players from the fight at lunchtime. They moodily cut out coloured sheets to make bunting out of.

"Detention," Hayley said before I could ask. "It must be part of the punishment."

"If that's the case," I said, looking around. "Then Walter must be here too."

"And Eli," Hayley added.

We spotted the brothers soon enough, standing to the side and refusing to participate. They each had a couple more cuts and both looked more alike when they were angry and standing stiffly with their arms crossed over their chests.

"Shall we go talk to them, or no?" Hayley asked hesitantly.

"I don't even know," I said nervously, thinking back to earlier today. I wasn't really expecting to see them still here, I'd thought they'd get suspended.

Walter made the decision for us when he caught our eye from across the room. He didn't smile as he started to approach us, and Eli eventually followed. I inched into Hayley and she tried to do the same to me. It wasn't long until we were face to face with the dark haired Simpson.

"You guys actually volunteered to do this shit?" Walter asked as he loomed over us.

I let out a tiny sigh of relief, he wasn't as angry as I thought.

"Well the teacher thought it would be *cute* to volunteer the whole class," Hayley answered.

Walter gave her a slight smile, "Have I met you?"

"No, not really," she held out her hand that was trembling a little. "I'm Hayley."

"So *she's* Hayley," Eli said, who'd just arrived to hear her introduce herself.

"Have I been mentioned before?" Hayley looked between me and the boys with a confused frown.

"It's a long story," I said with a tired smile, then added quietly. "I'll explain later."

She smiled and nodded, "Well, should we get started with some posters? Painting is the least boring choice."

"Agreed," I said, following her to the painting station.

The four of us started painting A3 posters that read things like 'Dog Show' and 'Who's the cutest pooch?' – Hayley's idea, not mine, and sure as hell not Walter's or Eli's.

"You call that a dog?" Walter asked Eli who had painted what looked more like a human on all fours.

Eli looked up from the painting to his brother, "Could you do any better?"

"Probably," Walter shrugged.

"Go on then," Eli scowled at him.

"Oops," Walter looked at the palette with a fake apologetic look. "We've ran out of paint."

"*Then get some more*," Eli said with a hardened jaw.

Walter looked at his brother with anger creeping into his features. I stepped in before things could escalate for another time too many.

"I'll get the paint," I said, putting my brush down.

I collected the almost empty palette before anyone could say anything, and hurried off to the paint station. Taking my time, I filled it with an array of colours, before balancing the palette carefully as I turned around to head back to the table, only to bump right into Walter's chest. The paint went everywhere. That was the *second* time today that his leather jacket had been ruined, and I didn't need to be reminded of what had happened the first time.

Walter looked down at the multicoloured sludge that slid down his front and then back up at me, *no* smile apparent on his face.

I started to shake.

I was definitely in for it now. He would beat me like he'd beat that boy, like I had been beaten back in my past. It didn't matter if everyone was watching, everyone had been watching the first time too.

Walter opened his mouth and started laughing. I was so shocked, my jaw hung open.

"Do I still...scare you...that much?" he held his stomach as he shook with laughter.

I was speechless.

"Sorry about your jacket," I said eventually once I'd found my voice.

"It already stinks of gravy," Walter said, finally catching his breath. "It's finished."

"Sorr – "

Walter cut me off by holding a finger to my mouth. Well he was about to. His hands were covered in the paint that he'd touched whilst he gripped his sides, laughing.

"Do I need to start telling you to stop saying sorry too now?" he said in a low voice.

"No," I shook my head with a small smile.

"Then let's get back," he said, throwing a smile back.

Returning to our table we continued to work, but I had lost concentration. That's what Walter did to me. He was sitting on a high stool next to me and I looked at my brush, then back at him.

Without thinking, I reached up and swiped my brush along Walter's jaw line.

Without moving the rest of his body, Walter flicked his eyes over to me and I could tell that he wasn't expecting me to do that.

His face broke out with an irresistible grin.

"That's twice now," he said. "Don't you think it's my turn yet?"

Before he'd even finished speaking, Walter played his move. Quickly. Swamping his brush with the closest paint he smeared it all across my cheek.

My eyebrows shot up and Hayley grinned on the other side of the table.

I hadn't really thought he'd do it back.

Walter and I reached for the palette with our brushes at the same time. It was only a matter of pure skill and agility that would allow me to -

Walter broke my thoughts by striking at me again, leaving a long trail of hot pink paint down my top. I put my paintbrush on the table and looked down at myself, pretending to be upset. I felt Walter touch my arm, and I looked up.

"Sorry," he said, and he looked it too.

"Look who's saying sorry now," I smirked at him, dropping my act and spreading my whole hand in the palette, spoiling the paint in the process.

I lifted my hand up and brought it down right in the middle of his chest. He had taken off his jacket and now I'd ruined the top he was wearing underneath too.

Walter shook his head from side to side.

"Coral..." he said my name in his sexy voice. "That's not funny."

"Serves you right," I shrugged.

"No, this serves you right," Walter said softly and he caressed my face, his eyes locked with mine the whole time.

The touch was so sweet I completely forgot that he was spreading yet more paint all over my face.

81

We were interrupted when Eli came up from behind me and slapped a hand of blue paint across Walter's cheek. I stepped away from Walter, expecting him to blow up, but he grinned instead and tried to get Eli back. Eli hopped out of Walter's reach and went round to the other side of the table to hide behind Hayley.

"I'm not playing," Hayley tried to get out of it, but she was grinning just as hard as the rest of us.

Eli put his hand round her mouth and probably got some of the paint in too, as well as leaving a blue handprint across it.

"You're playing now," he said in her ear.

Hayley blushed and pushed him away playfully as she tried to get paint off her lips. Eli sent her a dimpled smile and was hit in the side of the head by a squirt of paint, courtesy of Walter.

The boys went crazy after that.

Eli ran around the department, laughing as he went and squeezing paint into people's eyes. Walter followed Eli, throwing glitter at the victims afterwards so that it stuck to them.

Hayley and I chased the boys, laughing out our apologises to very unhappy looking students, and trying to stop the boys.

Walter paused to paint on an empty poster 'who's the baddest bitch?' and then he grinned and showed it to Hayley.

"I think my dog poster beats yours," he said to her with a smirk.

"On every level," Hayley laughed, trying to get her messy hair out of her face.

"Someone called the head," Eli came to a stop besides us, panting. "Again."

Walter touched the front pocket of his jeans and his brother shook his head at him.

"No," Eli said. "Let's get out of here."

"How?" I asked them. "They're already at the door."

"Ever heard of windows?" Eli flashed me a cocky grin.

"We're on the first floor," Hayley reminded them.

"Snakes don't die that easily," Eli said lowly and he ran for the windows.

Walter was on his heels and Hayley and I widened our eyes at each other. These boys were crazy, lots of fun, but crazy.

Eli pushed the window wide and sat on the ledge before pushing himself off. He landed on his feet, steadied himself with his hands and then stood up straight and turned to face us.

"Walter!" he cried up at him.

"Be careful," I grabbed Walter's shoulder.

"No need to be worried," he wiggled his eyebrows at me and then pushed himself out just like Eli had.

Walter landed safely enough and the headmaster along with his entourage reached the windows and started shouting down at the boys.

"Come back here now!" the head roared at them.

"Come catch us!" Walter shouted back.

"Fat arse," Eli grinned with his dimples and waved both middle fingers at him.

"You boys are in a lot of trouble," the headmaster growled in fury.

Eli stuck his tongue out at him and then the two started running. They jumped over the fence that surrounded the school and were gone.

"What an occasion," Hayley whispered, covered in paint and glitter from head to toe.

"You're a mess," I held back a laugh because I knew I looked the same as she did, if not worse.

11

It was Thursday after school and I was going home with Hayley for dinner. I'd let Walter know in advance that tutoring wasn't happening today, even though I wouldn't have minded doing both somehow. He hadn't been at school and neither had Eli, both were suspended and I'd heard it had even been close to an expulsion. I was glad *that* hadn't happened though.

"So popcorn and ice-cream for the movie, right?" Hayley was asking me. "We have drinks at home."

"What kind of drinks?" I sent her a sidelong glance as we walked to the central shopping complex with our schoolbags over our shoulders.

"Non-alcoholic ones," she assured me. "Unless you want them."

"No," I said quickly. "I'm fine with juice."

"Juice?" she laughed. "I'm talking at least fizzy drinks. Let your hair down Coral. Why drink OJ when you have *Coca-Cola*?"

I allowed a laugh, "I don't like *Coke*, but I'll have *Fanta*."

She grinned at me and gave me a push as we rounded the street corner only to walk right into a cluster of boys. I accidentally bumped into someone's back and it was only when the boys turned around to scowl at us, that I recognised the younger Santiago members. The twins, who I believed were around sixteen years old, and their younger brother who was, at fifteen, the most juvenile of the Santiagos.

84

"I'm sorry," I apologised, gripping Hayley's sleeve and trying to walk round them on the narrow pavement.

"Where are you going in such a hurry?" the one called Miguel blocked our path.

It was common knowledge that he was the twin with the scar across his chin, hard to spot, but up this close I was able to see the faint pale line against his caramel coloured skin.

A couple who had just turned the corner behind us froze when they saw the situation we were stuck in. The Santiagos looked at them and they quickly backed up and disappeared. I wish we'd been so lucky.

"My brother asked you what the rush was," Miguel's twin, Manuel demanded, staring down at me with his deep brown eyes.

"We didn't see you there," Hayley tried. "W-we were just going shopping."

"Well it's very *clear* that you can't see well, don't you think?" Miguel gave us a menacing look.

He reached into his pocket and drew out a knife. Keeping it down low by his side he narrowed his eyes slightly.

"Do I have to peel off those eyelids of yours so that you can see a little better?" he growled.

I was shaking violently and I locked my knees so that they wouldn't give out on me. Hayley's hand was as cold as ice and she gripped mine with a vice strong hold.

Manuel gave his twin a dark grin, "That's a cool idea, I haven't seen that done before."

The last Santiago who had been leaning against the wall the whole time, pushed himself off it and came up behind his brothers, putting his hands on both their shoulders.

"They're just girls," he said to them.

"Am I a sexist?" Miguel turned to give his younger brother a challenging look.

"No, but Carlos wouldn't – "

"Carlos isn't here Paulo," Manuel shoved his brother back. "I'll assure you that he wouldn't care about a couple of stupid school girls."

Paulo shook his head at the ground but didn't make another attempt to stop his brothers. Miguel stepped forwards, to me first. Lifting a strand of my blonde hair he tugged on it, making me flinch.

"This might sting a bit," he said lowly, smiling as he gripped my chin hard and lifted my head up sharply.

I saw the glinting knife, coming closer and closer to my face and I squeezed my eyes shut.

"Open them, you bitch," he grunted. "How can I cut them off when you've got them closed so tight?"

I kept them closed tight, and tighter so when I felt my right eyelid being kissed by the cold, sharp metal.

"*Hola putos*," said a familiar voice.

Miguel drew the knife away and let go of my face to look at the owner of it.

Gomez Simpson looked right back.

"What do you want, Simpson snakes?" Miguel spat at them.

"Sounds a lot better than Santiago *splinters*," Giovanni smirked at him, spinning a blade around in plain sight.

Severn was there too and he looked meaner than I'd ever seen him with a clenched jaw and hate in his eyes as he regarded his enemies.

"You seriously wanna start something right now, over those two?" Manuel questioned, getting out his own mean looking knife.

"If we have to," Gomez shrugged, looking so relaxed, which couldn't have been said for me or Hayley, who was clenching onto my arm again.

"You know them?" the youngest Santiago asked.

"Nope," Gomez didn't hesitate.

"Why would you help people you don't even know?" Miguel narrowed his eyes at him.

"I didn't know the triplets were all about protecting the weak now?" Manuel stepped forwards.

"We don't know them," Giovanni repeated in a hard voice. "But they're coming with us."

"And you think we'll let them go so easily?" Miguel smiled cruelly.

"Well the funny thing is, they weren't yours to begin with," Severn said, pulling out a serrated blade. "Stand down."

"Make me," Miguel laughed.

Gomez pulled out a gun.

I pressed my lips together to stop a whimper escaping. I didn't doubt he'd use it, and I didn't want to be anywhere near such violence.

Miguel's smile dissolved and he replaced it with a hard look.

"I'll kill you," he said.

"I'll kill you first," Gomez pointed out the obvious as he held the gleaming black metal.

The twins shared a look and then eventually, after a long silence, they put their knives away. Paulo, their little brother, did the same.

"Gracias," Gomez gave them a smile.

Giovanni pulled me by the back of my bag and almost sent me crashing into the concrete. I steadied myself and followed him, holding onto the sleeve of his jacket. I risked a glance behind me and saw that Hayley was gripping onto Severn, who had given her his arm, and Gomez was the last to leave, still holding the gun low by his side.

"We won't forget this," one of them called after us.

"This makes us even," Gomez threw back over his shoulder.

The triplets marched us away from the street corner and to the edge of a playground several minutes away.

"Sorry I grabbed you like that," Giovanni said as soon as he let me go. "I was keeping up the act."

I couldn't express how happy I was. I wouldn't have even cared if he had dragged me away face down over the dirty pavement. They'd saved us from a very possible mutilation.

"Thank you," I squeezed his hand so tight he had to pull me off.

"It's nothing," Giovanni patted my shoulder.

"Thank you all," I turned and faced Gomez and Severn, "so, so much."

"Yes," Hayley nodded. "We don't know what we would have done without you, turning up out of nowhere like angels."

"That would make us very deadly angels," Gomez smiled at her.

"No, I like the sound of that," Severn held a finger up. "You know, like angels of death."

Gomez laughed, "Don't get so carried away bro, Phoenix will kill us if he finds out we took the gun in the first place.

87

"It doesn't matter," Giovanni pushed it aside. "If it wasn't for that, we would have to fight, in front of the girls."

"Try telling that to him when he's bashing your face in," Severn scoffed. "Not that he'd hit us or anything," he added quickly when he saw Hayley and I wince. "He's a very *loving* big brother."

Gomez and Giovanni tried not to laugh.

"Where were you two going anyway?" Severn asked us.

"To buy popcorn," I smiled at the ground sheepishly.

"I can get that for you," Gomez offered with a sly look.

"No, no," Hayley declined. "I have money, and you've done enough to help us already."

"I didn't say anything about paying," Gomez smirked and then held up his hands. "But okay, that's cool, I guess we'll see you around."

"Yeah," we smiled. "See you around."

Gomez threw what I assumed were gang signs at us with a wide smile and Giovanni sent us the peace sign. Severn, last to go, gave us a flick of his wrist and then grinned before heading off after his brothers, leaving Hayley and I smiling hard.

***

Dinner with Hayley's family was better than I anticipated, after a shy start from my part. Her father was a business man and her mother was an accountant. Both were kind to me and asked lots of questions. Following a few failed attempts to try and discover more about my family life, Hayley's parents steered clear of it the whole night. I was grateful for that.

After desert Hayley and I went to watch a movie in her room. We chose a comedy, nothing too romantic and nothing too bloody - just something to make us laugh and forget about the worst side of life.

The movie ended and I checked the time.

"It's late, I should go," I said, widening my eyes.

"Why don't you just sleep over?" Hayley suggested care freely. "I could drive us to school in the morning."

"I shouldn't, I.." I said automatically and then trailed off because I had no proper reason behind it.

Hayley smirked at me, "I'll get you some pillows."

I allowed a smile back and settled down again in Hayley's comfy pillows, waiting alone as Hayley went to find me bedding. It was so foreign to have a sleepover. Something that I never felt I was even qualified to do, let alone actually have one. I got up and looked at all the pictures plastered on the walls, of Hayley and her group of friends looking all happy and drinking at parties. There were some pictures of them with guys, friends and maybe boyfriends too. I felt like I'd missed out on all that kind of stuff, friendships, parties, romance... But I was still eighteen; at least it wasn't completely over.

Hayley returned to her room, dumping a pair of pillows at me. We went to brush our teeth, me using a spare brush, and Hayley let me wear a t-shirt and a pair of shorts for bed. It was fun, how easy it was being with her.

"Get in then," Hayley motioned to her bed.

"Are you sure?" I asked hesitantly, I was expecting to sleep on the floor, not share her double bed.

"Of course I'm sure Coral," Hayley grinned. "Get in."

She went to turn her bedroom lights off as I got into her bed. Hayley flicked on some fairy lights, bathing the room in a soft purple glow.

"Childish, I know," Hayley said, hopping into the bed. "But I love them."

"Me too," I grinned, glancing up at the lights that she'd secured all over her room.

Hayley lay down facing me and I was about to turn and face the ceiling but found that I couldn't look away from Hayley's eyes.

"Coral," she said quietly. "What's wrong?"

I frowned at her, "Nothing's wrong with me."

There wasn't a shadow of a smile on her face, "What aren't you telling me? You can tell me anything."

I stared at her, unable to break the gaze as a thousand thoughts whizzed round my head. I wanted to tell her everything, I really did. I'd been holding my painful burdens alone, my whole life, and now I had a real friend, someone I could confide in.

"After my mother died," I said, dropping my gaze. "My life changed. Everything turned bad for me."

My hands were trembling as unwanted memories stared to arise and Hayley held them in her hands, squeezing them encouragingly.

"Long story short," I sniffed loudly and gave her a watery smile. "Sorry."

"Don't say sorry," Hayley said to me, giving me a sad look.

"Long story short," I repeated, rubbing my eyes. "I went into care and suffered abuse. I don't even remember which came first."

Hayley gasped quietly, pressing shaking lips together, "That's disgusting. I'm so sorry."

I tried to smile, "Don't say sorry, it's not your fault."

"It ended by the time I was ten after a slight change in situation, the abuse ended I mean, and by the time I was sixteen I got a part-time job and started renting a flat," I said. "It's cramped and in poor condition, but it's all I have and it's better than...than anything else I've had before. It's the reason why I get you to meet me for school somewhere else, away from my home. I'm ashamed of it."

Hayley pulled me into a hug and she didn't let go for a long time. I cried over her shoulder and although I felt a deep sadness, I felt deep relief too.

12

Wanna meet up today?

I rubbed my eyes and read Walter's text again. It didn't change.

It was Sunday and I'd had a long sleep following a tiring shift at work the day before. There had been no gunshots nearby or nightmares last night. Checking the time, I was surprised to see that it was midday. I rarely ever slept in this late and I actually felt well rested.

Walter had sent me the message around 9am, which had me imagining what he looked like first thing in the morning, all cute and sleepy eyed. I didn't feel like doing work and I didn't think Walter particularly wanted to either, but I would still agree though, I liked seeing him.

What do you want to study? I sent back.

His reply came just five minutes later:

Do we always have to do work?

Let's just chill

It seemed he had read my mind and knots started to grow in my stomach. Walter and I had never really just *chilled* before and I didn't know what to expect.

Sure, I replied. **What do you wanna do?**

When you're ready, meet me outside your place. We'll decide then.

I felt like a stone had dropped in my stomach and then I squeaked like a little girl, happy that there was no one around to hear me. After texting Walter that I was ready a while later, it wasn't long until he texted me to say he was waiting outside me. On stepping out of the block of flats I couldn't find him anywhere.

"Walter?" I called out in confusion, looking at the empty street.

"Round here," I heard his voice.

I walked the short distance to the side of the degraded building to see Walter standing on the overgrown grass with a black hoodie drawn over his head, looking up at the brick wall.

"I didn't know we did this," he said, gazing at the graffiti.

"Your gang sign," I said, looking at the old spray painting of the seven headed snake. "It's your territory isn't it?"

It wasn't as big and elaborately drawn as some of the others I'd seen up around the area, but it still symbolised the Simpson gang and showed that they operated in this part of London. It was weird thinking all those things and then seeing this eighteen year old boy standing next to me as he bit on his thumbnail. He seemed so normal. I just couldn't put the two sides of Walter together.

"Yeah," Walter rubbed his arm, looking like he wanted to say more. "Never mind."

"Okay," I gave him a smile.

"Have you eaten?" Walter suddenly turned his attention to me.

I shook my head, "I basically just woke up."

"Not accepting that," Walter folded his arms, pretending to be angry.

"Sorry I wanted to see you so I didn't bother having anything," I laughed.

Walter's face changed and I stopped laughing, dropping my gaze to look at the ground instead. I hadn't been able to read his expression, but his look had been so intense all of a sudden.

"Let's go eat," he said, taking hold of my arm.

I looked up at him in surprise as he walked with me like a gentleman. Walter caught my eye and grinned down at me, his injuries from previous fighting nearly healed.

"How has your day been?" I asked as we made our way to the shopping complex in the centre of the borough.

"I've been in bed," Walter replied. "It was pretty loud though, Phoenix got mad at the triplets. I heard the shouting and stuff."

I widened my eyes and kept my look down at the grubby slabs of pavement. I hoped the triplets were okay and were truly joking about Phoenix bashing their faces in for taking the gun.

"I don't know what they did this time," Walter was saying. "But I don't really care. They're annoying as hell."

"Young teens, huh?" I pulled a face.

"I'm pretty sure I wasn't as annoying as that," Walter mumbled. "They make so much drama and speak so much shit. I was quieter."

"You're saying all of this as if it wasn't just three years ago," I tried not to laugh at him.

Walter nudged me with a smile, "Hey, don't tease me."

I looked down, still smiling, and we soon arrived at the shopping centre. I glanced around cautiously for any Santiagos, even though I knew I was relatively safe with Walter. But still, it was only a couple of days ago when I'd almost gotten my eyelids cut off. That memory didn't go away so easily.

"Want coffee?" Walter asked me. "And a sandwich or something like that?"

"Sounds good," I answered.

I let Walter decide which cafe we went to and he took us to a fairly quiet one that I'd never been to before.

"Not busy enough for everyone to be hearing our business," he said as we sat down. "And not empty enough for anyone to hear everything we say."

"Fair enough," I shrugged, not really minding.

We ordered our coffee and I also ordered a slice of strawberry cheesecake, one of my favourite deserts. Walter had wanted me to eat 'proper food', like a sandwich or something, but I had insisted I was fine with the desert. After all, he was paying and I didn't want it to be a big bill for him. Walter himself just had a black coffee with no sugar, disgusting in my opinion. You needed as much sugar as you could get!

"So tell me more about yourself," Walter leaned forwards in his chair playfully.

"There isn't much to say," I decided to keep things short as usual. "Growing up wasn't easy. My mother passed when I was young and I went into care not long after."

Walter seemed surprised and didn't ask about my father, probably assuming that I didn't know him or want to talk about him.

"Do you remember her?" he asked softly, all traces of playfulness gone.

"Honestly," I took a breath. "No, not really. But I'd like to think she was a good mother."

"Me too," he smiled at me.

"What about you?" I asked, after taking a bite of cheesecake. "Tell me about your childhood."

Walter scoffed, "Mine isn't pretty either."

"I told you about me," I pointed my fork at him, pretending to threaten him. "So you have to tell me about you, doesn't have to be a lot."

"Okay," Walter surrendered, holding up his hands. "The first part is easy, my parents are dead."

"Oh," I raised my eyebrows. "I'm sorry to hear that."

"Don't be," Walter said with a look I didn't understand. "They weren't nice people."

"People say all sorts of things about your family, your gang," I said, unsure as to how he would take it. "But I've never heard that about your parents. It makes me wonder just how much of it all is true."

"How about you tell me what you know?" Walter suggested, taking a gulp of his drink. "I doubt any of the stuff you've heard is true."

"Probably," I agreed. "Well, everyone knows it's the Simpsons and the Santiagos who are the rivalling gangs in the area."

Walter nodded, listening.

"Phoenix is your leader, the oldest, and Carlos is their leader, also the oldest," I said.

"Yep," he murmured.

"As for what you do," I paused. "Well, apparently you rob, deal drugs and even kill people."

A half-smile slipped onto Walter's face, "Is that so?"

"That's what I've heard," I said quickly.

"It's accurate so far," Walter had my jaw drop.

"You *kill* people?" I hissed in alarm, staring at him.

He started to laugh, "You're too gullible."

I let my shoulders sink in relief, "You looked so serious."

"Do you really think there would be any of us left, if we all killed people and went down for murder?" Walter rolled his eyes.

"Yeah, that was silly of me," I smiled reluctantly.

"Exactly," he smirked, "which is why we get *other* idiots to kill for us."

"Walter," I blinked at him.

"*Walter*," I repeated when he said nothing.

"I don't want us to lie to each other," he replied simply. "You could go to the police with that information and report me, but I trust you."

"I trust you too, but...how could you do that? That's murder," I said quietly in disbelief.

"If you knew the type of people they *were* and the type of things they took pleasure in *doing*," Walter said in a relaxed tone. "Then you wouldn't be asking that."

"Okay," I said eventually.

I had asked for the truth and had gotten it. That's how the vicious world of drugs and criminality worked. It was just me, still being unable to comprehend this really dark side to Walter and his brothers.

"Are you mad at me?" Walter gave me a shy smile after a short silence.

"No I'm not mad at you," I replied after a thought.

"Good," Walter beamed. "Let's not talk about any of that stuff anymore, okay?"

"Okay," I smiled back, trying to push those thoughts out of my head.

Instead, Walter and I talked not about our pasts or even our present, we talked about our dreams for the future. Or at least I did. He had me telling him all about how my wish would be to become a designer, to create my own brand and style of bags, shoes and even jewellery. Stuff I had never told anyone, not even Hayley. Walter seemed genuinely interested and he asked so many questions that I forgot how carried away I was getting and blushed when I realised how much I'd been speaking about myself.

"I'm sorry," I said with a flushed smile. "I should ask about you. What are your goals, your dreams?"

Before Walter could answer, his phone sounded and he glanced at it. I could tell from the way his face hardened, that it was urgent and that our time together was over.

"Have to go?" I asked him with a bright smile despite feeling a little disappointed.

"Yeah," Walter frowned, tugging a hand through his hair. "I forgot about plans I had later...I'm sorry."

"It's fine," I said. "We've been here almost two hours, I've had fun."

Walter smiled sadly at me, "So have I. I guess I'll see you tomorrow, at school."

"Yep," I said, trying not to let my disappointment show.

We got up and then shared a smile before Walter led me out of the cafe and we walked out onto the street side.

"I had a good time," I said again to Walter honestly.

"And so did I," he replied. "We should do this again soon."

"Yeah," I nodded.

"I'm sorry I had to go like this," he apologised again.

"It's fine, seriously," I said with a shrug.

It just seemed like the two of us wanted the goodbye to last as long as possible. I smiled to myself and decided to make the first leave.

"See you then," I said and stepped back, giving him a smile and a wave.

Walter waved back and then he too took a few steps back, bumping into passerbys that didn't challenge him, and smiling at me before I turned the corner and he was gone out of sight.

***

I did a little shopping whilst I was in the centre and then went home to relax before school tomorrow which would be followed by work. I couldn't stop thinking about Walter, about why he had to go and what he was doing. Was he fighting somewhere? Dealing drugs perhaps?

I had a call from work asking if I could go in to do some overtime as it was getting very busy at the pub and I grudgingly agreed. I could do with as much money as possible, despite how bad my body would hurt afterwards.

Turning up at work in my uniform and getting out to take orders, I was shocked to see a few Santiagos there. Despite the pub being in neutral territory, neither the Santiagos nor the Simpsons visited the Dartfish. I guessed it wasn't their kind of thing, until now. There were three of them, Carlos the leader of the gang and his cousins Ario and Paulo. I didn't want to approach them, but I had to do my job and that meant serving them, as Tiffany was busy serving others.

"Can I take drink orders?" I asked, pen at the ready as I stood over the table.

I risked a peek at them from behind my small notebook and caught the striking blue eyes of Ario Santiago. I wasn't expecting such blue eyes, I had never been so close to him to notice that before.

"*Pepsi*," Paulo, the youngest, said to me, reminding me of the threats his brothers had given me and Hayley not too long ago.

Paulo had kind of stood up for us, not that the twins had listened.

"What beer have you got?" Carlos fixed his eyes on me. He had a cut on his cheekbone that looked fresh.

I swallowed, trying to moisten my throat that had gone dry before listing the beers we had available.

After Carlos had taken his order I waited for Ario, who also looked like he'd been in a fight.

"Give me what you'd usually have," he said eventually, looking up at me with a hint of a smile on his face.

I was very taken aback, but tried not to show it. Ario was my age, eighteen I believed, and the rumours had it that he was one of the quieter members of the Santiago gang. Not that one should underestimate him.

"You'll be pretty disappointed," I forced a smile. "I don't drink much."

"Then what do you have?" he leaned his chin on his hand that was propped up on the table as he looked at me with those vibrant blue eyes.

"*Fanta*," I gave him a genuine smile this time. "Gotta love it."

"*Fanta* it is then," he shrugged, rubbing his bruised cheek.

"Would that be all?" I asked after writing it down.

"That's all," Carlos spoke, looking down at the pub food menu.

The Santiagos left after having their drinks, they hadn't even ordered a main. Ario's eyes still lingered in my mind long after they'd gone and I was so relieved when it came to the end of my shift. I was tired again and needed my bed. After bypassing Tiffany flirting with a drunk man at the bar, I rolled my eyes and went into the staff room to get my belongings and leave.

It was on my way home when I felt that I was being followed. At first I thought it was me being paranoid. Then, when it continued I decided not to be so naive. I considered it being a couple of the Simpsons, the triplets perhaps, having a laugh. It could have even been the Santiagos from the pub.

I crossed into the west side of the area, Simpson territory and expected my pursuers to stop. Trespassing wasn't taken lightly, as I could gather from the gunfights that rang out all too often at night. But they didn't stop. And now I could hear their voices.

It wasn't the Simpsons, or the Santiagos, but vile drunk men who'd followed me all the way from the pub and were currently gaining on me now that the streets were a lot quieter in these corners. I walked faster as panic caused the hairs on the back of my neck to prick. I didn't want to lead them to my home, despite being fairly close to it, but I couldn't stay out here forever.

"We're gonna have a feast tonight," I heard one voice say, making the other chuckle.

My hands started shaking and my heart hammered in my chest when I passed my block of flats and kept walking, not giving it a glance. I didn't have much choice left, in fact I only had one. I wouldn't be able to outrun them for long and I needed to get to some refuge soon.

I had to go to Walter's house.

Before they got any closer, I broke into a run. I knew Walter's house was roughly ten to fifteen minutes from mine, and if I ran I could make it in maybe less than ten. As soon as I started, I heard the men following me pick up the pace until they were running too. They were shouting vulgar things and I was genuinely afraid for my life. If they caught me...I....I..

With tears falling from my eyes, I ran as fast and long as I could until the Simpson's unusually tall looking house came into view. I couldn't hear the footsteps behind me anymore, but I wasn't going to stop or look behind me.

I banged on their door and prayed that they were home and that *someone* would answer. My fists continued to bang on the solid oak door until finally it swung open and I ran right into the person, sobbing uncontrollably.

I felt strong arms circle me hesitantly and I buried my face into their chest.

"Who is it?" I heard someone yell from the living room.

It sounded like Landon.

"Walter's friend," the person who was holding me said.

I pulled away from him, and looked up into Phoenix's blank face. He had a couple of bruises which weren't there the last time I saw him.

"What are you doing here?" he asked me, although I could tell he wasn't really concerned.

"I-I...these- th-these..m-men.." I tried, but I was choking on my words.

Phoenix took hold of my arm, "I haven't got time for this."

He began pulling me towards the front door. Out there again.

"No," I cried, pulling myself away from the door. "Please, don't!"

Someone else grabbed me and pulled me off Phoenix.

"Hey, don't be a prick."

It was Landon.

"What's the matter?" he asked me slowly and Phoenix rolled his eyes, walking into the kitchen.

"These...m-men were ch-ch-chasing me.." I shuddered, trying to explain.

Landon simply hugged me, "You're safe."

I calmed down eventually, until I was only sniffing.

"Thank you," I said to him, swiping at my eyes.

Landon continued to look at me in concern and I saw that he too had some cuts and bruises. They must have been fighting with the Santiagos.

"No problem, but why the hell were you out there alone?"

"I was coming back from work and they followed me, I didn't want to go home and lead them there and I knew if they tried to come in here you guys would...would stop them," I said, trying to stop my shaking muscles.

"Smart move," Landon rubbed my arm. "Come in to the living room."

I followed him towards the living room and Landon opened the door, pausing in the doorway.

"Walter's not so good," he said to me over his shoulder.

"What?" I raised my eyebrows in alarm.

"Come in," he gestured for me to follow him.

I walked in and saw Walter's tall frame lying on one of the sofas. He was limp and pale, and I could see from where his hoodie was unzipped that he had bruises on his neck.

"What happened?" I murmured.

Landon looked down at his brother, "He got on the wrong side of a fight, wasn't watching his back well enough."

"The Santiagos right?"

Landon nodded, sucking on his lip piercing.

"Somebody tried to strangle him," I said as I took in the fingerprint shaped marks on Walter's neck.

"We can see that," Phoenix replied as he walked in.

He slipped a thermometer into Walter's mouth, and covered him with a blanket. It was quite cold this time of the night.

"We got back not long ago," Landon explained. "Look Coral, you can stay if you want. You don't need to go back out there."

"Thank you Landon," I said, and I really meant it. "I can stay down here, with Walter."

"If you want," Landon said. "Do you want to go ask the triplets if they have anything to lend you? I'm sure you don't want to sleep in your uniform, and their clothes will probably fit better than mine."

"Yes," I smiled a little bit. "Thanks."

I went up and knocked on the triplets' door, waiting for a reply.

"What do you want?" someone called.

I opened the door, and poked my head round it, "Hey it's me. Landon said it would be okay if I could borrow some clothes?"

Giovanni and Severn who were in their beds sat up to look at me, "What's the matter?"

I didn't know it was that obvious that I had been crying.

"I ran into some trouble," I told them.

"Did someone hurt you?" Gomez who was lying on the floor asked with a frown.

"No."

"Good," he muttered, sounding like Walter.

Giovanni hopped out of his bed. "You're staying over then?"

"Yeah," I said.

He searched through a chest of drawers and picked out a long sleeved top and jogging bottoms.

"Take this," he handed them to me and punched my arm lightly. "And cheer up."

I gave them a smile, "Thank you."

I sat on the floor by the sofa Walter was placed in and watched him sleep peacefully. My eyes were heavy, but I didn't want to sleep just yet.

"Hey, you okay?" Landon asked as he came back into the room holding a blanket which I was sure was for me.

"Yeah," I replied.

"Walter's fine," Landon reassured me.

"I know," I said, glancing at him.

"When you're ready to sleep help yourself to this," Landon held up the blanket.

"Thanks Landon," I said as he turned to leave.

"Has anyone ever told you that you say thanks way too much?" he looked back and smiled at me.

13

I woke up when I heard the door creak open. I didn't know when I had fallen asleep but I could tell it was late, or should I say early?

"Anyone awake?" I heard Landon whisper.

For some reason, I hesitated from answering and I dimly saw Landon's silhouette walk further into the room and sit down in one of the armchairs. It was silent for a while and I thought I would fall asleep again, until Walter groaned and I was instantly wide awake.

"Walter, you okay?" his brother asked.

Walter grunted. It could have been a yes or a no.

"Coral came to see you," Landon said.

"When?" Walter asked in a husky voice.

"She's still here."

"What?"

"She's asleep in one of the sofas."

"What happened?" Walter questioned after a pause.

"She was chased on her way home from work and came here for help," Landon explained.

Walter's tone immediately hardened, "Santiagos?"

"Not that I know of," Landon answered. "They had stopped following her by the time she got here so I don't think so."

Walter seemed to accept that reply and there was a silence, in which I felt myself slipping back into sleep.

"So tell me about the girl," Landon demanded.

"What about her?" Walter asked.

"What's she like?" Landon wanted to know.

Walter didn't answer for some time and I began to grow uneasy, wishing I knew what he was thinking about me.

"She's been through some shit," Walter finally answered. "I can tell."

"Has she told you about it?" Landon questioned.

"A little," Walter said. "But I know there's more that she hasn't said and I want to be the person she can confide in. You know? Sometimes that can help, and I care about her."

"Care? " I could picture Landon giving Walter a smirk.

"What?" Walter snapped back at him defensively.

"Nothing, I just haven't heard you say that about anyone before, let alone a girl," Landon commented. "You must like her."

"Shut up Landon," Walter muttered darkly, maybe embarrassed.

"No," Landon laughed. "I don't think I will. You don't even say that you care about us, even though I know it's true. But you never say it."

"And?"

"So I have come to the conclusion that my baby brother might possibly be falling in love for the first time," Landon said, I could literally hear the grin in his voice.

"Landon if you ever say something like that ever again, I will kill you," Walter growled.

Landon laughed silently, and I felt a smile split across my own face.

"I'll bear that in mind," Landon said contently.

"Night," Walter mumbled.

"You're going to sleep?"

"Yeah, my head hurts."

"Do you want some painkillers?"

"Nah, I'm fine."

"Sure?"

"Okay, get me some."

"Where's the please?"

"Landon!" Walter exclaimed. "*You're* the one who asked *me*."

Landon chuckled as he left the room, only teasing his brother, and I let myself fall asleep, knowing I wouldn't have any bad dreams tonight at all.

***

"You feeling okay, Walter?" Phoenix grunted at him.

"Headache," Walter mumbled back.

I sat up, blinking my sleep away to see Phoenix, Landon and Gomez standing over Walter who was still lying in the sofa.

"Morning," Gomez turned around when he heard me rise.

"Hey," I croaked, making him wince.

"Man, you sound like a troll," he started to laugh.

"Thanks," I said sarcastically, but smiled.

"Can you two be quiet?" Phoenix turned and gave us a look.

"Chill, Phoenix," Landon touched his arm with the back of his hand.

"Don't talk to Coral like that," Walter snarled, struggling to sit up.

Landon gently pushed him down again, "Relax."

But Phoenix didn't seem like his wanted to do any relaxing, "I'll talk to anyone in *my house* how *I like*."

"Not while I'm around," Walter gave him a fierce glare, despite the pallor in his face.

Landon and Gomez looked like they didn't want to go down that route, and neither did I.

"Guys, both of you, relax," Landon tried to cool the situation.

"He thinks he can treat anyone how he likes," Walter snapped. "And I'm not having that, not with Coral."

"Then she can get the hell out of my house," Phoenix glared at him and then gave me a similar deadly look.

"Thanks for having me," I squeaked and hurried to my feet, looking for my things I'd brought with me last night.

"Coral, sit," Walter looked at me. "Don't listen to him."

"No," I said quickly, all too aware of Phoenix's deep look. "I'm fine with leaving, I'll be late for school anyway."

"You're already late," Gomez checked his phone. "School started ten minutes ago."

Damn.

"All the more reason to leave," I gave Walter and Phoenix a tight smile.

I gathered my things and headed towards the door when Walter called my name again.

"Coral, don't leave."

I looked around to see him sitting up and gazing at me with determination in his face. He didn't want me to leave, just to piss Phoenix off. Nothing more. And there I was, foolishly hoping that he really did like me enough for me to stay just for the sake of having me around.

"I have to go," I said sternly, turning my back on him.

I opened the door and heard Phoenix mutter something under his breath. Walter got really mad then and he forced himself up, despite Landon and Gomez trying to keep him sitting.

"You wanna say that to my face?" Walter thrust his chest right up against Phoenix's.

Phoenix managed to look down on Walter even though Walter was only a couple of inches shorter. Phoenix pulled out a sharp switchblade from his pocket and held it up to Walter's bruised face.

"Get that bitch. Out my house," Phoenix spat each word loud and clear.

I was shaking, I wasn't supposed to be here, at all. Phoenix's words really hurt, not that he hadn't been saying things like that from the moment I'd woken up, but now I was near tears.

I left before anything else could happen, closing the living room door firmly behind me. I tried not to let the tears in my eyes fall and I marched to the front door and let myself out swiftly, not listening to my name being called behind me. I didn't belong there, I was out of depth and in danger. I didn't know why it took me so long to see it. Walter and his brothers were unsafe and I was a girl who needed to just get on by in life. The last thing I needed to do was affiliate myself with a bloody gang.

I was a couple paces down the street when Walter caught up with me.

"Coral," he stopped me, panting and out of breath. "Please wait, I'm sorry about - "

"Walter, I can't do this," I said to him, turning around and looking him straight in the eye.

"You can't do what?" he frowned in confusion, his chest rising and falling quickly.

"I can't see you anymore," I dropped my gaze, unable to hold it any longer.

"Coral, what?" I could hear the shock in his voice. "Forget Phoenix, he's a – "

"I don't want any trouble," I cut him off. "And he clearly hates me, although I don't know why. But that doesn't matter, I have to keep my distance. So we have to stop the tutoring...and just all of it."

"What are you saying?" Walter just stared at me, a look of dread on his face.

"Let's just go back to our old lives," I said, looking away and over his shoulder. "We're two different people and I don't want to be involved in what you and your family do."

Walter narrowed his eyes, "So this isn't just about Phoenix? It's about our lifestyle? *My* lifestyle?"

I nodded, swallowing nervously, "I just want to pass my exams and finish school – "

"And I'm not gonna stop that!" Walter cried. "I want the best for you too."

"Walter please," I tried to block the tears that I felt rising. "Don't make this any more difficult. I didn't know what I was getting myself into and I'm not sure if it's for me. If you're for me."

Nothing could erase the look of pain Walter had in his eyes after I'd said that.

"We were just friends, but you don't want that anymore? I'm too 'bad' for you? Not clean enough, is that it?" his voice grew hard and cold.

"I'm sorry," I whispered, turning and walking away.

He didn't try and stop me again and I didn't look back.

14

Walter stopped coming to school that first day.

A whole week had passed now, and it was Monday again. I had not seen Walter once in all that time and I didn't blame him, but I was hurting just as much as he was. I didn't want to stop seeing him, but I knew it was what I needed - the right thing to do. I still liked him, I still thought about him every day and I even thought about giving up and taking him back.

If he even wanted me back, that was.

"Coral, you should eat more," Hayley nudged my hand.

I took a bite of my apple, just to stop her going on about how little I was eating lately, and looked across the canteen at the triplets.

"I have to give his jumper back," I said blankly.

"Who's jumper?" Hayley frowned at me.

"Severn's," I replied. "I still have his jumper that he let me borrow last week."

"Oh," Hayley hesitated.

"Do you think he'll talk to me?" I sighed, meeting her brown eyed gaze.

"There's no reason why not to," she shrugged.

"He won't even look at me," I let my shoulders sink. "None of them."

"I'm sure that's not true, you're over thinking things."

I wasn't. Not one of the triplets would catch my eye for more than a second whenever they saw me. Of course they had reason to be mad, I had basically criticized their way of life. It hurt me more to imagine how Walter would act towards me if he and I ever crossed paths again. I put my apple down.

"Coral," Hayley looked at me, appalled. "Please."

"I'm not in the mood," I shook my head. "I don't feel well Hayley, I think I'm going to go and see the nurse and hopefully go home."

"I'll take you," Hayley said, concern all over her face.

"Thanks," I sent her a weak smile and got up from my seat.

We cleared our trays and Hayley walked with me to the infirmary, giving my hands a squeeze before she left. The school nurse told me to have a seat and I had a cup of water while I waited to see her or one of the other assistant nurses. My stomach was cramping and I felt hot and tingly. I knew eating would make it feel better, but I didn't have an appetite and I couldn't stomach anything.

"Coral?" the school nurse called me into her little private room.

I followed her in and sat down, looking at my lap.

"How can I help you today?" she asked me. "Not feeling too well?"

"No," I shook my head, wrapping my arms round my middle. "I've got bad cramps and I can't concentrate in class."

"Oh poppet," the nurse gave me a sympathetic look. "Would you like some painkillers?"

"Sure," I replied, hoping she'd let me lie down for a while and maybe go home early.

I took the tablets and luckily she did allow me to sleep in one of the beds, drawing the blue paper curtain around me. I tried to get as comfortable as possible in the thin, papery bed and I closed my eyes, not really expecting to fall asleep but hoping to daze out and not think about Walter.

I frowned slightly when I felt the air around me shift and tried to remember if there was a window above me. My eyes flew open when I heard the curtain being drawn back and I was shocked to see Eli Simpson standing there. He was slightly frowning, which I had come to understand was his normal resting face, and his dark blond hair was pushed up and out of his emerald eyes. I opened my mouth but words wouldn't come out. I had no idea what to say.

"You sick?" Eli was the first to speak.

My first thought was to ask him about Walter. If he was okay, what he was up to, if he was still hurting as much as I was. Anything.

"You can't be in here," I said instead. "This is the girl's section, if someone catches you in here we'll both get – "

"Oh please," Eli cut me off with a roll of his eyes. "Pin it on me, you won't get in trouble."

I shut my mouth and just looked up at him, waiting for him to explain why he was even here.

"Are you sick?" Eli only asked me again, looking at me with those green eyes.

"I..I don't know," I swallowed. "I don't feel well, but I don't think I have anything like a bug."

"Okay well that makes the answer a yes," Eli responded. "Not feeling well is the same as being si – "

"Eli why are you here?" I interrupted. "Aren't you mad at me, like Walter and the others are?"

Eli's face remained straight, "Why should I be? I'm not Walter or the others."

I was a little confused but I was certain he was being honest and it made me feel a bit more relaxed that he wasn't angry at me too.

"Are *you* sick?" I asked him, sitting up in the bed.

"No," Eli answered. "I'm just cutting class, told them I had a headache. I could go home but there are some interesting looking drugs here that I like the look of."

I frowned at him, "What?"

"Relax," Eli smirked. "They won't even notice they're gone."

"Eli," I stared at him, expecting him to smile and say he was joking, but he didn't.

"Stop looking at me like that, it's free," Eli said in the end. "And how much harm can penicillin do anyway?"

"Okay, okay," I said, waving my hands at him to try and get him to stop saying those things, just in case someone was listening.

Eli smirked widely and crossed his arms and I smiled faintly at him, knowing it was the wrong thing to do. I was meant to be staying *away* from these brothers.

"Well, um...I think I'm gonna go back to bed now," I said to him.

"Oh, yeah," he unfolded his arms and went to leave.

"Whatever you're doing, don't get caught," I told him, hiding another smile.

Eli rolled his eyes and then smiled back, "Get better soon."

"Thanks," I said, and he was gone.

I lay back in the bed and squeezed my eyes shut, sighing deeply. Eli, of all people on this Earth, had actually been pretty decent to me, which just made the whole keeping my distance thing even harder.

***

I was kept fairly busy at work which I preferred because it made the time pass quicker, however it left me feeling even worse than I was feeling before, and the painkillers had worn off. By the time my shift was over, my vision was coming in and out of focus and my stomach was really hurting. I stumbled out the back door and right into someone.

I went to step past the man, trying to smother the overwhelming strong feeling of déjà vu and my knees buckled as I became a little lightheaded. The man turned around and then quickly grabbed my arm when I started to lose my balance.

"Are you alright?" he bent down a little so that he could look into my face.

It was Ario Santiago who I'd bumped into and he had been talking to his cousin Carlos, the leader. I winced. I was trying to stay away from one gang, not land myself with another.

"I'm fine, thanks," I gently peeled myself out of his grip.

"You work here, right?" he narrowed his blue eyes slightly as he tried to figure out where he remembered me from.

"Yeah," I looked down. "Thanks again."

I quickly stepped away from him so that I wouldn't be asked to give any more information about myself, but it wasn't that simple.

"What's your name?" Ario fell into step with me.

I frowned and glanced behind me, seeing Carlos standing there in the dimly lit area alone. If he was planning to rob the place, I should have told the manager about it.

"Please leave me alone," I shivered, trying to walk in a straight line.

"Hey," Ario frowned at me. "I'm not going to hurt you."

"I don't know you," I murmured, keeping my gaze firmly on the ground. "Why would I believe what you say?"

"Fair enough," he replied. "I just wanna know your name though. I bet you know mine."

"I don't," I lied. "Please, leave me alone."

"Fine," he stopped walking. "But I just wanted to tell you, don't go to work on Wednesday."

That had my blood turn cold.

"Why?" I stopped to look at him in alarm. "What are you going to do?"

"I can't say," Ario spread his arms, and then glanced over his shoulder. "But I wasn't supposed to tell you that. I can't stop you from telling anyone else, but keep in mind that if you *do* tell someone, it would only make things worse. People might get hurt."

I was finding it hard to breath. They were going to rob the place, with knives and guns. Of course people would get hurt, the customers, my colleagues. They weren't safe and I wouldn't have been safe myself until Ario had just decided to tell me that.

"I can't not tell anyone," I said to him, trying to catch my breath. "You know that."

"You're not okay," Ario stepped towards me, frowning.

"Don't touch me," I said, stiffening and stepping back.

We were alone and it was late, I wasn't exactly in Simpson territory yet but I had been heading home, stupidly letting him know I lived on the West side. I was tired and not thinking straight, come to think of it I couldn't see straight either and I didn't even notice I was falling towards Ario until he caught me in his arms.

I held onto him as tightly as I could, scared and cold. He smelt good, felt warm and was a sense of comfort. I knew nothing was making sense right now, everything was upside down and jumbled – quite like my head.

"Hey, I've got you," he said, sounding nothing like a cold-blooded gang member but more like a normal, concerned person.

"I'm okay," I tried not to shake as hard. "I've got some water in my bag, please, help me get it."

I faintly thought about how this would be giving Ario the perfect opportunity to rob me, but he didn't go for my purse. He rummaged around and found my water bottle instead.

"Here," Ario unscrewed it and held it to my lips.

He was gentle and I drank the rest of the water I had. It made me feel better after a few moments and I let go of Ario, expecting him to do the same as he still had one arm clamped around my body, holding me up.

"Better?" he looked at me, his lips slightly parted as he frowned in what looked like genuine concern.

"Yeah," I said, taking a step back from him. "Thank you."

"No problem," he was still frowning, unconvinced.

"I have to go," I said, and I started walking away before he would suggest that he accompany me to make sure I get home okay. Or maybe I was thinking too much of Walter.

"Don't forget what I said," Ario called after me.

Walking home was long and hard but I made it back alright. During the journey I couldn't stop worrying about what Ario had said. I needed to call my manager and let him know that the Santiagos were planning something, else my conscience would never let me go if something terrible *did* happen. I couldn't help but also wonder why Ario had essentially saved me from potential danger, because I did in fact work Wednesdays after school and I wouldn't have had a clue about a thing. He was nicer than I'd ever thought, helping me like that.

I stopped dead in my tracks when I reached my block of flats. There on the path on several feet away stood Walter. I could have completely missed him, it was very dark and he was wearing a black hoodie drawn over his head.

I hadn't seen him in over a week and my hands started shaking. I was nervous, why was he here? Did he want to talk to me, or had he already tried buzzing my door? There was hope, hope that despite my reasons, he (like me) wanted to forget all the stuff I'd said and just start over again.

Walter's eyes bored into mine and I couldn't look away. He didn't smile.

"Walter," I breathed, but he was already gone.

15

I could barely sleep that night and the nightmares didn't help either. In my dreams he smelt so foul, so real, like I was truly back there in my past again. I woke up crying and gripping my pillow, wishing I had someone to comfort me. Ario came into my mind and I shook my head, I had to stay away from him just like I had to stay away from Walter. I had just liked how safe I had felt in his arms, that's all.

I sighed and got out of bed to do my homework. I wanted to talk to Hayley and tell her about what Ario had said, but she was definitely asleep. In the morning I would call my manager, I had to.

I was up all night and as I waited for Hayley to pick me up I held my phone in my hand and considered calling and telling my manager that The Dartfish could be in danger. I was about to press call when Ario's words entered my mind. Telling someone could mean contacting the police and if there happened to be something like a shootout, then I'm sure people would get caught between it. Maybe he was right, calling would make it worse. Hayley's small red car pulled up in front of me and I put my phone away. I just hoped the Santiagos weren't planning anything crazy.

"You look tired," Hayley said when I got in. "Not feeling any better?"

"Not really," I replied.

Hayley sighed, "You should call in sick, there's no way you can go to school if you're feeling so bad."

"You think so?" I asked her, wishing she could stay with me so I wasn't alone again.

"Yeah," Hayley nodded. "I have a half day today so I'll come round your place around lunchtime."

"You will?" I raised my brows.

"Of course," she took my hand and squeezed it. "Just give me your address."

I nodded, trying not to think about how shameful my place was. Walter hadn't said anything negative that one time he'd been upstairs, so I was hoping Hayley wouldn't either. I gave her my address.

"I'll tell school office you're ill," Hayley assured me. "Eat something and sleep, I'll see you soon."

"Thanks," I said, leaning over and giving her a hug before exiting the car. "See you."

***

Hayley came round after 1pm with some ringed doughnuts and smoothies. She didn't say a word about how tiny my flat was, we simply went and sat down in the cramped living room.

"Here," she offered me the box. "Have some."

I took a sugared doughnut and took a bite, "Thanks."

"Don't thank me," Hayley pointed a finger at me. "That's what friends do."

I smiled and then looked down.

"How are things going?" Hayley asked softly and I knew exactly what she was talking about.

"I haven't spoken to him at all," I replied. "I hadn't even seen him until last night when I was coming back from work. He was near my flat, but he didn't say anything to me, he just left."

"Oh," Hayley rubbed my arm. "It will get easier, trust me."

"I guess," I shrugged and then forced a laugh. "It's almost like we've broken up or something, but we were only friends, he said it himself."

She smiled sadly and handed me a smoothie, "Apple and passion fruit, thought you might like it."

I smiled back and took a sip, "Pretty good. Anyway, how are you?"

"Oh I'm fine," Hayley said, lying back in the small sofa. "Studying and stuff as usual. The girls want to go to Oxford Street on Saturday actually, maybe you could come with us? It will be fun, you could also get your mind off things with Walter and his brothers."

"I don't have any money to spend," I said, drinking my smoothie.

"I can buy you stuff," Hayley said. "I'm going to use some of my birthday money that I've been saving."

"No way," I argued. "That's yours."

"I don't mind, otherwise I wouldn't be offering," she gave me a challenging look.

I sent her back a half-smile, "I have work anyway."

"Oh shit," she remembered. "Yeah. But wait, what about Sunday? I'm sure they wouldn't mind if we moved it to Sunday."

"No Hayley its cool," I said to her. "I'll be too tired to have fun and I don't want to dampen the mood. You guys enjoy yourselves."

She sighed and gave me a defeated look, "Fine Coral, but next time, no excuses."

"Sure," I smiled sweetly.

We sat and talked about random things and I found myself laughing which I hadn't properly done in a while, not since I ended my friendship with Walter. Hayley stayed until dinner time and she asked me if I wanted to go and eat out in the mall but I said no. I needed to try and get some sleep and I was worrying again about Wednesday tomorrow. I wanted to tell her, but I didn't want her to freak out and insist we tell the police. The *last* thing we needed were the Santiagos against us, they weren't all a friendly bunch, as we already had personal experience of.

"See you soon," Hayley gave me a tight hug before she left. "If you want my advice, sleep in as late as you can tomorrow. I'll let them know you're still not well."

"Okay," I nodded. "I think I need it anyway."

"Yeah," Hayley smiled. "Get better soon hun."

"Thanks," I said, holding the door open for her. "For everything."

Hayley grinned and gave me another hug before she left and I closed the door behind her.

***

I woke up in the morning with a somersaulting stomach and the first thing I did was rush to the toilet to vomit. It was finally Wednesday and I was so nervous. I couldn't go to work, I didn't feel much better and I was a little scared. I felt so bad and guilty knowing that whatever was going to happen, could have maybe been prevented if I had acted.

I spent the day watching the news, napping in the sofa and drinking cups of tea in between. I called work and told them I was sick and couldn't come in, which almost made me throw up again, and when it got to the evening I was actually shaking. I stared at the small TV screen, waiting to hear anything about the pub, but nothing was announced. Maybe they would announce it in tomorrow's news, I thought.

On the Thursday, again nothing was said about anything like an attack or robbery at the Dartfish and I was just confused. I was well enough to go to work by Saturday and during my shift Ario turned up and took a seat. He wasn't alone. This time he had Carlos *and* Diego with him and my face crumpled. Diego was one of the worst, he had tried to touch me and I could never forget how horrible it had been. I knew they wouldn't leave here without speaking to me, at least Ario wouldn't, that much was obvious.

"Coral," Tiffany said my name like it was something nasty caught in the back of her throat.

"Yes?" I turned around and gave her a pleasant smile, just to annoy her.

"New customers," she pointed to the Santiagos. "What are you waiting around for?"

"I could ask the same about you," I muttered under my breath as I made my way over to the gang members.

"How can I help you today?" I asked, keeping my eyes on my notepad.

"I know you," came Diego's slimy voice. "That basic blonde bi – "

"Shut up, will you?" Ario cut him off. "Not all girls are bitches like you *love* to go on about."

I looked at them to see Diego giving his younger cousin Ario a scowl and Carlos leaning back in his chair rubbing his stubble like he was bored. I noticed that his cheekbones were immaculate and when he met my gaze with his deep brown one, I gulped and looked down again.

"Sorry about that," Ario said, his eyes searching for a name tag.

"We don't wear them," I said out loud.

"Wear what?" Diego glared at me.

"Nothing," I said quickly. "Would you like any drinks?"

I took their orders and hurried away as quickly as possible. I just knew Ario was following me and when I reached the bar, I turned around and there he was.

"Nothing happened," I said, looking up at him. "You lied."

"I was just testing you," Ario said, not even trying to deny it.

"Testing me?!" I cried and then lowered my voice before I drew any attention to myself, it's not as if people didn't know who I was talking to.

"Testing me why?" I demanded angrily. "And for what?"

Ario's lips turned upwards into a little smirk, "To see if you would tell anyone, and you didn't. Why was that?"

I shook my head at myself and for some reason, I wasn't afraid to show him how mad I was. When I didn't answer Ario leaned down and I thought he was going to kiss me, for one crazy second, making my heart race.

He spoke quietly into my ear, "Don't be pissed at me. Are you interesting in helping us?"

"Are you crazy?" I jerked away from him like I'd been burnt and stared in disbelief. "No, I am *not* interested in doing anything for you or your gang so just leave me alone or I'll tell my manager."

"Tell your manager what?" Ario smiled it made the pit of my stomach feel light.

"I'm working here," I said after realising that threatening these people was the *worst* thing I could possibly do. "Excuse me."

"Cool," he shrugged. "I'll be waiting for that beer, I'm feeling a bit peckish today so add today's special to the order. I might be here a while."

Ario *did* stay for a while and he tried and tried to get me to tell him my name. I busied myself as much as possible with other customers, but I'd always end up back there, taking yet another order from him. Carlos hadn't spoken to me much at all, but I knew more than to underestimate him. He wasn't a gang leader for nothing. I hated the way Diego's filthy eyes raked my body each time I approached their table, and I was pretty distressed by the time they finally left.

It had been very stupid of me to say those things to Ario. I had let my anger get the better of me which was such a shock because I rarely ever did that with people I barely knew. Maybe it was because I had let myself stupidly think that he wanted to help me, that he had chosen me of all people to make sure I was safe.

Screw that, I thought bitterly at the end of my shift. I walked home fast, fuelled by my emotions and when I arrived, something just told me to check the side of my building, the place where Walter and I had looked at their gang sign. I used my phone light to illuminate the wall and there, in front of me, was a spray painted bleeding finger with a splinter sticking out of it, on top the original image of the seven headed snake.

I knew I shouldn't have been so rude to Ario, because now the Santiagos knew where I lived.

16

I stayed up in my bed almost the whole night, just waiting for my door to be smashed in and for the Santiagos to abduct me. I thought so hard about how it would happen that I almost completely failed to realise that although Ario knew which block of flats I lived in, he didn't know my flat number. There were fifty flats in the building so they *could* have gone from door to door demanding for me, but it would take quite some time and they also didn't know my name. I'm sure I wasn't the only blonde haired girl living here and they must have known that too.

In the end I convinced myself that if the Santiagos were really coming for me, they wouldn't be coming tonight, and in the end I earned a couple hours of sleep.

***

I held Severn's washed and neatly folded jumper in my hands and took a few deep breaths to calm my racing heart. It wasn't a big deal, I tried to tell myself. All I had to do was hand it back and say thank you. If he ignored me, which was fine, I had done my part.

School was over and it was a Monday which meant I had work soon so I couldn't do what I was doing right now, which was called wasting time. I'd planned that on purpose so I could just get it done and over with.

I took one last breath and started marching towards the three brothers who were sitting under a tree not far from the school gates. Other students streamed past me but I kept my eyes on the blond Simpson boys who were laughing and talking and covered in dry leaves.

"Hey," I said, my heart in my mouth when I finally reached them.

The triplets stopped talking and looked up at me silently.

"I just wanted to give you this back. Sorry I had it so long," I stumbled over my words and looked at the pavement as I handed Severn his jumper. "Thank you."

Severn took it from me and I risked a glance at him as he did so.

"Thank *you*," he smirked, dipping his head towards me.

I blinked in surprise, he didn't seem mad at all.

"We're...okay?" I asked, glancing at all three of them. "You're not mad at me?"

"More like *you're* not mad at *us*?" Giovanni grinned.

"Huh?" I couldn't help but grin back. "But you were being so...distant, like you didn't know me."

"That's only because you were doing the same to us," Gomez said with a confused smile.

I laughed, shaking my head at myself. "I thought you were pissed off."

"Well we're not," Severn said.

I wanted so bad to just sit down and talk to them, ask them about Walter and laugh at their jokes, but then all of this would have been for nothing. I would have hurt Walter for no reason at all if I was going to just keep interacting with his family like nothing had happened. Two weeks had passed, and like Hayley said, it would get easier.

"I have to go," I said to them all with an apologetic smile. "Work."

***

It was Tuesday afternoon after school and I stayed in my flat, making sure only to go out when I needed to. The household bin was almost overflowing and I knew that I would have to go and dispose of it outside soon.

There was a buzz at my door and I jumped about ten feet in the air. I breathed deeply, trying to calm myself down. If Ario and the rest of the gang were going to kidnap me, I doubt they'd let me know they were coming. I checked the peep hole and saw no one was there, of course they were still waiting outside the building for me to let them in. The buzzer sounded again and I bit my bottom lip.

Taking more deep breaths, I put my mouth to the speaker and asked, "Who is it?"

"Me," the person replied cheerily.

I frowned, "Landon?"

"Yes, now unlock the door because my nipples are freezing off out here," he said, making me smile despite my confusion.

"Come up," I pressed the button which unlocked the main door, sighing in deep relief.

Landon must have known I lived at flat number seventeen, Walter had probably told him that. It made me wonder if Walter had sent him in the first place, because Landon showing up here was the last thing I expected. He was knocking on my door in seconds and I opened it for him.

"Hey," I said, trying to suss him out.

"Hey to you too," Landon walked in, looking around. "I made Walter tell me where you lived, I haven't been stalking you."

I scrunched up my toes in discomfort, imagining what was going through his head as he viewed my home.

"Have you been in a fight?" I took in the raw cut on his face.

"Huh? Oh yeah, nothing beats a good fist fight," he said breezily. "Keeps you fit."

"...Sure," I said. "Okay."

"So you wanna know why I'm here, right?" Landon turned to face me, chewing on his lip ring.

"Naturally," I shrugged back at him, all the while thinking about how my plan to break things off with gangs all together was failing miserably.

"Walter isn't himself," Landon said to me, making me feel even sorrier. "Let's sit down."

"Yeah," I blinked. "Sure. Do you want a drink?"

"Nah, I'm fine," Landon grinned and I led him to the living room.

"How is he?" I asked as soon as we'd sat down.

"Not happy," Landon answered, "which isn't much of a difference because he's often in a bad mood, but now it's a lot worse."

"I feel terrible," I said honestly. "I didn't want to hurt him but I – "

"No, I get it," Landon said. "You don't want to get involved in that kind of lifestyle, it's not safe. I completely understand, but my brother is finding it harder to get over."

I sighed, dropping my gaze.

"I didn't come to force you to try and fix things between you or anything," Landon told me. "I just wanted to tell you a little more about us, why we are the way we are. Things Walter probably hasn't told you."

I looked up at him in surprise, waiting to hear what he had to say.

"Our parents died when we were young," Landon said. "But before that happened, they dumped us."

"Dumped you?" I frowned. "How?"

"Well they abandoned us," Landon explained. "You see the house we're living in now, they bought it, dumped us there and moved on. We actually used to live in central London, but that was a long time ago."

"How old were you? If you don't mind me asking," I questioned him quietly.

"When they dumped us?"

"Um, yeah."

"I was thirteen, so that makes Phoenix fifteen, Walter twelve, Eli eleven and the triplets nine," Landon answered casually.

"That's horrible," I said in shock.

"They weren't the best parents in the world," Landon said, looking down. "That's for sure."

"You were right, I had no idea," I said, giving him an apologetic look.

"Yeah," he shrugged. "Well there's more. Phoenix found a way to start dealing. He began as a 'delivery boy' for a small organisation not far from here and as the years went on he worked his way up. Eventually he left and started his own thing, our gang. They didn't let him go so easily but things got complicated and those big guys ended up getting busted and their whole organisation went down the drain. When the hustle died down, Phoenix made new connections here in this area. He was probably eighteen by this time and it wasn't too long until we got our own supplier and our own demands.

"And well, that's what we've been doing ever since. It's what our father did, what he taught us, especially Phoenix. We don't know a lot better, you know? None of us have actually finished school. Phoenix dropped out when he was fourteen, and dropped out when I was sixteen, he made me stay and 'learn' longer than he ever did. Maybe Walter will even graduate – " Landon broke off laughing, "but seriously, with your help, it's not so impossible.

"So what I'm saying is yes we didn't have to choose the lifestyle we did, and yes there are plenty of other things, bad things, that I haven't told you about that we aren't exactly proud of, *but* it's who we are. It would have been very hard to not end up like our parents, they were the real deal in the drug world and, well, the apples don't fall far from the tree."

"I don't want any of you to end up dead though," I whispered.

"No," Landon laughed. "That's not happening. I was just trying to tell you that we are decent people, really. With Phoenix it's a whole other story, but you can't really blame him after all the shit he's been through. But we'll deal with *that* part when we get there, if you *do* change your mind about seeing Walter."

I was so torn, what Landon was saying was right. It wasn't completely their fault that they were who they were today, and they weren't all that bad – which I *did* believe when it came to all the brothers except Phoenix. But he had his reasons, which I also accepted.

"Thanks for sharing," I said eventually. "I know you didn't have to."

"It's okay Coral, anything to try and get you and my brother back to yourselves," Landon smiled widely. "I can tell that you haven't been getting enough sleep."

That was kind of normal for me, but maybe the break off was having an effect. I hadn't really linked the two.

"Will he even talk to me if I tried?" I asked Landon.

"Of course he will," he replied. "He doesn't hate you, you know. Still far from it."

I nodded smiling, "Well, I'll try."

"Good," he got to his feet. "Cheers."

"You going?" I stood up.

"Yeah, I have to go home and shower," Landon rubbed his chest. "I have a date tonight."

"Oh, well hope you have a good time," I smiled, leading him to the door.

"I know I will," he winked at me and hit his bum, making me burst into laughter.

Less than an hour after Landon had gone, I finally left the building to put my rubbish in the communal bin outside and jumped when I saw a tall figure standing near the wall.

"Oh hey," Ario's face lit up and he was alone as far as I could tell.

"What are you doing?" I stopped dead, fear striking up inside me but actually for the wrong reasons. Landon had *just* been here. "You're trespassing. If any of the Simpsons see you they'll shoot you."

"Then they won't see me," Ario said in frustration, clenching his jaw. "Those bitches have run home to lick their wounds anyway."

He must have been talking about the fight, and I wondered how Walter was doing. The last time they'd had a fight, he'd had slipped up. Ario walked up to me, wearing a loose denim jacket and a black top underneath. I didn't want to make him angry so I decided not to mention anything about gangs again. Just looking at him, I felt there was no immediate danger and decided to take a risk and trust those instincts.

"You followed me," I said to him accusingly. "That night."

"Because you looked like you were about to keel over and pass out at any moment," Ario threw right back. "I was looking out for you."

"And looking out for me meant you had to graffiti the building I live in?" I frowned. "Now the Simpsons will know your gang has been here recently."

"We're in their territory a lot more often than you think," Ario folded his arms. "Just like *they* are in ours."

I sighed and lowered my voice, "Well thanks for looking out for me...but what are you here for now?"

"To apologise," he mumbled, dropping his gaze. "For *testing* you."

I just stared at him, unable to believe my ears.

"Let me just..." I unlocked my knees to get my legs working again.

I walked past Ario to dump the rubbish and then went back to meet him face to face.

"So apology accepted?" Ario looked at me through his dark lashes. He was breathing through gritted teeth and he rubbed beads of sweat off his forehead. Come to think of it, his breathing had been a little laboured the whole time.

"Are you okay?" I touched his arm.

"Yeah," Ario shifted in discomfort. "I didn't think it was a problem, but it's kind of bothering me now."

"What is?" I widened my eyes. "I think I smell blood. Did you get cut?"

"Yeah, by that – " Ario cut himself off in anger and took a breath. "Walter."

I blinked in surprise, Walter had done some real damage this time.

"Come up," I said, not thinking through what I was really doing, just trying to help. "I know first aid."

Ario frowned at me but I pulled him into the building by his sleeve and up the stairs into my flat. I made him sit down at the two seater table I had in my kitchen.

Part of my mind was hissing at me in anger. After everything I was worrying about, I'd led Ario *straight* into my home and now the gang member knew exactly where I lived. But then I looked past all that, and all I saw was a boy my age who was hurt and bleeding and needed at least an inspection and then treatment as soon as possible.

125

Ario took off his jacket and pulled up his t-shirt and I lowered myself down to look over his injury.

"It's not very deep," Ario said, wincing. "But it hurts like a bitch."

I couldn't reply. I was transfixed by his tattooed abdomen. He had a tattoo on his side and I couldn't read all of it because of the blood but I guessed it read Santiago Splinters. I grabbed a napkin and wet it before rinsing it out and using it to clean his very toned stomach.

"Ow," Ario gripped my wrist, stopping me.

"Sorry," I said, looking up at him. "But I think you're right, it's not that deep. You have to let me do it."

He looked at me with his blue eyes and then let go of my wrist, "Okay, be quick."

I cleaned up the blood and saw a cut across his stomach about four inches long and thankfully not very deep. It would leave a scar, but Ario seemed to have quite a few of them already.

"I don't think it needs stitches," I said, tearing my eyes away from a bullet wound just under his ribs. "But I'm not sure."

"You have any plasters or something?" Ario asked, looking down at himself with a pain filled face. "It's still bleeding."

"You'll need more than a plaster," I smiled briefly at him.

I checked my medical box where I usually kept all my drugs, plasters and patches but didn't have anything the right size.

"I'm going to have to improvise," an idea came into my head and I turned to look at Ario who had been staring into space.

"Yeah," he pressed the napkin into his cut. "Sure."

I went to my room and found what I was looking for. It would do the job but I was worried about how Ario would react.

"I can try putting this over it," I held up the pad.

Ario stared motionlessly, "Is that a..."

"Yes?" I bit my lip in uncertainty.

There was a split second of silence and then Ario cracked up laughing. I stood in the doorway, shocked and then he winced, tightening this hold on his stomach and cutting the laughter short.

"You'll let me try then?" I smiled at him.

"Go on then," he shrugged and then creased his eyebrows. "If the boys see it and take the piss out of me, I'll blame you."

I laughed and got on with it. It was weird to imagine the Santiagos as just a close group of boys who had all the usual mixture of arguments and banter like any family would. Just like the Simpsons.

"Looks pretty stable," I said, admiring my work. "I think it will do for now. But still, get it checked out."

I had secured the pad in place with bandages I'd wrapped tightly around his waist and just hoped that it didn't move around too much when he walked.

"Thanks," Ario smirked, standing up.

"It's okay," I clasped my hands together in front of me shyly.

He went to wash his bloody hands in the sink and I did the same after he was finished. I turned the tap off, very aware of how close Ario was standing to me. He startled me when I felt his hand touch my shoulder and turn me slightly so that I was facing him. When his fingers cupped my chin and lifted it so that my gaze met his, my mind went crazy with all sorts of thoughts and feelings. Ario was very good looking.

"You're so beautiful," Ario breathed, his eyes searching mine.

A boy had never called me beautiful before and I knew not to get overwhelmed by any strong feelings just because of a couple words.

It wasn't so easy though.

I gripped the front of Ario's shirt, unable to look away from his captivating eyes and he leaned down to kiss me. He brushed his lips against mine, one hand firmly placed on the small of my back and the other stroking my cheek. None of it made sense but I felt myself going along with it, caught in the moment and not quite believing that any of it was real. Ario kissed me and I moved my lips against his, reaching up to cup his face. The kiss was warm and soft but when his tongue touched my lower lip and was about to slip into my mouth, I pulled away from him.

"I can't," I choked out, letting go of his shirt. "Sorry, I just can't."

"That's fine," Ario ran a hand through his hair, turning a full circle. "I – I shouldn't have. Not so fast."

I looked at him, trembling, "I still like him."

Ario looked surprised for a moment, but didn't ask who I was talking about, he only nodded.

"I'll go, thanks for the help. I won't bother you again," he gave me a half smile and went to the door.

I followed him there, trying to think of something to say and Ario opened the door and then turned around to face me.

"You never told me your name," he smiled.

"It's Coral," I blushed, looking away.

"Coral," Ario repeated. "I won't bother introducing myself, I assure you, you won't see me again."

"No, don't say that," I shook my head, starting to feel bad even though I knew I should have left it with that.

"Why?" he smirked. "You the kind of girl who's interested in seeing two guys at once?"

"No," I said quickly. "Not that, but we might cross paths, you never know."

"I guess," he said and then stepped out the door. "Well I'm Ario. *Adios* Coral."

"*Adios* Ario," I said quietly even though he was already out of earshot.

I closed the door after him and touched my lips. Waking up this morning I would have never seen this happening. Walter was who I wanted, I missed him so much and I felt like I'd betrayed him even though we weren't even talking.

I couldn't keep this up any longer. I needed to see him and talk to him before I got any more confused. I just hoped he wanted to see me too.

17

Walking up and down my apartment, I tried to decide what to do. In the end I couldn't wait any longer and I put on my shoes and grabbed my coat. I walked briskly to Walter's house, no longer feeling lethargic or weak. It was probably all the adrenaline in me and the faint feeling of Ario's kiss still on my lips. I reached the Simpson household in double time and knocked on the door loudly.

It was just my luck that Walter himself opened it.

He stood there and looked down at me with a grazed and bruised face, seeming to grow angrier by the second. I opened my mouth to say something but he turned and walked back into the house, leaving me outside. I followed Walter in and found him taking his shoes off and dumping them in a pile under the stairs by the basement door. He was wearing his leather jacket too and looked like he had just been out.

"Can I speak to you, please?" I asked, my voice terribly quiet and catching in my throat.

Walter continued to ignore me and I was starting to think that Landon had been lying when he said Walter didn't hate me.

"Was someone at the..." Gomez's voice dried out when he saw me standing by the stairs.

"Hi," I tried to smile.

"Hey," he replied, glancing between Walter who was still bent over kicking his shoes off and me who was feeling nervous as hell. "I think I'll leave you two to it."

Gomez disappeared upstairs and I turned to look at Walter who was standing up straight now.

"Walter," I said, trying to breathe properly as I looked right into his hazel eyes. "Please can we talk?"

He opened the basement door, "Down here."

I looked at him. He wouldn't hurt me, would he?

"My room's a mess and no one will hear us down here," Walter read my expression and explained in a deadpan voice.

"Okay," I said and headed down the stairs.

The basement was actually a lot bigger than it looked and it was stacked with a TV, bean bags, weights and a treadmill. Walter closed the door, drenching us in darkness before he turned on the light. I watched him descend the stairs, trying to figure out how I could put my feelings into words, but it seemed Walter had that already sorted though.

"Why were you with blue eyes?" he demanded immediately.

I was taken aback by his ferocity and looked at him wide-eyed, "W-who's blue eyes?"

Walter cursed under his breath, tugging hard at his hair.

"Ario Santiago," he spat with venom.

That's what they called him?

"When did you..." I was speechless.

"Just now!" Walter shouted, then lowered his tone when I flinched. "I was going to your flat to see you when I saw him leaving the building. I chased him with my knife out of our turf. I didn't have a gun on me or I would have killed him, I swear."

"I'm sorry Walter," I apologised. "He was outside and I invited him in to hel – "

"I don't want to know," Walter interrupted. "I don't want to blow up."

I thought that *was* him blowing up, I winced. Glancing at him, I determined whether or not I should tell him that Ario and I in fact shared a kiss. It was likely to be a very bad idea, but I wanted to put all the cards on the table, else I'd never stop feeling guilty.

"What?" Walter's voice softened, he must have been reading my face.

"Walter...I..." my eyes swam with tears.

"What did he do?" Walter stepped towards me and held my arms.

The touch made my tummy feel light and fluttery and I did all I could *not* to throw myself at him and bury my face in his warm chest.

"He kissed me, but I couldn't do it," I said quickly. "I like *you*."

Walter stared at me so long and so hard I wanted to run away and hide.

"Blue eyes *kissed* you?" he repeated, almost whispering.

I nodded, tears falling now and my throat burning.

"How long have you two been...?" Walter didn't let go of me. It was like all the energy had been sucked out of him, which was the opposite of what I'd been expecting. He was so unpredictable.

"We haven't been seeing each other," I told him. "He spoke to me a couple times before, at work – "

"He goes to the Dartfish?" Walter frowned, cutting me off.

"Yeah well a few of the Santiagos have been coming recently," I answered quietly.

Walter shook his head and I took the pause as an opportunity to continue.

"He followed me home and knows where I live," I managed to explain between heaving breaths. "And today he came round to apologise for – for testing me."

I broke off crying, unable to go on and Walter pulled me into a hug. He probably didn't understand what I was talking about but he seemed not to care about Ario, or blue eyes, anymore.

"I'm sorry Walter," I sobbed. "I don't want him, you're the one that I..."

"Stop crying," he rubbed my back. "It's okay."

He held me until I was able to contain myself and then he pulled me back so that he could look at me.

"Coral I like you too," he spoke gently. "But this isn't going to work with the both of us. You have to decide between him and me, even if it's just friendship, because this runs deeper than territory. He's one of my mortal enemies. If you want us to be friends again, you have to cut him and all the other Santiagos out of your life and I'd expect it to be the same the other way around too."

131

"No, I want to be *your* friend again," I said, rubbing my eyes. "Not his, that was a mistake and I was confused....and missing you."

Walter finally smiled, "I missed you too."

I smiled back, my lips still trembling.

"I'm willing to..to try and forget what you told me about Ario," Walter said, briefly clenching his jaw. "And we can go back to how we were before."

"Actually," I said shyly, rubbing away the last of my tears. "I kind of want to be more than friends."

I peeked up at him through my wet lashes and saw Walter raising his eyebrows before his eyes clouded over with something that looked like passion.

"You know," he caressed my face, making butterflies erupt in my stomach. "I've been thinking the same thing."

Walter kissed me and I parted my lips almost straight away to let him in. The kiss was slow and deep at first and I could feel Walter's lips trembling as much as mine were. I inhaled when Walter knotted his hand in the hair at the back of my head and kissed me harder. A small sound of pleasure arose from the back of my throat and I felt Walter smile against my lips for a second. I pulled back first, still breathless from all the sensations I was getting in the palms of my hands and the bottom of my stomach.

I looked into Walter's eyes and held his face in my hands, gently rubbing the fresh graze under his eye with my thumb. I cared so much for him, as I'm sure he did for me. Walter pecked me on the lips before taking hold of my hand and heading for the door.

"I think it's food time," Walter said to me. "If anyone's gotten any, that is. You'll stay to eat, right?"

"Yeah," I smiled, feeling so much relief and happiness flowing through me that everything was behind us now.

We stepped out of the basement, hand in hand still and the triplets, who were eating in the kitchen, turned and looked at us.

Severn's face broke into a grin first, "Finally. Now you can smile again Walter."

Walter intentionally stopped smiling and I laughed, pulling my hand out of his shyly. Landon swooped down out of nowhere and clapped his brother Walter on the back whilst grinning and wiggling his brows at me.

"I thought you had a date," Walter shoved him away.

"I do," Landon replied, unable to stop smiling. "I'm late."

"He's doing that thing when he starts showing less interest in the girl so that she starts to get the message," Giovanni explained with a mouth full of noodles. "That way when he breaks it off, it hurts her less...or something like that."

I was surprised. It didn't occur to me how harsh Landon could be towards other girls when he was so kind to me.

"I'm not a prick, I swear," Landon thrust his face down to meet mine, causing Walter to push him away again. "The girls I 'date' don't really value themselves, so if I do the same, it shouldn't matter, should it?"

Well when he said it like that....but still. It made me wonder why he didn't just settle for a real relationship when he clearly knew so much about how they worked.

"I think it does matter," Gomez considered. "But then again, to not see your face again would be a blessing."

"Hey," Landon said to Gomez and pointed at his face. "This face is getting some tonight and yours isn't."

"Can we *not*?" Walter frowned at them.

"Oh yeah," Gomez smirked at me. "Excuse my behaviour my lady, but since you and Walter are clearly a thing now, I suppose you'll be round here more often and well I'm not always a polite gentleman so you'll get used to it."

"Same," Severn said, giving me a thumbs up and Giovanni seconded it.

"Okay," I smiled. "It's your house, your way."

"So," Landon squeezed himself between me and Walter then put his arms around our shoulders. "Did I do my job right?"

"You did nothing," Walter scowled at him. "Shut up, Landon."

"But by the looks of things," Landon smiled down at me. "After all the waiting, it's a happy ending."

I blushed and smiled at the floor.

"Piss off," Walter growled, elbowing him off us.

I heard someone coming down the stairs behind us and Eli showed up at the end of them. I gave him a smile, expecting him to return it but Eli frowned at me and then headed into the kitchen

133

without a word. I looked up at Walter questioningly and he only scowled at the back of Eli's head.

"Don't mind him," Walter muttered.

"He's a weird one," Landon nudged my side playfully.

Weird was one way to say it. Eli was very bipolar and it sure was confusing.

"Let's eat something," Walter said, leading us to the kitchen.

The boys had ordered big pots of noodles each and the triplets had just finished theirs. I sat down at the dining table and was handed my own pot of noodles with vegetables and pieces of chicken in it.

"Walter no," I looked up at him sharply. "I can't have that. What will you eat?"

"There are lots of things in the fridge," he replied with a lazy shrug. "Don't stress, just enjoy it."

He wasn't going to take no for an answer, so I thanked him with a guilty look and started to eat.

"If you can't finish it," Giovanni was grinning at me. "You know where I am."

"Shut up Gio," Walter scowled at him as he opened the fridge to find some food. "Coral, eat as much as you want. Don't listen to him."

I smiled back at Giovanni as I ate another bite and when Walter had his back turned, I sent him a nod, agreeing to his proposal.

"Did you know Blue eyes was in our territory just after the fight today?" Walter murmured to his brothers, getting out some leftover pizza.

"Serious?" Landon raised his eyebrows at him.

"Yeah," Walter nodded, turning to face us all. "He had some nerve. I chased him out."

"That little bitch," Landon shook his head at himself.

"I swear you cut him?" Eli asked in a low voice.

Getting a proper look at him, I saw that he too had a couple grazes on his face and what also seemed like a forming black eye.

"I *did*," Walter growled. "But clearly not deep enough."

I winced and Walter must have noticed. He sighed, biting into his pizza cold.

"You're probably wondering who blue eyes is," Severn sent me a smile.

"Walter already told me," I replied. "I didn't know you guys had nicknames for the Santiagos."

"Of course we do. Did you really think we'd bless them with the courtesy of using their actual names? And besides, it just habit now," Gomez grinned, coming to sit down on the seat next to me. "Do you wanna know the rest of them?"

I copied his expression, "Sure."

"Okay," Landon took it from there. "So there's Carlos, you probably know him, everyone knows him. He's their leader and we call him skull face."

"Skull face?" I repeated, raising my eyebrows.

"Yeah," Landon nodded and Severn sucked in his cheeks then made cutting actions along his cheekbones as a demonstration. "Because his cheekbones are so sharp, his head just looks like a skull."

I laughed out loud, "Isn't that a compliment though?"

"Shut up," Gomez covered my mouth, laughing all the same. "It's   just   what   we   say."

"Okay," I said in a muffled voice, smiling hard. "Got it."

Gomez removed his hand and then he continued from Landon, "Diego is mop head. His hair is just so...."

"Moppy," Severn said and the triplets all shrugged at the same time. "No other word to describe it."

The mention of Diego was enough to make me uncomfortable and slightly afraid, but hearing him being referred to as a 'mop head' made him seem absolutely harmless and I laughed again.

"Ario is blue eyes," Landon said, nodding at Walter. "Walter's already told you that one."

I made sure not to say anything about Ario so as not to upset Walter, and the boys thankfully didn't notice.

"You may see that one as a compliment too," Landon went on. "But it's not. We call him blue eyes because he's the only Hispanic person we've ever seen with blue eyes and not brown - and I've personally seen a lot of Latinas."

"More than *seen* a lot of Latinas," Gomez said in a low voice, wiggling his eyebrows, earning a snigger from Severn and Gio.

"Who's next?" Severn scratched the back of his head.

"The twins Miguel and Manuel," Gomez made a face of disgust. "We call them blockheads."

"Yeah," Giovanni added. "Their jaws are so square, their heads might as well be cubes."

I'd been eating some of my noodles when I started to laugh at the same time, resulting in me inhaling food and coughing hard in order to breathe again. Gomez slapped my back and tears sprang to my eyes, mainly from the burning sensation in my chest. The Simpsons made the Santiagos seem a lot less threatening.

"Not so hard," Walter gave Gomez a look as he finished off his pizza.

"Last but not least," Landon smiled cheekily. "Batty boy."

"Batty as in crazy?" I questioned.

"No," Landon corrected me. "Batty as in gay."

"Paulo?" I arched my brows. "I didn't know he was gay."

"He's not. Well we don't think he is," Landon confused me. "He   just   *looks*   gay."

"I didn't know gay had a look," I commented.

"Yes, okay camp then," Gomez elaborated. "Like the stereotype gay guy. There are people like that who exist, or there wouldn't be a stereotype."

"Okay, fair enough," I shrugged. "Anyway I guess you know him more than I do. Which isn't at all."

There was noise at the front door and I glanced around, seeing all of the Simpson brothers, *except* Phoenix, which meant *he* was the one entering the house at that very moment. I stood up, scared and ready to run or hide if I needed to and Walter walked up to me, frowning in concern.

"What is it?" he asked me lowly.

"If Phoenix sees me back in his house..." I whispered, unable to finish my sentence.

Walter's face hardened, "I won't ever let him hurt you."

Phoenix walked into view and stopped when he saw me in the kitchen. The boys were all silent and Walter stood and faced Phoenix, partly shielding me. Phoenix's deep stare made my stomach knot in discomfort and Landon hopped off the counter and walked up to Phoenix without a word.

"You okay?" Landon asked his brother.

"Fine," Phoenix grunted, his eyes still on me and then he turned away and went up the stairs.

"I've lost my appetite," Walter grumbled, putting the rest of his third slice in the bin, despite Gio trying to reach for it.

"Here Gio," I gave him my noodles which I hadn't gotten very far with. "I'm full."

"Thanks," Gio grinned at me, eagerly taking the food. "Don't let Phoenix get to you. He doesn't like new people."

"Gio," Walter sent him an annoyed look.

"Sorry," he ducked his head. "I was just trying to be helpful."

Walter ignored him and he headed out the kitchen, me following him. I was very aware of Eli's sour look and it really made me wonder what was with him.

Landon checked the time on his phone. "I didn't mean to be this late, damn. I have to go. See you sooner rather than later Coral."

He gave me a wink and a cheeky smile before leaving the house.

"Wanna go upstairs?" Walter asked me, looking at the floor. "Get away from the noise?"

"Okay," I agreed, looking back at the kitchen where the triplets were laughing about something and thinking about whether we would kiss again or not.

We went up together and I looked at the various doors, wondering which one Phoenix was behind and why he was always so cold.

As soon as Walter and I entered his room, he blew up.

There was no other way to describe it, he went ballistic. He grabbed the handle of a wooden bat that had already been broken in two and started smashing it against a wall. Shouting angrily, Walter formed multiple dents in the plaster and when the bat splintered into tiny pieces, he started using his fists instead.

"Walter please, stop," I tried to get close to him without getting punched. "You're hurting yourself."

"I'm gonna *kill* him," Walter said, breathing deeply as he whirled around to face me. "I'm gonna kill that – "

"Please Walter," I cried. "Calm down."

His knuckles were dripping blood onto his dark carpet but Walter didn't even seem to notice. Of course he'd be mad, I thought.

It didn't seem real enough for him to have taken the news so calmly the first time.

"I've always hated Blue eyes, but *now*," Walter shook his head. "Now, I'm going to kill him for sure."

"Walter," I rushed to him and held his arms. "You can't kill him."

"I can do anything I want," Walter looked at me, fury still blazing in his eyes.

I had to calm him down.

"If you kill Ario, I'm sure Carlos and his gang won't take it so lightly," I said patiently, trying not to show how worried I really was. "The last thing either of us wants is one of your brothers dead."

Walter sighed deeply, "But he – "

"I know," I said, cupping his face. "And I'm sorry, but please don't let your anger make you do something you'll regret."

Walter scowled, "At least let me shoot him. I'll make sure he survives that."

I stared at him in horror, knowing full well that Walter was serious. I didn't want Ario hurt, let alone *shot at*, because I let him kiss me. I just needed to make Walter know that Ario was no longer a threat. I wanted to be with him and no one else.

"Don't shoot him," I said softly. "You said you'd put that behind you."

Walter's face fell, "It's not easy Coral."

"I know it's not easy," I said, searching his eyes. "But *please* don't do anything stupid."

Walter breathed slowly for a few moments and I said nothing, allowing him to hopefully relax a little.

"At least explain to me how you felt about it," Walter said eventually, "because I can't forget about it when I don't fully understand."

I took a breath, "I was confused most of all. Part of me wanted comfort and he was offering it to me, but part of me knew that it wasn't the right thing to do. He was in a gang and the whole reason I'd stopped seeing you was because you were in a gang too, so I was just contradicting myself. He...he called me b-beautiful and well...no one had called me that before and I guess I just let myself fall for it. I didn't know if he really meant it or not and I stopped the kiss before it....got heated or anything. You were all I could think about and I told him that I still liked you. I mean, I didn't say your name but he didn't ask anyway. After that, he left and said he wouldn't bother me again."

Walter had been watching me quietly and listening hard, and when I stopped talking he took my hands in his battered and bleeding ones.

"You're more than beautiful to me," Walter said, looking at every single inch of my face. "I'll write for you, because at the moment my mind is...just...jumbled and I can't get the words out right."

"Thank you," I said, trying not to smile so hard because I knew Walter meant it.

We gazed at each other for a couple of seconds until I noticed the warm wet feeling of blood on my hands.

"Walter, we need to fix that," I said, lifting his busted knuckles.

"Oh," he looked down. "It's nothing."

"It's not nothing," I said sternly. "Where's the bathroom?"

After I'd cleaned and patched up Walter's hands we went back to his room and this time I noticed how much of a mess it really was. His desk was smashed almost to pieces and the chair that went with it had been thrown to the other side of the room. Walter had stabbed his sofa multiple times so that it was covered in lots of slashes where the white stuffing within was showing. I tried not to think about it being a human body, or Ario Santiago in particular.

"You cold?" Walter asked me when I shuddered.

"A little bit," I rubbed the goosebumps on my arm.

"Hey," Walter turned so that he was standing in front of me, facing me. "I'm sorry if I scared you. My room I mean. I didn't want you to see it but..." he sighed. "What I'm saying is that I just get angry a lot, but I would never lay a finger on you. Believe me."

"I do believe you," I said to him.

"I'll protect you," Walter rubbed my arms. "I'll look after you. And when the time is right, I'll be there for you to talk to me. About all the things that trouble you, the things that keep you up at night. I want to be there for you Coral."

I gave Walter a wobbling smile before throwing myself at him, squeezing my eyes shut as he held me tight. I felt safe and loved, and happier than I'd been in a while.

"You wanna get in the bed?" Walter asked me, kissing the top of my head. "Just to lie down for a bit?"

"Yeah, okay," I agreed.

Walter kicked pieces of splintered wood out of the way as he walked to the bed and I followed his footsteps, still holding onto his hand. Walter and I lay on his bed, leaning against the headboard with pillows propped up behind our backs. Walter turned to look at me, brushing my hair over my shoulder and cupping my face in his hand. He leaned in and kissed me and I closed my eyes and let his lips, his tongue take me out of the room and to a place of euphoria.

"He knows where you live," Walter said after he'd pulled back. "And it won't be long until he finds out that you're with me. You're not safe Coral, and I can't have that."

"I'm safe with you right now," I replied, not wanting him to worry or get angered anymore by Ario and his gang.

I ran my fingertips along Walter's arm, which even though was relaxed, was big and powerful. In fact, Walter's navy blue t-shirt looked nice and snug on him and my eyes trailed down to his chest which was all to visible through the fabric. I couldn't believe we were together. We were each other's to kiss and hold. It was something new and exhilarating.

"Fine," Walter sighed, rubbing his face. "But later we have to sort something out, maybe I could come stay round yours some nights or – "

"Walter relax," I shushed him, putting a finger to his lips.

Walter looked at my finger and looked back at me, holding his breath it seemed.

"Right now - I'm safe - with you," I said, kissing him softly on the lips between each phrase.

Walter inhaled deeply before his hands grasped my waist and he held me closer to him, kissing me hard. He rolled us over so that he was on top and his lips devoured mine. I was soon breathless but enjoying how he felt. The kiss was rough and I could tell how much Walter was putting his feelings behind it. We broke away and I suddenly yawned.

"You're tired," Walter was immediately concerned. "Sleep in my bed, I'll sleep over there."

Walter pointed at the torn up sofa and I looked at him, trying to think. I didn't want him to have to sleep on the cramped and damaged thing, but I also didn't know if I was ready to share a bed with him yet. He had made the decision for me of course, but I still felt a little bad.

"Are you sure?" I asked him.

"I'll be fine," Walter sent me a reassuring smile. "Rest Coral."

He kissed my forehead and I smiled at him.

"Thank you Walter," I said.

"It's alright angel," he replied.

18

"Don't, please," I begged, trying to get away from his dirty hands. "Stop it, please!"

I fought against his rough grip, knowing it was useless but unable to stop myself from trying. He wasn't supposed to do this to me. It was all wrong but he made sure I kept quiet by enforcing a lot of pain. I jolted awake at the same time he shoved his hand down my trousers. The tears were falling before I'd even opened my eyes and I blinked in disorientation as the sobs raked through my body.

I didn't know where I was.

I didn't know where I was and I could still smell his horrible scent. It was suffocating me.

"Hey, Coral," I heard someone's voice. "Shh."

I was still struggling to breathe when I felt the person climb into the bed with me. Their arms went around my frame and they held me tight.

"It was just a dream," Walter said to me. "You're safe with me."

I cried into his chest, gripping onto his t-shirt in a tight fist as he rubbed my back rhythmically which eventually relaxed me and had me only sniffling.

"Feeling better now?" Walter pulled away slightly so that I could see his face.

It was dark but I could still clearly make out his features and the worry in his eyes as he searched mine.

"I'm okay now," I said, enjoying the warmth of another body. "Thank you."

"Don't thank me," he said, creasing his brows. "I told you I'm here for you, didn't I?"

It was all I'd ever wanted. Someone real, solid and warm to hold me and tell me I was just fine and that *he* could never hurt me again.

"Is it okay if I stay here with you?" Walter murmured quietly.

"Yes," I said, placing my hand over one of his arms.

There was a silence and I closed my eyes, snuggling into Walter's warmth. I was drifting off again when Walter spoke.

"Do you wanna talk about it?" his low tone ran through my chest.

"No, it's okay," I said to him, keeping my eyes closed. "It's not nice stuff."

"I know," Walter said. "But I'm be here to listen, whenever you want."

I sighed, "I know you are."

Walter tightened his arms around me, "I – I like you."

"I like you too," I smiled, blushing.

Walter kissed the top of my head, "Sleep well."

***

"Ah, shit!"

I frowned when I heard noises. Sleep was sweetest when it was time to wake up.

Walter shifted besides me, his hands leaving my waist as he turned over.

"Get out my room," he grumbled sleepily.

"I came to talk to you and I stepped on a piece of – " Landon's voice groaned in pain and anger. "Why is your room such a dangerous mess?"

Walter sighed loudly and felt him get up off the bed. I kept my eyes closed as he pulled the covers back on top of me and gave the top of my head a rub. I opened them a peek after a couple of seconds and shifted slowly as I stretched my legs. Walter had been sleeping in only a top and boxers the whole night and my eyes unconsciously focused on his behind as he walked up to Landon.

Landon was standing in the middle of Walter's bombsite of a room dressed in *even less* clothes than Walter. I couldn't help but trail my eyes down his topless body, which looked like something out of a magazine but with more of a rough finish. Landon had a colourful tattoo on his right bicep and a few bruises, from the fighting yesterday I presumed. It only made me want to know what Walter looked like under *his* top and if he had movie star abs or any special tattoos I had no clue about.

"What do you want?" Walter asked his brother, rubbing his eyes tiredly. "Do you even know what time it is?"

"Six," Landon answered, making a face of pain. "It's not that early. You have to wake up for school soon anyway."

"Not in almost *two hours*," Walter snarled, then he sighed again. "What's wrong with you?"

"I've got a splinter," Landon complained quietly as he tried look at the bottom of his foot.

"Sit down," Walter instructed, pointing to the torn up sofa.

Partially obscuring my face with the sheets, I watched the boys sit down and Walter took a closer look at the sole of Landon's foot, trying to dig the splinter out.

"Ow," Landon winced. "You got it?"

"No," Walter snapped. "Stop moving your foot."

I smiled at how cute they were being, especially from Walter's part. I wouldn't have expected him to be so...gentle with Landon, particularly when he'd just woken up.

"Got it," Walter said, pulling out a tiny splinter after another long pause.

"Thanks," Landon took his foot off Walter's lap.

"What do you want?" Walter asked.

"I was just coming to check up on how things are between you and Coral. They must be great if she's still here *and* in your bed for that matter," Landon bit on his lip ring as he smirked.

"Landon this isn't a three way relationship," Walter said, glancing over in my direction. "Stop asking me about her. If you think you can take her from me - "

144

"Nah of course not," he held up his hands, cutting in. "You're my brother, jeez, kill me for showing interest. That wasn't the only reason I came anyway, I want my blade back."

"So you needed this at six in the morning, why?" Walter said in annoyance.

Landon smiled, "If you must know, I had a bad dream, woke up early, and that's my second favourite blade. I need it or I won't be able to get back to sleep. It's very sentimental."

"Okay," Walter took that answer and walked over to his bedside table.

"Hey guys," I heard another voice at the door.

"What do you want Gomez?" Walter turned to face him with an unhappy expression.

"Good morning to you too," I heard the sarcasm in his voice.

Gomez walked into the room, sidestepping all the sharp debris left on Walter's floor and stood by Landon.

"Hey man, I – " Gomez frowned when he saw me and I shut my eyes immediately. "Coral is still here?"

I knew Walter was glaring when he spoke, "Get to your point, what do you want? Why are you even awake?"

I risked opening my eyes again and saw Gomez shrugging.

"Can't I come say hi to my big brothers?" he asked. "I heard voices and Gio and Severn won't be awake for hours. Especially Severn."

Landon cracked a smile and then rubbed his shoulder, "I guess Severn has an excuse."

"Here, take your blade," Walter interrupted and handed a sheathed knife to Landon.

"It was good, huh?" Landon grinned at him as he took it back.

"It was okay," Walter mumbled. "But mine did a better job cutting blue eyes."

"Well this," Landon held his knife in his hand, "has cut blue eyes, mop head *and* skull face. *And* this is just my second favourite. Don't get me started on my number one blade. I even have a name for it, I call her – "

"Woah Landon," Gomez cut him off with wide eyes. "What's that on your back?"

145

Gomez turned him around to show his taunt back which was covered in raw, red scratches from the tops of his shoulders to the bottom of his spine. I gaped at it silently in Walter's bed, imagining what kind of *rough activities* led to such marks.

"What can I say?" Landon shrugged with a smirk. "I'm good at what I do."

"Is that a bite mark?" Gomez made a face of disbelief as he looked closely at the top of Landon's shoulder.

Landon twisted his neck round to try and get a look, "Probably. She loved it when I - "

"Shut up," Walter hit his arm. "Enough about that."

"No," Gomez argued. "I want to know what you did. How you get them to like it so much?"

"Gomez," Walter stared at him. "You're fifteen. Don't be stupid."

"Landon did it first when he was around my age," Gomez smirked. "He's just fine."

"He's *addicted*," Walter said with a frown. "That's not fine."

"Yeah but – " Gomez tried.

Landon cut in, "I'm not addicted, I – "

"Shut up, all of you," Walter hissed. "Coral is sleeping. Just get out."

"Fine," Landon said, making his way safely back to the door. "Come on Gomez, I'll tell you all you wanna know."

Landon looked back at Walter with a cheeky smile and Walter scowled at him, shaking his head. Gomez only grinned. I shut my eyes again when Walter started coming my way and he sat on the edge of his bed. I gave up fake sleeping and pretended to wake up, scrunching my eyes and stretching my limbs.

"Morning," I smiled at Walter.

"Hey, good morning," he looked over his shoulder at me fondly. "Did they wake you up? God, they're so frustrating."

"No it's okay," I said, sitting up and pushing my messy hair out of my face.

Walter gazed at me a little too closely, making me blush out of nervousness. I'd just woken up, what could be attractive about that?

"Don't make fun out of my writing," Walter blurted all of a sudden. "Or even my spelling for that matter. I'm not a poet, but I'm willing to write hundreds of things just to describe how much you mean to me."

"Don't make me blush," I said, looking down and fanning my face as it burned.

Walter moved onto his bed and closer to me, "This is only the beginning too. Our feelings can get so much...so much....never mind. I don't know what I'm saying."

"No," I said softly, looking up and touching his face. "Go on."

Walter's cheeks were a little pink, he was so cute when he was embarrassed.

"I just wanted to say that in time, our feelings can get so much deeper," he dropped his gaze. "I can't imagine how that would feel. I mean, I like you so much already and it's only the star – "

I cut Walter off when I leaned forwards and kissed him on the lips. He widened his eyes in surprise before smiling briefly and moving his lips against mine.

"Let's just get back in," I said quietly, my forehead against his. "We don't have to get up for a while, huh?"

Walter didn't hesitate and he smashed his lips against mine so that our noses brushed. We laughed a little bit, falling back into the bed and kissed like we had nothing else to live for.

***

When I arrived at school, I said goodbye to Walter and went to my first lesson of the day which was Textiles with Hayley. She didn't even let me sit down when I got to class. I had texted her beforehand saying that she shouldn't pick me up because I was with Walter and she wanted me to explain the sudden dramatic change of events.

"Let me sit down first," I said, trying not to grin.

"Okay," she pulled out a chair for me. "Sit down."

"Thanks," I took the seat and then looked across the table at her. "Okay so we're together."

"Yeah I figured," Hayley grinned at me with excited eyes. "I want to know how! What happened to all the 'I need to keep my distance' stuff?"

147

"Well it got too much I guess," I said, pulling at my sleeves. "And well I went to his house so that we could talk, then we decided to scrap all that I said before and just do what we were prolonging all this time. Get together."

"Well that sounds adorable," she leaned on her arm, watching me. "And then you two had a really heated makeout session."

"Ugh," I cringed, hiding my face. "Don't say it like that Hayley, it just sounds less appealing."

"Well I'm happy for you, either way," Hayley hit my arm playfully.

"Thanks I guess," I looked down shyly. "It's Friday so I'm tutoring him after school."

"Not that you wouldn't have gone back there anyway," Hayley winked at me.

"Okay let's just do our work," I said, getting up out of my seat, trying not to show her how much I was blushing.

Hayley grinned at me and squeezed my arm as we went to get our materials. All throughout the class I was thinking about Walter and what he was doing in his Philosophy class. Sleeping probably, I smiled to myself. He'd told me that all the 'stupid' rhetorical questions made him tired.

"Perfect," Hayley said, looking at my finished handbag. "As usual."

"Thanks," I smiled. "Your polka dot dress turned out really nice too. Shame its November."

She laughed, "I'll wear it with tights if I have to. Don't tell me you're going to let the teacher keep your bag again. You let her keep everything you make."

"Well, I've already got a bag," I replied with a shrug.

Hayley gave me a knowing look, "Seriously, take it. It's yours and it's beautiful, just like you are."

I didn't know how to react. She'd scold me for saying thank you again.

"You don't have to say anything," she gave me a side hug. "I'm just being honest."

"I'll keep it," I said, nodding to myself. "This one I'm keeping."

"Great!" Hayley cried. "Make a dress next, one you'll look amazing in."

I rolled my eyes, "I'll think about that."

"Walter would like it," she sent me a coy look.

"I'll think about it," I repeated, genuinely considering whether to make something that I'd actually keep and wear myself.

Maybe I *would* do it for Walter.

"You look convinced," Hayley was looking at me closely. "Good."

"Shush Hayley," I waved my hand at her playfully and we laughed.

***

Back at Walter's house it was hard to believe that a whole day had passed. Walter had tidied his room up and gotten rid of all the sharp pieces of wood whilst I was down in the kitchen with the triplets. We were currently sat at his desk studying some maths, well it was easier said than done as Walter and I kept getting distracted by each other.

"Stop jiggling your knee," Walter placed his hand on my thigh under the table.

"I can't help it," I smiled down at the page of the textbook.

"Are you nervous?" he said lowly in my ear.

"No, it's just a habit," I said, unable to look him in the eye. "What do you think about question seven?"

"I don't know the answer," Walter ran a hand through my hair, brushing it away from the side of my face and over my shoulder. He brought his lips up to my ear and kissed my earlobe as he gripped my thigh with his hand.

"Walter," I said quietly, not sure whether to try and stop him or not.

"Forget the maths," he murmured. "I'm distracted."

I gave up trying to fight and succumbed into his warm coaxing, touching the side of his face and trying not to smile so hard.

"I'm distracted too," I had time to say before Walter bit on my bottom lip.

"That tickles," I pulled away, giggling like a kid.

Walter smiled and started chuckling too, "It does?"

149

He did it again and I laughed, pushing him away.

"Walter stop," I couldn't stop laughing, for now he was biting on my earlobe and actually tickling my stomach.

"Nah I'm good," he murmured into my neck, tickling me relentlessly.

Walter's door was opened and we both turned our faces to look at it while I pushed his hands away from me.

It was Phoenix. The last person I was expecting to see.

He was watching us with a face like he had disgust itself stuck in his throat and when he swallowed, it was like he was trying to swallow a mountain of hatred. Gomez, Giovanni and Severn were all behind him, looking over Phoenix's shoulders at me with interest. I too wanted to know what was going on and that feeling only intensified when I realised with a strike of fear that they were all looking at me, not Walter.

Phoenix spoke then, in a low and frankly terrifying voice.

"I came to make a proposal."

19

"You wanna marry her?" came Giovanni's voice.

"Couldn't even smile when you popped the big question could you?" Gomez muttered, shaking his head.

"He didn't even take her on a single date first," Severn looked at his two brothers with fake disappointment.

"Hell, he didn't even get down on his knee!" Giovanni cried in realisation.

"Shut the hell up you three," Phoenix turned and gave them a scowl.

The three of them looked at him for a second and then broke into laughter, unable to keep up the pretence any longer. I wished that I could laugh too but I was so scared, it was impossible to join in. They quietened down after a second glare from Phoenix and I waited silently to hear what he had to say. His eyes locked with mine and I found that I couldn't dare look away.

"I want you to spy for me," Phoenix said, completely serious.

I was speechless and Walter seemed to be too because neither of us said a word.

"The Santiagos don't know you're involved with us and they have no reason not to trust you," Phoenix said, walking further into Walter's room. "The bonus is that Ario and you are somewhat acquaintances, so I've heard, therefore getting through to them would be easy."

"No," Walter snapped, finally finding his voice. "I don't want her anywhere *near* them, *especially* not blue eyes, and don't even get me started on her being in the same *building* as Diego."

"Yeah," the triplets murmured amongst themselves. "Mop head *is* a bit of a perve. Not gonna lie."

"*You*, Phoenix, can go shove your proposal up your – "

"Walter," I said, putting my hand over his. "Relax, please."

"Think about it," Phoenix said to me.

"Do you even know her name?" Walter growled at him, standing up and pushing his chair back.

Phoenix didn't answer, he only cast me a look and left the room, pushing the triplets out of the way as he did so.

Walter muttered insults under his breath and I held his hand, trying to calm him down. Maybe that was my only chance to try and prove myself to Phoenix, perhaps he would have started to like me more...but I couldn't go behind Walter's back nor did I even *want* to get close to the Santiagos anyway.

Ario included.

I could do without ruining my relationship with Walter.

"Coral, listen to me," Walter said after taking a deep breath. "I don't want you involved with the gang in any way. The less you know, the better. You understand where I'm coming from?"

"Of course I do," I said, looking down at my lap.

"It's not safe and we both want the best for you," Walter went on. "I'm not the kind of gang member who manipulates and makes their girl commit crimes for them, and I will never be that kind of guy. The last thing either of us wants is for you to get arrested for any kind of gang affiliation. I wouldn't be able to forgive myself."

"I know Walter," I said, catching his hazel eyes. "I understand."

"Don't let Phoenix scare you into it," Walter's eyes bored into mine. "No matter what."

"I won't," I said, but inside I tried to imagine what it would be like if Phoenix Simpson actually smiled at me for once. And I guessed to achieve that, it required doing what he wanted and truly impressing him.

***

Severn yawned, scratching the back of his head, "Man I'm tired."

"You're always tired," Gio muttered at him as he snacked on a packet of cookies.

"He's lazy too," Gomez smirked as he looked at a silver ladies watch. "When was the last time you worked out again, Severn?"

"Shut up," Severn gave them a look.

We were sitting in the kitchen, me, Walter and the triplets, and it was only about six in the evening. Phoenix wasn't around, and I hadn't seen Landon or Eli either. Severn was sitting on a chair at the dining table, resting his chin on his folded arms, and Gomez was sitting opposite me and Walter. We had eaten another takeaway and I had told the boys that one day we'd have to cook something proper, rather than eat out. It was so strange how they were in such good shape when they basically ate fast food every night.

"Yo Walter," Gomez said, showing him his latest 'catch'. "How much do you think I'll get for this?"

Walter took it and looked at it closely, "I don't think it's a fake, probably a couple hundred."

A grin split across Gomez's face, "Good."

"Don't take my word for it," Walter scoffed. "I'm not an expert."

"Well I would have sold it online as the real thing anyway," Gomez said. "I don't care."

"So that's what you do with all the stuff you...obtain?" I raised my brows at Gomez. "Sell it online?"

"Yep," he nodded. "I make quite a lot from it, sometimes I get away with selling stuff as brand new.

"And sometimes they really *are* brand new," Severn added, lifting his head from the table with a sleepy look.

"Go to sleep if you're so tired," I smiled, touching his hand lightly.

"I *am* sleeping," Severn said, smiling back at me.

"What, right here?" I arched a brow. "Isn't it noisy?"

153

"Severn can sleep anywhere," Giovanni said, spraying out cookie crumbs, which landed on the table, as he did so.

"Thanks, Gio," Walter sent him a dry look.

Gio in turn gave Walter a cheesy grin and where Walter glared at him, I returned his smile slyly.

Eli came down and went straight to the fridge, ignoring every single one of us.

"S'up dawg?" Giovanni winked at him.

Eli cast him an unimpressed green-eyed look and after rummaging through the almost empty fridge, he slammed it shut and turned around to face us.

"Is there anything to eat?" he demanded.

"Not if you ask like that," Walter replied in a low voice.

"I'm not in the mood for your shit," Eli scowled at his older brother.

"*My* shit?" Walter narrowed his eyes. "You're the one who's been acting like a complete prick for some unknown reason."

Eli surprised me by not even responding, he just stared at Walter then after a couple more moments he walked out. Walter sat back in his chair, growling under his breath and Severn snored a little as he slept on the table.

"Is there any food for Eli?" I asked the boys. "I hope you didn't give his share to me."

"No," Gio said. "Eli's is in the microwave."

"Why didn't you tell him that?" I asked, appalled.

"He was being rude," Gio shrugged.

When none of the brothers made an attempt to do anything, I got up and went to the microwave. Taking out Eli's still warm takeaway meal, I left the kitchen and went up to find him. Only problem was, I realised once I was upstairs, I didn't know which room was Eli's.

Knocking on the first door I came across, which wasn't Walter's or the triplets', I waited nervously for a response, desperately hoping that I hadn't picked Phoenix's.

"What?" I heard Eli grunt, making me sigh a breath of relief.

"It's me, Coral," I replied. "Can I come in?"

There was a long pause, and when I thought he was just going to ignore me, he grumbled a yes. I opened the door slowly, poking my head round. Eli's room was surprisingly tidy. After seeing the state of Walter's room and the triplets' room, I wasn't expecting a spotless carpet and a tidy desk.

"Hey," I said softly. "I got your dinner."

Eli was sitting on his bed, near the window, "Mine?"

"Yeah," I nodded. "It was in the microwave."

Eli shook his head to himself, probably muttering about his brothers and I smiled softly, treading quietly into his room.

"Here," I handed it over to him, not sure whether to take a seat or not.

"Thanks," Eli said, looking at me through his long lashes.

"No problem," I shrugged. "You doing okay?"

He sighed, putting his meal down on the bed beside him, "No."

I honestly wasn't expecting him to be so open and it took me aback a little bit.

"Do you um...do you want to talk about it?" I sat down next to him, knotting my fingers together in my lap.

"Stop acting uncomfortable," Eli nudged my hand with the back of his. "You don't have to stay you know."

"No," I said, placing my hands flat on my knees. "I'm fine. Tell me what's wrong with you."

Eli sighed, looking down at his lap to that his dark blond hair hung over his emerald green eyes.

"They...well every one of them have someone thing that I want."

"Your brothers?" I asked. "What do you mean?"

155

"Phoenix, he has the authority. He calls all the shots, does what he wants whenever he wants to. It's just...it's not always fair. Sometimes *I* want to make the choices for us...or do whatever *I* like."

"I personally think he's too big headed," I attempted a joke. "But don't tell him I said that."

Eli smiled slightly at his lap and I wanted to grin so wide at the sight of his adorable dimples.

"But in truth, he *is* the oldest, so it makes the most sense for him to take that leading role," I said honestly. "I don't know how he calls the shots, but maybe talk to him about considering your opinions sometimes."

"As if," Eli rolled his eyes. "You don't know him like I do. He thinks he's always right. The only person he would ever really ask advice from, is Landon."

"Okay," I said. "Well what does Landon have that you want?"

The seventeen year old started clenching and unclenching his fist, "Landon gets so much attention from girls. It doesn't really bother me much, but that being said...I wouldn't mind having some attention myself at times."

"Listen Eli, I know without a doubt that girls find you hot," I said, unable to look him in the eye in fear of blushing. I was never really this forward with people, but I was trying to get a point across to him.

"The problem is," I spoke. "You kind of push them away. With your attitude I mean. Girls...and guys I guess, are scared of you."

"Scared of me?" he looked at me with a smirk.

"Don't act as if you don't know Eli. They are very aware that you're part of a gang and the rumours don't help either," I grinned. "Smile more often, it will put them at ease and you'll get talking and stuff."

"Sure," he shrugged, sounding unconvinced.

"Hayley would talk to you," I suggested with a smile. "She's really friendly, she talks to just about anyone."

"Okay," Eli nodded.

"You do remember Hayley, don't you?" I had to make sure.

"Yeah of course," Eli said to me. "Dark hair and red lipstick."

"Yeah," I raised my eyebrows at how much he remembered from just one encounter. "That's her."

"I'll think about it," Eli chewing his lip.

"So um, what about Walter and the triplets?" I questioned.

"Walter isn't included," Eli said with a scowl. "I don't want anything that he has."

"Okay," I said quickly, trying not to fire his temper up too much.

Eli and Walter had a pretty rocky relationship and I guess I would never know why that was.

Eli continued with a bitter expression, "The triplets have fun and they have each other. That kind of relationship is priceless."

"You mean triplets and twins?" I asked him.

"Yeah," he answered. "It's just different to how it is with normal siblings. I wish I had that."

Eli looked really upset for a second and I didn't know what to say about that one. You couldn't choose to be a twin or a triplet, nor could you conjure one out of thin air. I didn't know what the relationship between normal siblings was like in the first place, as I was an only child, let alone understand what Eli was saying about twins and triplets. I asked myself how he knew himself anyway, but knowing Eli's volatile mood and the expression on his face, I decided not to mention it.

"All I can say is make do with what you've got," I shook his knee playfully, sending him a smile. "And you've got six brothers. That's a lot more than most people have, including me. I'm an only child."

"Then you won't know what being the middle child feels like," Eli half-smiled back at me.

"Being loved from both directions?" I grinned at him.

Eli shook his head, but he kept the smile and I touched one of his dimples which I thought were so cute.

"Eat your food," I said to him. "It's gone cold I bet."

"As if it wasn't cold when you gave it to me," Eli shot me an incredulous look that had me burst out laughing.

"That wasn't meant to be funny," he said, laughing himself.

I only laughed more, feeling the most relaxed I'd ever been when it came to being with Eli Simpson.

It was rewarding.

20

I lay in Walter's bed, wrapped up in his arms and listening to his heart beat as he slept. I knew it was early but I felt wide awake. I stroked the neckline of Walter's t-shirt with my fingertips and glanced at his lips as he breathed slowly. Walter woke suddenly with a jerk, making me jump too.

"Are you okay?" I murmured to him in concern.

Walter swallowed, a little short of breath, "Yeah I...I was dreaming."

"Oh," I sighed in concern, rubbing his chest through his shirt. "A nightmare?"

"Yes, it was my....my Dad," Walter ran a hand down his face and sighed deeply. "I just hope I become nothing like him. That guy was a....he was a...."

I cupped his face and made him look at me.

"Walter," I said. "I never knew your father, but I'm telling you, you're not going to be anything like him."

Walter nodded, gazing into my eyes before he pulled me into a very tight hug. Walter didn't say anything and I didn't either, I just held him like he held me and it seemed to be enough.

Hours later, we woke up again and I got out first whilst Walter lay propped up in his bed watching me. I felt comfortable in the top and shorts I had been sleeping in and didn't mind Walter's gaze that followed my bare legs as I went to open the curtains. It was late November now and even though it was chilly at night, Walter's body had kept me warm.

"Do you have to do that?" Walter moaned before I'd even opened them.

"What's the problem? Are you a vampire?" I turned around and smiled at him.

"No, but – "

I threw the curtains wide and was almost blinded myself by the blanket of white I saw. Having to blink hard a few times first, I looked again and sure enough it was snow covering the whole of Walter's huge back yard.

"Walter! Walter it snowed," I span around grinning at him whilst he had his head buried in his pillow, still groaning.

"It snowed?" he lifted his head and frowned at me.

"Uh huh," I nodded excitedly, almost like a child would.

Walter groaned again, "I hate snow."

"Oh," I bit on my lip. "So you don't want to go out in it with me?"

Walter took one look at me and then sighed before he got out of bed and going to the window to see for himself. As soon as I saw his face start to form a grimace I grabbed his arm and pushed my bottom lip out.

"Please Walter? For me?" I batted my eyelids.

Walter slowly blinked at me whilst a smile crept onto his face, "Fine. Twenty minutes."

"An hour."

"What?" he exclaimed. "Coral, are you serious?"

"Very," I smirked at him.

"Thirty minutes," Walter said.

"Forty five."

The longer he looked at me the more I saw in his eyes that he was fighting a losing battle.

"Okay," he finally agreed. "The things you do to me."

He took hold of me by the waist and before he could kiss me, the two of us jumped when we heard what sounded like a shout of joy from one of the next rooms.

"The triplets," Walter rolled his eyes, letting go of me. "If we're going to go out in the snow we have to go now before they all come and ruin it with a snowball fight or something."

A snowball fight sounded like fun to me but I didn't want to put Walter off completely, so I nodded in agreement. We went and brushed our teeth and got dressed into warm clothes. Well I only had what I had worn the day before so Walter gave me some of his to wear.

"I don't think I'll be able to run in this," I laughed, looking down at the oversized jogging bottoms and jumper sleeves.

"Who said anything about running?" Walter cocked his head to the side. "We were just going to walk, right?"

"Uh yeah," I said quickly. "No snowball fight or anything like that."

"Coral," Walter narrowed his eyes playfully at me. "What are you planning?"

Instead of replying, I started rolling up the sleeves and then bent over to do the trouser legs too. As soon as I was done, I took off running as fast as I could manage without unravelling it all. Walter was laughing in what sounded like disbelief as he chased me down the stairs and I raced for the back door.

I didn't see Phoenix until it was too late and I crashed right into him. The force I hit him with actually made Phoenix stumble back a little bit and he looked down at me with what I could describe as loathing.

"Oh my," I stared at him with wide eyes, taking a couple steps back. "I'm so sorry."

Walter caught up with me and took hold of my hand, pulling me back slightly and positioning himself in front of Phoenix instead.

"Excuse us," Walter muttered.

Phoenix wouldn't say anything and it made me want to know what he was thinking. All Phoenix did was give me the same look that had me feeling like I owed him, like I should take up on his proposal to spy on the Santiagos. Walter moved past Phoenix, who didn't move a budge. He made sure not to touch Phoenix which would have probably started an 'argument', and I did the same.

"That prick," Walter balled his fists once we'd let ourselves outside.

"You did well," I said to him encouragingly. "Not starting a fight or anything."

"It's a new day," Walter shrugged. "I can do without getting angry first thing in the morning."

That's when the triplets burst out of the back door behind us, already laughing, yelling and pushing each other over in the snow. Walter clenched his jaw and exhaled deeply through his nose and I tried not to grin.

"Snowball fight?" Giovanni came up to me and Walter.

"Umm, sure," I tried to make it sound like I had to think about it and gripped the sleeve of Walter's jumper before he could turn around and head back inside.

Knowing that he had been caught out, Walter smiled down at me and made a defeated expression before glaring at Giovanni and his triplets.

"We gotta sort out teams," Gomez was saying as he packed a snowball in his hands, aiming it for the back of Severn's head.

All three of them were wearing identical snow hats, which I thought was adorable.

"Where's Landon?" Gio asked.

"Well it's Saturday morning, so probably asleep," Severn said before getting hit on the back of the head by Gomez's snowball.

"There's only five of us," Gomez came to join us. "And Phoenix isn't going to play, he thinks he's too good for us."

"What about Eli?" I asked.

"Oh yeah, where's he?" Severn questioned, rubbing snow out of his hair.

"Don't care," Walter stretched his arms out. "Let's just play this thing and get it over with."

"We need even numbers," Gomez made a point.

"What about Hayley?" the thought popped into my mind. "It's a Saturday, she might be free."

The boys paused for a second and then the triplets started nodding and telling me to go and invite her to come over *'now, right now!'* I went back inside the house laughing as I went to retrieve my phone and sent her a text asking if she was free and wanted to come round to the Simpson's house. Hayley replied within a couple minutes saying how she'd love to come over and how nervous she was about it. I told her it was fine, Phoenix hopefully wasn't going to be around. She said she'd be there in half an hour and after asking Eli, who was in his room, I sent her the address.

"Are you coming to play too?" I asked Eli after I put my phone in my pocket.

Eli sat on the edge of his bed, rubbing his hair sleepily, "Later."

"Make sure you come," I sent him a smile. "It would be a great chance to talk to Hayley."

Eli smiled tiredly, "I hear you."

I turned to go, "See you down there."

"Yeah Coral."

When I got back outside, I was surprised to see that Landon was also out in the snow. The boys seemed to be waiting for me, and when I arrived to join them, Landon told everyone to gather round.

"Nice outfit by the way," Landon pointed at me with a smirk.

"Thanks," I felt my face warm slightly.

"So teams," Landon said, glancing around at us with excitement in his eyes, as if he *didn't* just wake up a couple of minutes ago.

"Walter and Coral together," he motioned to the two of us. "One of the triplets with them."

"Coral how good are you at throwing snowballs?" Gomez asked me. "With precision and force?"

I stood there, taken aback, "Average?"

To be honest, it was barely even that. I had poor aim and a short throwing distance, but it didn't stop me trying and having fun in the process.

"Yeah, I'm on Landon's team," Gomez concluded. "Sorry Coral."

"Sorry to yourself man," Walter said darkly. "You've got my *precision* and *force* to play against."

"Bring it on," Gomez smirked, folding his arms and Gio hooked his arm around his shoulders.

"I'm with Gomez and Landon too," Gio lifted his chin at us.

"I was going to go on your team anyway," Severn smiled at me. "But do bear in mind that I'm not much of a runner."

I laughed, "It's all just some fun anyway, it doesn't matter who wins."

Landon started laughing, "Of *course* it matters who wins."

"Oh...uh okay," I glanced up at Walter who was smirking threateningly at Gomez and Gio.

"Rules," Landon spoke.

Giovanni cleared his throat, "Rules are, there are no - "

"Rules are," Walter cut him off, putting his hands down on my shoulders. "No one throws any at Coral's head, or I'll end them."

"Okay," Gio nodded, swallowing. "That's a cool rule."

"Rules are," Landon started again. "The team to get the most bruises on the opposite team wins."

"Wait, what?" I blinked at him in alarm.

Maybe I shouldn't have been in such a hurry to play this game with the Simpson brothers. They clearly took everything to the next levels. How did I not see this coming?

"Okay, girls, not included," Landon quickly added after a look from Walter.

"That means when Hayley get's here, she has to be on my team," Gomez wiggled his eyebrows suggestively. "Makes it even."

"And you guys can have Eli when he comes," Gio grinned. "You're going to lose by the way."

"Keep saying that," Walter said to him, pointing at him. "Feel free."

By the time Hayley arrived, Eli had also come down and had actually been the one who let her into the house. They came out into the massive back yard together, smiling about something and I grinned, happy to see Eli trying.

"Hey," I waved at Hayley and she came and gave me a hug.

"I can't believe I'm really here," she whispered in my ear as she squeezed me.

I laughed and let go of her and Walter smiled and greeted Hayley too. The triplets sent her grins and Gomez beckoned her over to his side. After sending me a nervous smile, she went and joined the other team.

"Hayley," Landon said, holding his hand out to her. "I'm Landon, nice to meet you."

"Landon," Hayley's eyes rounded as she looked up at him and put her hand in his. "Nice to meet you too."

"I hope you are good at throwing," Landon shook her hand and grinned. "We have to win."

"I'll try my best," Hayley laughed.

"So can we start now?" Giovanni asked.

In answer, Eli chucked a ball of snow I didn't realise he was holding, right into his face and the game started. Walter, who didn't even want to play, was throwing balls snow that he'd moulded into ice at Gomez and Gio and I was just trying to avoid getting hit. Severn was lying in the snow after being knocked over, making no attempt to get up at all and Hayley and Landon seemed like they were having fun. Every time I looked over at them, they were either using each other as shields or down in the snow laughing.

To my disbelief, Phoenix came out the back door during the game and actually joined in.

"Who's team are you on?" Eli asked him after throwing a massive ball at Landon.

"Doesn't matter," Phoenix replied, aiming for Walter.

"Walter's on our team," Eli said, deciding for Phoenix. "Landon, Gomez, Gio and Hayley are on the other team."

"Who's Hayley?" Phoenix frowned, looking at her who continued to play obliviously.

"Coral's friend," Eli answered, making my stomach tighten.

"So she thinks she can invite her friends round to *my* house now?" I heard Phoenix say and I quickly avoided his gaze and busied myself in running away from him and making it look like I was dodging snowballs.

"You okay?" Walter came over to me, packing snow in his hands.

"I'm cold," I smiled sheepishly. "I think I'll head inside for a bit."

"I'll come with you," Walter replied. "I'm done with this anyway. It's been about forty five minutes, right?"

"Probably," I said, glancing around as the others played. "Did you get hit?"

"A couple times," Walter shrugged. "You?"

"Lots of times," I grinned.

Walter frowned, "Hard? Who did it?"

"No," I assured him quickly and then jumped out of the way before I got hit again by another snowball. "It didn't hurt much."

"Are you sure?" Walter creased his eyebrows.

"Yeah, I'm sure," I replied. "If we're going in, let's go before Landon or someone throws ice at us."

On our way back inside I saw that Severn was still lying in the snow like he had been about half an hour ago.

"Do you think he's okay?" I frowned in worry. "He's gonna get sick if he stays there for too long."

"He's fine," Walter said.

"No, I have to check," I went over to Severn and Walter grudgingly followed.

The boy was fast asleep by the looks of it.

"How?" I gaped. "It's freezing. He's gone a bit blue."

"No he hasn't," Walter wasn't even looking, he was throwing balls back at Gomez.

I bent down and woke up Severn, shaking his shoulders. He'd been in the snow for way too long and he was extremely pale.

166

"You have to get inside, now," I said once he'd opened his eyes.

"What?" he shivered.

"Severn, get up," I said to him. "Come on."

I helped pull him up into a sitting position and called Walter to aid with lifting him up onto his feet. Walter hooked his arms around Severn's chest and got him standing up and he walked Severn, who was shaking violently, back to the house.

"I'm cold," Severn shuddered, wrapping his arms around himself.

When I expected Walter to make a snide comment about how it was his own fault for falling asleep in the snow, Walter only said he was going to get some blankets. I sat down in one of the sofas with Severn who really had turned a pale blue and put his hands under my armpits, which would warm him up faster.

"Thanks," Severn breathed through chattering teeth.

"It's okay," I replied with a smile, although I was thinking in my head how he should have been more careful.

Walter came back down with a two blankets and a change of clothes. He pulled Severn's hands out from between my underarms and told Severn to take off his wet clothes. Severn stood and slowly started pulling off his sodden jumper with trembling hands and Walter decided to speed things up by taking Severn's jumper off for him, followed by his soaking jogging bottoms, socks and....well I looked away for the last item of clothing. After Severn had gotten into some warm clothes, Walter wrapped him up in the blankets and pushed him down into the sofa. I got up so Severn could stretch his legs out and he closed his eyes, asleep *again* in seconds.

"He has narcolepsy," Walter explained, looking down at his brother. "It's a sleeping disorder."

"I haven't heard of that before," I raised my eyebrows. "Is it common?"

"No, not really," Walter replied. "He has irregular sleeping patterns, which means he doesn't always get enough sleep at night so he's tired throughout the day and just falls asleep randomly. Or he can also fall asleep if he feels strong emotions like anger or joy...it's weird like that."

"That's definitely something new," I looked down at sleeping Severn. "He's so cute."

"Huh?" Walter stepped towards me, almost bumping his chest in my face. "What was that?"

"He's cute," I repeated, smiling cheekily up at him.

"You're cute," Walter said, tipping my face up more with his finger under my chin so that he could kiss me.

We only kissed for a few moments before the back door opened and everyone piled in. I stepped back from Walter and stuck my still freezing hands under his armpits, instructing him to do the same with me.

Gomez and Gio walked on by, dropping chunks of snow (from God knows where) onto the floor as they passed. Landon was blowing into his hands to get them warmed up again when he saw me and Walter.

"We're counting the scores later," Landon said to us as he walked past. "Give a bit of time for the bruises to *really* come out."

Hayley I noticed was talking to Eli, the two of them trembling from the cold, and Phoenix was last to come in, glaring at Hayley which made me shift my gaze because I knew that I was next to be glared at.

After a couple of hours, everyone was warm again and ready to count scores for each team. Severn (who was feeling a lot better) was awake once more and he sat next to me drinking hot chocolate in one of the sofas, with Walter on my other side and Eli on the carpet.

Landon stood up, "My team first. Someone needs to count and someone else needs to add up the score."

"I'll add up the score," I volunteered.

"And a counter?" Landon asked. "I can't do it myself."

"I'll do it," Hayley said shyly.

"Good," Landon winked at her.

He then proceeded to take off his shirt and Walter put his hand over my eyes, making me giggle.

"Don't get any funny ideas," Walter said in my ear jokingly once he'd removed his hand.

"I will when I see you," I grinned, blushing at the same time.

Walter raised his eyebrows when he too remembered that I hadn't ever seen him topless and then he smiled.

"That's the only exception."

Looking back at Landon, who had finished stripping, I was surprised to see his body actually marked blue in multiple places. Exactly just how hard had the boys been throwing those things?

"I count one," Hayley pointed to Landon's chest., and then to his toned stomach. "Two, three....is that a bullet wound?"

"Yeah," Landon rubbed the spot on his side briefly. "Doesn't count."

No one seemed shocked, but I was, and I could tell Hayley was too. Even though I heard the Simpsons and Santiagos shooting at night, I never really thought that anyone actually got shot...and well even when I'd seen a bullet wound on Ario, it didn't really appeal to me how real and how dangerous what they did was. Perhaps it was sinking in now, because I had gotten to know and like Landon a lot more and he seemed like such a nice, funny guy...nothing like a thug.

"Turn around," Severn said and Landon did, showing more bruises scattered across his broad back.

"Four...five....six," Hayley raised her eyebrows.

"And drop them pants," Gomez said.

"*You're on my team,*" Landon gave him a look. "The lowest score wins, remember? Do you want us to lose?"

"Oops," Gomez bit his lip with a grin.

"Drop the pants," Severn called when Landon didn't do so.

"Fine," Landon said, pulling his trousers down.

I didn't know where to look and Hayley didn't either. Standing right next to Landon, who was just in his boxers, she looked like she wanted to sit down and let someone else take the role of counting.

"One on the back of his thigh," Walter spotted.

"Okay, so that's seven," Hayley concluded, blushing like mad.

Landon noticed it too and he grinned at her, holding the eye contact as he pulled his trousers slowly back up.

"This isn't the strip club," Eli called. "Sit down."

Landon slapped his butt in Eli's face and laughed before jumping back into the sofa.

"Gomez," Landon said. "You're up."

Gomez got up to his feet in excitement and then took off his jumper. Neither Hayley nor I could disguise our disbelief when we saw that Gomez had a body as built as Landon's. He was only fifteen.

"Okay," Hayley didn't know where to look. "Two on his chest and...turn around?"

Gomez turned and I saw that he also had dimples in his back.

"Don't say it," Walter said, reading my mind. "It's not cute."

I grinned and said nothing, and Hayley counted three more bruises on Gomez's back before Gomez took off his trousers and basically waved his bum in Hayley's face.

"Are you trying to tell us that you got hit from behind?" Gio smirked. "My Gomez, I didn't know you swung that way."

"Shut up," Gomez rolled his eyes, wiggling his brows at Hayley instead.

Hayley laughed and counted two more on Gomez's legs which made the total seven, like Landon. Gio had six bruises.

"So what's the total for my team?" Landon asked me.

"Twenty," I replied.

"Okay. You're up Eli," Landon pointed at him.

Eli sighed and got up. He pulled off his shirt and I noticed how curious Hayley looked, and how I most likely had the same expression on my face too. Eli's body was slim but muscled all the same, and he also had a few scars here and there.

"One," Hayley touched Eli's bruised ribs lightly.

"Two...three..four," she brushed her fingertips over his chest. "Turn around?"

Eli turned around without a word and Hayley touched his back, counting two more bruises.

"Drop your pants?" Landon said.

"No," Eli spoke. "Don't have any bruises there."

No one challenged him, probably because no one was in the mood to argue and up next it was Walter's turn.

I found my stomach fluttering in anticipation as Walter stood up to take off his shirt. When he pulled it off I simply stared, drinking up every part of his sculpted physique. Walter *did* have a tattoo, and it was of a thorny heart which was on his left hip with the letters E.S in it. I was inquisitive as to who E.S was, Eli? An ex? Walter also had a couple scars scattered over his body which I tried to memorise so that I could ask him about later.

170

Hayley counted only four bruises for Walter, who also decided not to take his trousers off and then it was Phoenix's turn. When it came to Phoenix I found myself holding my breath. I didn't think Phoenix would actually comply, but he started to take off his top and I looked away out of fear before shifting my eyes back again.

The first things I noticed were the gold chain around Phoenix's neck and the scar that ran down his side. Phoenix's body radiated power. He had no doubt gotten the mean looking scar whilst spending time behind bars. Phoenix also had more bullet wounds than I could count. At first they were hard to notice, but once I noticed one, they all became apparent and I held back a gasp. Phoenix barely any bruises and Hayley was done counting in no time. Phoenix didn't take off his trousers, and nobody really asked him to, he put his shirt back on and sat down.

"That was just two," Hayley said to me, so I could add it to the total.

"Severn," Landon called next.

Severn shook his head, "Nope."

"What do you mean 'nope'?" Gomez frowned at him.

"I'm not taking my clothes off," Severn shrugged.

"Then we'll have to do it another way," Landon rubbed his hands together. "Stand up."

Severn put his hot chocolate down and stood up with a frown.

"Every time you wince, that counts as a bruise," Landon said, grabbing Severn's shoulders.

Landon did next what I could only describe as a *very thorough* body search, making sure to press hard so that Severn would definitely wince each time Landon found a bruise under his clothes. Landon went behind his younger brother and squeezed his butt cheeks making Severn shout and me and Hayley burst into laughter.

"Was that another bruise?" Landon smirked.

"Just get this done and over with," Severn gave him a dead eyed look.

"Well I make that six," Landon concluded after feeling down Severn's legs. "So what's their total Coral?"

"Sixteen," I said. "So that means we win."

171

"Damn," Landon hit the arm of his chair.

"We had more people than you and we still won," Severn laughed at his brothers.

"The girls didn't do it though. Can't we like...strip search Coral and Hayley too?" Giovanni suggested. "It would make it fair."

"Are you crazy?" Walter asked him in a low voice.

"I might be a little bit," Gio made a thinking face.

"I agree with Gio," Gomez said. "I guess that makes me slightly bonkers."

"Same here," Severn smiled. "Sorry Coral and Hayley, but like Gio said, it would only make it fair."

"We're on the same team," I said incredulously to him. "And we *won*."

"Start running," Walter said.

"Wait, what?" Giovanni faltered.

"When the man says start running," Landon said with a carefree smile. "It means: start running."

As soon as he finished speaking, Walter jumped out of the sofa, slapping Severn on the side of the head first then going for Gio and Gomez who upped it and ran. I was laughing so much at the way the triplets were screaming that I couldn't even see straight from all the tears in my vision.

***

That night after Hayley had gone home, the older Simpson boys told me that they were going out on patrol. Landon and Walter explained to me that patrol meant going through their turf, sniffing out any Santiagos who might be trespassing. At first I didn't really have a problem with it, but when I saw the guns I started to worry.

"Walter, do you really need that?" I pulled him aside and asked him quietly.

I knew Phoenix was looking at me as he stood by the door waiting for Walter with Landon, but I ignored him. Out of the corner of my eye I saw Phoenix step outside, probably so he wouldn't see any possible signs of affection.

"We don't stab or shoot to kill," Walter said to me. "The guns are used as warnings when they are trespassing, or vice versa."

"I've seen bullet wounds on nearly all of you," I said. "And judging from the sounds I hear at night sometimes, they aren't just warnings."

"I know you're worried," Walter caressed my cheek. "But it's unlikely that any of us will meet death anytime soon. There are only seven of us and six of them after all. If we kill them all, there'll be no fun around here anymore."

"Not to mention," Landon came over to add. "They'll kill as many of us as they can in retaliation. Then, there would be no one left at all. And well..that's not how you play the game."

They had a point, but accidents happened. How could one shoot a gun at a moving target, in near darkness, knowing that the shot wouldn't be fatal?

"Landon, go," Walter pushed his arm in annoyance.

"Be careful," I pulled Walter closer to me once Landon had joined his brother outside. "Please."

"I promise," Walter said to me.

I cupped Walter's face and gave him a firm kiss, "I'll be waiting."

"I'll be late," Walter took my hand and kissed my knuckles softly. "Don't stay up for me."

I nodded, knowing I wouldn't be able to sleep anyway and then gave Walter a hug.

"See you later then," I told him.

"Later," he kissed my forehead and rubbed my hair before leaving.

21

It was around 5am when I heard the boys return from patrol. As I'd suspected, I hadn't been able to fully get to sleep, but instead I had been drifting in and out, worrying about Walter in my broken dreams.

Walter entered his room quietly, not turning on the light. He fumbled around in the darkness and I heard him start to remove his clothes. I didn't know he was topless until I felt him slide in the between the sheets next to me and his bare chest brushed my arm.

"Walter," I whispered. "Are you okay?"

"Coral," he sounded surprised. "I thought you were asleep. Yeah, I'm fine. Have you been up all night?"

"I couldn't sleep," I said, snuggling closer to him.

Walter put his arms around me, "I'm sorry I worried you so much."

I couldn't get over how warm Walter's skin was. It felt smooth but I knew it wasn't flawless, he had all sorts of scars littered all over his body. I rubbed my hand over his chest, right above where his heart was and I felt Walter shiver.

"Are you okay Coral?" Walter murmured.

"I'm okay now," I said, breathing him in. "Did you find any Santiagos?"

"Not tonight," Walter replied tiredly. "It was kind of boring actually. Fighting keeps me awake, but this time I was struggling to stop yawning, and Landon almost collapsed from fatigue. He sleeps late so that makes it worse I guess."

"What about Phoenix?" I found myself asking out of curiosity.

"Phoenix was fine. As usual," Walter replied bitterly. "He would never show that he was tired. He thinks of it as being weak."

"Weak?" I frowned. "It's normal."

"I know," Walter said, tightening his grip around me in anger. "But apparently he's too strong to appear remotely human. Let's just...not talk about him."

"Okay Walter," I kissed his neck. "You're tired, we both are."

"Yeah," I felt him smile. "Goodnight."

"Night."

Walter was rubbing small circles into the back of my shoulder and I opened my eyes, sighing pleasantly. We had slept in fairly late and as it was Sunday morning, no one was in a rush. Walter, sensing my movements, opened his hazel eyes and he smiled at me.

"Morning beautiful."

I knew it was something lot's of guys said in lots of books and movies, but hearing it from Walter and having it directed at me, made it feel so much more special.

"Morning," I smiled warmly at him.

Now it was brighter, I could see up close all the marks on Walter's body. The first thing I noticed were the bruises from the snowball fight the day before.

"Wow," I said, gently touching one of the dark blue marks. "It looks so painful."

"Nah," Walter reassured me. "I've had much worse."

I winced, not exactly feeling put at ease. Allowing my eyes to trail down his topless body I saw what looked like old stab wounds, some of them short and others long, as if someone had slashed across Walter's body, rather than stuck the blade right in him.

I touched a pale white line on his chest, "What happened to you?"

Walter felt where I was feeling and thought a little, "This one was last year. Skull face got me in a fight. It wasn't so bad. A couple of inches to the left and a little bit deeper and I would have died for sure."

"And it wasn't so bad?" I raised my eyebrows, staring at Walter.

"I've had worse," he shrugged.

"Worse than almost being stabbed in the heart?" I made a pained face.

"Yep. Blue eyes got me here," Walter pointed to a scar across his side. "Smashed two of my ribs with a baseball bat and I had to have surgery. They put metal plates in there to help them heal quickly and slightly less painfully. But it still hurt like a bitch for weeks."

I'd never seen Ario very angry so I couldn't imagine him causing Walter such a serious injury. It was frightening.

"Which one was your worst?" I had to ask.

"This one," Walter put his fingers over a bullet wound on his stomach. "Diego got me right in the stomach. I was sixteen, had two surgeries and spent a month in hospital. I'd never seen the triplets cry so much, not since...well not since we were younger. They thought I was gonna die...and well from all the shit I gave them, I was surprised how much they'd miss me if I really did die."

Walter smiled fondly and the memory and I tried to imagine how scary it must have been for him and his brothers whilst Walter fought for his life in hospital only two years ago. Diego had caused that. No wonder the boys hated the Santiagos so much...but the Simpsons had likely done the same to them throughout the past too.

Without a word I gently kissed Walter's chest, then planted my lips on his side and lastly a soft kiss on stomach too. I saw, once again, the tattoo on his hip and I wondered who or what E.S was.

"Coral," Walter pulled me up so that we were lying on our sides, face to face. "It's okay, you don't have to do that. I'm fine."

I couldn't really speak in fear of actually crying. Walter's life had been on the line more times that I could have thought, and it wasn't just him. I bet his brothers had been in similar situations...and Ario and his family too. They were all lucky to be alive, and it made me wonder what the point was for taking such risks just over territory to sell drugs. There was more to life than that, and it wouldn't ever be right if anyone so young died because of it.

Walter held me as I tried not to tear up. He never mentioned his tattoo, so I didn't ask.

"I'm sorry. I shouldn't have ever said any of that," Walter murmured quietly.

"I'm the one who asked," I replied shakily into his shoulder. "Don't apologise."

Sunday at the Simpsons' house was oddly quiet. It was 1pm and all of Walter's brothers were just waking up, except Phoenix who had been working out in the basement apparently since the crack of dawn like he did almost every day.

"Coral I think you should bring some of your stuff over here," Walter said after we'd finished eating.

"You mean come and stay with you and your brothers?" I widened my eyes.

"Yeah," Walter nodded, looking serious. "Like I said before, the Santiagos are going to find out you're with me and they know where you live. They do home invasions all the time Coral, and I don't want you getting hurt."

"Do your gang do home invasions too?" I asked him instead.

"We're not thugs," Walter shook his head.

"You just get other thugs to do it for you?" I questioned with a smile.

He grinned at me, "No actually. We just don't play the game like that."

"Okay," I said, not completely sure I understood.

"It doesn't have to be permanent," Walter said, taking hold of my hand. "But you've been alright staying here over the weekend haven't you?"

"Yeah," I nodded. "I like it here with you guys, it beats being all alone. But Phoenix – "

"I'll talk to Phoenix," Walter interrupted. "Let's just go and get some of your things from your place."

"So I'm moving in before you've even talked to him about it?" I said in fear. "Walter, what if he just throws me out?"

Walter clenched his jaw, "I'll make sure he doesn't do that."

"Walter," I looked down in worry.

"Trust me," Walter squeezed my hand. "I've got this."

"Okay," I nodded. "I don't have a lot of things, so it won't take long."

"That's fine," Walter smiled. "We could go out afterwards."

I nodded, "That would be nice."

"What would be nice?" Landon asked as he strolled into the kitchen half naked.

"Don't you have any clothes?" Walter immediately stopped smiling and frowned at his brother.

"Nope," Landon winked at him. "I sleep naked so you're lucky I was bothered enough to put some pants on."

Walter scowled in disgust as I let out a laugh.

"So what would be nice?" Landon got a carton of orange juice from the fridge and sat down next to me.

"That's none of your business," Walter snapped at him.

"Coral?" Landon smiled sweetly at me.

"Well..." I tried not to smile so much. "Walter and I are going to go and bring over some of my stuff."

"You're moving in?" Landon looked surprised.

"Not forever," I said quickly.

"The Santiagos know where she lives," Walter explained. "They'll see us together before long and I don't want her in danger."

"Fair enough," Landon leaned back in his seat. "You're rash, so they'd love to get at you by using her."

"Don't piss me off Landon," Walter balled his hands into fists.

"I wasn't trying to," Landon backed off. "I'm just saying it's a good idea."

Eli came down into the kitchen in a loose fitting jumper and some jogging bottoms.

"You look like Severn, dressed like that," Landon said when he saw him.

"I don't," Eli muttered. "I'm just cold."

Landon smiled, "How would you like to join us on a trip?"

"What?" Walter frowned at him.

"A trip where?" Eli glanced at me and Walter with curious green eyes.

"To Coral's place," Landon offered. "To help bring some of her stuff back here."

"Landon," Walter growled in anger. "None of you are coming."

"I can drive you though," Landon said, turning to look at him. "It would be a lot easier. Come on, you know it's true."

Walter hesitated, still furious, but Landon was right. Taking a car would speed up the process and then Walter and I would have even more time to have for ourselves afterwards.

"It's a good idea," I said when Walter wouldn't answer. "Thanks Landon."

"Well we're going now," Walter stood up. "So get ready."

"Demanding," Landon only laughed. "Maybe you should learn how to drive and then you wouldn't have to boss anyone around."

"*You're* the one who offered," Walter's fists shook.

"He's only winding you up," I said to Walter gently. "Let's get our shoes."

I pulled Walter out of the kitchen by his sleeve and Landon went up to go and get changed. Eli came out after us, eating an apple.

"So Phoenix is okay with this?" he asked the two of us.

"I'll talk to him," Walter muttered, shoving his shoes on.

Eli raised his eyebrows but didn't push it. Instead he said something much worse.

"What happened between you and blue eyes anyway?" Eli questioned.

I widened my eyes and looked at Walter who had a reserved look on his face. You'd be a fool to think he was really fine though. I could tell he was close to blowing up.

"Nothing happened," I gave Eli a look. "We only talked a few times at work."

"Where's work?" Eli asked me.

"A pub called the Dartfish," I replied, not expecting him to have heard about it.

Eli looked at Walter with an expression I didn't understand and I frowned, feeling like I was missing something.

"What?" I asked them.

"Nothing," Eli shrugged. "I'm gonna get a scarf."

He disappeared upstairs and I looked at Walter, "What was that?"

"I don't know," Walter rolled his eyes. "I guess he's just cold."

That wasn't what I meant but I knew it was futile trying to press any further. A couple of minutes later, Landon returned fully dressed and spinning his car keys around his index finger. Eli came down moments after and I frowned slightly.

He wasn't wearing a scarf.

"Let's go," Landon said, heading for the front door.

We followed him out into the already melting snow and out of the corner of my eye I saw Eli slip something to Walter, a knife most likely. Did they always have to carry weapons? If the police caught them with a knife or even worse, a gun, they wouldn't get off lightly.

Landon's car was in a garage on the side of the house that I'd never noticed before. There were two cars in there, both looked expensive indeed. Landon opened the slightly less flashy one and we climbed in.

"Show me the way Coral," Landon said as I sat in the passenger seat.

"Don't touch her," Walter threatened from the back seat.

I looked down and saw that Landon's hand was reaching out and about to feel my thigh.

"Its habit," Landon chuckled and put his hand back on the steering wheel. "Sorry."

It made me think about how many different girls Landon had had sit in the passenger side of his car. It had to be a lot if he was about to feel up his brother's girlfriend without even noticing.

I directed Landon to my home which took no time at all and I was shocked that I had missed it a little bit, but I was also happy to be finally moving on. I hadn't said I would stay with the Simpsons permanently, but I knew it was what Walter wanted, and to be honest once the Santiagos found out about us, I didn't think I *could* go back anyway.

We got out of Landon's car and walked slowly towards the rundown block of flats. I was aware it was Eli's first time seeing where I lived, but I didn't mind anymore. It was no longer all that I had.

"I'm pretty sure I tagged this building," Eli said as he tried to remember. "On the side somewhere."

He started heading round the side of the building where I knew Ario had sprayed his own gang sign on top of the Simpsons'. I decided to stand back and wait near the front of the building as the boys round the side.

"Blue eyes," Walter snarled, cursing furiously when he no doubt saw the Santiago sign.

"Well that's just rude," I heard Landon mutter.

I walked around in the sludgy snow, thinking about the last time I'd seen Ario out here when I'd been taking the rubbish out. I stopped dead and frowned when I saw something in the snow. I bent down and wiped the snow off the item to reveal what looked like a switchblade. The handle was brown and had something scratched into it, and there was a small knob on the side which would cause the deadly blade to spring out if I pressed it.

I just knew it belonged to Ario.

"Coral, you okay?" I heard Walter's voice.

I slipped the knife into my pocket and span around to face him.

"Yeah, shall we go in?" I smiled at him.

He nodded and turned to Landon and Eli who were walking back to join us.

"Remind me to spray over that tonight," he said to them.

"I'll do it myself," Eli spat. "Stupid shits."

I smiled slightly, thinking how protective the boys were being over their territory and...well over me. I didn't know why I had hidden Ario's knife or what I was planning to do with it. I doubted I would have a chance to talk to him again now that I had chosen the Simpsons, and Walter had made it very clear that the two sides were immiscible.

I tried not to worry as I led the boys up into my flat and we started loading some of my things into Landon's car. Ario's knife felt a lot heavier than it was in my pocket and it was hot, as if it was burning me through the fabric. It was probably my nerves that had me feeling that way and I told myself to calm down.

All I had to do was give it back to him, it didn't require actually talking.

***

Walter and I returned home after an evening meal together in the shopping complex. Walter had told Landon and Eli to leave my stuff in his room and that he would talk to Phoenix when we got back.

And now we were back.

I still had Ario's knife in my pocket, but that wasn't what was making me feel edgy. It was Phoenix's reaction that was making my stomach tighten more than anything. I could hear his voice in the living room and I somehow sensed that everyone was in there.

Walter opened the living room door and sure enough all the Simpson brothers were there and they seemed to be having a heated rant. Well Phoenix was. He was clearly mad about something and when he saw me he fixed me with a dark look before ignoring me completely. The boys looked serious, even the triplets, and when I heard the Dartfish being mentioned my back stiffened and I widened my eyes.

"What's going on?" I asked in a quiet voice.

Phoenix turned his gaze to me, "You really want to know?"

I frowned, "I work at the Dartfish. So yes."

Walter was shaking his head at Phoenix and I touched his knee, wanting to know what he didn't want to tell me.

"What is it Walter?" I asked him.

He looked unhappy, "Remember when I told you the less you knew about the gang, the better? Well this is what I meant. I don't want you to know."

"But I'm connected to it somehow aren't I?" I looked round at the straight faces. "I work at the Dartfish so maybe I could...help...with whatever the problem is."

Phoenix paused and then glanced at Landon who seemed to be his second hand man as well as his younger brother. Landon nodded and half shrugged and Walter again shook his head.

"Don't tell her anything," Walter said to them.

"I want to know," I argued. "Walter, please."

"She wants to know so I'll tell her," Phoenix said. "You're either in or out."

"She's joining the gang?" Gomez widened his blue eyes in shock.

"She's not joining the gang, that is to say," Phoenix said. "But I'm taking it as her agreeing to my proposal to be an accomplice."

"Coral," Walter looked at me closely. "Think about it."

"I can help you Walter," I said to him. "All of you. Right?"

Phoenix nodded and I looked back at Walter with wide eyes, "Please?"

Walter bent his head when he said, "Okay. You can tell her, but she's not doing anything stupid for you Phoenix."

Phoenix nodded again and I looked at him, waiting to hear what he had to say.

"Don't repeat this to anyone," Phoenix said to me. "Not your family or your friends, the authorities or anyone."

"I won't," I shook my head. "I promise."

"I'm going to explain to you how our gang works," Phoenix's eyes bore into mine. "From now on you're with us and you can't turn against us."

"Doesn't that mean she's in the gang though?" Gio raised his hand.

"She's not part of the gang," Phoenix snapped at him. "The gang is just the seven of us. Family only."

He probably didn't mean for his words to hurt me, or then again maybe he did, but I understood what Phoenix was saying. I couldn't be a member of his gang because I wasn't blood, but I could be a partner, someone who helped. I'm sure I wasn't the only person with this role. Phoenix probably had a lot of connections to ensure that everything he had set up ran smoothly. I knew it was dangerous but I was clearly in too deep already and I didn't want to turn back.

This was the *closest* to family I'd ever had.

I wanted in.

22

"There are several levels to the drug networking system," Phoenix said. "Those in the top level are members of South American drug cartels. They produce massive amounts of pure illegal substances and smuggle it out, usually into the US."

I knew I shouldn't have been surprised, but hearing it like this from Phoenix (who I knew was being completely serious) made everything feel so much more real and so much more dangerous. It wasn't just what happened in movies, it was happening in real life too. Walter and his brothers were really criminals.

"Those in the second level," Phoenix went on, "are regional distributors and consist of people who are linked to the cartels, more often than not, by blood. They are in charge of distributing the product within large cities, both within the US and overseas. Understand?"

I nodded, aware that all the brothers were watching me closely, seeing my expression as I discovered more of their dirty truths. Walter still looked upset, but he didn't stop Phoenix, he knew I wanted to understand.

"Those in the third level, known as top dealers – "

"That's us," Gomez sent me a grin.

Phoenix cast him a glare and continued, "They tend to cut their product with other substances and sell it in bulk to make greater profits. All three of these top levels run like businesses. They rarely ever use the product they sell and they insulate themselves from the authorities by using others to do the dirty work for them. Although we work slightly differently, but I'll come back to that."

"Okay," I said quietly.

"The fourth level, called mid-level dealers are individuals who have been in the drug world for some time and often sell to support their own addictions. They again cut their product so they can make more profit, but as they are more visible they are easily caught out by the law."

"The fifth level, made of your average dealers, have usually made their way up from users to dealers so that they can support their addictions. The products they sell have been cut multiple times."

I immediately pictured scruffy looking people, walking the streets and slipping small packets into their buyers' hands in return for decent amounts of cash.

"Those in the sixth and last level are small-time dealers and also users who are held so tight by their addictions that they always need a fix and will cut their product with anything they can get away with. They will also tend to deal to anyone, just so they can support their own addictions. They are so deep in it, it's almost impossible to get themselves out of that lifestyle and they can very easily fall prey to the authorities."

"So you get the gist of it?" Landon sent me a smile.

"Yeah," I breathed. "I think so."

"So back to what makes us different from most other top dealers," Phoenix didn't take time to pause.

"The third level?" I tried to remember.

"Yes," he nodded and I realised that this was the most Phoenix had ever said to me, and he wasn't exactly angry at me either. "Instead of dealing to other dealers, we deal to legitimate businesses."

"What?" I stared at him, forgetting to be afraid of holding his eye contact for more than a second.

"It's not that hard to understand," Phoenix snapped and Walter looked at him with a frown.

"We get the product from our supplier," he broke it down. "We cut it, we then give it to small businesses like cafes or pubs, such as the Dartfish, to sell it for us."

I widened my eyes as realisation struck.

"The Dartfish? I've been working these past two years for a pub who deals drugs to people?" I blinked at him.

Phoenix shrugged, "Yeah."

"Why would businesses agree to do that?" I blurted. "If they get caught...they'd get prosecuted. It would be all over the press! They'd lose everything, and so would their employees."

"All it takes are a few threats," Phoenix said with no care at all. "Of course they don't know they're working for me or that any of my brothers are involved. I use some of my men as messengers to pass it to them and collect the profit from them. The businesses get a small proportion to keep and all they have to do is not get caught and make sure I get all my money."

"So they really don't know you're behind it?" I frowned.

"Of course not," Phoenix replied. "All they know is that they are working for X. Most people in this area think I'm a thug who directly deals to my users. You probably thought the same, from all the rumours, but if that were really true, I would have most likely been arrested, charged and found guilty of a lot of shit a very long time ago. My brothers and I are shielded by the people who work for us...and from the examples I set, they know never to cross me."

I didn't want to know what *examples* Phoenix was talking about. I didn't underestimate him, not one bit.

"Our method is a lot more sophisticated than the Santiagos who just get other dealers to deal for them the regular way," Phoenix said sounding a bit angry, "which is why it's going to be a big problem if they're catching onto us."

"We think they are trying to get the Dartfish to collaborate with them," Landon said, playing with his lip ring. "They've been going there a lot more often, we've heard from our sources and also from you."

It made sense now why Walter looked surprised when I'd first told him that I'd met Ario at work and how weird Eli acted when he'd found out this afternoon.

"So the Santiagos don't know that the Dartfish is already working for you?" I asked, my question sounding so unreal to my own ears.

"No," Phoenix said. "We don't make it as obvious as they are making it. The idiots."

It was true.

I had never seen any of the Simpsons at the pub throughout the time I had been working there and now I was suddenly seeing the Santiagos a lot. I froze as another thought popped into my mind. Which of my colleagues were in on it? I couldn't imagine any of them slipping packets of pills or powders to any of our 'customers'.

"So what do you want me to do?" I asked, feeling my stomach knot.

Walter fixed Phoenix with a hard look but Phoenix looked unfazed.

"All I want you to do is find out if that's what the Santiagos are really planning," he replied. "Get information out of Ario and report back to me. As soon as you get an answer, I'll do the rest."

"Okay," I nodded, letting it settle.

"Don't let it slip that we are already dealing to them," Phoenix spoke. "Can you do that?"

He had already told me that I didn't have a choice, once I was in, I couldn't get out. I only nodded, but it was a lot easier said than done.

"Good," his lips formed a very faint smile.

Where I thought he was going to thank me, Phoenix only got up and walked out. Walter stood up too and headed out the living room, making me frowned and follow him out.

Walter was standing at the bottom of the stairs and Phoenix had already gone upstairs.

"At the beginning," I said quietly to Walter, "when I first met you...you pretended that you didn't know what The Dartfish was."

"I know," Walter mumbled.

"And that cafe," I spoke. "The cafe you took me to that one time. They work for you too, don't they?"

Walter had said that it was a fairly quiet place with not enough people to listen into our conversation. They seemed like the perfect partner, someone not as well-known, who might risk their reputation by working with criminals to get a cut of the profits.

"They do," Walter sighed.

"You said you didn't want us to lie to each other," I said to him, a frown forming on my face.

Walter looked at me sharply, "I didn't lie....I just didn't tell you the whole truth. And that was because it's private and like Phoenix said, I couldn't just go around telling anyone."

"Anyone?" I looked at him blankly.

"You know what I mean," Walter creased his brows, looking surprisingly upset. "Coral, I didn't want any of this to happen, but you've made your choice...and Phoenix won't let you back out that easily."

Walter's words were worrying me and I wouldn't be able to help them if I was scared.

"I can do it," I said to him. "I'll help Phoenix and you and your brothers."

"Be careful," Walter said to me, hardening his jaw. "Don't let Blue eyes do anything to you again."

"I won't Walter," I said firmly and took hold of his hand. "Trust me."

Walter looked down at me and I could see all the emotions whirling though his mind. I saw anger, worry and pride.

Even though he wouldn't admit it, he was proud of me.

Before I could even start to smile, Walter had pressed his lips against mine and he kissed me hard. I was breathless in seconds but Walter was fuelled with so much passion, he didn't notice.

"I don't know what to do with you Coral," Walter broke off and shoved a shaking hand through his hair as we both panted.

I looked at him with blazing eyes and pulled him back down, "Don't stop."

***

The next day was a Monday and I went to school knowing that I had work afterwards. I thought I would have a lot of time to prepare myself on how to approach Ario when I next saw him, but I clearly didn't.

"So how is Eli?" Hayley asked me as we sat together in class.

I'd told her that I was temporarily living with Walter and his brothers so there was no need for her to pick me up in the mornings anymore. She had been shocked at first but then thought of it as extremely sweet of Walter to suggest such a thing. I hadn't mentioned anything about Ario and the Santiagos, nor did I bring up how Phoenix had given me a death glare when Walter had discussed it with him.

"Showing interest in Eli, are we?" I perked up in excitement.

Hayley blushed, "No, I was only being polite."

"Sure," I grinned. "He's good. Good-looking huh?"

"You're not being very discrete with your hints," Hayley cocked an eyebrow at me as she smirked.

"Oops," I bit my lip and grinned. "Did you enjoy the snowball fight then?"

"It was...an interesting version," she tried not to laugh. "And the rumours are right, Landon is such a flirt."

"I know," I smiled, remembering how he almost touched me up the day before. "He can't help it."

"Well with a face and body like his," Hayley lowered her voice. "I wouldn't be able to help it either if I were him. I mean, who would say no?"

"He's a player Hayley," I said to her before she started getting funny ideas.

"I can tell," she murmured, playing with a strand of her hair. "I never said I was falling for it. He just seems like a nice guy. Anyway, how are you and Walter? It must be serious if you're moving in with him already."

I mentally sighed. It was more difficult trying to explain what the rush was for when I had to avoid the truth. It would be unnecessary if Hayley knew all about how I could someday be in danger just because of my relationship with Walter.

"I don't know how to define serious," I shrugged. "But I care about him a lot, and he does for me."

Hayley was giving me a sneaky smile.

"What?" I asked, pressing my lips together in an attempt not to grin.

"You're blushing," her smile widened. "What else have you done with him?"

"Nothing!" I cried and then glanced around at the other students before lowering my voice. "Nothing at all."

In truth, Walter and I hadn't done more than kiss which was just fine for me. I loved kissing him, feeling so close to him as our tongues entwined. Thinking of it and daring myself to think of *more* made my cheeks burn and I covered my face.

"You're lying to me," Hayley started laughing. "Coral!"

"I'm not lying," I looked at her, still covering my cheeks. "He's really patient. We haven't even talked about...any of that stuff yet."

Hayley clasped her hands together, "That's so nice of him. Walter isn't as scary as I used to think."

"You're telling me!" I laughed. "I was *terrified* of him."

Hayley smiled, remembering the early days and I wondered if she had had any boyfriends in the past. I knew she was single now, but how much experience did she have?

"Hayley," I murmured, trying not to blush again. "Have you had any boyfriends?"

"Not any serious ones," she replied. "Only the thirteen year old crush kind of thing, you know?"

I didn't know. When I was thirteen I was still very afraid of men and didn't speak to anyone at school, let alone the boys. There was no such thing as early teen infatuations for me.

"Yeah," I lied, throwing in a shrug.

"I'd love to know what real love is," Hayley said sincerely.

"Me too," I said looking down at the desk.

"Well you're not far from it," she wiggled her eyebrows at me, dropping the serious tone. "Now come on, let's actually do some work before the teacher notices."

***

Walter kissed me goodbye after school finished. He didn't say anything about Ario again, but I knew it was weighing heavily on his mind.

"Don't worry about it. I'll see you tonight," I said to him.

"See you later," he said, nodding.

I made my way to the pub in neutral territory thinking of ways to start conversation with Ario. How could I possibly find out what kind of illegal objective he and his gang were after at the Dartfish? *Hey Ario, so is Carlos possibly trying to pass on drugs to this pub?* I silently scoffed at myself. As if.

I was so busy thinking about it, that I was completely thrown off when I arrived at work and saw Carlos and the twins: Miguel and Manuel, but no Ario. Thankfully someone else was already serving them, so I concentrated on avoiding their eyes at all times whilst checking the door each time it opened and people entered.

Ario never came.

I finished my shift and was about to head out the back door with bitter disappointment when I heard a familiar voice.

"Why the long face?" Ario was leaning on the bar in a dark jacket.

I blinked in pleasant surprise and then smiled at him. I wanted him to trust me. The faster I got information out of him, the more pleased I would make Phoenix.

"I'm just tired," I said to him.

192

"But you're finished right?" he arched a brow. "So you should be glad about that."

"I guess so," I replied. "It's been a while since I've seen you."

"Well I did say I wouldn't bother you again," Ario smiled, rubbing one of his blue eyes tiredly.

In fact, he didn't look so well. His eyes were rimmed red and he looked a little bit pale and clammy.

"Are you okay?" I asked him.

"Yeah," he wiped sweat off his forehead. "I'm fine."

He wasn't, but I didn't push it. Ario glanced back at the table where his older cousin and brothers were sitting and then he turned back to me.

"You wanna step outside?" he asked me. "It's hot in here."

"Sure," I replied, already with my bag in hand.

The both of us walked out into the cool, dark night and stood near the back doors where I'd bumped into him the very first time. It made me think of Walter and how similar it had been to the first time I'd met him too.

"So you like the Dartfish?" I asked Ario once we were outside. "You've been coming here quite often recently."

"Do we really catch your attention that much?" he smirked.

"Of course," I tried to play it cool even though I was starting to panic.

"Well it's alright," Ario said neutrally. "Just another pub, isn't it?"

"Yeah," I nodded, mentally kicking myself. I had to be smoother than that.

"Do *you* like the Dartfish?" Ario turned my question back at me.

"Yeah, it's cool," I replied. "It's always got the right amount of people inside. Not too many, but it's never quite empty either. Do you know anyone who works there? Except me?"

"No?" Ario frowned. "Why would I?"

"I don't know," my palms started to sweat. "But some people...like Tiffany for example, you know Tiffany don't you?"

"I don't think I do," Ario looked at me with a dull face.

193

"Well I was going to say she really makes effort to get to know our customers," I was aware I was just rambling now. "And she tends to go for men...you know?"

Ario smiled, "I don't."

"Oh never mind then," I said, taking a deep breath. "Ignore me."

"What's with all the questions?" Ario looked amused and my heart started hammering. "You're acting weird."

Maybe he had sussed me out already. I was being terrible at trying to be sneaky. Phoenix would kill me if Ario worked out that the Simpsons were already selling to the Dartfish...and Ario would probably kill me if he found out I was helping the Simpsons.

"I found this," I said, delving my hand into my bag and changing the subject.

Ario's face instantly lit up like daybreak on a bleak morning and I grinned at him, handing him back his clearly loved knife.

"Graci – thank you," he caught himself, looking up from his knife to me.

"I knew it was yours," I looked at him.

"Yeah," he nodded, smiling at it in disbelief. "I thought I'd never get it back."

"You've got it now," I beamed at him. "So that means you owe me, right?"

Ario's happy expression faltered, "I owe you now?"

"Yeah," I said as confidently as I could. "I didn't have to give it back to you, but I did."

"Okay," he said slowly, slipping his switchblade into his pocket. "What do you want?"

"I want to know you," I made a point to look right into his bright blue eyes.

Ario seemed convinced by my act and he nodded slowly, "So you *are* interested in seeing two guys at once?"

"I guess," I looked down so he didn't see the lie through my eyes. It seemed to be working. "But for now, I just want to know you for you. You seem like an interesting guy, someone dangerous...and...I like dangerous."

I prayed that he didn't see right past those cringe-worthy lines and looked up at him through my lashes.

He'd taken the bait. I knew it as soon as I saw his expression.

"I'll see you around Ario," I turned to leave. "Make sure to have some dirty little secrets in mind the next time I see you."

"You too," he called lowly after me.

23

I was freaking out.

As soon as I was well out of sight, I dropped the facade and clutched at my chest, struggling to get my breath back. Where the hell did all that talk at the end come from? It was just so unlike me! But...but it had worked, hadn't it? Wait! What did Ario mean by 'you too'?! He wanted to know *my* dirty little secrets? *What the hell was I supposed to say to that?!*

I must have been muttering to myself out loud because I heard someone call out to me in the dark. The streetlights didn't work well in the area and it would be a five minute walk until I reached the closest lit path.

"Manuel? That, you?"

I widened my eyes and shut my mouth. The only people, who I assumed would address Manuel Santiago by his first name like that, were his family. I couldn't see anyone and I'm sure they couldn't see me, but all the same, I started walking faster.

"Where you running to?" the person must have noticed my increase of speed. "Why aren't you saying anything? Trying to scare me?"

I was so afraid of them actually catching me, I flat out started running. I immediately picked up a second pair of footsteps chasing me and I my heart felt like it would give out. They were gaining on me.

"Manuel, why are you so slow?" the voice made me jump. "You been eating too many *cachapas*?"

I didn't even know what *cachapas* were and was busy trying not to trip over my own feet when they grabbed me from behind, muttering Spanish in a teasing tone. It was only when their hands felt my chest and realised that I wasn't exactly *male*, that they let go of me with a shout of shock.

"What the hell?" they exclaimed. "Who is that?"

I didn't answer, instead I just turned and ran again. I could see the streetlights up ahead and knew that once I reached them, I would be visible to whoever it was I'd left behind me. As long as they quit the chase, I would manage. Or so I thought.

I felt them clamp onto my hand and I gasped.

"Get off me!" I shouted, turning around to see Paulo, the youngest Santiago.

Paulo let go of me, "Why didn't you say anything?"

"I...I just wanted to get home," I replied.

"I thought you were my brother," he said, looking at me with those wide brown eyes. "Sorry."

He was apologising just like that? He was so unlike his brothers Miguel and Manuel who, I was very sure, would *never* apologise, yet similar to his brother Ario who came all the way to my home just to say sorry for his wrongdoing.

"It's okay," I tried to relax. Paulo didn't strike me as a threat.

Paulo was frowning as he searched my face, and I knew he was seconds away from recognising me from the time his brothers Miguel and Manuel tried to cut me and Hayley's eyelids off.

"I have to go," I turned and started walking away.

"I know you," to my dismay Paulo fell into step with me. "You're the waitress at the pub."

197

He was actually a couple of inches taller than me, despite being about fifteen years old. Just like the triplets.

"Yeah," I murmured, avoiding his eye.

"Am I bothering you?" Paulo asked, sounding strangely like his brother Ario.

I couldn't find it in me to just say yes. I didn't want to anger the kid, he wasn't exactly known as a sweetheart.

"I'm just tired," I said to him. "Weren't you looking for your brothers?"

"Oh," he stopped. "Yeah...well, later."

He must have not realised that I had been walking West and probably wouldn't see him later as we lived on opposite sides of town. If I were to ever see him in the town centre, I wouldn't exactly jump out to greet him, and especially not if he was with his brothers.

"Later," I said anyway and even threw a smile over my shoulder at him.

I had already turned away from him when I heard the voice of either Miguel or Manuel, which had my blood running cold.

"Who is that?" they questioned Paulo.

"No one," Paulo responded. "Let's go back."

***

I was probably still sweating profusely when I arrived back home, home being the Simpsons house, that was. I knocked and waited outside as my hands trembled in my pockets.

"Hey you," Gomez opened the door and literally pulled me in. "You hungry?"

I blinked in surprise, I *was* actually.

"What is there to eat?" I asked, following him into the kitchen.

Gomez didn't answer, he only gave me an innocent smile and I returned it uncertainly. He led me to the kitchen and as soon as I saw bare flesh, I slapped my hands over my eyes.

It seemed that I had just walked in on a game of strip poker.

The butt naked boys laughed back at me and Gomez slapped my back as he died of laughter.

"How's it going Coral?" Severn waved at me from his seat at the dining table.

"Hi," I was relieved to see that he was wearing boxers and a singlet.

The same could *not* be said for Landon, who was *of course*, completely naked and fanning himself with his cards like he was in a palace. God knows how grateful I was that he'd had the decency to cover his crotch with his shirt.

"You wanna play?" Landon winked at me.

"No thanks," I said, still standing in shock. "Walter, you too?"

Walter got up, holding some of his clothes over his crotch and smiling as he came up to me. Gomez was wearing jeans and a singlet and Giovanni too was one hundred percent nude, in fact, Eli was the only one with both his trousers and shirt still on.

"How was it with Blue eyes?" Walter asked me quietly.

"Walter I can't take you seriously when you're naked like this," I tried not to smile so hard.

His face split into an even wider grin and he slipped past me to the downstairs bathroom to put more clothes on. I looked at the table to see what the boys were betting with. There were stacks of real money and also knives of various shapes and sizes.

"Eli you must be really good at this game," I commented, raising my brows.

"Or he just has a resting bitch face which means you never know when he's bluffing or not," Walter said from behind me, already back from the bathroom and thankfully dressed.

Eli only shrugged a shoulder and smirked.

"I'm pretty sure Landon chose to strip even when he didn't have to," Gomez murmured as he went to get a drink out of the fridge for me.

He handed me a can of *Fanta*, "He's just that kind of guy."

"That's true," Landon spread his arms out.

"Sit down," Walter pulled his chair out for me.

"Thanks," I joined the brothers at the table.

"So what's the update?" Severn nudged my arm. "You get any info on the Santiagos?"

"Not yet," I said, lowering my gaze. "But I'm getting there."

I didn't want to give out all the details of my encounter with Ario to all the boys, but I would share it with Walter later on. As for Paulo basically feeling me up by accident, well it was best not to mention that one to anyone.

"So Gomez," I glanced over at him. "There isn't actually any food?"

"There will be," Gomez answered. "Phoenix is out getting it."

Landon started putting his clothes back on, and Giovanni did the same.

"No hard feelings," Eli grinned at Landon as he collected his winnings from the table.

"I'm getting my blade back," Landon only shrugged. "You'll see."

"You can trade it back," Eli said, taking what I assumed was one of Landon's knives. "Or just give me money."

"You're just lucky it's not an important one," Landon said to him as he pulled his shirt back on.

There was a sound at the door and Giovanni was the first to leap up, still in a partial state of undress.

"Gio," Gomez groaned. "We have a lady here. No one wants to see your white butt."

Phoenix appeared in the doorway and Gio, after pulling his pants on, took the bags of food from his hands.

"Thanks," he said to his brother.

Phoenix didn't reply, he looked at Gio in disgust and then glanced at the table and at Eli with his stack of winnings.

"You lost the least rounds?"

"Yeah," Eli answered. "I won."

"I should have been here," Phoenix grunted. "You can't win against me."

"Well you weren't," Eli smirked. "Gio, pass the food. I'm starving."

As the boys started sharing out boxes of Chinese takeaway, I noticed Phoenix looking at me. When our eyes met, he made his way round the table towards me.

"How did it go with Ario?" he asked me, looking down at me in a pretty intimidating way.

"It was okay," I said, looking away. "Slowly getting there."

"The very fact that they were back at the Dartfish again means that they are definitely planning something," he grumbled in annoyance. "Carlos, what the hell are you thinking?"

I noticed how Phoenix didn't use the nicknames that the rest of his brothers did, and I wondered if that was because he saw himself as more mature.

"Where did you guys get the idea for your gang symbol?" I asked after Walter passed me a box of noodles.

"The seven headed snake?" Severn murmured, eating some chicken. "Phoenix of course."

I turned to glance at Phoenix who was now standing by the fridge.

"It's pretty self-explanatory," he commented. "There are seven of us and we aren't your nicest people."

"Wanna see our gangmarks?" Gio asked whilst stuffing his mouth with rice.

Walter glared at him as rice rained down on us.

"Do you *want* me to hit you?" Walter asked in a low and angry voice as he picked a couple of grains out of my hair.

Gio was about to answer (food still in his mouth) when Gomez slapped his hand over it for him.

"I'll show you," Gomez said to me, elbowing Gio back.

Gomez leaned across the table, holding his hand out towards me. I frowned in confusion, reaching out to take his hand and I heard the brothers chuckle.

"No," Gomez laughed. "Look at my little finger."

"Oh," I smiled in realisation when I saw a number of little scratches down the outside of his pinky. "Are those scars?"

"Yep," Gomez grinned. "Hurt like hell but it was worth it."

"Wow," I said, looking more closely. I counted seven lines. "How did you do it?"

"Landon did mine," Gomez laughed again. "After Phoenix made Severn cry when he did his, I was like no way. Landon's doing mine."

"I didn't cry," Severn smiled, looking at his finger.

"Sure you didn't," Gomez smirked at his triplet.

"So how is it done?" I pulled a pain filled face.

"You basically heat a sharp knife in a flame, press it into the skin, *et voila*," Landon explained casually as he held a spring roll in his hand. "It forms nice scars when it's healed."

I shuddered, "I don't blame you for crying Severn."

"I didn't cry," he groaned, making me laugh.

After dinner, Walter and I went upstairs for the privacy I'm sure we were both craving.

"So what really happened with Blue eyes?" Walter sat down in the edge of his bed.

I sat next to him, looking at my upturned hands that I rested on my knees.

"I think I started to earn some of his trust," I said. "I didn't touch him, but I...I did imply that I may have been interested in him, which isn't true."

"You don't have to be afraid of me Coral," Walter touched my hand. "I know it's not true."

I looked up at him in surprise. I was expecting him to grow angry.

"I'm not going to do anything with him," I told Walter. "I just want him to think that I will, just until I get what I need."

"Okay," Walter nodded, squeezing my hand in his. "Just...just don't let Phoenix turn you into someone you're not."

I thought about what he was saying and I knew I could never let that happen. I knew myself and I wouldn't be able to cheat on anyone, let alone Walter who I had deep feelings for.

"Don't be scared of that happening Walter," I said as I reached up to brush my fingers across his face. "I only have feelings for you."

Walter looked at me with that fervent expression of his and I smiled at him warmly, cupping the side of his face and moving slowly so that I was straddling him. I brought my lips close to his, so close, but not touching.

"I want you, so bad," Walter breathed quietly.

Hearing that made my stomach flutter, making me feel nervous yet exhilarated at the thought of venturing somewhere I'd never been with him.

Walter tried to catch my lips, but I moved back a little, teasing him.

"How bad?" I whispered.

Walter grabbed me by the waist and smashed his lips against mine. I let him in and his tongue went rifling through my mouth, making me gasp in bliss. I ran my fingers through Walter's dark hair, making him moan quietly against my lips. He broke off and started kissing down my cheek and then trailing my neck and down to my collarbone.

Walter started unbuttoning my black work shirt and for a second I saw someone else on top of me. Walter opened my shirt, his eyes filling with desire when he saw me underneath and when started pulling my shirt off me, a second flashback struck me. The horrible smell started to pick up in the back of my throat, as if I was really back in my childhood and as if *he* was really there.

"Walter!" I cried suddenly, pushing against his chest. "Walter, stop."

Walter froze, letting go of me immediately.

"What's wrong Coral?" he frowned in concern.

I was shaking. I couldn't do this.

"I can't," I said, sitting up and wrapping my shirt around myself. "I can't do this."

It was the first time I'd been slightly undressed in front of him, and I couldn't do it. How shameful.

"I'm sorry," I looked down, tears filling my vision.

Walter was alarmed, "Don't be sorry Coral. I shouldn't have rushed you."

"But you didn't," I cried and then covered my face as I sobbed. "You didn't do anything wrong...I just...I just couldn't do it."

He touched my shoulder hesitantly and when I didn't stop him, Walter wrapped his arms around me.

"It's okay," he said, kissing my hair. "Don't worry about it."

24

Ario was waiting for me outside the back door at the end of my shift after school on Wednesday. It was half eight and very dark, but I wasn't too scared. I was nervous more than anything.

Nervous of Ario catching me out.

"*Hola*," Ario nodded at me when he saw me step out the back of the pub.

"Hey," I smiled at him.

"Let's go to the park," Ario suggested, shoving his hands into his pockets. "It will be empty around this time, and if not...I'll make it empty."

"Sure," I looked down, following him.

The walk to the park was less than five minutes and Ario and I made a bit of small talk on the way.

"Looks like it's just us," Ario smirked as he opened the small gate into the dimly lit playground area.

He went and sat on one of the swings and I joined him on the other.

"So about my secrets," Ario said lowly, looking at his shoes.

I waited for him to speak, not sure what to expect and thinking about what exactly *I* was going to say to *him*.

"Sometimes...when I'm...you know, I like to use mango scented lube...it's actually really erotic," Ario said, still gazing downwards.

I was glad he wasn't looking at me or he would have seen my eyes bulge out of my head in shock. That was *not* the kind of dirty I had meant!

"Your turn," Ario lifted his head and glanced at me and then frowned in confusion, "...what?"

"I didn't mean *that* kind of dirty," I managed to squeak out. "I meant dirty as in...illegal, not dirty as in..."

I trailed off into an uncomfortable silence. I was mortified and I bet the same thing could be said for Ario. My face was burning so bad and I was extremely grateful for the semi-darkness we were sitting in.

As soon as I dared to look up, we caught eye contact again and just burst out laughing. I was half crying from embarrassment but Ario didn't notice and if he did, then he must have thought they were tears of laughter.

"Well that's a relief," Ario breathed out, stretching his back.

"Of course," I exclaimed.

"I was surprised at how forwards I thought you were being," Ario said, shaking his head at himself. "I should have realised what you meant."

"Yeah, that was my fault, I wasn't clear enough," I mumbled, remembering how I'd implied that I was interested in two-timing.

"I want to know about your gang," I said plain out, hoping this tactic would be more successful. "All I hear are rumours about you and your family and I'm curious to know how much is true...what you're all really like."

"Well in that case," Ario said, swinging himself lightly backwards and forwards. "You can just come over."

"Huh?" I started blankly at him, I must have misheard.

"You can come over," Ario repeated, a smile starting to spread on his face again.

I didn't know what to say to that. I was shocked. I mean, wait till the boys heard about that!

"You scared, Coral?" Ario smirked, pushing my seat so that I started to swing gently.

"Yes," I grinned, answering honestly.

"You'll be safe with me," he pushed my seat again, making me laugh and cling onto the chains on either side.

"Ario stop. Please," I cried which only made him laugh and hop off his seat to get behind me.

"Only if you say it in Spanish," he teased me, putting his hands on my back and pushing me harder.

"Come on," I pleaded, laughing as I was swung sky high. "I don't know any Spanish."

"Not good enough," Ario chuckled and pushed me even harder.

"Ario!" I shouted, genuinely afraid I was going to be flung off.

"Just look up," I heard him say. "It's pretty mesmerising."

I wasn't quite sure what he was talking about, but I looked up and saw the stars whirling by. It wasn't just mesmerising, it made me feel like I was flying.

"This is great," I cried.

"I know," Ario replied.

He continued to push me back and forth and I kept my head tilted back so that I could watch the brightly lit night sky.

"I'm getting a bit dizzy," I said, looking away from the spinning pricks of light. "Can you stop now?"

"*No hablo ingles*," came Ario's deep response.

"Yes you do speak English," I couldn't help but let out a little laugh. "Stop....*por favour*."

"Good," Ario exclaimed. "And you were saying you didn't know any Spanish."

He grabbed the bottom of my seat, pulling me to a stop and I smiled to myself.

"I don't really remember where that came from," I said honestly. "Most likely primary school, which was at least seven years ago."

"Credit to *Dora The Explorer*," Ario mocked me playfully, ruffling my hair.

I went to nudge him with my shoulder but as he was standing behind me, and I was still sitting on the swing, I miss calculated the force of my nudge and ended up falling backwards off the seat and knocking Ario to the ground.

"My stomach," he groaned beneath me.

"Oh yeah," I widened my eyes in alarm and rolled off him as I remembered Ario was still healing. "Are you okay?"

"I am," he winced. "Don't worry."

"Well you have to be, considering how much you've been laughing," I said, getting up to my feet and holding a hand out to him.

"You think you can lift me up?" he smirked. "One handed too?"

"Don't underestimate me," I only arched an eyebrow back at him, not knowing what crap I was speaking.

Ario didn't even take my hand. He moved swiftly and grabbed my legs which almost had me landing on my butt again.

"What are you doing?" I looked down at his brown haired head.

Ario lifted his face to look at me with his blue eyes, "Thanks for the knife. Again."

"You don't have to say it twice," I smiled, looking away before I got embarrassed. "You can let go of me now."

Ario let go of my legs and got up to his feet and brushed himself off.

"You're so small," he said.

"You're so big," I folded my arms in response.

We looked at each other and then grinned, neither of us wanting to be the first one to laugh again. Ario lost and cracked up.

"I think I'm drunk to be honest," he said to me with his eyes alight.

"Probably," I shrugged a shoulder, smirking at him.

"What do you mean probably?" Ario pushed my shoulder jokingly, making me laugh again. "You didn't even serve me tonight."

I didn't know how Ario was feeling at that very moment, but I felt like I'd found the sibling I'd always been looking for.

And it felt good.

"So when can I come round?" I asked him, picking up my bag.

Ario thought about it, "I don't know yet. But I can text you or something."

"Give me your phone," I said, holding my hand out. "I'll put my number in."

"I've been invited over."

The Simpson brothers blinked at me. Even Phoenix looked completely taken aback.

"You're going to their house?" Severn had to clarify. "Their actual home?"

"Yes," I said, sharing a grin. "It's a great step in the right direction."

"How?" Landon asked, sitting on the arm of Phoenix's seat.

"Well I said I wanted to know if the rumours about his gang were real or not, and he just said come over and basically see for myself," I said simply.

Walter scowled and started calling Ario all sorts of foul names.

He looked at me, fury still blazing in his eyes, "Coral if any of them put their hands on you, I swear..."

"I'll be okay," I said confidently, deciding not to mention Ario's word to keep me safe. It would only make Walter angrier.

"When are you going?" Phoenix questioned me.

"I er...I don't know yet," I said, avoiding his hard look. "But I'll know soon."

"I wish I could go with you," Walter grumbled, balling his hands into fists. "It could be a trap or something like that."

"They don't even know me," I tried to assure him. "I'm no threat to them."

"I still don't trust them," Walter said lowly.

I didn't blame him, they had been rivals for a long time.

"We can't risk following her there," Landon made a valid point. "If they spot us, not only will the whole operation be ruined, but she'll be in danger too."

"I'll call you if anything," I said, looking at Walter.

He didn't look like he wanted to settle for that, but he sighed, not having much of a choice, "Okay."

"You're really good at this Coral," Gomez grinned at me, getting to his feet. "I've never been anywhere close to their lair before."

"I'll send you a postcard," I joked.

"Bring back some Venezuelan food if you can, yeah?" Giovanni gave me the thumbs up.

When his brothers shot him looks of disgust, Gio only shrugged and scratched his hair, "I know it would be cooked by those stupid splinters....but I like Venezuelan food."

"Have you even tried Venezuelan food before?" Eli gave his brother another look.

"I'll see what I can do," I said quietly, sending Gio a sly smile.

He too stood up and grinned back.

"Is it time to go already?" Severn asked his brothers, rubbing his eyes.

"Yeah," Gomez was checking his phone. "It's ten."

"Where are you going?" I asked as the older boys started to rise too.

I wasn't told about anything.

"We have a fight," Walter said, coming over to me.

"Right now?" I gawked at him.

Walter nodded, "Every so often we arrange a fight. Tonight's one of those nights."

So all that time I was spending with Ario, laughing and hanging out, he was going to go out later that same evening to fight with the Simpsons?

"Don't look so worried Coral," Landon put his hand on my shoulder. "No guns allowed."

"That's a rule you two gangs agreed on?"

"Unfortunately yes," Eli said darkly as he passed me on his way upstairs.

"Knives, bats, chains, knuckle dusters," Gomez listed for me. "Anything but guns, you have to be up close and personal whilst fighting, and the guns make it unfair."

"Okay," I said, trying not to wince. "You can still do a lot of damage with things like that though."

"Oh trust me," Gomez started laughing. "We know."

"We *all* know," Landon smirked. "Every one of us has been in the hospital at least once, and those were just the really bad times. Phoenix has been shot over – "

"Just go and get your shit," Phoenix cut him off as he pushed past Landon.

Landon sent me an apologetic look which only had me wanting to know how many times Phoenix had been shot. I remembered seeing a lot of bullet wounds when he'd taken his top off after the snowball fight.

"Blue eyes is all mine tonight," Walter said to his brothers as he headed for the stairs.

"When are you two *not* all up in each other's faces?" Severn said sarcastically. "You two were made for each other."

"Don't say it like that," Walter shot him a dirty look. "I couldn't hate the guy more."

"*We know*," Landon and the triplets said in unison.

"So you're all going?" I followed Walter as he went up the stairs.

He looked really guilty for a second and rubbed the back of his neck, "Yeah..we won't be too long. Sorry."

"It's fine," I said quickly. "It's what you do."

I looked down so Walter that wouldn't be able to see the sadness in my eyes. What they did was so dangerous and I wouldn't be able to handle any of them getting seriously hurt.

"I'll be here," I said, sitting on the edge of his bed smiling. "Waiting."

"I'll be back before you know it," Walter said after making a pained face.

"Be safe," I said, wringing my hands together.

"I will," Walter rubbed my hair and kissed my forehead.

I lifted my head so that he could kiss me on the lips too and Walter didn't hesitate. We kissed for a short time as the boys were already set to go. Walter grabbed an aluminium bat he had leaning on the wall near his window, and I knew he had a couple of knives stashed in his pockets.

I got up to see them off.

"Don't open the door to anyone," Landon was telling me, waggling his finger in the air like I was a six year old child. "We have keys so we won't be knocking."

"Got it," I said dryly.

"There's some pizza in the fridge if you get hungry," Gio slapped my shoulder. "Pepperoni."

"Nice," I smiled, though I didn't really think I'd be able to eat whilst worrying about them.

"Why would you eat when you could just sleep?" Severn yawned, looking adorably innocent, nothing like a boy who was about to go and have a pretty rough gang fight.

"Sleep is good too," I commented, again knowing I wouldn't get any.

"See you later then," Eli said to me, being the first to leave through the door.

"Bye," I called after them until it was Walter left.

"Don't worry Coral," he smiled at me, stroking my cheek. "You try to rest, I'll try not to wake you when I get back."

I nodded, "Okay."

"Sleep well," Walter leaned down and kissed my cheek.

"Thank you," I replied and then with a final smile I watched him leave and close the door behind him.

I couldn't decide how I felt about Walter and Ario viciously fighting each other. I needed them both to be okay, but the fact that they hated each other so much didn't make things easier. In fact, thinking about how Ario would react, when he found out I was dating Walter, made me feel a little nauseous.

I just hoped that tonight, when it came to the two of them, there would be no clear winner.

25

I knew something was wrong as soon as I heard the boys return.

There were a lot of loud voices and someone was groaning. I got out of my bed in a hurry and ran down the stairs to see Eli and Walter laying out a large plastic sheet on the kitchen floor and Phoenix holding up a badly beaten Severn. But it was Giovanni who was bleeding.

"Gio," Landon said, slowly walking him to a chair in the kitchen with the support of Gomez. "Sit down."

Gio was moaning in pain, scrunching his face up as he was lowered gently into the chair. His blood dripped onto the plastic sheet that was spread on the floor and Landon gently tried to peel Gio's clothes off him.

"What happened?" I whispered.

Somehow Walter sensed my presence and he turned to face me with a worried face. He was holding me in an instant and I could feel his body trembling from the cold and probably also from adrenaline. I let go of him when I felt him wince.

"Are you okay?" I frowned, looking up into his bashed up face.

"My ribs," Walter gripped his side. "But don't worry about it. It's Severn and Gio who we have to worry about."

Despite Walter's injuries, it didn't seem like he had exactly 'lost' against Ario and although it made me relieved, I wondered if that meant Ario had suffered the worse hand.

"What can I help with?" I asked, putting on a grim face as I looked past Walter into the kitchen.

"I don't know," Walter looked distressed.

In the kitchen, Phoenix was wiping down Severn's bruised and bloody face with wipes and disinfectant. I could only imagine the pain Severn felt as the alcohol came into contact with his cuts. Eli was the one who let Severn hold onto him each time he needed to cry out in pain, and from the looks of it, Eli had a few scratches himself. His cheek was bleeding and it made me wonder which one of the Santiagos had given him that wound.

Landon had successfully removed Gio's shirt and I immediately felt light headed when I saw the bleeding wound in his side. Gomez was crouched down and talking to Gio, holding his face and forcing him to keep looking at him, to stay awake.

"Walter," Landon barked, turning to look at us over his shoulder. "Get me the kit."

Walter went to a cupboard in the corner of the kitchen and got out a first aid bag, quite like the one I had at my flat but a lot bigger and full of a a lot more than just plasters. I snapped out of my daze and went to the sink, filling up a cup of water and passing it to Gomez who was closest to me.

"Thanks," he looked up at me, rubbing sweat from out of his eye.

I filled cups for all the boys, except Severn who had fallen unconscious and Gio who wasn't able to drink. I don't know how long it took for Phoenix to clean Severn up or for Landon to *stitch* Gio's wound, but eventually it was done.

"So what happened?" I asked after the two boys had been put to bed.

Landon was washing blood off his hands in the sink and Gomez was plastering his cut knuckles. I was sitting next to Walter who was sitting at the dining table looking tired and Phoenix was drinking ice cold water. All of them had an array of busted lips, bruised eyes and cut cheeks. And that was only what you could see on their faces.

"Diego and the twins went at them," Landon said, "for how bad Severn got batty boy the last time."

"Batty boy?" I looked at him.

"Paulo," Landon reminded me.

"What did Severn do?" I asked in shock.

"He beat Paulo senseless," Gomez said, inspecting his plastered hands. "He didn't even use a weapon or anything, just his bare hands...and a knuckle duster."

I was astonished. Severn could do something like that?

"Why?" I had to ask.

"Does he need a reason?" Phoenix grunted, putting his empty glass down. "They're our enemies."

"But Severn doesn't strike me as the kind of person who would do that. Unless he was angry, but I don't know," I mumbled, looking down at my hands.

"Well you don't know him well enough then," Gomez muttered, grabbing a drink from the fridge. "I'm going up."

"Night," the boys muttered after him as he left the kitchen.

"I thought I knew Severn as the one who got angry the least easily," I murmured to myself, frowning at what Gomez had said.

"He just doesn't like Paulo," Landon shrugged. "He never has. It might be because they are both the youngest in each of the gangs, so there might be more competition? I don't know."

"It doesn't matter," Walter snapped. "Diego got involved when he shouldn't have. He stabbed Gio and knocked down Severn which gave the twins the chance to have their own back."

Walter cursed angrily and I sighed, running my hands through my hair. I wished none of this had to happen but it was their lifestyle and I had made the decision to jump on board.

Eli came down from upstairs in a fresh change of clothes and a tired expression.

"Are they sleeping?" Phoenix asked Eli.

"Yeah," Eli nodded his dark blond head. "Severn seems fine. Gio was sweating a little so I opened the window wider. Gomez is with them now. I'm going to bed."

215

Phoenix nodded, seeming satisfied and it made me admire the brotherly love they all had for each other throughout all of the drama.

"Goodnight," I said to Eli.

"Night," he replied, turning around and heading back up.

"I'll see you guys in the morning," Landon said rubbing his hair. "I need a long, hot shower."

"We don't need to know that," Walter said to him, making Landon smile before he left.

Phoenix walked past us and left the kitchen without a word, and Walter balled his hands into fists.

"Don't let him bother you," I soothed him quietly. "Are you going to get your ribs checked up on?"

"No," he gave me a half-smile. "I'll be okay in a couple weeks. I don't think they're even fractured or anything, just a bit sore."

I knew he was only playing his injuries down so as not to worry me so much, and I squeezed his hand.

"Let's go to bed," I said.

***

The next morning, the boys slept late. None of them went to school and I decided to stay home too. I sent Hayley a text saying I wouldn't be in and she replied asking if I was okay. I told her that I was fine and would talk to her soon, just to reassure her.

Sitting up in Walter's bed, I put my phone down and glanced over at him.

"How are Severn and Gio?" I asked Walter who was cleaning his knives on his bedroom floor with his back to me.

"I haven't seen them yet," he replied, not looking up as he wiped down the cold metal.

I knew better than to assume he hadn't seen his little brothers yet because he couldn't be bothered. Somehow I thought it was because he was afraid, afraid of finding out that they had gotten worse, especially Gio. I was surprised with Landon's skill to be able to cleanly close a stab wound like that. I would have panicked and taken him to hospital, but then again me and Landon were pretty different people.

"Do you want to go now?" I asked him, getting out of my bed and rubbing the top of his dark head.

Walter turned and looked up at me and I knew I had been right. There was worry in his eyes, but I was there to give him that push that he needed.

"Let's go," I put a hand on his shoulder. "It's almost eleven, they might be awake now."

"Okay," Walter got up to his feet, putting his knives on his bedside table behind him.

I knocked on the triplets' door and waited.

"They might be sleeping," I murmured to Walter who only smiled at me before pushing it open and walking right in.

Two days later and things had really improved. Severn was back to himself almost straight away. He had healing wounds on his face and sore ribs which made him slow, but he joked about it, saying that he already moved at a snail's pace anyway. Gio was walking around little by little and he was actually pleased about the scar that his stab wound would leave. The boys didn't seem so angry at Diego or any of the other Santiagos anymore which I found strange, but it was probably because they had hurt them just as bad, if not worse in the past.

I had just come back from my Saturday shift at the Dartfish and none of the Santiagos had been by. It was the day Ario and I had arranged that I come over and nervous was a massive understatement for how I was feeling.

I had been given spare keys to the house and let myself in. It was quiet, which I was coming to understand was normal for the weekend. I trudged up the stairs, wondering where Walter was, and was confused when I saw his room was empty. I put my bag down and walked to the bed where I found a piece of paper.

Picking it up, I smiled as soon as I read the first line.

My Coral,

I've never told you any of this stuff, but I hope you'll accept me writing it for you.

You are such a smart, beautiful and amazing person. From the moment I met you that night, I was hooked. I didn't even know you then, but I'm glad you let me get closer to you. Even now your smile still makes my stomach feel like it weighs nothing, and your laugh makes me warm inside. Really. I love it. I feel really strongly for you and I know I don't deserve you at all, but even so, it's 100% true when I say you make me content. (See. Content was the best word I could come up with. Even the dictionary doesn't have the words to describe how you make me feel.) But yeah, I'm falling so hard for you and I'll be there for you always.

Love Walter.

I had just finished reading when Walter came into his room. I would have sworn he'd planned it out like that, if it wasn't for the towel around his waist and his wide eyes when he saw what I had in my hands.

Walter blushed so hard.

"You weren't supposed to read that yet," he dropped his gaze. "I was going to put it under your pillow or in your bag or something. You were meant to read it when I wasn't there."

"Well you weren't," I grinned at him.

Walter still couldn't look at me and I couldn't stop smiling. He was so cute!

"Thank you Walter," I walked up to him and was going to hug him but stopped when he stepped back.

"I'm all wet," he looked down at himself.

Looking at the water droplets all over his gorgeous body made me want to hug him even more.

"I don't care," I said, throwing my arms around his neck.

I heard Walter laugh as he held onto me, lifting me off the ground. He smelt great and I loved the feel of our bodies pressing against each other. I told myself Walter was Walter, and *not* the monster of my past, nor would he ever be.

"You *do* deserve me," I said quietly, remembering the only thing that had made me sad in the letter. "Never say you don't."

Walter sighed, but he didn't let go of me, "Okay. I won't."

I wanted to say: I love you.

It felt so right, so natural, and not to mention the perfect timing, but I chickened out. I was also pretty scared of his reaction. Yeah, he'd said he had deep feelings for me...but that was on paper, and pretty different from saying the L word out loud like that. I imagined he was feeling the same way I was and I felt my stomach knot continuously. I pulled back from the hug and kissed him instead.

"You going to see Blue eyes soon?" Walter murmured after he'd set me down on my feet again.

"Yeah," I nodded. "He said he'd meet me at the playground."

Walter wasn't happy, but he knew it was beneficial for him and the gang to figure out what the Santiagos were doing.

"Take one of my knives," Walter said. "So if anyone tries anything - "

"But they might recognise it's yours," I said quickly, ignoring the fact that I'd never be able to harm anyone with a knife.

He sighed, "That's true."

"I'll be fine Walter," I smiled, cupping his face.

He couldn't help but return the smile.

"Be back before nine," he gave me another squeeze. "Just so I can relax."

"Okay," I agreed.

Walter and his brothers (namely Severn, Gomez and Landon) made sure I had long sleeves on, and they even tried to get me to wear multiple layers, but I told them I'd melt if I wore three jumpers on top of each other, despite it being late November.

"Don't forget your aim," Phoenix, who had been silent the whole time, finally spoke.

"Find out what they want with the Darfish," I said.

His gaze was so intimidating, I wasn't able to say that I didn't think I'd be able to find all of that out from the first visit, but I kept quiet.

"See you soon," Walter hugged me tight.

"See you," I kissed his cheek.

"And one for me?" Landon joked, tapping one of his cheeks.

"I'll bruise it for you, if you like," Walter threatened him with a smirk.

I laughed and waved at them, then I was off.

***

The Santiagos lived in a big, detached house on the very edge of our area. It was quite remote, the closest neighbours lived at least

219

a five minute walk away, making it as far East as East went for our part of London.

"You're lucky today," Ario said as he opened his front door. "All the boys are home."

Lucky? He must have been kidding me.

I caught a glimpse of his blithe smile and tried to relax. He would keep me safe if anything. I'd already told him I had to be home by nine and Ario joked about being bossed around by parents. I'd only laughed, imagining how normal it was for people to have parents to depend on. Little did he know that my situation was far from that.

Ario's fight with Walter seemed to have been a fair one, because Ario too had a few cuts and bruises and he was limping a little bit. I had asked him if he was okay, but he'd brushed it off with a joke.

He opened the door and I immediately heard Spanish music being played from somewhere inside. He limped in and I followed him, trying to push down the nerves that were rising.

"Want something to drink?" Ario turned to asked me over his shoulder.

I nodded with a smile, looking around.

The walls were painted with homely shades and I could smell something that was probably the Venezuelan food Giovanni had wanted me to bring back so much. The whole place, minus those who lived in it, seemed so relaxed and not as hostile as I'd thought it would be.

"I'll take you to the kitchen," Ario said, turning into the first room on the left.

I wasn't expecting to see the blockhea – I mean – the twins in there.

They stopped, halfway through their meals, and stared at me. I was silently praying that they didn't recognise me from all those weeks ago when they'd stopped me and Hayley, and tried to cut our eyelids off. It was a memory *I* wasn't going to forget anytime soon.

"Who is that?" Miguel, who had the scar on his chin, demanded at Ario.

Ario ignored his brother and went to the fridge to get me a drink, but the twins obviously weren't letting it drop.

"Why are you bringing *gringas* into our house?" Manuel asked, looking me up and down with a frown.

I remotely recalled that term being used to refer to people who weren't Hispanic and were therefore foreigners. I didn't know if it was meant to be rude, but his tone of voice had made it.

"Shut up, will you?" Ario cast him a dark look.

I dropped my gaze and looked at the floor, hoping Ario and I would leave the kitchen as soon as he had gotten me a drink.

"I think I recognise her," Manuel put his fork down and got off the high stool he was sitting on. "Miguel, isn't she one of the girls we saw in town, when we got into a little incident with the clones?"

Damn. They remembered me. I should have been more afraid than I was, but I was busy trying to figure out who the clones were. Surely he wasn't talking about the triplets?

"Oh yeah," Miguel nodded and stood up. "That damn bastard Gomez. I told them we wouldn't forget that, but then we did."

"Good thing we got them back in the last fight," Manuel grinned. "That felt really good."

I was surprised. The Simpsons weren't the only ones who had nicknames for their rival gang members. What 'til they heard about that!

Before I registered it, the twins were already heading towards me and I avoided their brown eyed gazes hoping that they wouldn't dare try to hurt me in front of Ario.

"I don't know what you are talking about," Ario said, stepping in front of them. "But she's a guest, my friend. So piss off."

I looked at Ario's back and saw his younger brothers scowl at me from over his shoulders. I was safe for now, but what about the next time when Ario wasn't there?

"If I hear that you've bothered her," Ario must have read my mind. "Then I'll deal with you."

"Yeah?" Miguel challenged him. "Deal with us how?"

Ario replied in Spanish and even though the twins didn't look fazed by what he was saying, after giving Ario a few snide responses, they turned their backs on me and went back to their food.

"Sorry about that. Let's go to the living room," Ario said to me, holding two cans of *Fanta* in his hand.

It turned out Paulo was already in the living room, watching TV. He looked completely relaxed and at ease, and would have been a perfect loungewear model if it wasn't for the bruises and the busted lip.

Paulo asked Ario something in Spanish and Ario replied. From what I could hear, it didn't sound like anything rude, but I did wish that I could speak Spanish too.

"Hey again," Paulo sent me a smile and I raised my eyebrows.

"Hi," I smiled, realising it was the first thing I'd said aloud since I'd entered the house.

"I didn't realise you and Ario were friends," Paulo said, rubbing his hair. "We don't normally bring people home, so this is just a surprise."

He probably meant 'outsiders' when he said people, and I was happy that he didn't want to possibly offend me.

"What are you watching?" I turned to the TV, opening my can and taking a swig.

"Discovery channel," Paulo looked embarrassed. "It's something about the Amazon."

I liked watching animal and plant documentaries and didn't judge him for liking it too.

"Does the Amazon cover Venezuela?" I asked them. "I know it covers a lot of Brazil, but that's as far as my Primary school knowledge goes."

"It does indeed," Paulo nodded. "I'd say about half of Venezuela is Amazon rainforest."

"Half?" I arched my brows. "I didn't know that."

"Yeah, neither did I," Ario frowned at his brother.

"Maybe you shouldn't have quit school when you were a foetus," Paulo smirked at him.

"I was sixteen," Ario corrected. "That's a decent age. They just didn't teach us shit about Venezuela."

"It's our country," Paulo said, gazing at the TV. "You shouldn't need to be taught about it. Look for the information yourself. That's what I did, and I was basically a baby when we left."

"Good for you," Ario sunk deeper into the sofa, watching the TV with a childish sulky expression on his face.

"So you were born over there?" I asked Paulo.

"Yeah," he nodded. "I thought everyone knew that about us."

"Yeah, but how much of the rumours are actually true?" I raised the question.

"Fair enough," he replied.

We talked a little bit about Venezuela and its history, and I had to admit Paulo knew a lot about the politics of his country of origin, a lot more than I knew about mine, and I was three years older than him. He didn't mention anything personal about his past and I didn't ask.

"So you don't plan on quitting school when you're sixteen?" I asked him with a grin.

"I barely go as it is," he surprised me by saying. "I hate the teachers telling me what to do, and the other kids are scared of me and my older brothers and cousins. I can do without all that shit."

"Oh, well that's fair enough," I said. "But you seem to like learning new things, so when you do go, try to look over that and think about the learning."

Paulo scoffed and rubbed his brown hair, "Sure. I'll try that."

I sent him a smile and then caught Ario's sapphire eyes.

"What?" I gave him a confused look.

"Did you intentionally choose a subject of conversation that bores me?" he said to the two of us flatly.

"Oh shut up man," Paulo laughed. "You should care about our homeland."

"I do care," Ario muttered, frowning to himself. "I just don't wanna talk about it."

To me, it seemed like Ario didn't like thinking about it where he came from and the fragmented country he had left behind, not that it bored him. But that was just an observation.

We all looked up to the door when we heard laughter. I noticed that the music had stopped playing and now I could hear voices, and I recognised Diego's. He was talking to girls, I heard their high-pitched giggles and even though I didn't understand what they were talking about as they came down the stairs, I knew it was vulgar. I didn't want to think about what sounds the music had been drowning out earlier.

After seeing whoever it was off at the door, Diego's footsteps headed our way and I wanted him to turn into the kitchen so bad, but he didn't.

"Waitress," Diego's eyes homed in on me immediately.

He stood in the doorway, only in some trousers and a vest that showed his hairy chest and defined arms. He didn't have many cuts on his face, but he had one of his hands plastered up and I was happy to see that at least one of the Simpsons had gotten at him for stabbing Gio.

"Why are you here?" Diego looked me up and down in a way that had my skin crawling.

"Because I said she can," Ario said to him before I could answer, not that I would have said a word to him anyway.

Diego smiled in an unsettling way, "You sleeping with her?"

Whereas I flamed up red, Ario didn't even blink, "There's more to life than sex, you know."

"Okay," Diego held up his hands. "I hear you. That means that she's available for me to grab."

That, Ario didn't take so lightly, and he shot up out of his seat in the sofa in a flash to face Diego, defending me. The two argued in Spanish and it was the first time I'd seen Ario seriously angry.

It felt so guilty.

I was lying to him. If he found out I was working for the Simpsons, let alone going out with Walter Simpson, I doubt he'd be cool with it.

"Would you like me to translate?" Paulo leaned over the arm of his chair to ask me with a grin.

"Um..nah, I'd rather not know what he's saying," I replied.

"Good answer," Paulo said, looking over at Diego and calling out something to him.

Diego gave Paulo the finger and then pushed Ario back before leaving, still angry. Ario sat down in the sofa, muttering curses under his breath and then he sighed deeply.

"I guess it's time for you to see Carlos now," he said to me.

"What?" I widened my eyes.

Since when was that part of the agenda?

"You said you wanted to know more about our gang and I'm not sure how much I should tell you, so he's the man to ask," Ario explained.

"Okay, sure," I said, trying to ignore the several beats my heart skipped.

"I'll take you to his office," Ario stood up.

"If he's busy then it's fine," I started, but Ario cut me off with a shake of his head.

"He's not busy," he said. "He just goes there to get peace and quiet."

"Okay," I squeaked and then glanced at Paulo who was still slouched in the sofa.

"Later," he smirked at me.

"See you," I replied.

"Don't be scared," Ario said as he led me out of the living room and to the office. "Carlos is usually chill."

"*Usually*," I repeated with emphasis.

Ario laughed lightly, "You'll be fine, I'll come and get you so that you can get home before nine."

"Okay," I said, breathing deeply.

Ario stopped in front of a closed door. "Want me to introduce you?"

"Yeah, please," I said breathlessly.

"Relax," Ario laughed again. "Seriously, Carlos is alright."

But he was still a gang leader, and with other people no doubt working for him, he had respect which could only be gained through power...and most probably fear.

Ario had knocked on the door before I had prepared myself and I looked up sharply at him.

"What?" he looked at me blankly. "You were taking your time and I really need to pee."

I didn't have time to answer when I heard Carlos call a 'come in'.

"Come on then," Ario said, grinning at me and I took a nervous breath before following him in.

225

26

Carlos was sitting behind a black desk, wearing a shirt that was unbuttoned to midway down his chest. He raised his thick eyebrows when he saw me and I looked down at the floor.

"Hey, I didn't think you'd be busy, so I came to make introductions. This is my friend Coral," Ario said, nudging me so that I would look up.

"Hi Coral," Carlos smiled at me and I swallowed hard.

"Hello," I replied quietly, wishing I could be more confident.

"Don't be shy," Ario smiled at me.

"Easier said than done," I whispered back.

He chuckled quietly, then walked up to Carlos and said something to him in Spanish. Carlos murmured back, his eyes on me the whole time.

"Come sit down," Carlos said to me. "I would offer you a drink, but you haven't finished that can yet, have you?"

"No," I said in a dry voice, walking forwards and sitting on a chair opposite him.

"I'll see you later," Ario said, touching my shoulder as he left.

I wanted him to stay so badly but I knew I couldn't show even more weakness by asking him in front of Carlos. And besides, he needed to pee.

"Okay," I said instead.

As soon as Ario closed the door behind him, I felt my palms starting to tingle as they began to sweat. I looked up when Carlos got out of his seat and walked to a table on the other side of the office.

"I see Phoenix is getting unsettled," he said as he poured himself a glass of water, "now that he's getting little girls to do his work for him."

My jaw dropped. I couldn't even mask my shock.

I knew if I even attempted to deny being involved with the Simpsons, I would only make a fool of myself. Carlos knew.

"I'm not little," was all I could think of saying.

Carlos turned to look at me with an amused smile, "How old are you?"

"Eighteen," I answered.

"Ario's age," he murmured. "That's little."

"How old are you?" I took a sip of my drink, hoping he didn't notice my trembling hand.

"Twenty three," he walked back to his seat with his glass in hand.

"Are you going to tell Ario?" I blurted, unable to continue ignoring the pressing question that had been burning in my mind as soon as Carlos had called me out. Then something even worse dawned on me. "Or does he already know?"

Carlos took a drink, "He doesn't know and he won't find out from me, so don't worry. It will teach him a lesson, not to let a pretty face fool him."

I bowed my head although I was having very mixed emotions, "Thanks."

"You do realise he will find out eventually," Carlos arched a brow at me.

I nodded, "I know."

"Good that you know," he said. "So what does Phoenix want from me?"

"He...he just wants to know why you have a sudden interest in the Dartfish pub," I said, knowing there was no other way to explain it without Carlos calling out a lie.

227

"I know they work for him," Carlos shocked me again. "So there's no need to be afraid of letting that out."

"How do you know all this?" I looked at him in disbelief.

"As highly as he thinks of himself, Phoenix is predictable," Carlos smirked. "Sending a girl here to try and get information out of us? I bet even the twins would have seen through that. And Ario? Well like I said, he'll learn his lesson when he finds out the truth."

I dropped my gaze, feeling terrible and a little bit nauseous.

"So what should I say to Phoenix?" I knotted my fingers together in unease.

Carlos rubbed his stubble as he smiled to himself, "Tell him...tell him it's finally come to the end of our little fun and games."

Even though I didn't completely understand what Carlos was getting at, this sounded bad.

"That's all," Carlos smiled at me.

"O-okay," I got up stiffly, still holding my can of drink. "Thanks for...having me."

I turned and started to walk out of the office when I thought to ask Carlos something, knowing this was probably my only opportunity to get an answer.

"Can I...can I ask you a question?" I spun around and said to him.

Carlos looked curious, "Depends on what it is."

"Oh, right," I said, rubbing my wrist. "Well I just wanted to know why you seem to know Phoenix so well? Could it be that you were...I don't know, maybe friends in the past?"

A smile stretched across his face, "Somewhat, yes."

That was as far as I was going to get with that, so I thanked him again and let myself out.

***

Phoenix was pissed.

Not that I expected otherwise. Carlos had not just called him out about me spying, but also with Phoenix using the Dartfish to distribute his drugs. He sat in an armchair in the living room, shaking his head to himself as he muttered under his breath. Landon

228

was sitting on the floor, also with a serious expression on his face and I sat next to Walter who was silent.

Eli and the triplets weren't present when I'd gotten home. So much for Gio getting his Venezuelan dinner. I decided to leave the container of rice, beef and beans in the kitchen for him.

"So what does Carlos mean when he says it's the end of your fun and games?" I asked quietly, interrupting the silence.

"He's *implying* that we are no longer going to run in this area. That there won't be any more fighting over whose territory is whose," Phoenix grumbled, "that the Santiagos are going to take total control."

I blinked, "Can they even do that?"

"They can try," Walter said through a clenched jaw.

"What I'm thinking," Landon said as he fiddled with his lip piercing, "is that something must be happening if they sense a change is gonna come. Something we don't know about."

"Like what?" Walter snapped.

"I don't know," Landon said. "But it's clear that Carlos doesn't call the shots, he takes his orders from above."

"Really?" I raised my brows, unable to imagine anyone giving Carlos 'orders'.

"That's what we think," Phoenix said.

"So where is this...shot-caller?" I questioned.

"Prison, most likely," Phoenix answered, rubbing his stubble. "So maybe they're getting out soon."

"What?" Walter growled. "And so they think they can take control of *our* businesses that we worked so hard to establish?"

"That will never happen," Phoenix said firmly. "I'll deal with it. Coral...your work is done, even though Carlos had already worked me out, it wasn't your fault, he probably knew before you got involved."

"That's how he made it sound," I commented.

Phoenix nodded, clenching his jaw.

"Um...he also said that you two had been somewhat friends," I said in a hushed voice. "What did he mean by that?"

Landon looked over at me and Walter was still. I immediately felt a rock drop in my stomach. Perhaps that had been something I shouldn't have asked about.

"We are *not* friends," Phoenix said lowly. "We never were."

"You kind of were," Landon mumbled.

"If you count unsuccessfully trying to work together, a *friendship*, then fine," Phoenix cast him an angry look. "But I don't."

Carlos and Phoenix had tried to work together? Under what circumstances!

"You remember that time I told you a bit about 'the history' of our gang?" Landon said to me.

"Yeah," I replied, recalling the time Landon had come to my flat during the time Walter and I had not been speaking.

"Well do you also remember when I told you about the time when Phoenix was working as a delivery boy for another gang that used to function near here?" Landon tried to jog my memory.

I nodded. Of course I did. Phoenix had left that gang and it hadn't been long after when the members had been bust and imprisoned. After that was when Phoenix first began to form the gang he had now.

"Carlos had been in that gang too," Landon shocked me. "He was also a delivery boy. The two of them planned to work together to form a new gang after they both left the old one, but it didn't work out and well...each of them basically formed what we have now. The Santiago Splinters and the Simpson Snakes. Rival gangs."

It made sense once he'd said it, but no way would I have ever guessed a story like that ever even existed.

"Bet you weren't expecting that," Landon grinned at me after seeing my mind-blown expression.

I shook my head in silence, then I risked a glance at Phoenix himself to was looking right at me with a hard face.

"Well," Phoenix said, making me look down. "Good job. You've done all I've asked for you to do, for now."

I nodded, "It's okay."

Phoenix then got up and left the living room. It was like a king departing from a room of his subjects.

Walter sighed beside me and checked his phone.

"Gio says we should go join them at the pizza place," Walter read a text message. "You wanna go?"

"I'm meeting someone," Landon said, still sitting on the floor and looking into space.

"I wasn't asking you anyway," Walter sent a dirty look to the back of his head and then turned his attention to me. "You're hungry aren't you?"

"Yeah," I nodded. "I did actually manage to bring back some Venezuelan food, but Gio clearly didn't have enough faith in me."

Walter chuckled, "Or he's just a greedy shit and wanted to eat both pizza and Spanish tonight."

I shrugged, "That's also a possibility."

Walter smiled and got up to his feet. I knew he was trying to take our minds of the gang stuff. Phoenix said he'd sort it out, but it was still weighing on my mind so of course it would be even heavier on Walter's, Landon's and the other boys once they heard. Phoenix had the most pressure of all, deciding to figure out what to do next, how to plan for the Santiagos' next move. I could see Landon giving him sound advice, but Landon wasn't always around when Phoenix needed him, for instance right now, he was going out for another date.

"You ready?" Walter asked me.

"Yep," I said, really starting to feel the hunger now. "Landon, do you want us to bring you back anything?"

Landon looked up at us as if he was coming out of a daze with a chilled smile on his face, "Nah, I'll be dining on something else tonight."

Walter swore at him and called him something dirty and I blushed, giving Landon a wave and heading for the front door with Walter right behind me as Landon chuckled to himself.

We stepped outside and Walter grabbed my hand, making me smile up at him. He gave me a little smile in return whilst not completely catching my eye. I loved it when he got shy like that, it was so sweet.

"What are you thinking about?" I asked him.

Walter looked down at the floor as we walked hand in hand, "I just was actually just thinking about going for another date. Forget Eli and the triplets, let's do our own thing."

"Walter," I laughed. "That's cheeky of you."

"They wouldn't mind," he shrugged. "Eli would probably love it if I didn't join them."

"Don't say that," I scolded him. "Why do you and Eli always seem to have some sort of...thing between you?"

"He's incredibly annoying, maybe?" Walter suggested.

"So does that make you annoying from his point of view?" I smirked at him.

"No," Walter smirked back. "I get angry quickly, but I'm not annoying like he is. He's always so snide and quick to start fights. I know I start fights too, but with him...it's just different."

"Why do you think that is?" I frowned slightly, looking at the dirty slabs of pavement that we walked over.

Walter sighed, "I have no idea. He's just like that."

I thought for a little bit and then raised my head, "You know, I talked to him for a little bit one time. He told me that he didn't really like being the middle child. So that probably has something to do with it. He might feel ignored."

Walter made a flat expression, "Eli makes sure he's never ignored by starting shit with anyone."

"Walter," I groaned. "You're not getting what I'm saying."

"No," he squeezed my hand gently and then lowered his voice. "I am. I just....I don't really talk to him about personal things. I don't talk to any of my brothers about personal things...except maybe Landon...sometimes."

"That's fair enough," I squeezed his hand back. "You'll get there bit by bit if you try."

Walter scoffed, "Sure."

"Hey," I gave him a look.

Walter smiled warmly at me, "*Okay*, I will."

"Good," I smiled back.

It didn't take much longer to reach the shopping complex where we would find Eli and the triplets at the pizza place. It was strangely nice walking with Walter in the night and I was smiling like a fool as I held onto his warm, gentle hand.

That was until Ario Santiago stepped out of a store onto the street a couple paces ahead of us.

I didn't even notice until Walter stiffened and I looked up. Ario was looking right at us, his blue eyes wide and utter disbelief on his face. I couldn't even imagine all the thoughts whirling around in his head as he saw that I had been involved with Walter Simpson from the very beginning.

Walter gripped my hand tighter as anger fired up within him and I did the same to him, in an attempt to stop him going after Ario.

"What are you looking at?" Walter snarled at him.

Ario didn't reply, he just looked at me with an expression that made me want to disappear into thin air, then he turned and walked off.

"Is he going to come back?" I looked up at Walter with wide eyes.

"I don't know," Walter was trying to stay calm by taking deeper breaths. "We need to go home, you're no longer safe."

"Right now?" I asked him. "But we didn't find Eli and – "

"It doesn't matter," Walter cut me off, his hazel eyes searching the streets as passerbys strolled past us. "You're not safe anymore."

"Okay," I swallowed, unable to get Ario's expression out of my head.

Walter turned us around, continuing to take cautious glances over his shoulder.

"I didn't want to make him so upset," I said to myself, as Walter reached into his pocket for his phone, or a knife.

He froze when I said that.

"Why do you think Blue eyes and I hate each other's guts so much?" Walter asked with a grim look on his face. "It's because we are both more similar to each other than we'd like to admit."

I frowned at Walter, unable to get where he was going with this.

"What I'm saying is," Walter looked at me. "Ario doesn't *do* upset, he does furious."

27

Walter and I walked fast back the way we came. For all we knew, Ario could have been gathering his gang to come after us right at that moment. We would be safe not just in Simpson territory, but in the Simpson household itself. That was one place the Santiagos wouldn't dare get close.

"You guys need to get here now Eli," Walter barked on his phone as he gripped my hand with his free one. "...Forget the bill, since when did you care if you've paid or not? ...If it's that much of a problem, just leave the money on the table. I...I need you. Now."

Walter cut off and put his phone back in his pocket.

"They should be coming soon," Walter told me. "In case the Santiagos are after us. I can't fight and protect you at the same time, not if there's more than one of them."

"I hope it doesn't come to that," I said, too scared to even glance behind me.

I never thought for one second that Ario would find out the truth so soon. I could barely even register what had just happened. Everything had changed, in a single second. Ario, who I had considered a friend, was now an enemy.

He hated me.

When Eli and triplets arrived, they made me feel a bit relaxed, even though the situation hadn't changed. It was just so hard to be shit scared when the triplets were so excited. They formed a protective shield around me, laughing and joking all the while, as well as making playful threats towards 'Skull face' and the others. Walter didn't share the same enthusiasm, he was grim faced and held my hand in a tight grip.

"Did Blue eyes say anything?" Eli asked me, looking straight ahead as he walked on my other side.

"No," I winced. "He said nothing."

Eli looked over my head at Walter and I didn't need to ask them what it meant. It was very clearly: not good.

"Are you going to fight?" I asked the boys in a worried voice.

It was the last thing I wanted, especially with Walter's ribs and Gio's healing wound.

"If they come after us, yes," Walter grunted. "But if not, it will be another day. Blue eyes won't let it rest without a confrontation."

"And by confrontation," Gomez turned to grin at me as he walked backwards. "He means a pretty good fight."

"But you just had one," I said in dismay.

"It's okay," Walter said to me.

"Relax," Severn smirked at me, throwing at arm around Gio's shoulders. "We got this."

Eli rolled his eyes at them and I tried to take the whole situation lightly, like they were doing. Impossible. I knew it was only a matter of time until Ario responded, and I got his message loud and clear.

The Santiagos didn't show.

It was what I had wanted, but it meant I'd be carrying the fear for day after day until Ario gave me what I deserved. Whatever that *was*. He wouldn't really hurt me, would he? I thought I knew him well enough, but when Walter had told me about Ario's temper, I was taken aback. I realised then, that I couldn't guarantee my safety.

The triplets had gone upstairs, talking in disappointed voices about how they didn't get to fight the Santiagos and Eli sent me a goodnight before going up to his own room.

I was still shaking, half from the cold but probably more from the fear of what was going to come next. Walter made me a cup of tea and he sat with me in the kitchen until I finished it. It calmed me considerably and I took one long deep breath.

"You want to shower before we go to bed?" Walter stood up, holding my hand.

I nodded silently and fell into his chest, trying not to cry. I was upset, scared and confused. I wished that I knew what Ario was thinking. Whether he was planning to attack, or if he was alone and hurt more than anything.

"Walter, I'm scared," I closed my eyes.

Walter held me close, kissing the top of my head, "I've got you. I won't ever let any of them hurt you Coral."

I knew he meant it. I could feel it from the way his heart was pounding.

I had a hot shower and washed my hair too, just to try and feel that little better. Walter was in his room waiting for me to finish so that he could go and have a shower and when he saw me enter only in my towel, his eyes filled with desire.

He wordlessly got up from his bed and approached me. He held a strand of my damp hair in his fingers and then looked down at the water droplets that ran along my collarbones and down past my towel. I felt my cheeks getting warm and my palms starting to tingle. My stomach started to feel light and I didn't understand why my body was acting so strange because of a look Walter had given me. It wasn't as if I'd be able to venture any further with him if I wanted to, I was shameful.

"I'll let you get dressed," Walter glanced up at me and smiled, before he left to go to the bathroom.

I knew he was taking things slow because of me, and he still didn't know the full story. He'd never directly asked me...the same way I hadn't directly asked him about the tattoo on his hip, which still played on my mind every now and then.

When Walter returned, I had already changed into some pyjamas as well as half-dried my hair with my hairdryer. I sat on the edge of his bed, facing away from him as he stripped and got into some boxers and a t-shirt. He crawled onto the bed behind me and kissed the back of my neck when he was finished. I turned and faced him, before kissing him hard on the lips, putting in all my emotions, knowing that Walter was the only one who could have my heart, despite the guilt I was feeling towards Ario. He had become a brother to me, but I knew better than to think I'd been nothing more than a sister to him.

Walter broke off the kiss, breathing raggedly against my lips.

"Don't worry him," he said huskily to me.

I nodded, "I don't want to talk about him right now. I...I want to know more about you Walter."

Walter raised his brows for a second, before smiling softly at me. I'm sure there were still plenty of things I didn't know about him.

"Let's get comfy," he said to me, getting out of his bed to turn his light off so that the room was dimly illuminated by his desk lamps.

I got in under the sheets and Walter slid in beside me, letting me lean on his chest as he held me close to him with his arm.

"What should I tell you about myself?" Walter murmured to himself under his breath with a faint smile on his face.

"Anything," I put a hand on his solid chest through his shirt.

Walter looked up at the ceiling and then his eyes seemed to change. They shone for a brief moment before he turned his face down to look at me.

"When I was growing up, back in central London, there were eight of us," he said, making me widen my eyes in disbelief.

Eight Simpson brothers?! *Were*. I refused to believe where Walter was going, and desperately hoped that the last sibling simply lived somewhere else even I knew it wasn't the case. If anything, they would have all stayed together, at least for now.

"My sister Eunice died when she was eight," Walter said gently, playing with my fingertips in his hand. "I was a year older than her...she was Eli's twin."

I gasped, unable to contain the mountain of shock that came with those two sentences alone. Maybe that was why Eli was so bipolar sometimes, because he'd lost a twin sister. Eunice Simpson. E.S.

"Your tattoo," I whispered. "It's for her."

"Yeah," Walter smiled, despite the crack in his voice. "It's for her."

"I'm sorry Walter," I said to him. "I had no idea."

"It's not your fault," Walter hugged me, burying his face in my hair.

When I heard Walter sniffing, I widened my eyes before almost breaking down and crying myself. Instead I pressed my trembling lips together and tried to be the strong one, as I rubbed Walter's dark hair.

"Sorry, Coral," he mumbled over my shoulder. "I'm eighteen years old...this is pathetic of me."

"No," I said sharply, gripping his hair. "No Walter. It doesn't matter how old you are, you can cry if you have to. I can't imagine what you've been through. It's not pathetic at all."

He laughed whilst crying and I felt my heart swell with so much love and emotion for him. I wanted him to stop hurting, I wanted to make him feel okay.

Walter pulled back and rubbed his eyes with the back of his hand. I wondered what Eunice had looked like. If she had dark hair like Phoenix, Landon and Walter, or blonde hair like Eli and the triplets? What had she been like? A joker just like her youngest brothers? Or more serious and reserved like her eldest one?

"What was she like?" I asked him quietly.

Walter smiled again, looking up at the ceiling once more.

"She was so friendly," he said fondly. "She never really got angry, even though we teased her all the time...well all of us except Eli. She was the only girl so we loved to try to rile her up, but Eli would always defend her, fight for her even when she wasn't bothered about it. I guess he misses her a lot. They shared a lot of secrets, I could hear them whispering at night all the time."

I smiled along with Walter at the cute childhood memories. Eunice had been a lucky girl, having so many good brothers.

"What did she look like?"

"Like Eli," Walter answered. "Even though they were different genders, they had the same eyes, same hair, same smile. Basically everything."

"Wow," I breathed, wishing that I'd gotten the chance to meet the only Simpson sister. "I bet she was a lucky girl to be loved by so many brothers."

Walter half-smiled, "Yeah, I guess. I know it's childish but...I wish...I wish she never had to go. She was only here for a short time, there was so much more she could have done. Stuff we could have all done together."

"Oh Walter," I looked at him. "It's not childish."

He had tears in his eyes but he kept smiling, being so strong.

I gently cupped his face and kissed his right cheek and then his left one, before kissing his forehead and finally his lips.

"She's in a good, safe and happy place," I said softly. "That's what I believe."

He nodded, chewing on his bottom lip.

"Enough about me," Walter said eventually, after he was certain he wasn't going to cry again. "Tell me something I don't know about you."

Walter had been so open with me, about something so deep, personal and painful. I felt like I was finally ready to do the same.

"I've told you a bit about my childhood," I said, recalling the first date we'd had in the cafe a while back. "But this time I'll tell you all of it."

Walter looked at me silently, knowing I was about to tell him about the horrible things that kept me up at night. He held my hand and that small gesture gave me the courage to go ahead with it.

"My mum died when I was three years old," I said, looking down at our entwined fingers. "I was in social care until I was seven when I was adopted by my father, who I'd never met, who turned out to be a...very horrible person. He....he..."

I broke off, swallowing as I tried to moisten my suddenly dry throat as well as push down the sickening memories that were trying to arise.

"It's okay Coral," Walter rubbed my hand with his thumb. "You can do it. I'm here."

I nodded and took a breath before continuing. "He abused me for years...he said I couldn't tell anyone because they wouldn't believe me, and if I ever did, he said he'd kill me. I don't know why I was scared of death, I mean, surely it was better than the living hell I was going through."

239

Walter made such a pained expression when I said that, I almost wished that I hadn't added that last part. I quickly kept going.

"I don't remember a lot," I said, "but it comes back to me in my dreams. One thing I can't ever forget is his smell. Some sort of aftershave he always wore, I think. It was very distinct."

Walter was plain disgusted, he wasn't angry at all. He was holding my hand so tight, I didn't think he'd even noticed he was doing it.

I gave him a wobbly smile to try and put him at ease, "It went on until I was ten, and then one day out of the blue, he just didn't come back home. So I stayed on my own for a couple of days and was picked up by the social services again when I started a small fire whilst trying to cook on the stove. I was in care for six years, which wasn't exactly a sanctuary either, and it was when I was sixteen that I got my job and moved into my little flat. I've been there ever since, barely scraping by, until I met you...and things changed. And that's it. That's my childhood."

Walter blinked a couple of times, the anger starting to show in his features as he continued to grip my hand in his.

"You're stronger than you think Coral," Walter told me firmly. "You've been through a lot of things other people wouldn't have been able to survive. You kept going, and for that, I'm proud of you."

"Thank you Walter," I said, looking into his hazel eyes. "You've made me very happy."

Walter's face split into a smile, "You have too."

He suddenly dropped the smile and his gaze, then started blushing. I knew what he was going to say before he said it, and even then, I still couldn't believe my ears when Walter confessed.

"I love you," he said, looking into my eyes at the last second.

He looked so nervous, I wanted to squeeze the life out of him. I grinned and my eyes stupidly decided to fill with tears. I wiped at them quickly and Walter smiled, caressing my face.

"I love you too," I said quietly, my voice breaking.

Walter pulled me into his arms and he held me in a warm, safe embrace. I was happy. So inexplicably happy.

28

"It's trashed," I said, devastated. "All of it, ruined."

Walter and I stood outside the mess of what my flat used to be.

In my bedroom, my curtains had been slashed into shreds and so had my pillows and duvet. The Santiagos had ripped the stuffing out so that it was dispersed all over the house like little fluffy clouds. The word 'PUTA' had been carved into the headboard with such force that I didn't even care what it translated as, the hate that I picked up from it alone, made me afraid.

In the kitchen, every single one of my plates, bowls and mugs had been smashed to pieces and lay all over the floor like a frenzy of sharks' teeth. The eggs in my fridge were now half dried on the walls and on top of all that, they'd also stuffed the sink with tissue and left the tap on so that water had overflowed onto the floor. Walter had made me stay by the doorway whilst he went and turned the tap off, his shoulders stiff with anger and his shoes making the water ripple.

My tiny living room was destroyed, my little sofa torn up, no doubt with the use of their knives. My small TV had been smashed beyond recognition and lay discarded, off its stand and on its side.

As soon as we'd entered my bathroom, Walter told me to cover my nose. I didn't realise why until I saw the piss all over the floor and almost retched in my mouth. My bottles of perfume had been emptied into the sink and my toothpaste was squirted all over the walls.

Upset was an understatement. I was shattered.

I tried to imagine how different the whole situation would have been if I had been present in my home at the time the Santiagos broke in. It was a very frightening thought indeed. It had definitely been more than just Ario who'd trashed the place, but the thought of him being in the lead, hurt. I hoped it had made himself feel better.

"We need to take you away for at least the weekend, maybe longer," Walter said in a clipped voice as we stood outside my flat.

To be honest, I was surprised by how well he'd kept his temper in check.

"I'm not arguing with that," I said to him, sighing. "I really pissed him off."

"He's more pissed off with *me* than anyone else," Walter touched my shoulder, as if that was an assurance.

"Let's just go home," I said to him, leaning into his side. "I'll give my landlord a notice that I'm moving out."

"I'll help with the rent until that's sorted out," Walter said to me.

"Walter, I've been managing with the rent for two years, its fine," I gave him a smile. "Let's go."

"Alright," he said, mirroring my expression.

We walked down the flight of stairs and let ourselves out of the building and into the cold wintery afternoon. We'd come here straight after school, as it was on the way to Walter's house and he'd had the smart idea to check to see if the Santiagos had played any moves yet.

And they certainly had.

Walter and I had only taken a few steps when I felt myself being roughly grabbed by my elbows from behind and ripped away from him. Walter barely had time to turn to me before Ario had hit him right in the jaw.

"No, stop!" I cried quickly before things got out of hand.

Walter must have been hit hard because he fell onto his hands and knees and struggled to get back up. Ario stood over him, holding his knife – the one I'd returned to him – in his hand. Diego was walking around Walter, grinning and laughing as he insulted him in Spanish and Miguel stood to the side, watching with a straight face.

"Don't let her go Manuel," Miguel said to his twin brother.

"She can try," Manuel chuckled cruelly from behind me.

I searched for Paulo, hoping he'd be sane enough to try and talk sense into his brothers and cousin Diego, but Paulo wasn't there and neither was Carlos. The only two slightly calm ones were nowhere to be seen.

Ario, Diego and the twins had waited for us in an ambush. They must have known I'd come back sometime and what was even better for them, was that Walter was there too. Why hadn't I considered that this could have happened?!

"You're trespassing," Walter only muttered to them, spitting blood out of his mouth.

"So?" Miguel barked at him. "Are you going to shoot us? Where's your gun?"

"Walter," Ario grabbed a fistful of his hair and yanked his head up so that Walter was in a kneeling position. "You knew all along? I bet you were all smug as you got your girl to use me, to get information on us."

Walter didn't say a word. He tried to look at me from the corner of his eye but Ario wouldn't let him so much as turn his head an inch in my direction.

"What are you going to do?" Ario held Walter's chin firmly and snarled in his ear. "I could kill you right now....I could kill the bitch too."

I couldn't stop the gasp that escaped my mouth. Ario was behaving in a way I'd never imagined he could behave. Walter didn't seem fazed, Blue eyes must have been like this a lot when he was faced with his enemies...and now I was one of them.

"Stop with the small talk and bash his face already," Diego urged his younger cousin on with a menacing grin.

"Don't rush me Diego," Ario scowled at him.

"Then let me rough him up a litt – "

243

"No. He's all mine," Ario cut him off and held his knife to Walter's cheek.

"Ario please," I pleaded. "I'm sorry, I really am. Please don't hurt him."

Ario looked at me properly for the first time and I saw a whole mixture of emotions in his blue eyes. I was hoping that I could get through to him, hoping that even though he was angry, he wouldn't take things too far.

"Asking on his behalf makes me sick Coral," Ario said blankly. "You should know that."

I tried to pull myself out of Manuel's grip which only caused him to hold me even tighter, if that was possible. I hissed in pain and that caused Walter to shove Ario out of the way with his shoulder, before rising up to his feet.

"Don't you touch her," Walter aimed a deathly glare at Manuel.

Diego laughed and punched Walter right in the side where his ribs were healing. Walter dropped to one knee, groaning as he breathed with difficulty.

"Let go of me, please," I tried begging quietly to Manuel.

"Why would I do that?" he scoffed. "Just shut up and watch your boyfriend take what he deserves."

"Come on Ario," I looked at him instead. "Tell him to let go of me. I'm not going to run. Not without Walter, and you know he would never run away from this."

Ario glared at me for a few moments and then he finally sighed and nodded at Manuel who released me with a push forwards.

"Don't think about doing anything stupid like calling the police," Diego spoke as he waved his knife at me. "Because I'll kill you before they get here, I guarantee you."

"I won't," I said, trembling.

"Get this done and over with," Walter snapped angrily. "I've got shit to do."

"No," I argued. "We can talk this out. There's no need to fight."

Diego laughed again, "You're a funny bitch, you know that? Walter is a pain to us all, so why would we 'talk this out'?"

"Don't call her that you – " Diego cut off Walter by punching him right in the face.

"Diego!" Ario shouted. "I told you he's mine."

"You're taking your time *hermano*," Diego replied. "We are in their territory, like he rightly said, the others could show up anytime. And besides, the guy pisses me off too."

"Yeah, hurry up Ario," Miguel said, looking up and down the street. "I get the feeling our time is running out."

I hoped so bad that Walter's brothers were happening to be passing through this way. I didn't want Walter getting hurt anymore than he already had been.

Ario spat out curses in Spanish and the gripped Walter's face again, holding the tip of his knife under his chin.

"Today you're lucky," he said to Walter. "I don't feel like killing you in front of your girl. It wouldn't be nice of me."

Walter smirked and spoke in a low voice as blood trickled out his nose, "You wouldn't kill me anyway. If I was dead, who would you have to hate so much?"

Ario pressed the knife harder into Walter's flesh and I held my breath, not wanting to say anything to cause Ario to actually cut Walter.

"Don't test me," Ario growled. "Don't take our hate for each other as some sort of friendship. One day this will end and only one of us will come out of it."

Walter spat in Ario's face and I internally crumbled.

"Good to know you've accepted your death," Walter replied.

Way to make the situation even worse, but then again, this was Walter and Walter's temper wasn't to be reckoned with.

"No one has to die," I said in a trembling voice.

"Shut up, bitch," Diego snapped. "You're interrupting."

"Stop calling her that," Walter yelled at him, and Ario didn't stop him.

"You aren't in the position to make demands," Diego looked down at Walter teasingly. "And waitress, I enjoyed taking a nice, long piss all over your bathroom floor. It was refreshing."

I felt anger fire up inside me, but I knew not to act. What could I do? Probably get myself hurt, or maybe killed. People like Diego were best to leave ignored.

But it seemed Walter had trouble doing that.

Still on his knees, he punched Ario in the gut, despite Ario's knife still hovering by his face, and got to his feet a second time.

245

Walter ran at Diego and got in one punch before Miguel and Manuel pulled him off and rained heavy kicks down on him.

"Stop!" I shouted in a shrill voice, knowing I was being heard (and ignored) by anyone in their homes nearby.

They only stopped to let Ario through and Walter lay panting on the floor, holding his damaged ribs in agony and looking up at Ario with loathing. Walter's free hand reached into his pocket to get his own knife, but Diego saw and stepped on it before he could. Walter gritted his teeth in pain as Diego ground his hand into the pavement and my legs were shaking so hard in fear and adrenaline.

"Diego stop," Ario said to him.

Diego pushed his hair out of his face and gave his cousin a frown, but still took his foot off Walter's hand.

"Walter," Ario bent down in front of him. "I'll see you around, man. But until then, take this as a parting gift."

He pressed his blade into Walter's cheek and drew a red line down it from Walter's cheekbone, down to his jaw.

"Hopefully that should give you a nice scar," Ario smiled, "to add to your collection of special souvenirs from me."

Walter held his face and gritted his teeth as blood trickled through his fingers and I stood rooted to the ground, stunned.

"*Vamos chicos*," Ario murmured to the boys and they walked away from Walter and towards the East Side.

I watched them leave and just before they were out of sight, Ario turned around and looked right at me. I thought he was going to give me an apologetic look in, but instead he gave me the middle finger and disappeared.

***

I'd made Walter go to A&E to get his cut stitched up, despite him disagreeing. He'd said Landon could do it for him, but I'd reminded him that Landon might not have been at home, and then what?

Walter had frowned, in discontent rather than pain, throughout the period it took for the doctor to put in six soluble stitches to close the wound down the side of his face.

"You should rest," I said to Walter when we got home.

"I need to talk to Phoenix," Walter shook his head, "about leaving for the weekend. I don't have a car, remember? If he agrees it's a good idea, then I think we'll all probably go."

"Okay Walter," I said, knowing I couldn't get him to lie down for even a second while he was determined like that.

The basement door opened and Eli came up with a towel draped over his shoulder. He was dripping with sweat and looking quite fatigued. I had forgotten about the home gym the Simpsons had in their basement.

"What happened to your face?" Eli frowned at Walter.

"None of your business," Walter snapped back.

I wanted to interrupt the pair of brothers before they started arguing. Was it really that hard for Walter to see that Eli was actually just concerned?

"Get out of my way then," Eli said to him blankly.

And then again, Eli had a strange way of showing it.

"Walter," I put a hand on his back to try and settle him. "Phoenix?"

"Yeah," Walter nodded and cast Eli a glare before he moved on.

Eli narrowed his green eyes at the back of Walter's head before he went upstairs.

"Where's Phoenix?" Walter demanded at Gio and Gomez who were in the living room watching TV.

"He just came in," Gomez didn't even look up at us. "Went up to his room I guess."

Gio, who was rifling through a packet of crisps, sighed when his hand came back empty. I just knew he was going to ask us to get him more before he opened his mouth.

"Walterrr?" he looked up at us with a cheeky smile and then widened his eyes when he saw the state of his brother. "What happened?"

"Nothing," Walter rolled his eyes and turned around. "Let's go Coral."

"Okay," I backed up and went to stand at the bottom of the stairs. "I'll wait in your room while you talk to him."

"Don't let him scare you," Walter said to me. "Let's go together, you don't have to say anything to him if you don't want to."

"I won't be," I smiled.

I followed Walter up to Phoenix's room and waited outside with him while he knocked. I noted that Phoenix's door was the only one Walter actually knocked on before entering.

"What?" we heard Phoenix call, and Walter opened the door.

Phoenix's room was spacious, but not because it was really big, rather because it was quite bear. He must have kept all his weapons and things tidy and organised in one of the big chest of drawers he had, because something told me Phoenix didn't have enough clothes to fill all three of them.

Landon was lying on Phoenix's bed and Phoenix himself was sitting up against his headboard. For a split second they just looked like normal brothers just chilling after a day of college or something like that.

"What do you want?" Phoenix looked at us.

"Don't tell me you haven't seen the size of that plaster on his face," Landon gave Phoenix an incredulous look. "Do you have stitches under there, Walter?"

"Yes," Walter grumbled, looking away. "That's not what I came to talk about – "

"But I'm still going to ask," Landon cut in, getting off Phoenix's bed and walking up to Walter to touch his chin. "Which one of them cut you?"

Walter turned his face, pushing Landon's hand away, "Landon, don't touch me. We need to leave for the weekend. They destroyed Coral's flat, completely messed it up...and if she'd been in there at the time, I don't know what they would have done."

"Are you okay, Coral?" Landon asked me. "You weren't hurt, were you?"

"No," I replied, shaking my head. "It was Walter I was worried about."

"Hey, I'm fine," Walter touched my elbow discretely. "So Phoenix, are you driving us or do we have to take the train out of here?"

Phoenix sighed and then to my surprise, he simply nodded.

"I've been needing a break myself. Trying to figure out what they are planning to do is wearing on my mind," Phoenix said.

"How long are we going for?" Landon turned to ask Phoenix. "We can't leave our turf unpatrolled for long, especially when the Santiagos are already trying to take our businesses from us."

"We leave on Saturday morning and come back on Sunday night," Phoenix said. "It's not long, but it's a break."

Landon and Walter nodded, and I was curious about where we were even going, but I was afraid to ask Phoenix.

"The coast," Phoenix spoke, looking right at me. "Eastbourne is where we're going, if you were wondering. We have an apartment there."

"Eastbourne," I smiled. "Sounds nice, I've never been there before."

"It's only a three bedroom," Landon wiggled his eyebrows at me. "It's kind of a safe house, so we didn't want anything that would draw a lot of attention."

"I understand," I shrugged. "Umm, can I ask a question?"

The boys looked at me, waiting for me to speak, which only made me feel more nervous about asking. Nervous of Phoenix's answer anyway.

"Can my friend Hayley come?" my voice dropped in volume. "I mean, if she's free that is."

Phoenix shared a look with Landon who started counting on his fingers.

"Yeah, there's room," Landon nodded.

"So, yes?" I raised my brows.

"Okay," Phoenix grunted. "As long as you make sure she doesn't go around saying anything about it to anyone. Because if she does, I'll personally see to it myself that she *forgets* all about us."

I tried not to show fear and only nodded, "She won't. She's trustworthy."

"Walter?" Phoenix spoke. "You know her?"

"Yeah," Walter shrugged a shoulder. "She's a good one."

"Fine," Phoenix nodded.

"Thank you," I sent him a smile. "I guess we'll all be sharing somehow."

"You just read my mind," Landon smirked and Walter gave him a look.

"I don't find that funny," Walter mumbled.

"You don't find a lot of things funny," Landon replied before throwing himself back on Phoenix's bed.

"Come on," Walter said to me, taking my hand.

"Bye guys," Landon called after us, and Walter ignored him.

"Landon, get off my leg," Phoenix was grumbling as Walter shut the door.

"So Eastbourne it is," I smiled up at Walter's bashed up face and then frowned. "I'm sorry they hurt you."

Walter shook his head, "Please Coral, don't waste your breath talking about them. I'll get my own back on them when the time comes. That's how it goes."

"But your face," I gently touched the plaster that covered the stitched up wound.

"Doesn't hurt that bad," Walter touched the side of mine. "I'll take some painkillers later before I go to bed."

"Be honest with me Walter," I folded my arms. "You're in pain now, so take the painkillers now and rest."

Walter took a breath and nodded, "Okay."

"Not just okay," I said to him. "I want you to be honest and say how you're feeling."

Walter looked at me through his dark lashes, a tiny smile on his lips.

"My ribs hurt a lot and it's hard to breathe. My face feels like its burning and it stings when I talk or try to smile," Walter started listing. "And my hand, the hand that bitch ground into the dirt, is still pounding. I've got a headache, from the punching in general...and I think that's about it."

I blinked at him slowly and then opened my mouth, "Go to bed."

"Wait, Coral – "

"I'll bring you medicine and food. Just stay in your bed," I touched Walter's sore hand. "We're travelling tomorrow. I want you to be okay."

He sighed and nodded, "Okay. I love you."

I blushed, not expecting to hear that at all. It was still very new to me and Walter had completely caught me off guard.

"I-I love you too," I tucked some of my hair behind my ear, dropping my gaze. "Walter get into your bed."

He chuckled softly and winced, before I physically had to push him to his bed and make him sit down.

"I'll be right back," I kissed his forehead.

***

I called work and took the Saturday off before calling Hayley to see if she was free and wanted to come with us for the weekend. I hadn't really spent a lot of time with her recently and I missed her. I just hoped she'd be available.

"Hayley," I cried when she picked up, trying to keep my voice down a little because Walter had thankfully fallen asleep.

I heard her laughing down the line, "Coral, what's up?"

"Please, please, please, please – "

"Please what?" I could hear the confusion in her voice. "Are you talking to me?"

"Yes," I smiled. "Please say you're free for the weekend."

"Hmm...let me see," she murmured.

I was still chanting a multitude of pleases in my head whilst I waited for her to reply, just thinking how Eli much would like it if Hayley were to join us too. I think anyway.

"I'm free," Hayley interrupted my thoughts. "I was just kidding when I said I had to think about it. I don't have to think about shit. I have nothing planned, it was just gonna be an empty weekend with a bit of babysitting. Glad to get out of that."

"Great," I grinned.

"So what's the plan?" Hayley asked me, excitement in her voice.

"You're gonna think I'm crazy for inviting you, but here's the deal...."

29

"So this is Eastbourne," I said as I looked around after getting out of Landon's car and stretching my legs. "It's cold."

"What do you expect?" Landon came and ruffled my shoulders. "It's almost December."

"The sea looks lovely," Hayley said as she came to join me, wrapping her arms around herself.

"Yeah," I nodded in agreement. "Landon, you never told me the inconspicuous apartment had an amazing sea view!"

Eli scoffed as he came to join us, "It would only be amazing if it wasn't freezing."

I cracked a smile, "That's true."

On hearing snickering and hushed laughter from behind us, we turned to see Gomez and Giovanni carefully sticking cheese sticks up a sleeping Severn's nostrils, who lay in the back of Landon's car, blissfully unaware.

"He's gonna fall out the car," Eli commented indifferently.

Severn was leaning dangerously close out of his seat and something told me his triplets wouldn't have caught him if he did happen to fall out of the open car door. Phoenix walked on by and shook Severn's shoulder roughly, rousing him from his sleep.

"What's your problem?" Severn frowned as he opened his eyes.

"You would have fallen on your face," Phoenix muttered, giving Gomez and Giovanni straight looks.

Walter came up from behind me and hugged me, holding me close.

I smiled, putting my hands over his, "Did you miss me?"

Walter nodded, "A whole two hours without you."

"I'm going inside," Eli scowled and turned away.

"I want to see inside," I turned around and grinned at Walter.

He half-smiled on the good side of his face, "Alright."

"I'll show you around," Landon said to Hayley, looping his arm around her shoulders in an expert move.

She sent me a nervous smile over her shoulder and I tried to give her a metal message not to let Landon's flirting affect her. I had a hunch that Eli liked her more than he was letting on.

The flat was a decent size, a lot bigger and grander than my tiny one bedroom had been. Phoenix had already claimed a room by dumping his bag in there, and Landon was showing Hayley around whilst Eli hung back with a more pronounced glower on his face than usual.

"Fight for your girl Eli," I whispered to him with a cheeky grin as Walter and I passed him.

Eli gave me an amused smile and I was glad I'd kind of cheered him up a little bit. Walking into the living room, Walter and I discovered that Severn had already gotten comfortable (fast asleep) in one of the leather sofas and Giovanni was moaning in the kitchen about how there was 'no food'.

"Well what do you expect Gio?" Gomez said to him as he used his phone. "We haven't been here in about four months, have you seen the dust everywhere?"

"Landon," Giovanni walked out of the kitchen and pushed out his bottom lip. "Can we go get food?"

"We only just got here," Landon rolled his shoulders as if to loosen his muscles. "Give it some time."

"Its lunch time," Gio said and then a sly smile spread across his face. "I'm only spending money on myself, which is why I asked you in the first place. I'm going to get food. Wanna come Gomez?"

"You not gonna get me anything?" he asked.

"I can make exceptions," Giovanni allowed.

"Okay then," Gomez said. "It will be busy in town on a Saturday afternoon anyway, prime time for some work."

"Sticky fingers," Landon shook his head at him.

"It's a way of life," Gomez shrugged. "We'll be back in a few hours."

"Cool," Landon nodded.

Eli went to turn on the TV and after successfully locating the remote, he started flicking through the channels.

"Where are those two going?" Phoenix frowned as he walked out of a room to join us.

"To do what they do best," Walter answered. "One is going to eat and the other is going to pick people's pockets."

We spent the majority of the day doing different things. Landon went out on his own, probably to find a girl to charm. Hayley and I watched movies with Walter, Eli and Severn (who drifted in and out of sleep), and Phoenix was in one of the rooms, alone for all I knew. I felt a little sad for him because somehow I had the idea that if I wasn't there, he would be in the living room with his brothers. When I told Walter, he shook it off, saying Phoenix liked solitude and he would join when he wanted to. He would never let anyone stop him from doing anything he wanted, which sounded just like him, so I took Walter's word for it.

When evening came, Landon returned with shopping (which was a change from fast food) and Hayley and I cooked dinner together, laughing as we did so. It was a big challenge, cooking for nine people (seven of them being males who ate large portion sizes), but it was doable. It wasn't anything special, not that we knew how anyway. I'd never been taught how to cook by my mother or anyone at all really. Hayley only knew a few things that she'd picked up over the years. The boys enjoyed the mash and chicken anyway. They said the last time they'd eaten real mash potato was back when they were kids. The same could probably be said for me too.

After dinner, which even Phoenix ate all of, Hayley and I suggested we play a game together. It was a kind of bonding game, primarily for me and Hayley to get to know the boys better and vice versa. I'm sure they knew each other very well, to say in the least, already.

"Two truths and a lie," Hayley sat on a cushion and explained.

The triplets had brought a couple of beanbags from the house and were sitting on them, and I sat in one sofa in between Walter and Landon, whilst Eli and Hayley sat in the other one. Phoenix was sitting in the armchair and we'd moved the furniture around so that it was in a circle shape.

"I'm sure you've heard of it before," Hayley was saying, "but you say three statements about yourself. Two of them are true and the third is a lie. You can't tell us which ones are what and we have to guess. Got it?"

"Got it," Gomez slapped his hands together. "Let's go."

"Wait," Severn held his hand up. "Can we have an example? I've never played this before."

"Okay sure," Hayley beamed at him. "So for example I could say: I like grass, I hate dogs and I'm a natural blonde. You'll have to guess which one is the lie out of the three and once you've all guessed I'll reveal it – which is the third one by the way."

"See," Gomez gave Severn a dry look. "It's not that hard."

"I'm tired, okay?" Severn elbowed him back.

"So," Gomez thought for a while. "The first time I drank alcohol was when I was thirteen. The most I've ever stolen was a watch worth £1000. I used to fancy the *Powerpuff Girls*."

"The watch one is probably true," Landon said as he tried to work his brother out.

"So is the alcohol one," Giovanni said. "I'm pretty sure I drank with you."

Gomez shrugged, "I can't say, just guess which one is the lie already."

"What are the *Powerpuff Girls*?" Phoenix frowned.

I smiled, "It was a cartoon about superheroes."

"They probably still show it," Walter murmured beside me.

Giovanni sent me a grin, "You make it sound cool by skipping the fact that they were less than a foot tall and the show was basically purely for girls. There were too many hearts."

"Well for a show you clearly *never* watched," Eli spoke up. "You sure do remember a lot of the detail."

We laughed teasingly and Gio pulled a defeated expression.

"Only because Eunice made us," he shocked me by saying so easily. "I guess it wasn't so bad once you got used to it."

I sensed Hayley's confusion, but she didn't say anything and none of the boys did either. They simply continued as if Hayley and I knew the full story anyway, which Hayley had absolutely no clue about.

"So what's your guess?" Gomez was smirking.

"I think the watch one was a lie," Phoenix said to him. "No way could you successfully bag a watch worth that much."

Gomez only continued to smirk and then he looked round at the rest of us, "You agree?"

"Nah," Severn argued. "*Powerpuff Girls* was the lie. It was all about *Totally Spies*, they were the full package."

"I don't know," Landon said. "It could be the watch or the *Powerpuff Girls*."

"Watch," Walter called out. "Gomez was a weird kid, I wouldn't put it past him to fancy little cartoon characters."

"Girls?" Gomez asked me and Hayley.

"Watch," I reluctantly agreed with Walter and Phoenix. "I think one worth £1000 is a bit much for someone to easily 'lose'."

Hayley nodded, "Yeah, the watch is the lie...but then again, alcohol at the age of thirteen?"

"Thirteen isn't that young," Giovanni said. "Lots of kids start experimenting at that age."

"Fair enough," she shrugged.

"Okay," Gomez folded his arms, looking smug. "Well...I fooled you all. The alcohol one was the lie. The first time I drank wasn't when I was thirteen, I was eleven."

"Huh?" I widened my eye and dropped my jaw. "Gomez."

"When your parents don't care what you get up to, you tend to grow up pretty fast," Gomez said with a carefree smile.

"But I don't remember that," Gio gave him a sharp look.

"That's because you weren't there," Gomez smirked back at him. "I did it on my own. Drank half a small bottle of lemon vodka and had a headache for the whole of the next day. I didn't even get drunk."

Walter scoffed and Phoenix shook his head with an unsurprised face.

"Wow," Hayley said, blinking back her disbelief.

"So Gomez," Severn questioned. "Which *Powerpuff Girl* did you fancy?"

"The green one," Gomez mumbled, scratching his face as he sank deeper into his beanbag. "I don't remember her name, but she was badass."

"Me next," Gio called. "I once dated a girl called Cookie. I'm scared of spiders. I've been picked up by the police three times."

"Gio those are shit," Gomez called him out immediately. "I *know* you're scared of spiders, I met that girl who called herself Cookie but who's really called Cassandra, and I've been with you nearly every time we've been caught by the police and that was at least four times in our lives."

Giovanni swore at his brother and Gomez smiled triumphantly.

"Next time, be more creative," Gomez said, and Gio tried to kick him off his beanbag.

Severn gave smiled cheekily, "Well I've got some good ones, I'll go next."

"Go ahead," Hayley smiled at him.

Severn began, "The most awkward place I've ever gotten turned on was in a library. I love chocolate cake. When I was young I wanted to be an Olympic runner – "

Landon, Gomez and Gio's cut Severn off with their loud laughter and I had to say even I was surprised about the last thing Severn had said. An Olympic runner? Could that really be true?

Severn kept a straight face and I couldn't read him at all.

"Walter?" I murmured. "What do you think?"

"The runner thing would be too obvious if it was really a lie," Walter responded, watching Severn closely. "But then again, maybe he wants us to think that."

"I don't care," Giovanni said. "I'm calling it a lie, it has to be."

"Yeah," Gomez nodded.

"Walter has a good point," Landon said. "The running thing could be true, I mean, we all wanted to be stupid things when we were kids. I'm pretty sure Eli genuinely wanted to be a – "

"Hey," Eli interrupted Landon with a flick of his emerald eyes.

"What?" Landon smiled blamelessly. "It's not that bad."

Eli shook his head, "Whatever."

"Come on Eli," Hayley nudged him with her elbow. "I'm sure it wasn't something like a fish or something. That would be embarrassing."

Eli cracked a smile, "I wanted to be a star."

"See?" Hayley grinned. "That's so cute, what kind of star? A singer?"

"No," Eli smiled wider so that his dimples appeared. "Like an actual star. The ones that burn in the sky."

"Oh," Hayley pulled an interested face. "Well that's different."

"It's cute Eli," I said to him.

"I never thought it was," Landon was frowning. "I thought it was lame as – "

"This isn't about Eli," Severn coughed. "Guess which one was a lie."

"The chocolate cake," Phoenix said in a low voice and we all looked at him.

"So...is he right?" Gomez looked back at Severn.

"Yeah, I hate it," Severn nodded, watching Phoenix with a confused look. "How did you know that?"

"You're my brother," Phoenix sent him a frown. "Why wouldn't I know something as simple as that about you?"

"I didn't," Giovanni said. "And I love food...and him of course."

"Yeah," Gomez said. "Neither did I. I don't know why, I guess it's because we never really have chocolate cake anyway."

Severn laughed, "Whatever. Excuses, *excuses*."

"Wait so are we all going to ignore the fact that Severn got turned on in a library?" Landon said in a deadpan voice.

"Oh yeah," Gomez looked at his brother in disgust almost. "What were you doing in the *library* in the first place?"

"Well," Severn smiled to himself. "I was following this girl. She's really hot – "

"Who?" Gio cut in.

"Ashley Coleman," Severn replied.

"The brainiac?"

"Yep. So I was following her at school one day...I don't know, I just wanted to see her. She went into the library," Severn told us. "Now I look back, she must have known I was after her because the next thing I knew, she'd gone down a quiet aisle and 'accidentally dropped' her books...and well...when she bent down to pick them up..." Severn broke off with a boyish grin.

"How long ago was this?" Gomez looked pale. "I thought you were a virgin man."

"I am," Severn laughed. "Come on Gomez, sex in the library? She's way classier than that."

"And you're not?" Walter and Eli said in unison.

"Sex is sex," Severn shrugged. "I don't care when or where."

"That's the spirit," Landon grinned and nodded. "And the library actually sounds strangely appealing to me. Pinning her down in the middle of all the spilled books and – "

"*Can you not, Landon?*" Walter sent him the most disgusted look he could manage with his injured face.

Landon held up his hands, "I was just saying."

"Well we're moving on now," Walter said. "I've already thought of mine so here it goes. I used to have a pet frog called Sid. I once cut a girls hair off at school when I was four. I used to fancy my teacher in Year 7."

"What was her name?" Landon was first to ask.

"Miss Francis," Walter replied.

"Oh yes I remember her," Landon grinned. "That one is definitely true. Whenever she took us for History, I used to imagine I could – "

"How old were you in Year 7?" I interrupted him with an arched brow. "Twelve?"

"Eleven to twelve, yeah," he nodded. "That's the time when a boy's hormones are especially fired up – "

"Yeah, we get the idea," Eli said. "Yours never cooled down again."

Landon half-smiled, "You could say that."

"I *did* say that," Eli replied flatly.

"Okay, so if the teacher one is true," Severn said, "which I take your word for Landon, which one is the lie out of the pet frog and the hair cutting?"

"What kind of question is that?" Phoenix smirked. "Did Walter ever have the compassion as a child to care for an animal of any kind?"

"Excuse me?" Walter frowned at him

"Oh right," Phoenix feigned a smile. "Does he even have compassion now?"

Walter decided to give him a small smile, thankfully taking Phoenix's comment as a joke, which I believe it was, and the mini crisis was averted.

"I think the hair cutting is more...you," I had to admit. "It's the perfect way to vent anger, I would have done the same to so many girls at school if I had the guts."

"But age four?" Hayley asked. "Isn't that a bit young to be acting so...mean?"

"No," every single one of the Simpson boys replied.

"So that confirms it for me," Gomez said. "The frog thing is bullshit, that's the lie."

"No," Eli said, narrowing his eyes as he looked down at the carpet. "I think that one was actually true."

"What?" Gio said sarcastically. "So you're telling me you remember Walter having a pet frog called Sidney?"

"Sid," Walter corrected.

"I remember something about a frog...or some tadpoles or something," Eli frowned faintly as he thought back. "I think the hair cutting one is the lie."

We all looked at Walter expectantly and he smiled faintly, shaking his head at Eli.

"You got me," Walter said. "Eli was right, I found a frog in a pond and took it home and kept it for a day. He was a cool guy."

"And why Sid?" Landon had to know.

"I don't even know," Walter replied. "But yeah, I didn't cut a girl's hair when I was four. I cut the teacher's hair when she bent down talking to another kid, not paying attention."

I didn't know what surprised me more, Walter having a pet frog and calling him Sid or baby Walter cutting his *own* teacher's hair off with a miniature pair of scissors.

"You're serious," I said to Walter when he didn't say anything else.

"Yeah," he shrugged. "She told me off, so I got mad."

Hayley couldn't hold back and was already laughing, laughing so hard I had to laugh too and soon all the boys were at it, except Phoenix who kept himself to a smile.

"Coral," Hayley said as she got her breath back. "Your turn."

"Okay," I smiled and rubbed my hands together, already knowing what I was going to say. "I was adopted. My favourite animals are penguins. I've never been outside of England."

"Adopted?" Giovanni blurted. "Isn't that a little far-fetched?"

"I can see that," Gomez said as he looked at me closely. "I don't know anything about your family, so it could be very possible that you were adopted."

I didn't say anything, only spread my hands and smiled at them. Hayley and Walter already knew that my mother had died and I had been taken into social services when I was young. It was easy for Hayley to assume I'd been adopted into a foster family at least once in all that time I was in care, and as for Walter, he knew I'd been adopted by my father.

"What's it about penguins?" Landon asked. "If that one did happen to be true?"

"They're cute?" Severn suggested. "The baby ones anyway."

"Never been out of England sounds like a lie," Eli said, "but it could also be true at the same time."

"Exactly," Walter murmured. "I've never been outside of England myself."

"Yes you have," Phoenix said to him.

"When?" Walter gave him a bewildered look.

"When you were young," Phoenix answered. "We went to France."

"You're lying," Walter stared at him. "I have no memory of that at all."

"You were a kid," Phoenix shrugged.

"And you weren't?" Eli muttered.

"I was old enough," he said neutrally.

"I don't remember that either," Severn said.

"You weren't born," Phoenix explained. "Eli was a year old, Walter was two...Landon was sick so he didn't go, and I was five."

"I don't remember this at all," Landon said blankly. "But okay. Back to Coral, I can also see you having a mysterious background and possibly being adopted too. So I'd say never being

261

outside of England is a lie...because to be honest, girls find all animals cute, making that one the truth as well."

"Final answer?" I looked around at everyone.

They seemed to agree for the most part so I revealed the answer.

"Landon's right," I said. "I have been outside of England, but only to Scotland so it was nothing too far away and exotic. It was a school trip."

"Wow so you're really adopted?" Giovanni widened his blue eyes.

"Yeah," I nodded. "By my biological father who I had never met at the time."

"Sounds cool," he smiled.

If only he knew that it hadn't been.

"Where's your dad now?" Gomez asked me.

"I don't know," I gave him an honest answer. "He was an unlawful person so probably in prison or dead or living some place completely different."

"Kind of like our dad," Severn smiled. "We have more in common than I thought."

"Our dad is dead," Eli explained to Hayley who was again, unsure of what was being said. "He was....well he was definitely a criminal."

"Enough about him," Landon brushed the subject away with his hand. "I'm next."

"Let me guess," Walter said. "I like sex. Sex is great. Girls love to have sex with me."

"Which one would be the lie in that?" I laughed.

"Shut up Walter," Landon shook his head. "So, I've slept with over a hundred women – "

Hayley started choking on thin air, it appeared, and it was Eli who patted her back to try and get her to stop coughing and spluttering.

"That can't be true," Hayley wiped at her eyes once she'd regained herself. "You're only nineteen."

"Let me finish and then you'll have to guess," Landon replied with a smirk. "I've slept with over a hundred women. I lost my virginity under the legal age. I had sex for fifty minutes straight once."

"Fifty minutes straight?" Giovanni, Gomez and Severn shared looks of surprise and admiration.

"Just because he says it, doesn't mean it's true," Phoenix burst their bubble.

"I ain't saying anything," Landon leaned back in the sofa.

"Fifty minutes straight can't be true," Gomez was shaking his head. "How does a guy go at it for that long without...?"

"Exactly," Severn agreed.

Giovanni thought a little longer, "Landon is too smart to make the lie that obvious though."

That made us all hesitate and think again.

"Still impossible," Gomez refused to believe it.

"It's possible," Walter argued. "A lot of things are when you're addicted, like Landon is."

"And it's clearly true that he lost his virginity before he was sixteen," Eli added. "Just look at him. The way he's smiling and shit. That one, at least, has to be true."

"I'm still not sure the over a hundred women thing is true though," Hayley mentioned. "Maybe the fifty minutes is possible, like Walter said, but to have been with that many women? Only aged nineteen?"

"You don't know him if you think that's impossible," Phoenix mumbled.

"Yeah," Eli hesitantly agreed. "I can see that actually being true too."

"Hurry up and decide," Landon cried out of impatience and excitement.

"Fifty minutes," I just decided to side with the triplets.

"Fifty minutes," Hayley agreed and the others reluctantly nodded too.

"You're right, but for the wrong reasons!" Landon grinned and started laughing at us. "It was *one hour* non-stop, not fifty minutes."

"Landon, come on," Gomez was shaking his head frantically. "No way. How do you do that?"

"I don't want to know," Walter said before Landon could answer.

"I do," Gio and Severn demanded, and to be honest I was curious too.

"Well the girl can climax multiple times, we all know that, so that's what I kept doing," Landon explained. "Making her climax again and again for an hour."

"And how did you not climax too?" Giovanni asked. "That's what we want to know."

"I just had to...you know...exit when she was having her climaxes or else there would have been no way I could have not...climaxed too," I could tell Landon was choosing his words very carefully. "Exit and enter, exit and enter."

"Why?" Walter asked. "What did you get out of it?"

"It was simply a personal challenge," Landon shrugged. "It wasn't about the girl at all, I just wanted to test myself for the fun of it. But of course she felt I was treating her special or something."

And once again I was reminded of how mean Landon could be towards women, even though he seemed so clueless about his actions. He was a genuinely kind guy, but he needed improvement if he was ever going to be nice all around.

"When did you lose your virginity?" Giovanni asked him.

"It doesn't matter when," Landon looked down. "It was before I was sixteen."

"So can you also explain how it's possible that you've been with over a hundred girls?" There was no way Hayley was letting Landon off with that one.

"Easy," Landon said. "You 'date' a different girl every week. There are fifty-two weeks in a year, so that's fifty girls which is easily achievable. I've been doing this for a number of years now, it didn't start off as that many girls a year but now that I'm older that's how it's come to be. So it's easily over a hundred, and I have absolutely no STDs. I get tested every month."

"Thanks for telling us that," Walter said with a straight face. "We were just *dying* to know."

Hayley only blinked in shock and nodded.

"Well, I guess it's my turn now," she said, shaking herself out of her disbelief and then smiled at us. "One, I have a tattoo. Two, I'm a sucker for dimples. Three, I've been with a girl before."

The last one threw me off and as I thought about it, I could imagine Hayley being bold and stepping out the box like that. I heard a lot of girls experimented with other girls, to try how it was like, at some stage in their youth. But then again, Hayley was

264

probably good at this game (as she had suggested it) and was trying to fool us.

"Please let the girl on girl action be true," Landon pleaded. "That would be so hot, especially if it was with – "

"Say it," Walter said in a low voice, keeping his gaze forwards. "I dare you."

Landon swallowed and smiled at me instead, before turning his gaze away and talking about how he'd also love Hayley to have a tattoo. I tried not to laugh and after catching the triplets' eyes, I knew they were struggling to do the same.

"I'd love to see you make lady love," Gomez smirked as he bit his lip at Hayley who grinned back at him.

Eli was frowning at his brother, "Don't say shit like that."

"Oh Eli," Hayley touched his arm. "I don't mind, it's just play."

"Sure," he replied.

"Phoenix, what do you think?" Hayley was bold enough to ask him.

Phoenix regarded her with his intimidating gaze, "You seem like a risk-taker, both the tattoo one and the girl one could be true, but I think the gay one is the lie, I just have a feeling."

"Phoenix you're good," Hayley nodded at him. "I've never been with a girl, that was a lie."

"So let's see your tattoo," Gio cried before Landon could and Hayley laughed.

"Alright then," she started to get up.

Hayley pulled up her jumper and there on her lower abdomen was a line of butterflies, flittering across her tanned skin from one side to the other.

"Nice," Landon was nodding to himself, and Eli glanced up at her for a second before he looked away as if he was scared of getting caught looking.

"Your turn," Hayley poked Eli in the side as she flopped back down into the sofa again.

Eli nodded, "I don't want kids. I first smoked when I was five. My mother once dressed me in a skirt."

"Five is a *bit* young Eli," I arched an eyebrow.

"Yeah, that's such a lie," Giovanni was shaking his head. "You not wanting any kids? Well that sounds right up your alley."

265

"What about the skirt?" Severn asked. "Why would mum do that? That must not be true."

"Skirt is the lie," Landon shrugged. "Taking a guess here."

"I wouldn't put it past her to dress him in a skirt," Walter said. "I think smoking at five is a lie. He was probably older, like ten."

"You're all wrong," Eli said to us. "I don't want kids, was the lie."

The boys were taken aback, and they couldn't hide it. I thought it was so sweet that Eli would want to have children and I even tried to imagine what his kids would look like.

"Are you gonna explain the smoking thing?" Gio asked.

"Dad let me smoke some of his cigarette once," Eli said.

"He didn't smoke," Walter frowned.

"Yes he did," Eli replied. "Sometimes."

"Yeah," Phoenix nodded. "Occasionally."

"And you were really five years old?" Hayley had to clarify.

"Yes," Eli nodded. "I practically coughed up my lungs. It put me off which was good. It's a bad habit."

"And the skirt?" Walter brought up. "Aren't you going to explain that one?"

Eli only shrugged, "Not much to say. It was early in the morning and we were getting ready for school. She must have thought I was a girl, I had kind of longish hair when I was young."

I bet what Eli *really* meant was that in her sleepy state, his mother had actually mistaken him for his twin sister Eunice. Walter had mentioned they had looked alike.

"Phoenix," Landon said. "You're up."

Phoenix kept his straight and reserved face, "My favourite flavour ice-cream is strawberry. My first scar was given to me by my father. I once slept with a nun."

There was a pause as we tried to catch out Phoenix's lie.

"I wouldn't be surprised if dad cut you," Walter said, much to Hayley's alarm, "so that one could be true."

"I'm pretty sure you don't even like ice-cream," Landon frowned at Phoenix.

"He doesn't," Gomez agreed. "Does he?"

"I've never seen him eat it," Gio murmured.

My question was how they were all able to ignore the *sleeping with the nun* part?

"You guys are taking too long to answer and I'm tired," Phoenix cut us all short. "The nun one was the lie. She was a mother of two who was cheating on her husband. I didn't know that at the time, but I wouldn't have cared."

"You were drunk, weren't you?" Landon questioned.

"Of course," Phoenix said, as if it was the most obvious thing in the world.

In fact, I wouldn't have even been able to imagine Phoenix sleeping with anyone before he'd come out with this. It was a real eye-opener and he's surprised me for sure.

"Where did your dad cut you?" Hayley was frowning in concern.

Phoenix leaned forwards in his armchair and held out his hand, palm up.

"That line," Phoenix traced his finger along a fine white line that ran across the inside of his palm. "It was like some initiation thing, I was seven."

The boys weren't even moved by that.

"Since when did you like strawberry ice-cream?" Gomez demanded to know.

"I sometimes like to buy it when I feel like something cold," Phoenix replied earnestly, sounding adorable for a second.

"Maybe you should try tasting yourself when you feel like that," Gio said in a quiet voice, knowing that Phoenix wasn't going to let a cheeky comment like that slide.

Phoenix didn't.

Giovanni's screaming and laughter as Phoenix chased him round the apartment with his slipper was loud enough to wake anyone in the flats around us, not that we cared. I was glad we were having a good time, and I was glad Hayley was there too. I didn't think Phoenix would have gotten so comfortable with talking about himself if it had been me alone. She was a great asset to the family.

30

I gently ran my fingers over the patch that covered Walter's cheek and he shivered a little bit as we lay down in the bed, facing each other.

"Does it hurt?" I asked him quietly.

He took my hand and kissed my knuckles, "Not much."

I leaned close to him and kissed him softly on the lips and Walter's hands found my waist and held me against him. He slipped his tongue into my mouth and I uttered an airy moan as I let him in. Walter's touch fired up my senses and left me gasping for air in seconds, only to want more of it.

Walter groaned as he pulled away from me for air and I smiled at him, "Good thing we got our own room."

"Yeah," Walter half smiled with his good side. "After you invited Hayley, she must have thought you were going to share with her."

I giggled, "I'm sure she's doing just fine with Eli and the triplets, I can still hear them laughing in the next room."

Walter paused for a second and then nodded, "Me too."

"Do you think Eli and her would be good together?" I asked Walter with an excited smile.

He raised his eyebrows as if he'd never considered it before.

"I don't know," Walter replied, playing with my hand. "Eli with any girl is weird."

"Why?" I questioned him.

"Well, Eli's just Eli," Walter dismissed it.

"So? He can still find love," I smiled and Walter laughed darkly.

"If he doesn't drive the girl away first, that is," Walter responded. "He's hard to get along with."

"I kind of see what you mean," I said as I thought about Eli's bipolar attitude. "But at the same time he can be great to be with when he wants to be."

"I guess so," Walter mumbled. "I think he likes Hayley anyway, as a friend."

"I think it might be something more," I squealed.

"You mean you *want* it to be something more?" Walter smiled fondly at me.

I grinned back and then yawned, causing tears to rise to my eyes and I blinked them back tiredly.

"You're exhausted," Walter stroked my hair. "Sleep, Coral."

"But what are we going to do tomorrow?" I asked, putting my arms around him as I breathed him in.

"Hmm," Walter murmured, sending a soft hum through my chest. "Go to the town and look around, do some shopping if you want. We can go to the beach too, if it's not too cold."

"Yeah," I smiled into his chest. "We can go skinny dipping."

"Are you serious?" Walter started laughing and then stopped when he winced. "I bet you Landon would do it."

"Maybe I should ask him then?" I pulled back to look at him as I teased Walter sleepily.

"You'd rather see him naked than me?" he cocked an eyebrow at me.

"Of course not," I blushed, not quite sure where I was going with that.

"Is that so?" Walter picked his head up off the pillow, a daring look in his eyes.

"Did you want me to say *yes*?" I asked incredulously. "What kind of response is that?"

Walter tried not to laugh so much and then he unexpectedly sat up and pulled his t-shirt off. I found myself holding my breath as I watched his muscles shift underneath his taunt skin.

There was no way I could lie and say I wasn't attracted to him.

"You didn't have to do that," I tried not to smile. "I already said I choose you over anyone."

"I know," he nodded and lay back down so that he was facing me. "Come here."

I didn't need telling twice.

I fell into Walter's arms and I rested my face against his warm skin as I felt his heart beating steadily. He always knew how to make me feel safe and loved. Two things that had been missing throughout my past and up until now.

"Good night," I said quietly.

"Night," Walter kissed the top of my head.

In the morning Walter was gone and I knew it was past noon. I hadn't had a single nightmare and had possibly been one of the best sleeps I'd had in a while. I sat up and looked at the unfamiliar room. It was medium sized and had basic furniture which I had wiped down to get rid of all the dust the day before.

I lay back down and looked up at the ceiling, feeling content. I guessed the triplets were still sleeping and perhaps Phoenix was off working out or running somewhere like he did on Sunday mornings. Somewhere in the flat I could hear Landon speaking to someone in an overly friendly voice and I frowned in confusion, wondering who the hell he was talking to.

Getting out of the bed I went to the bathroom, which was thankfully unoccupied, and brushed my teeth. I considered changing out of my pyjama bottoms and t-shirt, but decided to wait as my stomach had suddenly decided that it was famished.

Walking into the kitchen I stopped in my tracks when I saw Landon talking to a curly haired baby who he had standing on the counter so he was face to face with her. The baby, or toddler I should say, couldn't have been older than two or three years old and had a face of made of gold. She was adorable, but what was she doing here?

"Oh hey," Walter said when he saw me, holding two cups of tea in his hands. "I was going to bring this to you."

I hadn't even noticed him standing in the other corner of the kitchen, and smiled as I took in his bed-head and laid back look.

"Thank you," I said and forced myself to take my eyes off the young child to take the drink from him.

"Hi Coral," Landon turned to face me, still supporting the little girl so that she didn't fall off the kitchen counter. "This is Melody."

'Melody' smiled at me and my heart almost exploded at how cute she was. She only had eight front teeth.

Judging by how relaxed Walter was, this wasn't the first time Melody had been around and I refused to believe that this was in fact Landon's child. The longer I looked between the pair, the more I noticed how identical their rich brown eyes were. She was definitely his daughter.

"She's mine," Landon gave her a little tickle which made her laugh.

I only stood and blinked at him.

"Why don't you explain to her?" Walter spoke for me, smirking as he drank from his mug.

Landon laughed and picked his daughter up from the counter so that he could lean against it and face me whilst he held her on his hip.

"There isn't a lot to explain," Landon said. "I dated a girl here in Eastbourne a couple of years ago and she got pregnant and had our kid."

"But you said you always used..." I said in confusion and trailed off as I wasn't sure how much to say in front of the sweet little girl.

Landon shrugged, "We got careless, I guess. I thought she was something different, I wanted to be with her...like forever and shit. But that didn't work out."

"The bitch cheated," Walter added.

"Hey," I widened my eyes and motioned to Melody.

Walter shrugged a shoulder and took another gulp, "She'll get to know all about those words someday, it doesn't matter."

I shook my head at him and took a step closer to Melody.

"Hi," I grinned at her.

She grinned back and even waved at me. She had freckles sprinkled over her nose and her hair was almost like a big fluffy afro.

"She's so cute," I looked up at Landon. "I just wanna ruffle her hair."

"Go ahead," he smiled. "You can take her if you want, I wanna make her lunch anyway."

"Okay," I said in excitement, putting down my tea and holding my arms out to Melody, hoping she'd let me take her.

To my glee, she leaned towards me with her arms also outstretched and I took her from Landon's hold.

"How old are you Melody?" I asked her, touching her big soft curls.

"Can she speak?" I asked Landon when Melody only smiled and then started pointing at Walter who was standing behind me making funny faces at her.

"She understands most things and she can say mummy," Landon said as he went to the fridge. "And stuff like yes and no, please and thank you. But apart from that, she's still learning."

"Do you see her often then?" I asked him, tickling Melody and making her giggle.

Landon paused, still facing away from me.

"As often as she lets me," he said, making me crease my brows in confusion.

"The bitch, not the baby," Walter explained.

"Walter stop," I cried at him, making him smile.

"I'm sorry," he leaned down over my shoulder and squeezed Melody's cheeks playfully.

"I wish it was more frequent, but such is life," Landon sighed and then continued making his daughter's lunch.

"You can take her back with us," I suggested excitedly. "Then she could spend more time with you."

"Maybe," Landon's voice hitched up. "I haven't tried that before."

"She better say yes," Walter said darkly. "I mean, we could always *make* her say yes."

Landon turned and gave Walter a look over his shoulder, "That won't be necessary. Her mother is a drama queen and its best not to provoke a reaction from her that would probably lead to being arrested."

"Don't say stuff like that," I said, not sure if Melody was picking it up or not.

Landon smiled at me, "It's not going to happen, I was just saying."

"Mummy," Melody held her arms out to her father.

"Mummy?" I arched an eyebrow in confusion.

"That's what she calls me," Landon said giving his kid a bright beam.

"Mummy!" Melody leaned out of my arms towards him, wanting him to pick her up.

Landon brushed the crumbs off his hands and took Melody back, "I'm waiting for the day she calls me Daddy or something."

Hayley walked into the kitchen in a loose fitting t-shirt and jogging bottoms, her dark hair tumbling down her face messily.

"Hey guys, morning," she smiled at us, rubbing her elbow.

"Good morning," Landon smirked back and that's when Hayley noticed Melody.

She widened her eyes, "Is this your..."

"Yeah," Landon rubbed his hair with his free hand. "She's my kid, her name is Melody."

"Hi Melody," Hayley reached out to shake her little hand.

Melody smiled at her and put her hand in Hayley's which made me want to squeal at how adorable it was.

"I had no idea you were a dad Landon," Hayley looked up at him with a surprised face.

Landon shrugged a shoulder and before he could even say anything the triplets and Eli came into the kitchen, the triplets heading straight for Melody who started screaming in glee and trying to climb over Landon's shoulder to get away from them.

"Does she even remember us?" Gio paused to say as Severn and Gomez continued to tickle her.

"Probably not," Gomez laughed. "The last time we saw her, she was a lot smaller and had no teeth."

"She *still* basically doesn't have any teeth," Severn said and then looked at Landon. "Why?"

"How am I supposed to know?" Landon replied. "Every kid grows differently."

Eli stood back and looked at Melody with a smile, "She kind of looks like you Landon."

"I'm glad," Landon responded. "And if she could talk, I know she'd be agreeing with me."

"Hey," I started to laugh.

Eli sent him a look. "You can't be complimenting yourself at every opportunity you get."

"Ah leave him alone Eli," Hayley grinned, lightly hitting his arm. "You'd do the same if somebody complimented your kid."

That caught the attention of the triplets and Gomez cut in, "And don't say you're not having any kids because you told us last night, that that was something you wanted."

Eli blushed and the boys jeered, causing Hayley to pull him down into a hug.

"Leave Eli alone," she cried playfully over his shoulder. "You guys are so mean."

"Group hug!" I called just for the fun of it and Gomez, Gio and Severn even beat me to it.

They crushed Hayley in a wall of muscle and I didn't even bother trying to get in, I was just trying to control my laughter from seeing Hayley's expression the second before she was engulfed. To die for. Walter leaned on the back counters, smirking as he finished his drink and the triplets jostled Hayley and Eli and Landon threw Melody in the air, her hair brushing the ceiling.

"What's wrong with you people?" Phoenix muttered as he came and stood in the doorway.

He looked like he'd just come back from a run, and sweat was dripping down the sides of his head and down his chest, soaking the front of his shirt.

"Everything," Eli said as he pushed his younger brothers off him and Hayley. "There's seriously something wrong with them."

Phoenix wasn't even listening anymore, he had caught sight of Landon's daughter and watched her closely.

"You managed to get her to let you take the kid for the day?" Phoenix asked his brother.

"Yeah," Landon nodded. "But I'll talk to her about taking Melody back to London with me too."

"Really?" Phoenix looked sceptical.

"Yeah," Landon said. "For a week maybe."

"It would be good for the two of them," Walter backed him up.

"Okay," Phoenix said. "If you think you can handle it Landon."

Landon frowned slightly, "It will be fine. She's a good girl."

"Sure," Phoenix muttered.

"So Phoenix," Giovanni said. "What are we doing today?"

"Whatever you want," Phoenix said.

"What are *you* doing?" Walter asked him, probably to get on his nerves a little bit, knowing how argumentative he could be.

"I don't know," Phoenix replied. "Go to the town. Or even to the beach to clear my head, anything to get my mind off those Santiagos."

And just like that, Phoenix had brought back all the frightening memories of my trashed flat, the ambush and Ario slashing Walter's face. I had actually managed to forget all about how much hate Ario was feeling towards me, and now I was feeling guilty and also apprehensive about going back home tonight.

"Yeah," Hayley said. "Let's go to the beach - "

" - beach, let's go get away," Severn continued her sentence in a *Nicki Minaj* voice.

Hayley laughed and pushed him playfully. She was aware of our current situation with the Santiagos and like I'd assured Phoenix before, Hayley wasn't going to spread any gossip around. I knew she was a trustworthy person and she had been very sympathetic when I'd told her about the state my flat had been in and how Ario had injured Walter.

"Beach sounds good to me," I said and the boys murmured in agreement.

We decided to eat and then go to the beach, even though it was very cold. We dressed in thick layers and headed out together.

Not that we stayed together long.

Phoenix splintered off alone and went into the town centre whilst the rest of us stayed on the beach front. Landon started chasing Melody around in the sand and soon we all joined in, laughing as the two year old squealed with excitement. When she got tired, I picked Melody up and ran with her in my arms, her long brown hair flying everywhere. When I got tired, I passed Melody to Hayley who carried her for a while as the boys chased them. Melody loved it.

"I need a drink," Severn coughed, doubling over.

"You barely ran," Gio slapped his back.

"I still need a drink," Severn cast him a look.

"Let's go to town then," Gomez said, chewing on his bottom lip as he looked towards the shopping areas. "I wanna get to work."

"Bye then," Walter said to the triplets, looping his arm around my neck.

"See ya," Gio waved and the three of them left together.

"I feel like shopping," Hayley said to us. "Anyone wanna come?"

Landon, Eli and Walter pulled faces of discomfort and Hayley and I grinned at them.

"We can go together," I said to her. "Leave the boys to themselves."

Walter looked like he wanted to disagree but then he said, "I'll see you guys around then."

"Bye," I waved and smiled at Melody who was trying to play with Landon's lip ring.

Hayley and I crossed the road and walked along the busy streets full of people doing their weekend shopping. It had been a while since we'd spoken together, just the two of us, and I was looking forwards to knowing how she was feeling towards certain people such as Eli Simpson.

"This isn't so bad, is it?" I asked her, nudging her side.

"No, it's fun," she smiled at me. "I already knew it would be fun. The only thing I was uneasy about was Phoenix, but he's not even around that often. And he doesn't seem so bad either."

"Yeah," I agreed. "He keeps himself to himself."

"I also can't believe Landon has a kid either," Hayley cried. "He's only a year older than us."

"I know," I said. "I was pretty surprised too. I still am. Melody is so damn cute."

"And Eli...." she trailed off with a little smile on her lips.

"I didn't even have to ask," I smirked at her. "Go on, tell me everything. Anything happen when you were sharing the room last night?"

"No!" Hayley started laughing. "Three of his brothers were in there! And I'm pretty sure Gomez has night vision, can you imagine that he asked me if he could guess whether I was wearing a bra or not? And that he actually guessed right?!"

"Were you?" I had to ask.

"No," Hayley said. "It was dark, and him calling me out like that made me super embarrassed, so then Eli swore at them and told

276

them to shut up, you know, like he does. I made a joke out of it to lighten the mood of course, but he did ask me if I was okay quietly afterwards, which was really sweet."

"He is really sweet at times," I smiled, nodding in agreement.

"And good looking," Hayley widened her eyes in emphasis.

"So you like him?" I asked, glancing at her out the corner of my eye.

"I don't know," Hayley gave me a confused look, seeming really serious all of a sudden. "He's so nice to me, but if we were to go out or whatever, I don't know if I'd like him fighting the law all the time. I'd be worried about him getting arrested or something like that. And I don't even know if *he* likes *me* anyway."

What she was saying was all correct and she hadn't even mentioned how dangerous it was for the boys to be fighting their rival gang, which could lead to worse that arrest.

"I get what you mean," I said, looking down as we walked the streets.

"How do you manage with Walter? Don't you worry about him?" she asked me.

"Of course I do," I replied. "He got badly hurt just a couple of days ago and I'm still scared the feud between the gangs will lead to something regrettable."

Hayley was nodding, seeing exactly where I was coming from.

"It's so deeply ingrained in them all," I went on. "If I *did* ask them to stop doing what they were doing, I doubt they'd make a change. They wouldn't be able to let the Santiagos take over everything they'd worked for....and I understand that too."

"Boys huh?" Hayley sighed with a smile. "Eli's exactly the type that my parents wouldn't let me date. The kind of boy they'd tell me to stay the hell away from. You can do a lot of time for drug related crimes."

"Don't let the rumours fool you. They don't even handle the drugs themselves," I said to her. "The boys are smart. They know how to shield themselves from the law when it comes to that kind of stuff."

Hayley looked impressed, "Phoenix's smart thinking, I bet."

"You got it," I grinned at her. "I wish I knew what was in that guy's head. He's always so reserved."

"He's been through a lot," Hayley agreed. "I don't even need anyone to tell me that. I can tell."

The two of us went into a couple of shops after that and Hayley bought some clothes, and then the two of us went trying makeup later on. I didn't wear makeup often, but Hayley was an expert (not that she wore a whole lot herself) and she picked out a really nice shade of pink lipstick for me.

"In case you *do* decide to make the dress in Textiles class," she said. "This is your colour. Make sure the fabric matches."

"I actually forgot I said that," I laughed. "But yes, I will remember that."

We went around some more shops when I got a call from Walter.

"Hey," he said. "Eli and I are in a cafe, are you and Hayley free to join us?"

"Yes," I replied, knowing Hayley wouldn't mind seeing Eli.

Walter told me the name of the cafe and it wasn't long until Hayley and I were able to locate it. The brothers were sitting at a four seated table and both of their faces lit up when they saw us enter.

Walter squeezed my hand under the table as I sat down next to him, and Hayley grinned at Eli and Walter both as she took her seat.

"How was your shopping?" Eli asked, motioning to Hayley's shopping bags.

"I got a couple nice things," Hayley replied.

"I love your lips," Walter said to me and when Eli sent him a scowl, Walter blushed a little bit and corrected himself. "I mean your lipstick...it's a really nice colour."

"Thank you," I smiled back. "So what have you guys been doing?"

"Landon disappeared with the baby," Eli said. "He said he'd be back, but we didn't bother waiting."

"Landon has no sense of time," Walter muttered. "We would still be waiting for him now, and that was two hours ago."

I cracked a smile, "At least you saw it coming."

"Yeah," Eli smirked. "So we just sat in here for a while, and thought you could join us when you finished your shopping. And Landon too, but I doubt he's gonna make it."

"Do guys want anything to drink?" Walter asked me and Hayley. "Or some cake or something?"

"I just had a drink," I said. "So not at the moment but maybe later – "

"That's great then," Walter stood up, pulling me up with him. "Let's go."

I frowned in alarm, "Wait, what – "

Eli nodded a goodbye at Walter who returned it and I glanced at Hayley who looked just as surprised as me. If I hadn't understood correctly, I would have just said that Walter had actually helped his brother Eli get some alone time with Hayley, which was totally unexpected. My words about setting the pair up together must have gotten to him last night.

"Bye," I grinned at Hayley and Eli over my shoulder as Walter pulled me away by my hand and Hayley sent me a nervous grin back.

As soon as we were back out in the chilly air, Walter pulled me close to his side and we walked together so that our arms were touching.

"So you think they'd make a good couple after all?" I smirked up at him.

"This wasn't just for them," Walter replied. "It was for us too."

Before I could ask him to explain what I already knew he meant, Walter's phone started ringing and he rolled his eyes before answering it, "Hey."

"Who is it?" I whispered at him.

"Landon," Walter said and then sighed, listening to this brother on the other end. "Fine, black."

Walter turned to me and pulled the phone away from his ear, "Landon is buying everyone onesies, he wants to know which colour you want."

I raised my brows in excitement, "What do they have?"

He shrugged, "Everything?"

"Okay, sea green," I replied.

"Oh come on," he cracked a smile. "Is that green or blue?"

"It's both," I smiled back.

"They don't have both."

"You don't know that."

"Coral."

"Okay," I laughed. "Green."

"Did you hear that?" Walter put the phone back to his ear. "Yeah, green. Yeah, bye."

Walter cut off the call and I looked at him.

"Wasn't that a bit abrupt?" I asked.

Walter shrugged his shoulder indifferently, "He was talking too much."

"But he doesn't know my size," I realised.

"He's gonna have to guess," Walter smirked. "I'm not calling him back."

I shook my head at him, "Walter, Walter, Walter."

"Seaweed, seaweed, seaweed," Walter mumbled back, making me widen my eyes at him with a challenging look.

"Are you referring to me?" I gaped at him.

"No," Walter sent me a cute smile and then engulfed my smaller frame in a big hug.

I tried to pull away from him, still playing mad, but he held on tight and when he started tickling me, I gave up and laughed out loud.

"Hey, you can stop now," I cried. "Please Walter."

Walter paused the tickling and we kept walking, back towards the beach. After crossing the road, we found a fairly quiet spot and sat down on a bench, huddling close to keep warm from the cold sea breeze.

"You're so beautiful," Walter touched my cheek, his eyes homing in on my painted lips.

I didn't wait for him to lean all the way in to kiss me, and I went straight for it and kissed him right on the lips. Walter smiled a little bit against my lips before he started to kiss me back hard. I lifted my hands to cup his face, taking care with his healing wound, and Walter ran his hands through my hair, opening his mouth and letting me rub my tongue against his.

We broke off for air and sat back, watching the sea.

"This is perfect," I said to Walter, who was still holding my hand.

"I know," he put his arm around me, and we continued to look out at the big blue sea.

***

We were setting out to go back home in the night, so we decided to have one last little game before we left. Dressed in our onesies, we sat in the living room once again and readied ourselves to play a classic game of Truth Or Dare as Melody slept in one of the bedrooms, dressed in her own little pink onesie.

"I'm spinning first," Gomez reached forwards and span the empty wine bottle.

We watched it turn and I hoped it would land on Phoenix so that Hayley and I got the chance to know a little bit more about him. It landed on Landon instead, his red onesie unbuttoned down to the middle of his torso.

"Truth or dare, bitch?" Severn grinned at him.

"Uh, what was the need?" Landon pretended to be hurt as he placed a hand on his bare chest.

"Who do you think drank all the wine in that bottle in the first place?" Giovanni smirked.

"That's a stupid question," Gomez hiccupped. "We did."

"I wasn't actually asking you," Gio sent his brother a look. "Lightweight."

"Just answer the question," Phoenix grunted. "We need to be on the road by ten latest."

Phoenix had actually surprised me by wearing the onesie that Landon had bought for him, which was a grey colour and looked good on him.

"Dare," Landon said. "You didn't have to even ask."

"Okay," Hayley said, who was in a purple onesie which really suited her figure. "I've got one."

"It better be a good one," Landon grinned wide.

"It's adequate," she tried not to smile. "I dare you to kiss Walter."

Walter, who was sitting opposite me, dropped his jaw at the same time I did.

281

"Cool," Landon didn't even seem bothered. "Come here baby brother."

"I'm not doing that," Walter looked at Hayley with wide hazel eyes, with the black hood of his onesie drawn over his head.

"A dare is a dare," Hayley smiled innocently.

"Why me?" Walter cried.

"Because your reaction would be the best," she grinned.

"I thought we were friends," Walter said before he looked over at Landon with disgust.

"How about on the cheek then?" I came to the rescue. "Landon can kiss Walter's cut better."

Walter almost dry heaved at the sound of that, but he didn't argue. It was a good compromise. Landon crawled over to him and licked his lips, just to piss Walter off and make the rest of us laugh (the triplets a bit too hard). Landon's lips barely brushed the plaster on Walter's cheek before Walter pulled away and called it done.

Hayley had to take it.

The bottle was spun again and this time it landed on Phoenix.

"Truth or dare?" Giovanni asked.

I hoped so bad that he'd choose truth, he didn't strike me as the person who would ever give his brothers the opportunity to dare him to do something that would make him look stupid.

And surely enough I was right.

"Truth," Phoenix answered.

"Let's ask him about his preferences in women," I whispered to Hayley who was sat next to me.

"Alright," Hayley said with surprising confidence, perhaps she'd had a little bit of the wine to drink too.

"Phoenix," Hayley said before anyone else could. "What do you like about a woman? As in, what attracts you to her the most?"

Phoenix frowned at her so long, I was expecting Hayley to shy away like I wanted to, but Hayley only blinked at him as she waited for him to answer, and that confirmed for me that she was indeed a little bit tipsy. Or she'd just gone and lost her mind within the last couple of hours.

"The face," Phoenix muttered eventually.

"Come on man," Severn called. "Be more descriptive!"

"Shut up," Phoenix snapped at him. "If I catch you drinking again, I'll smash the bottle over your head for you."

"You make it sound like I intended to do that to myself," Severn frowned in what looked like genuine confusion.

"Shut up Severn," Walter pushed him. "Phoenix answer the question properly."

"Maybe he likes men," Gomez mumbled, still hiccupping.

Phoenix fixed him with the deadliest glare known to man, I was so glad I just wasn't sitting in his line of sight. I took that as a definite no then.

"I answered, now spin it again," Phoenix said.

Nobody challenged him, and Landon leaned forwards and gave the bottle another spin.

It landed on Hayley

"Truth or dare?" Landon asked her and a smirk on his face.

I saw Hayley try not to ogle at Landon's muscular body too much as she answered the question.

"Dare, of course," she said boldly.

"Kiss Eli," I said and then covered a really wide smile.

Eli stared at me in what looked like disbelief and then he glanced at Hayley who was smiling at him. I could tell she was just as nervous and not drunk enough to dampen that.

Walter gave Eli a shove towards Hayley and Eli steadied himself on his hands and knees, looking at Hayley with stained pink cheeks. Hayley shuffled closer to him and the two of them knelt on their knees so that Eli was looking down at her slightly. I was so excited and I didn't know why.

"Go on then!" Severn shouted and Giovanni pushed his face away with his foot.

Hayley smiled at Eli again and Eli smiled back, his dimples showing. Without warning she leaned in and kissed Eli on his stunned lips. She had her eyes closed and Eli's green ones were wide open only for a second before he started to kiss her back, both of their cheeks burning.

We cheered, me just as loud as the boys, and I thought they were going to pull away but Hayley reached up and knotted her hands in Eli's dark blonde hair, lengthening the kiss. Eli's hands held Hayley's face for a moment before they broke apart, panting and not knowing where to look.

"My boy, my boy," Gomez cried, grabbing Eli and holding his face to his chest.

We were laughing so loud, Melody woke up in the next room and got out of her bed to join us. She sat herself in Landon's lap and smiled at us all, as if she knew what was so funny. Eli looked like he'd passed out to be honest, as he didn't pull away from Gomez like I thought he would.

I squeezed Hayley's shaking hand and she gave me a look that said both: I want to kill you, and thank you.

I grinned and winked back.

31

"So you and Eli have a date?" I asked Hayley with wide eyes.

She grinned back at me in excitement nodding her head up and down frantically. We were in Textiles class sitting at the table, pretending to sketch up new designs for our next projects.

"I'm really starting to like him Coral," she said, biting the end of her pencil as she grinned.

"Starting to?" I raised my brows. "You kissed him like crazy in front of everyone that night!"

"I was a bit drunk," she tried to duck her head.

"Drunk in love, you mean," I corrected. "So what are you going to wear?"

Hayley and I spent the rest of the lesson talking about choices of clothing and sounding like complete girly girls. Apparently even Hayley's other friends couldn't believe she and Eli Simpson were sort of together. They had even asked Hayley to invite me to their next outing so that they could get to know me and hopefully some more of the Simpsons.

In the end, Hayley decided that she'd wear a black cocktail dress she had worn to prom at the end of secondary school. Something sweet, but simple. I wondered what Eli would wear. I hadn't really seen him in anything other than jeans, t-shirts, hoodies and leather jackets. Hayley said whatever it was, it would be a nice surprise.

When school ended, I knew Hayley couldn't wait to get home and start getting ready for this evening. I wished I could join her, but as it was a Monday, I had work straight after and I was dreading it. I really didn't want to see any of the Santiagos.

"I can come with you," Walter suggested after English.

"Its fine Walter," I discretely touched his hand as we walked down the packed hallway. "I won't be able to talk to you, it get's busy. You'll be bored."

"I wouldn't mind just watching," he smiled with a shrug.

He'd taken off the plaster on his face so that now his healing wound was visible to all. It looked painfully sore, but Walter was still able to smile and laugh, even more than before.

"Okay then," I smiled at him, threading my fingers through his.

Walter and I walked to the Dartfish together, talking about anything except Ario and the other Santiagos. We both knew it was on our minds, but neither of us wanted to sour the mood. Not that that lasted long.

I wasn't surprised to see Paulo and Carlos already sitting near a window as we walked in, drinking beer and juice. I did my best to ignore their looks and I knew Walter was scowling right at them. I dropped my gaze as I walked to the staff room behind the counter.

"I'll be right here," Walter stroked my hair and gave me a quick kiss on my forehead before he sat at the bar.

"Alright," I said.

Walter squeezed my hand warmly and I smiled back before heading into the back to change.

Ario never showed up during my shift, as I knew he wouldn't, and I had mixed emotions about it. I was partly relieved that I wouldn't have to face him, but also I angry at him for how he destroyed my home, and then there was also the guilt about him finding out that I had been using him.

"You okay?" Walter asked me as I went and served him another drink at the bar.

I nodded, cautiously looking over in the direction of the two Santiagos and caught Carlos's warm brown eyes. He smiled, and it wasn't exactly a reassuring one. It reminded me that they were at the Dartfish for a reason, a reason that we still didn't know.

"Walter we need to know what they are planning," I said to him quietly as I filled his glass. "It's bothering me."

"Oh trust me, it's bothering me too," Walter shook his head to himself. "And it's bothering Phoenix probably most of all."

"Carlos said a change is going to come," I said. "But how will it happen? And what do we do to prevent it?"

Walter sighed, "Don't let it hold you down Coral, it's nothing you should be worrying about. Focus on studying, don't let this gang shit distract you. I don't want you involved."

"Well that's hard when I'm living with the Simpson brothers," I touched the end of his nose and then handed him over his drink.

Walter laughed as I turned and went to serve someone else. As I did so, I noticed Tiffany, my colleague, giving me a look and then sending Walter a glance I didn't like. My grip tightened on the glass I was holding as I saw Tiffany move in Walter's direction out of the corner of my eye. Instead of showing my immense annoyance, I tried to focus on remaining calm and friendly as I handed the customer their drink.

As soon as I was finished, I marched back towards where Tiffany was leaning over the bar, trying to flirt with my boyfriend (who was very unresponsive) and I cleared my throat loudly.

"Tiffany someone's trying to catch your attention back there," I said to her firmly.

She turned and looked at me with distaste on her face and I tried so hard not to scowl or curse at her. After she left, Walter looked at me with what I could describe as intense longing and he ran a hand through his hair.

"Coral, you're so sexy when you're all mad like that," he said, looking at me through his lashes.

"So are you when you give me that look," I mumbled back, dropping my gaze as my cheeks warmed up.

Walter groaned, hitting his fist on the table, "When are you finished?"

I laughed, "Two hours more."

My laughter was cut off when Paulo appeared behind Walter, holding a menu in his hand.

"Hey," he said to me. "Can I have a bowl of onion rings and a lemonade?"

Walter's smile turned into a grimace and Paulo even went as far as to sit down on the stool one seat away from him. I entered his order into the till and he remained seated even after he'd paid.

"What do you want?" Walter eventually asked in a clipped tone, not even turning his head to look at him.

The youngest Santiago knew exactly who Walter was talking to and he didn't bother to look back at Walter either.

"I want to talk to Coral, not you."

Walter immediately balled his hands into fists and clenched his jaw and I was thinking in my head how brave Paulo was being to provoke Walter in such a way. Maybe because they were in a public place, he was thinking Walter wouldn't lash out? But then again, even I didn't know for sure that Walter wouldn't lose his temper whether he was in the pub or not.

"I'm working," I said to Paulo, looking at him earnestly as I filled up his lemonade glass.

"I know, but...I just thought I should let you know..." he gave Walter a sidelong look.

"Whatever you tell me, I'll tell him anyway," I made myself clear to the fifteen year old.

Paulo nodded, "Ario's sorry about your flat. He won't say it, but I know he is."

"And she needed to know that, why?" Walter turned and gave him a deathly glare before I could reply. "Do you think sorry is going to repair all the shit you damaged?"

Paulo held his hands up, "Hey, I wasn't part of that."

"I don't care," Walter snapped. "You're all part of the same family."

"Okay, whatever. I'll wait for the onion rings at the table," Paulo stood up. "*Adios*."

"*Adios* yourself," Walter said over his shoulder, tossing in a few curses too.

"Please, calm down," I said to him quietly. "He wasn't trying to annoy you."

Walter smiled cynically, "Don't be fooled by his youth. He's just as bad as the rest of them."

But I'd seen a side of Paulo that I doubted any of the Simpsons had. He was just a fifteen year old kid who was following in the footsteps of his older brothers and cousins. I hadn't heard anything about their parents, so I assumed they weren't in the picture, and for that, I couldn't really blame him.

I was trying not to imagine how sorry Ario apparently was, on the way home with Walter when I remembered that Hayley and Eli were going on their little date, and that really lifted my spirits.

At the house Eli was already down in the hallway, dressed in navy jeans and a smart black shirt. He looked like a completely different person and I knew Hayley wouldn't be disappointed one bit.

"Looking sleek," Landon put his arm around Eli's shoulders.

"Don't crease my shirt," Eli frowned at him, shrugging Landon off.

"Ooh, okay," Landon threw himself back against the wall. "Don't touch the shirt guys."

Giovanni came out of the kitchen, slurping noodles into his mouth and Severn was behind him, holding his niece Melody, whose mother had miraculously let her come and stay with us for a little bit.

"Wow Eli," Gio sprayed out noodle juice at us all. "You look good."

Eli rolled his eyes in disgust, "Can you all get out of my way? I need to go and pick her up."

"Are you excited?" I grinned at him.

"Of course he is," Gomez said, sitting on the bottom step with a smirk on his face. "He can't wait to see his girlfriend."

"It's not a thing," Eli mumbled, looking at the ground.

I smiled up at him, making him meet my gaze and blush slightly.

"If it's not a 'thing', make it one," I said to him. "Even Walter ships you with her."

"Ships?" Walter frowned down at me.

"It's when you want two people to be in a relationship together," I explained to him.

Walter raised his eyebrows, "Interesting."

"Anyway," I said, shaking Eli's arm. "Don't keep Hayley waiting, it's meant to be the other way round."

"What?" Eli scoffed. "The lady is meant to make the guy wait?"

"Exactly," I beamed at him.

Eli sent Walter an apologetic look and Walter tried not to smile.

"See you then," Eli said to us, heading for the door.

"Bye Eli, good luck!" I gave him a hug.

"Bye!" Severn cried, Melody copying him and waving at Eli.

"Good luck," Landon said to him but Eli was gone and had already shut the door.

"He better smile at her," Gomez mumbled.

"Of course he will," Landon grinned and then ducked down to face his daughter in Severn's arms, tickling her sides and making her scream with laughter.

"Aw Melody," I went and ruffled her curly hair as Walter made his way to the kitchen, passing behind me.

"How are you?" I smiled at her.

"Fine," she smiled shyly at me, putting her finger in her mouth.

"You love me, don't you?" Severn hugged her closer to his chest.

Melody didn't reply, she just kept smiling and Landon played with her hair.

"She is adorable," I told him.

"Isn't she?" Landon said. "I've missed her."

"How did you get her mum to say yes again?" Giovanni asked as he finished his noodles.

"I told her that me and Melody needed to spend time together and that I didn't want my child to grow up, not knowing her dad. She was saying that I didn't know how to look after her etcetera etcetera and also that I would be putting her in an unsafe environment."

"What did you tell her?" Walter asked, making him and me a sandwich on the counter.

"I told her I wouldn't put her in danger. Simple," Landon replied. "She wouldn't stop going on about it until she finally agreed when she saw that Melody didn't want me to leave. Melody started crying when I went to go, so I guess that showed that I was right, the two of us needed to spend more time together. That's when she packed Melody's bag and let me take her with me."

"I'm glad you two are happy," I said fondly.

"We're all happy," Walter said, handing me a cheese and ham sandwich.

"As long as she doesn't start crying," Gio joked.

"I don't think I've heard her cry at all yet actually," Severn thought aloud.

"It's only the first day," Landon cracked a smile. "Don't bet on it."

"That's very true," Severn laughed and looked down at Melody's innocent face.

Melody, sensing that we were all looking at her, fixed us with a cheeky grin and we just couldn't help but laugh.

***

"Walter," I said, sitting on the edge of his bed.

"Yes?" he murmured, standing by the windows as he shut the curtains.

I sighed, rubbing my wrists.

"What's up?" Walter turned and gave me a concerned look.

"I'm...I'm scared," I said honestly, feeling my throat start to burn. "I'm scared of what Ario is going to do next."

Walter crossed his room in two strides and sat down next to me, immediately engulfing me in his arms.

"I will never let him hurt you," he said to me firmly. "Ever."

"But Walter," I looked up at him with watery eyes. "I'm not scared about me, I don't want him to hurt you again either...and I feel bad for using him."

Walter stiffened, his muscles bunching up tight.

"It's okay to feel bad I guess," he said after a long pause. "You don't know him like I do but at the same time, I didn't know him like you did. He was nice to you...so yeah, it's normal to feel bad."

I smiled at him a put a hand on his toned chest, "That took a lot of strength for you to come out and say that, didn't it?"

Walter chuckled and I felt him relax, "Yeah."

"Please be careful Walter," I said to him, laying my head against his chest again. "I don't want you or any of your brothers to get badly – "

"I know," Walter cut me off, rubbing my hair. "We'll all be fine, whatever happens. I love you so much, you have to trust me on this."

I wanted to tell him that he couldn't be sure. He didn't know what dirty tricks the Santiagos had up their sleeves, or when they could next strike out. At the same time, I wanted to put my total trust in him and say to myself that no one could ever hurt Walter and that he and his brothers would always be safe.

"Do you trust me?" Walter asked me softly when I didn't respond.

"I trust you," I murmured back. "But anything can happen."

"Do you believe in God?" he deeply surprised me by saying.

"Do you?" I widened my eyes and looked up at him.

"I don't know, sort of," he shrugged, still holding me.

"I'm not sure either," I replied, thinking about all the horrible things I'd endured and the things Walter had also endured but hadn't told me about. I knew his childhood hadn't been a piece of cake.

"Sometimes I pray," I said quietly. "I don't know why, it wasn't as if I was brought up in a religious family or anything like that. But I just feel like maybe there is someone listening to me somewhere...and maybe they might even decide to turn things in my favour for once."

"Yeah, I get exactly what you mean," Walter smiled. "If you feel afraid sometimes when I'm out there...you know, about my safety or anything...if you want, you can pray, I can pray...maybe we can do it together if it's possible. It's harmless after all, and I guess we have nothing to lose."

I nodded still slightly shocked that this was coming from Walter, the hot-tempered boy I thought I knew pretty well, "I know. I love you Walter."

"I love you too," he said, squeezing me tight. "Now, I know you're very tired, so I'm going to turn off the light so we can go to sleep."

"Yes Sir," I smiled warmly, lifting my head up to kiss his scarred cheek.

292

Walter caressed mine back before he got up and went to turn his room light off. The two of us snuggled into his bed, dressed in t-shirts and shorts, and me with socks, him without. His arms went around me and we seemed to fit together like two puzzle pieces, sleepy and content. I almost fell asleep instantly when I was pulled out of my daze by the loud sound of a crying child.

Walter and I sighed and then we started to laugh. Could little Melody's timing be any worse?

32

It was after school and I was in the kitchen looking through the cupboards, trying to write a list of things the house would need for shopping. I had decided that we needed more home cooked meals and not just take-aways and the instant foods. I closed the fridge when I heard someone enter the kitchen behind me and saw Eli standing by the dining table.

"Hey," I greeted him.

"Hey," he murmured back, looking a bit down actually.

"What's wrong?" I frowned, walking up to him. "Didn't the date go well?"

Having already heard from Hayley, the date had been 'fantastic' and the two of them had shared a few more kisses. She didn't know if Eli wanted her to be his girlfriend, as he hadn't asked her straight out, but then again maybe Eli was the kind of guy who felt that he didn't need to ask.

"The date was good," Eli smiled faintly as he gazed downwards. "It's just...ah, it's nothing."

"Eli," I said softly. "You can tell me what's bothering you."

He frowned sharply and I took a step back from the sudden anger in his features.

"It's not 'bothering' me," he scowled. "How could my sister ever 'bother' me?"

I widened my eyes in surprise on hearing his words and I quickly tried to dissolve his irritation.

"I'm sorry Eli," I said to him. "I didn't mean to make it sound like that, I didn't know it was her who was on your mind."

Eli let out a long breath and hung his head so that his hair fell forwards, "No, I should apologise. I shouldn't have snapped."

Looking up at Eli's crestfallen face made me want to hug him and tell him that him missing his sister was normal and that she was happy.

"You can talk to me, you know," I said, trying to approach the subject gently.

Eli nodded and I asked, "Do you want to go outside?"

"It's too cold out there," he said quietly. "Let's go to the den."

The two of us went down into the basement and sat down on one of the small sofas, surrounded by beanbags, that faced the plasma TV and DVD case.

Eli sighed and looked down at his hands and I waited patiently for him to say whatever he wanted to.

"Eunice and I were really close," Eli said lowly. "It was better than having a best friend. That's how it felt like anyway."

"You never fought with each other?" I asked him, curling up in the sofa and listening to him speak.

"Yeah, we fought," Eli said. "But not as much as she and everyone else did actually, which was weird, because we were nearly always together so you would have thought we fought the most."

I smiled at his memories. It sounded like a lovely relationship.

"Ever since she left," Eli tugged at his hair. "I've felt lonely. She was my other half, we did everything together, shared the womb and all. Then one day, she was just...gone. Forever."

I felt my throat tightening and tried not to let my emotions overwhelm me. If I was struggling, I couldn't imagine how Eli was feeling and Eunice had been his fraternal twin. Irreplaceable.

"Eli," I took his hand. "I know nothing will replace the space Eunice left in your heart, but you still have all your brothers and they still have you. It makes me sad that you feel lonely, so please, please let your brothers in more. Don't shut them out as much as you do.

Maybe you'll feel better if you do that. I've talked to Walter about it too, he agreed that he'd try harder not to argue with you so much."

Eli didn't even deny that he often pushed his brothers away, especially Walter with whom he fought with a lot, and he nodded, swallowing. The tip of his nose had turned red and his hands were shaking. I squeezed his hand, trying to give some encouragement. I knew he was trying so hard to hold himself together.

"The day Eunice died," Eli said in a shaky voice. "We had an argument, and I never got to make up with her. I think that's what...hurts me the most. I..I didn't get to say a proper goodbye. She died angry at me and I can never forgive myself."

I didn't know how Eunice Simpson had died, but I imagined it had been quick if Eli hadn't been able to talk things over with her or say goodbye. It was heartbreaking that he thought her last memories she had of him would be bad ones.

"Children fight all the time," I said to him, still holding his hand. "I doubt it was so serious that she'd never be able to forgive you Eli. She loved you, and that's the most important thing."

Eli nodded, but I could tell he was unconvinced. I pulled him into a hug when I saw tears falling from his green eyes and I held him tight, trying to give him at least a little comfort. Eli hugged me back after a few broken sobs and I felt his body shuddering as he poured out his emotions. I tried not to cry. Him hurting, made me hurt....we had become family. I knew all the boys missed their sister and I wondered how they dealt with her loss. None of them had really spoken about her, except Walter – and seeing him cry had been very painful.

After what seemed like a while, but was probably just a couple of minutes, Eli pulled away, rubbing away the last of his tears.

"Sorry," he mumbled as he dried his face.

"No," I frowned, shaking my head. "There's nothing to be sorry about. We're all human, it's good to cry."

Eli's dimples shows as he gave me a watery smile, "Anyone who says that is a cry baby."

I smiled back at him, "Well I'm the biggest cry baby you'll ever meet then."

Eli smiled again and looked down in space, thinking. I didn't say anything, not wanting to interrupt his mind's thoughts on his sister.

"Thanks Coral," he said after a silence and then added a smirk, "and don't tell me there's nothing to thank you about either."

I laughed this time and pushed his shoulder playfully, "Come on Eli, let's go and get something to eat."

***

"Hey," Walter said to me, hugging me from behind as I washed up in the kitchen.

"How was your workout?" I smiled, enjoying the feel of his warmth.

"It was good," he replied. "Have you already eaten?"

"Not dinner," I said back. "This was a snack me and Eli had, I was thinking we should go out and buy food to cook with."

"You and Eli had a little snack together?" Walter repeated, with a hint of amusement in his voice. "What are you, nursery kids?"

"Well excuse me, Walter," I said, drying my hands and turning around to face him as he continued to hold be round the waist. "We were peckish."

Walter only half-smiled, his eyes staring at my lips. I leaned into him, wrapping my arms around his neck, and kissed him on the lips. Walter sighed in pleasure as he closed his eyes, instantly parting his lips to let me in. His heart was pounding and he gripped me harder as the intensity of the kiss increased. I broke off, breathless and trying not to blush. I'd felt his *passion* in more than one way.

"Is that Melody crying?" I changed the subject, moving past him and heading for the living room.

Opening the door, Melody seemed restless and she kept whimpering and pulling on Landon's hand, nearly in tears. Landon himself was lying in the sofa trying to get some sleep it looked like.

"Come and lie down," Landon held his arms out to her, but Melody shook her head, being difficult.

She kept pointing and rubbing her eyes as tears threatened to spill from them.

"Melody," Landon rubbed his face tiredly. "Daddy needs to sleep. When I wake up I can take you to the park, okay?"

It was already four in the afternoon and would be getting dark out very soon. I doubted Landon would fulfil that promise and Melody didn't seem to want to take any chances either.

"Mummy," Melody continued to moan, her beautiful brown eyes wide.

Landon sighed and then looked up at me and Walter in the doorway.

"She couldn't sleep because of her cold last night," he said to us. "So I was up trying to make sure she was okay and now she's had enough rest, she's bored and wants to go out, but I'm exhausted."

"You know," Walter said. "You didn't need to explain, we would have taken her so you could sleep anyway."

Landon smiled, "Thank you."

"Come on Melody," I went to take her hand.

"Mummy," she shook her head, reaching for Landon's hand again.

"Aunty Coral and Uncle Walter are taking you to the park," Landon said to her. "Go and get your shoes, alright? And don't forget your gloves, okay?"

"Okay," she replied in an adorable voice and allowed me to lead her out of the living room to put on her shoes and coat.

"Aunty Coral and Uncle Walter?" I heard Walter ask his brother in a dry voice.

"Its respect, isn't it?" Landon replied after a yawn. "When she grows up do you want her just calling you Walter? I wouldn't want your kids doing that to me."

I blinked to myself as I bent over to zip up Melody's coat. Landon casually talking about the children Walter and I would have in the future like that? It actually made me happy. I tried not to beam so much when I went to stand in the doorway by Walter's side.

"We're ready," I said to him after I'd gotten myself ready too.

"What's so funny?" Walter sent me an amused smile.

"Nothing," I said, brushing it away. "Go and put your shoes on, Melody can't wait any longer and it will be getting dark soon."

"Okay Melody," Walter crouched down and gave her cheeks a little squeeze before he went to get his shoes and jacket.

Melody was already pulling her gloves, which I had just put on her, off again. She sure was a stubborn child.

"Landon are you comfortable sleeping in the sofa?" I asked him before we went to leave.

He gave me a thumbs up, "I'm good, don't worry about me. Thanks for taking her out, I appreciate it loads."

"Not a problem," I grinned at him and turned off the light for him. "Later."

Walter and I took his niece to the playground in the central part of the borough where all the shops were. It was also the same playground that Ario and I had gone to one night, which seemed like such a long time ago. Thinking about that was sad. I'd really had fun and Ario had become like a brother to me after that, though it didn't last for long.

"Let her go," Walter said as Melody grinned excitedly.

Melody herself had already ripped her little hand out of my grip and was running to the climbing frames. I laughed as I watched her run, it was insanely cute. Walter and I helped her climb the steps and we cheered with her every time she went down the slide. To the few other people around, we must have looked like one happy family.

"We should go," I said to Walter as I swung Melody in the swing a little while later.

He looked up at the darkening sky, in fact, we were the only people left in the young children's part of the park.

"Yeah," he agreed, catching my eyes as he lowered his gaze from above.

I pulled Melody out of the baby swing and set her on the ground, only to catch Walter's gaze still on me. He smiled at me and I smiled back, a little bit confused.

"What?" I asked him patting my hair down in case it was a mess.

"You're perfect," he pulled my hand down and held it instead.

"Walter," I said, feeling embarrassed. "No one's perfect."

"You are to me," he grinned.

"Thank you," I said, leaning in closer to him so that our chests touched.

Walter held me around the waist and he ducked his head down to kiss my neck softly. The feel of his warm lips, so unbelievably gentle, against my cold skin made me shiver in pleasure. It was like we were magnets, unable to stay away from each other.

"Walter, kiss me properly," I whispered, getting caught up in the massive effect he was having on me.

Walter didn't need telling twice. He kissed me like crazy and wrapped myself up in him, feeling his hair, his face, his shoulders. It wasn't until I registered that I hadn't heard Melody for a while, that I pulled back sharply.

"She's gone," I said, my heart pounding like mad as I looked around the empty ground by our feet.

"Walter," I stared, feeling my blood freeze in my veins.

Melody was on the far side of the playground, running towards Miguel and Manuel Santiago who were standing by the fence, beckoning to her with mean smiles on their faces.

"Shit," Walter swore, already running after her. "Coral stay here."

I couldn't just stand and watch, so I started running after Walter, hoping that he would get to Melody before the Santiagos had her in their grips...hoping that I could help somehow.

"Melody!" Walter was shouting. "Melody, stop right now!"

Melody's steps faltered as she heard Walter's voice and Miguel Santiago ran forwards, trying to get to her before Walter did. Walter swore at him, yelling out threats but Miguel kept smiling, not even listening to his words.

Melody tripping over her own little feet was what saved the situation. Miguel and Walter reached her at the same time and Walter grabbed her first, spitting in Miguel's face furiously. The child had grazed her hands on the ground from the fall and had started to cry, and the angry shouting only made her cry louder.

Walter turned his back on the twins who were throwing back their own rude remarks and I took Melody from his arms, knowing how enraged he was. Melody clung onto me, wailing in my ear and I rubbed her back comfortingly, trying to get her to calm down.

"Come at me then," one of the boys called out to Walter. "*Hijo de puta!*"

"I need a distraction," Walter said, his chest heaving. "Coral, please. Distract me so I don't go back and kill those little shits. I'm trying so hard."

Without thinking, I stopped walking and grabbed him by the back of his hair with my free hand, kissing him hard. I could feel Walter's whole body shaking as hard as mine was, and I knew he was fighting against the urge to react to the Santiagos the way they wanted him to.

In my other arm, Melody had reduced her cries to quiet sniffing and I pulled away from Walter, making sure he was okay. I touched the side of his face, right where his healing wound was, and leant his forehead against mine.

"Are you okay?" I asked him quietly.

Walter nodded wordlessly, looking deep into my eyes as I did to his.

That was when I heard one of the twins say Ario's name.

"Hey Ario, you see that?" Miguel said with a laugh. "I think that one was for you."

I turned to look behind me and saw Ario standing by the gates with his younger brothers. Looking at him, I just knew he had been around the whole time and had seen everything. He knew what his brothers had tried to do, and he didn't do anything to stop them.

Did he really hate our guts so much that he'd put an innocent child in danger?

For the first time since everything had turned sour between us, I felt angry at him. So angry, that I didn't care if he'd just seen me and Walter kiss. Angry enough even, that I wouldn't have tried to stop Walter if he decided to go after him, but then I realised that was rash and unnecessary. I told myself not to care about Ario or his feelings anymore, and that there was no way Paulo had been correct in saying that this very same Ario Santiago was sorry about how he'd destroyed my home.

"Blue eyes isn't worth our time," I said to Walter, holding his hand hard as he turned and looked back at them. "Let's go home."

***

301

"Where have you been?" Landon jumped up from the sofa he was sitting in as soon as we got home. "It's so dark out and you've been gone for ages. I've been calling you Walter, but you didn't pick up."

Landon was already worried, and his brown eyes rounded when he saw Melody's glove-less, grazed hands and her tear-stained face.

"The Santiagos know about her," Walter explained.

"Come here," Landon said to her softly.

"Mummy!" she cried, elbowing me to get to her father.

Landon was mad now, I could tell by his clenched jaw and trembling hands. He handed his daughter to Phoenix, who held Melody at an arms distance before placing her down in the sofa.

"What the hell happened?" Landon growled at Walter.

Walter took breaths through his nose, trying to stay calm and it only caused Landon to grow angrier. He slammed Walter backwards, so that the door banged shut from the impact.

"Tell me what just happened," Landon demanded, his face just inches from his brother's. "Why was my baby crying? Why did you allow her to be put in danger?"

"Landon, get off me," Walter said in a tight tone.

"Talk then!" Landon shouted, jostling him.

I knew Walter was about to snap, which would have started a proper fight between them in an instant, and Phoenix knew that too. He stepped between the two, pulling Landon's hand off the front of Walter's jacket.

"Just talk Walter," Phoenix said calmly.

"I let her out of my sight and the blockheads almost had her," Walter muttered. "She fell over, that's why she was crying. I caught her before they could."

Landon narrowed his eyes at Walter, "Do you know what would have happened if you hadn't have caught her first?"

Walter didn't answer, he hardened his jaw and looked right back at him.

"That's not the point," I said, trying to dissolve the situation. "Melody is safe and we're so so sorry we almost let that happen."

Landon sighed and stepped away from Walter, forcing himself to breathe.

"I'm going to get them," he said, his voice shaking as he was still so angry. "I'll get each and every one of them who thinks they can try to abduct my child, with the idea that I'd be fine with that."

"Landon," Phoenix said quietly.

"No," Landon snapped at him. "I'm going after them right now. I'll even put a bullet in Carlos' head if I have to. Thinking it's a decent thing to allow members of his gang to harm a child, a *two year old* child?"

I'd never heard Landon speak like that before, in fact, I didn't think I'd even seen him that angry, and Melody was seeing it too, sitting in the sofa and watching him silently with her innocent brown eyes.

"I'm going," Landon was saying, heading for the door to most likely gather some dangerous weapons.

"Landon," Phoenix stopped him and put a hand on his shoulder. "Wait for the right time. They'll be expecting it otherwise. Come on, don't be rash."

Landon hung his head and Phoenix did what I thought as the nicest thing ever when he pulled his little brother into a hug.

"The baby is fine," Phoenix said. "It was an accident, but she's okay. I know you were worried and very upset, but don't let her see you like this."

"Okay," Landon's voice cracked as he put his head down on Phoenix's shoulder.

"Mummy," Melody pushed herself out of the sofa and ran to hug Landon's legs.

"It's okay baby," Landon smiled softly and bent down to pick her up. "Daddy's fine. Let's go and wash your hands and have a bath, okay?"

"Okay," Melody leaned her head on Landon and the two of them left.

Phoenix looked at Walter after Landon had gone, and Walter said nothing. I thought Phoenix was going to rant about how we should have been careful (ignoring me the whole while, of course) and telling us how stupid we were for almost allowing Landon's child to be taken by their mortal enemies.

He didn't.

"Be careful next time," was all Phoenix said and after a sigh, he too left.

33

"Coral?" Walter asked me at lunch. "Are you working after school today?"

"No," I shook my head. "It's Friday today. How come?"

"No reason," Walter shrugged, giving me a smile. "I lose track of the days you work, that's all."

"Did you have any plans?" I smirked at him.

"Well," Walter said, dipping his head forwards. "I'm not going to give anything away."

"Good," I beamed. "Well in that case you can go shopping with me, maybe we can get Landon to drive us."

Walter hesitated, clearly having something else on his mind.

"Landon is busy this evening," he said. "Phoenix is too."

"Damn Walter," I threw a piece of lettuce at his arm. "You should really learn to drive."

"Yeah?" he cocked an eyebrow at me. "And what's your excuse not to?"

"Um...I..."

"Exactly," he grinned triumphantly. "Neither of us can be bothered."

I had nothing to say, he was right. My silence, along with my defeated face made Walter laugh loud.

"Aren't those the triplets?" I frowned when I noticed action outside behind him, "...and a dog?"

Walter turned around in his seat to see Gomez, Gio and Severn running across the school fields laughing as they got chased by the School Marshal and the Deputy Head. Gomez had a little dog in his arms which looking like it was enjoying the game of chase.

"What have they done now?" Eli muttered as he came to join our table with Hayley.

"Must be serious," Hayley craned her head so she could get a better look. "They've even got big man Steve running."

Big man Steve, or the Deputy Headmaster, was clearly struggling to keep up and the triplets kept splitting up and running in circles, dodging the much more agile School Marshal.

"I can tell they won't be coming to school after this for a while," Walter said, turning his back on them and getting back to his lunch.

Walter had been right.

The triplets all gotten expelled that very same day for the attempted theft of the Headmaster's dog, which had been in school for the day, as well as for verbal abuse directed at senior members of staff. To be honest, the whole thing was too funny to be taken seriously. I knew the triplets wouldn't try to enrol in another school and it was a shame because they needed as much education as they could get at their age. The only thing that bothered Severn about it was not seeing the girl he liked as often anymore.

After school, Walter had gone out with Phoenix for business he hadn't want to tell me about. I assumed that I didn't want to know. He didn't want me mixed in with the illegal side of the gang and I wasn't complaining. I was only worried about him.

"Gio," I said, leaning in the doorway of the triplets' room. "We still up for the food shopping?"

"Yep," he got to his feet.

"We have to eat balanced," I said to him, trying to make sure we were on the same page.

"Yeah," Gio nodded. "Fifty percent carbs and fifty percent meat, my kind of balance."

I shook my head at him playfully and waved goodbye to Melody who was playing on the floor whilst Gomez and Severn supervised her. I'd asked Gio to come with me because I needed someone to help me carry the shopping and I knew he'd be enthusiastic about food.

"Let's go," I said to him.

"After you," Gio held the door open for me as we walked out.

"Thanks," I smiled at him.

"No problem," he said, closing the front door after him.

"So what possessed you to try and steal the Headmaster's dog?" I had to ask as we walked in the wintery afternoon.

"Oh that," Gio grinned widely.

"What do you mean, 'oh that'?" I cried. "You're telling me you forgot you got expelled today already?"

Gio started laughing, "Only momentarily. We didn't go that often anyway so it doesn't make that much of a difference."

"Okay," I raised my hand. "Fair enough."

"We were going to kidnap it and make him pay a ransom," Gio explained.

"Right," I blinked in utter disbelief. "Gio, even if that plan had worked...you've got enough money anyway, what do you need ransom money for?"

"It was Gomez's idea," he said. "He's always after things. He loves taking, I'm pretty sure he's a kleptomaniac."

"Don't say that," I couldn't help but smile in amusement.

"I'm not joking," he cried. "Gomez can't stop stealing, he always wants more. Nothing satisfies him, ever."

"Well that's something he'll have to address someday," I said, "before he ends up in jail."

"Oh juvenile detention?" Gio said casually. "That's bearable."

I shook my head to myself, "Will any of you ever learn?"

"No," he responded without delay.

When we reached the supermarket, Giovanni literally grabbed me by the arm and pulled me to all his favourite aisles. It took longer than I thought it would, mainly because Gio wouldn't stop talking about random things like frozen calamari and pickled gherkins. In the end I told him we had to stop because we wouldn't be able to carry it home, which made him start stuffing the smaller items in his pockets.

"That's stealing," I said quietly.

"Coral, it's calm," Gio grinned at me. "What do you like? *Mars* or *Snickers*?"

"Neither," I said before he could grab any more. "Let's go and pay."

I paid with the money Phoenix had given me after he'd asked me why I was writing a list. I had told him that I was planning to buy proper food for the house and he had simply told me not to use my own money before leaving the kitchen only to return with a large amount of cash. 'For the house', he had said, and even muttered a little 'thank you'.

On the way back home, Giovanni asked us to walk fast so that he could get home and eat quicker (as he was currently unable to because he had both hands occupied with the shopping). I couldn't stop laughing because I knew he was being genuine and I asked him to allow me to just pop into work for me to collect my payslip as it was now the end of November.

But things never turned out that way.

It was already dark out when The Dartfish came into view and Gio and I were still a small distance away when we saw a couple of the Santiagos leaving the pub and entering the street lit pavement outside. I recognised Diego immediately, his unkempt hair and cocky gait was unique only to a scumbag like himself. With Diego, was a slightly taller man, and Giovanni murmured 'Skull face' which confirmed that it was Carlos. The blockheads were also there, and they weren't the only ones who were surprised when Landon Simpson and his brothers jumped out of the shadows at them.

I stood in disbelief, watching the fight unfold itself on the street. Walter was there and he was fighting Diego as Eli battled one of the twins. Landon already had his knife out, and he was slashing expertly at the other twin, like he was playing a deadly game of fencing. He was amazing, very skilled at striking and dodging. But not as good as Phoenix...who of course I had built up to be one of the best fighters.

I sure wasn't let down.

Phoenix hit Carlos with his bare fists and Carlos struggled to shield himself at first, as he was caught unaware. I saw metal glinting on Phoenix's knuckles and realised that he had knuckle dusters on and was most likely doing a lot of damage to Carlos' exceptional facial structure. The force at which Phoenix rained down his blows was frightening, and now I knew why Walter had wanted to make sure I was nowhere near work when this happened.

Carlos didn't falter for long. He too had a mean reputation for a reason and he had slipped out a blade quicker than I could blink. He lunged at Phoenix and for a second I'd thought Phoenix had been impaled right in the gut. It was a miss, but only just. Phoenix had been cut, but not as badly as Carlos had wanted.

My attention was brought back to Landon as he cried out, punching and violently kicking one of the blockheads in a mad frenzy. The kid didn't stand a chance. Landon knocked him out cold and stood over his limp body, his chest rising and falling as he caught his breath. He swore and spat on the Santiago before turning his attention to fighting the other twin along with Eli.

"Let's go," Gio nudged me. "As bad as I want to join the fight, the ice-cream is melting."

I blinked a couple of time as he brought me back to my senses. Ice-cream was another one of the things Giovanni had insisted on. Who else would buy it in the dead of winter? We took another route out of the town centre and into West side territory.

"Did you know that was going to happen?" I asked Giovanni, still unable to take in the level of anger I'd just seen coming off from all the Simpson brothers and not just Walter.

"Yeah," he answered. "But I didn't think we'd walk right into it."

"Walter didn't tell me," I said, feeling dejected.

"He didn't want you to worry," Gio gave me a smile.

I knew he was right, but it didn't make me feel much better.

I fixed up a quick stir-fry when we got home and the triplets ate so much, that I had to make a second batch just for the others when they got home. Melody sat and copied the boys as they purposely slurped their noodles messily, getting sauce all over her face.

"Yes, that's right," Gomez said to her. "Show your mum that beautiful way to eat your meal next time."

"Yeah, well who's gonna clean her face?" Severn questioned. "Didn't think about that did you?"

I smiled and tried not to think about how Walter hadn't been so honest with me. That's what was bothering me, not the fighting, but the way he'd led me to believe he was going out to handle something that concerned illegal substances. I don't know why he hadn't just told me the truth, I wouldn't have tried to stop him. I was mad about the near abduction of Melody too.

When the older boys finally arrived home, they acted like normal. Which I guess a fight *was*, for them. I looked for any signs of serious injuries and was relieved when I saw none. I noticed Phoenix applying pressure to his abdomen, but I knew he'd decline any help, so I didn't ask.

"Melody," Landon beamed brightly when he saw his daughter sitting in the living room sofa watching TV with us.

"Mummy," she cried, pushing herself off to go and give him a hug.

Landon got down to his knees and engulfed her in a massive bear hug. When he let her go he pulled out a cuddly animal from his back.

"Look what Daddy got for you," Landon widened his eyes and grinned.

Melody took the toy dog and smiled so widely, I would have squealed if I wasn't upset with Walter.

Melody just had no idea what her daddy had been up to today.

"Hey," Walter came and sat on the arm of my chair.

He had a forming bruise under his right eye and I was just so relieved that Diego's fist hadn't found the healing cut that was on the other side of his face.

"Hi," I greeted him, dropping my gaze from his wounds and looking back to the TV.

Walter immediately sensed something and he gave me a concerned look.

"What's wrong?" he asked me.

I refused to say anything in front of those in the living room, so I stood up and asked him to come with me. Walter did so without a word and we went up to his room where it was quiet.

"Why didn't you just tell me you went to fight?" I asked him quietly.

Walter swallowed, "I didn't want you to – "

"It's not about that," I cut him off. "You were dishonest Walter, and that hurts. Everyone knew except from me, and I wouldn't have even tried to stop you going."

Walter sighed, giving me a heartfelt look, "It wasn't my intention to make you upset, like I said, I was trying to do the opposite."

I nodded, "I know, but I just wanted to tell you how I felt about it."

"I understand," Walter said, looking down at his carpet.

"I made dinner," I said after a pause. "It's in the kitchen."

Walter glanced up at me, "You've eaten?"

"Yeah," I nodded, sitting on the bed. "I'm gonna get an early night."

"Okay," Walter stood there for a second longer and then he turned to leave. "Sleep well."

"Night," I said, looking at the back of his broad shoulders before he closed the door after him.

Well, there was our first 'fight'.

It wasn't really an argument or anything explosive, but neither of us were feeling too great about it. I was half asleep when Walter returned hours later, and it was strange not cuddling up like we usually did. I felt awful and I knew he did too. Hopefully tomorrow it would have washed over. I didn't have the courage to try and speak to him in fear of making things worse.

I woke up with a jerk as my sleep was torn apart by nightmares. Panting in the dark, I tried to breathe properly and relax. Beside me, Walter was still asleep, breathing deeply. He would have woken up if he'd been holding me, he would have told me that I was okay, I was safe with him.

Letting out a shaky sigh, I sat up and got out of the bed. I couldn't face trying to go back to sleep only to be plunged right back where I'd left off. It was strange not being at home in the middle of the night when I used to do my homework. I walked out of Walter's room and into the darkness in the corridor. I jumped about three feet in the air when one of the bedroom doors opened and a shadowy figure walked out.

"Coral?" I recognised Severn's voice.

"Yeah?" I tried to make him out in the gloom.

"What are you doing?" he walked up to me.

"I couldn't sleep," I whispered, able to make out his blond hair and smiling face.

"Same here," he replied. "Usually it's just me, but tonight I've got company."

"Count me in," I joked, swinging my fist in an arc-motion across the front of my body.

"Were you going down to have a midnight feast or something?" Severn asked me.

"Oh, no," I shook my head with a little laugh. "I was going to get some water."

"Well I'll escort you," he grinned, holding out his arm.

I was glad I had him to hold onto, because the walk down the pitch black stairs would have been treacherous alone, and I wouldn't have wanted to have to turn on the light and burn my eyes as well as risk waking anyone else up.

We got into the kitchen and Severn flicked on the light.

"What time is it?" I asked him as I poured myself a glass.

"It's three in the morning," he replied, not sounding like he'd been asleep one bit. Severn was wearing grey jogging bottoms and a loose white t-shirt.

"So you've been awake all this time?" I asked, leaning against the sink to face him.

"Yeah," Severn sighed. "It's annoying as hell, but that's what my condition does to me."

"Narcolepsy," I said. "Walter told me about it once."

"Yeah," he nodded. "That's the one. I slept like six hours during the day so I couldn't get to sleep in the night."

"Don't worry," I smiled. "Like you said, you've got company this time."

"Wait," Severn rounded his eyes. "You're not going back to sleep at all?"

"No," I said, trying to make a light subject out of it. "I'll catch up some other time."

"Sure," Severn said, shrugging it off. "Well do you want to go sit in the living room? It's kind of cold in here."

"I agree," I said, hoping that it wasn't evident through the front of my shirt.

Severn didn't seem to notice and we walked into the living room and sat in one of the sofas.

"I wonder what's on at this time," I murmured to myself as I pointed the remote towards the TV.

"Nothing but shit and teleshopping," Severn said in a bored voice, clearly having gone through the same thing hundreds of times.

I didn't even bother switching it on and turned to look in the corner where a small coffee table was placed.

"Anything interesting to read?"

Severn gave me a dull look, "Do I look like I read?"

I laughed, "Reading isn't that bad, you should try it sometime, I bet you'll find something you really like."

I leaned over to the coffee table, rifling through the messy pile of magazines found there, as Severn pleaded with me not to. I didn't find a single reading book, but ended up picking a wine coloured folder which looked like a photo album.

I turned to face Severn with a grin, "Will I find embarrassing baby pictures in here?"

Severn's face said it all, and I jumped back into the sofa next to him with the album on my lap.

"Warning," Severn said in a monotone voice. "The following piece includes plenty of nudity, some of which viewer may find disturbing."

I laughed, trying (and failing) to keep my voice down.

"I hope you're joking," I bit my lip, opening the first page.

"You know I'm not," Severn replied with a childish grin.

Stuck in on the inside of the front cover was a picture of a couple. The man was tall and well-built with dark hair and the woman had long blonde hair and dimples. They were both wearing expensive looking clothing and no smiles. The picture had been taken from too far away for me to see the colour of their eyes, but there was definitely a resemblance between them and all seven of their boys.

"Your parents," I murmured, staring at the photo.

"Yeah," Severn nodded.

The only clue that would show that they were criminals ruling a mini drug empire, would be the cold expression Severn's father held on his face and the similarly vacant expression on his mother's.

"What were their names?" I asked quietly.

"Dennis and Cassandra Simpson," Severn said, looking at the picture with a frown. "They died in a road accident after they left us here, just like my sister had died a couple of years earlier."

I sighed, the same thing twice? How tragic. No wonder Eli hadn't had the chance to say goodbye to Eunice, she'd probably died instantly.

"Can we turn over now?" Severn said impatiently, looking away from the image of his parents.

I did so and saw that the next page was filled with pictures of Phoenix. Being the oldest, it made sense that he came first. In some of the photos, he was his age now, but others he was considerably younger. His expression was always reserved, even from when he was a young teen. It reminded me of the picture I saw of his father and it was a little bit sad.

Flicking over the next couple of pages, I came upon Landon's pictures. The first photo made me laugh. Landon was about two years old, stark naked and posing with his hands on his hips. Severn grinned.

"Who took this?" I asked still smiling.

"Mum. She took a lot of baby photos."

We looked at the photos of Landon. There was one where he was maybe thirteen, holding up a magazine with a girls butt on it. The boys must have taken some of the pictures themselves. Landon had an amazing smile and he must have gotten his piercing when he was fourteen, fifteen. In another photo he had his hand down his pants and was giving the camera a sexy wink. I laughed, looking forwards to Walter's pages.

"Who organised all this?" I questioned Severn.

"Me and Giovanni, it took ages," he replied.

"You did a great job," I praised.

"Thanks," Severn said lazily and then he groaned. "Enough of Landon, turn the page."

I rolled my eyes playfully at him and I did as he requested. Turning onto Walter's section, I found there were only a few pictures, much less than what Phoenix and Landon had. In the first one, he was a tiny baby and was being held by his mother I assumed. I couldn't be sure, because her face had been scratched out, but the woman had blonde hair.

"Did Walter do this?" I asked, rubbing the damaged material with my finger.

"Yep. He hates them," Severn said. "He pretty much destroyed all the pictures of them...and the ones of Eunice too, but Phoenix saved some. I guess seeing her face is...too much for Walter to handle."

The next picture of Walter was one where he was maybe around four or five. He was red in the face with his arms tightly crossed around his small body. Severn smiled widely, his greeny blue eyes alight.

"I don't remember why he was mad, but it's funny," he chuckled.

I gave a faint smile. Walter had had his attitude from a very young age. There was another photo where Walter was mad again, older this time. He was sitting on the floor, in his early teens and was glaring at the person holding the camera, his dark hair a mess. In fact, the only photo of Walter smiling was one where we was side on from the camera, wearing only jeans and an unzipped hoodie, underneath which he wasn't wearing anything. In his hand he held a penknife and the smile on his face was frightening, but sexy all the same.

Turning over to the Eli's part, I almost scrunched my toes in delight. Eli was easily one of the cutest babies I had ever seen. The blond hair and the dimples did it for me. In one picture, Eli was staring intently at someone to his left in annoyance, the camera picking up all the detail in his tousled hair and the muscles in his clenched jaw. Eli didn't have many pictures, but he smiled in more of them than Walter did.

Looking at the triplets when they were just toddlers, I definitely could not tell the difference, but they were all adorable. In one picture two of them were wearing only nappies and hugging, while the last was crossing his arms, as if to say he wasn't taking part. In another, all three of them were reaching for the camera. There were a few more pictures were the triplets were older, smirking, winking, and throwing hand gestures. They just had so much fun together.

Turning through the last few occupied pages I came across group photos.

Eli and Phoenix, their arms round each other as children. Walter and Landon fighting outside, Walter with his hands wrapped around Landon's neck, and Landon kneeing Walter in the gut. They looked so similar when they were angry.

I started laughing when I saw the photo of Severn sitting in the sofa, being kissed by a much older girl with dyed black hair in a very tiny dress and stiletto heels. The next one was of Severn again, this time slouched asleep in the same sofa up against Giovanni who was in hysterical laughter and Landon who was crouched down at the front, pointing at Severn and looking at the camera with a massive grin and wide eyes.

"You need to explain this one to me," I said to him, laughing so hard I almost cried.

Severn smiled, trying to hide his face.

"Landon's girlfriend of the week came round and he knew I thought she was hot so he asked her to kiss me and well...I was really thrilled one second and asleep the next," Severn said, looking at the memories. "It happens sometimes."

"You kill me," I held my stomach tightly as I struggled to control myself.

"Yeah, no one let it rest for quite a while afterwards," Severn shook his head.

I grinned turning back to the album. A young Phoenix showing a tiny Walter how to put on one of those kiddie watches. It was the sweetest thing ever. Eli and Walter hugging, the sides of their toddler faces pressed together. Landon and Phoenix were having an arm wrestle, both their biceps double the size they normally were. There was a photo of a fight, this time it was Giovanni and Eli, and Landon was pulling them apart, then another of the triplets trading knives. A photo of Landon and Gomez shirtless, posing at the beach. Walter and Eli sharing bed as little kids, Walter was not happy about it one bit. Another with Eli and Landon sharing a bubble bath, baby Eli putting a load of foam onto Landon's head, who was crying.

The last couple of photos made me really smile. There was a picture of all seven of them, walking together wearing snapbacks with hoodies drawn over them. Phoenix was younger, they all were. Severn was giving the camera a lazy grin and Giovanni and Gomez giving hand gestures. Landon was grinning, his arms around Walter and Eli. Walter wasn't even looking at the camera, but he looked absolutely gorgeous.

The rest of the pages were empty and so I began to close the book. The back cover had come apart and in trying to find a way to fix it, I saw a corner of another photo poking out. I slowly pulled the hidden picture out and felt shivers run up my arms.

The photo was of all the Simpson children, including Eunice. She looked seven or eight and so I guessed it must have been taken at a time close to her death. She had her little arms hooked around Eli and they were both grinning showing their identical dimples. They really did look so alike. The triplets couldn't have been more than six years old and they too were smiling widely. Walter was even smiling and so were Phoenix and Landon. It was the cutest, yet saddest photo because none of them knew that their dear sister would be ripped away from them so soon afterwards.

I slipped the photo back in its hidden place and closed the album, feeling my throat tighten. I just had so much emotion for the beautiful girl I'd never had the pleasure to meet.

34

I was not happy.

That time of the month had arrived and my mood had taken a downwards swing along with getting no sleep last night at all. It took my everything to keep smiling and continue with a good attitude as cramps tried to tear my stomach apart. None of the Santiagos showed. I assumed they were recovering from the vicious onslaught the Simpsons had laid on them the night before.

When my shift finally came to an end, I was up and out the back door in an instant, almost forgetting to even take my payslip. Grabbing it, I scowled to myself as I marched to the exit, thinking about having a long hot shower when I got home.

It nearly made me smile.

Until I came face to face with no one other than Blue eyes.

He was standing outside the back door, hands deep in his pockets and his face looking serious and a little bit red from the cold. I didn't even attempt to say anything to him, I wasn't in the right frame of mind.

"Coral," he called after me as I walked right past him.

In fact, right now was the worst time that this could be happening. I didn't want to snap at him, but I knew that was what would happen if he kept going.

"Wait," Ario grabbed my arm in a firm but not too tight grip.

"Get off me," I snarled, not even able to look him in the face.

"Relax," he frowned, releasing me. "I wanted to talk to you."

"About?" I lifted my gaze to give him my full attention.

Ario hesitated and I shook my head at him, "I have to go."

"Coral," he said again, looking at me with sad eyes.

"I'm not in the mood," I frowned, looking away.

"Is this because of that kid?" he asked me.

"Do you even have to ask?" my frown intensified.

I went to leave again, but Ario took hold of my wrist and I snapped. Shouting at him, I yanked my arm from him angrily and even went back to give him a shove in the chest.

"Was that really necessary?" he asked, barely taking a step back, which only made me madder. Today just wasn't my day.

"Leave me alone!" I yelled in his face so hard that my voice cracked and tears sprang to my eyes.

My throat hurt and I refused to let him see that I was close to tears. Ario looked down at me in surprise, his lips parted as if he was about to say something. He paused for too long, because I was already gone. Storming down the street, I chose not to think about what had just happened.

***

"How was wor – "

Walter cut himself off when he saw my thunderous expression. I didn't say a word to him and I went straight into the bathroom, locking myself in. I tore my clothes off in frustration and turned the shower on, waiting for it to warm up.

"Coral," I heard Walter's voice outside, soft and gentle.

"Yes?" I answered in a clipped tone.

"What happened?" he asked me.

"I don't want to talk about it Walter," I called back.

He paused and to my alarm I heard him unlocking the door from the outside.

"Don't!" I cried, throwing myself against the door as he began to open it.

I heard him grunt as I caught him off-guard. I'd probably hurt him, he had gained a few more bruises after the brawl last night.

"Talk to me, dammit!" Walter yelled.

"Don't raise your voice at me," I shouted back at him, feeling hot with anger.

There was another long pause and I leant against the door, my body shuddering as I fought to control my emotions.

"Coral," Walter's voice sounded so close.

I gave up. I wanted to feel his body against mine, to ask him to forgive me. I felt tears fall from my eyes involuntarily and I didn't bother brushing them away. Fluctuating hormones and extreme lack of sleep didn't go well together. I gripped my stomach as another cramp took me by surprise. Gritting my teeth and waited a couple agonising seconds until it had passed, before getting into the shower.

Walter waited for me in his bedroom and when I got there, he looked up at me from his bed with a confused expression.

"What's going on?" his voice was barely above a whisper.

I stood there in my towel with my underwear underneath and my hair still dripping wet, before I burst into tears.

Walter's eyebrows rose and he instantly got up and walked towards me swiftly. He stopped himself abruptly when he was a foot away from me and I knew he was trying not to make me nervous or uncomfortable as I was practically in a state of undress.

I closed the distance between us and threw myself at him, crying hysterically as my body shook like a leaf. I was tired, angry, in a whole lot of pain and confused about Ario's intentions.

"I'm sorry Walter," I sobbed into his shoulder. "I didn't mean to snap at you."

Walter held me tightly, not giving a damn that I was making his clothes damp.

"Tell me what's going on Coral, I don't understand," he murmured into my hair.

"I didn't sleep last night," I choked as I struggled to get my words out. "I've got cramps...and Blue eyes just tried to speak to me but I just...I flipped out, I don't want to talk to him or any of the Santiagos."

Walter loosened his grip on me so that he could pull back to look at my face. As he did so, my towels slipped and before I could grab it, I was seized by another painful cramp and gasped, unable to move as I bound my arms around my waist. Walter didn't look at my body, he quickly whipped off the t-shirt he was wearing and put it over my head. He bent down and scooped me up into his arms, carrying me the short distance to his bed as my muscles clenched in pain. Laying me down and pulling the sheets over me and sat on the edge of the bed, rubbing my damp hair out of my face.

"Are you okay?" he asked me.

"Yeah," I nodded, able to breathe again.

"When did Blue eyes try to speak to you?" Walter asked me softly.

"After work," I mumbled as soon as I was able to speak again. "He said he wanted to talk to me but I shouted at him and pushed him. I think he was trying to apologise...about the flat. Like Paulo said."

"Apologies aren't going to change anything," Walter said, keeping his voice level and calm. "He's not important anyway Coral, what's important is you. You need some sleep."

"I need painkillers," I replied, closing my eyes.

Walter paused, probably imagining what sort of experience I was going through.

"I'll get you some," he said, getting up.

Walter was back in minutes with a glass of water and painkillers in his palm. He helped me sit up and swallow them and when I was done, I lay back down. This time Walter slipped in next to me.

"I'm sorry you're hurting," he said over my shoulder, holding me from behind.

"It's not your fault," I replied, curling my toes in discomfort as more cramps came.

Walter rubbed my stomach as the contractions gripped me, while I groaned quietly in pain. His circular hand movements actually started to sooth me after a while and every time a cramp came, Walter would feel my body clench and he would rub my stomach until it went away.

"I love you Walter," I said quietly as he lulled me to sleep.

"I love you too," he replied.

***

The next time I awoke, it was early evening and I could hear a lot of noise in the house.

"What's happening?" I asked sleepily.

"I don't know," Walter started to rise, still lying behind me.

I smiled and turned over so that I could face him, "Did you fall asleep too?"

Walter rubbed his eye, "I think so."

We lay together for a few more moments, listening to each other's beating hearts, until the noise grew so great I just had to see what it was all about.

"You look so good in my shirt," Walter said, smirking at me from his bed.

I blushed, looking down at myself in Walter's grey t-shirt that swamped my frame. To be honest, I liked wearing his clothes.

Walter and I got dressed and we ventured out of Walter's room. The first thing I saw was little Melody running past stark naked and laughing. Landon was chasing her, crying with laughter, and I could hear the triplets chuckling as well as Hayley?

"Is Hayley here?" I asked Gomez as he came up the stairs, still laughing.

"Yeah, she's downstairs," he said.

"Melody, bath time! Your mother will be here soon," I heard Landon call from somewhere upstairs.

"Melody's leaving?" I stared at Gomez in surprise, I hadn't been expecting her to go so soon.

"Yeah," Gomez sighed. "She's going today."

"Already?" Walter murmured, seeming to have not known either.

"Yep," Gomez replied.

We turned our attention to Landon who had come out of Phoenix's room with his daughter still kicking in his arms. Phoenix shut the door firmly behind them, making me smile to myself.

"Why did you go in there?" Walter asked him with a laugh. "You probably distressed the Phoenix."

Landon laughed loudly, "The Phoenix? Melody is a naughty girl, I tried to stop her but she knew exactly what she was doing."

Walter shook his head at his sweet little niece, who grinned back at him.

"I smell food," I said, rubbing my stomach which was now rumbling.

"Hayley made cupcakes," Gomez said. "They're really good, I've had like five."

"Well she must have made a hundred in the first place then," I scoffed, following him down the stairs. "Think about how many Gio's had."

"Very true," Gomez said over his shoulder.

Downstairs Hayley was in the kitchen with Eli, who was helping her with what looked like a second batch of cupcakes. Eli was creaming the butter and sugar together and Hayley was filling a tray with cupcake cases. The sight was simply adorable.

"Hey," I grinned at her, so happy to see her at the house and knowing that it had been Eli who'd invited her.

"Hi Coral," Hayley turned and beamed at me, coming up to me to give me a hug. "How have you been?"

"Okay," I squeezed her back, feeling so much better now that the painkillers were doing their job.

"Walter, you good?" Hayley gave him a hug too.

"I'm good," Walter smiled, hugging her back.

"It's really nice to see you here," I said to her. "A lovely surprise."

"Well," Hayley shrugged a shoulder and looked back at Eli. "He gave a proposal I couldn't decline."

"What?" Walter and I gave her a questionable look.

"All I said was: do you want to come round and eat something sweet?" Eli turned to explain to us in a deadpan voice. "Apparently that sounded dirty or something and she couldn't stop laughing on the phone for about five minutes straight."

Hayley looked like she was about to start laughing again and I grinned, "You gotta admit Eli, it does sound a bit dirty."

"I'm sorry Eli," Hayley leaned up and kissed his dimpled cheek with her red lips. "Did I embarrass you darling?"

"Not at all," Eli rolled his green eyes and put his arms around Hayley's shoulders from behind, leaning on her so that she stumbled around complaining about how heavy he was.

We spent just under an hour baking (well instructing the boys how to) and icing the cupcakes with pretty designs. I ate so much afterwards that I felt a bit sick and Walter almost threw up after Eli decided it would be nice to punch him in the stomach for commenting about Eli's virginity. Surprisingly, Walter didn't pursue a fight and Hayley whispered to me that she thought Eli being 'innocent' was cute.

Melody joined us after her bath and she ate some of the cupcakes, licking the sugary icing off her lips.

"What's my name?" Walter said to her as he held her on his lap.

Melody smiled, refusing to answer him.

"Looks like she doesn't know it," Eli said sarcastically.

"She does," Walter insisted, smiling at Melody. "What's my name?"

"I wouldn't expect an answer from her to be honest," I started to laugh. "She still calls her dad 'mummy'."

"She does?" Hayley grinned in amusement.

Landon himself was in and out of the kitchen, packing little snacks in Melody's bag and making her laugh by tickling her under the chin every time he passed her. He looked a little sad, but that may have just been me over interpreting things.

When there was a knock at the front door, the triplets came running down the stairs and I wondered what was going on.

"She's here," Eli scowled.

"Who?" Hayley looked confused.

"The bit – "

"Melody's mum," I cut Walter off.

"Aw," Hayley pulled a sad face. "Melody is going?"

"Yep," Landon said, going towards the door. "Say goodbye Melody."

"Bubye," Melody cried, laughing for the fun of it.

"Aw bye baby," I reached over Walter and gave her a tight hug.

Melody was pushing me away after a couple of seconds and then Hayley gave her a hug, followed by Eli and the triplets. Phoenix was even downstairs too and he waited in the kitchen doorway whilst Landon spoke to Melody's mother at the door.

"Time to go," Landon came back into the house after a few minutes.

He took Melody from Walter and carried her to the door. Phoenix patted Melody on the back, which I guessed was his version of a hug, and the triplets hurried out after Landon.

I walked out of the kitchen and saw a tall woman with tanned skin and curly hair standing about a couple centimetres into the house. I'm very sure Landon had offered her to come inside out of courtesy, but she'd refused.

She was looking behind Landon with nervous glances and I didn't blame her.

The triplets were brandishing knives.

Giovanni was checking his white teeth in the reflection of one blade, whilst Severn used another sharp edged knife to get the dirt out from under his nails. Gomez was sheathing and unsheathing his switchblade over and over again slowly and I tried not to grin my head off. They were truly hilarious.

"Come here baby," Melody's mother said, holding her arms out to Melody who was up in Landon's arms.

"Daddy," Melody turned away from her and held onto Landon, gripping her little hands into his shirt.

"I'll miss you Melody," Landon held her tight, closing his eyes as he hugged her. "See you soon, okay? I love you."

Walter, who was standing a couple steps behind Landon, must have been fixing Melody's mother with a deathly look because she glanced at him and quickly averted her gaze, then proceeded to try and pull Melody away from her father. Melody started kicking at her and she even cursed which she must have picked up from the boys. I was shocked and her mother was in complete disbelief.

She snatched Melody from Landon, despite her starting to cry, and raised her hand to slap Landon who made no attempt to stop her. Walter did, however. Melody's mother pulled her hand out of Walter's grip and stared at them in anger.

"How could you allow her to pick up such language Landon?" she glared at him accusingly. "She's only two years old!"

"I'm sure she knew a lot of it before she came here," Landon replied evenly. "She's a stubborn kid, you never taught her to stay away from strangers."

"So that's all my fault then?" she retorted.

"If you'd let me be in her life a lot more often, then maybe things would be different," Landon said, trying not to get angry.

Melody's mother laughed bitterly, "You mean worse? Look at them – " she gestured to the rest of us, "why would I want my child in such a dangerous environment."

"They're my brothers," Landon replied. "I'm no different."

"Exactly," she said with disgust in her features.

"She's perfectly safe here," Walter added, balling his fists in anger by his sides.

"Look," Landon held up his hands. "Let's not do this here, in front of her. I'll call you Felicity, we'll talk about this."

"Whatever," the woman scowled at him and pulled Melody's little bag from Landon's free hand. "We'll talk."

"Daddy!" Melody was crying. "Walt-er!"

Landon kissed her wet cheek and Walter reached out and ruffled her curly hair with a sad smile as her mother gave the rest of us one last frown before she turned and left, taking a screaming Melody with her. She was still crying for her dad when Walter closed the door and everyone's shoulders slumped in sorrow. I felt so sorry for both Landon and his little girl, we all did. Landon turned away, ignoring Walter's comforting hand and heading upstairs for his room.

"What a bitch," Hayley muttered, looking down with a sympathetic expression.

Eli put a hand on her shoulder with a similar sour expression on his face.

"Do you think someone should go and talk to him?" I murmured to Walter and Phoenix. "To see if he's okay?"

Phoenix thought about it, "He wants to be alone."

There was a shout and a smashing sound from upstairs and we all jerked in alarm.

"Was that glass?" Severn looked at his brothers with wide eyes.

Giovanni and Gomez started running up the stairs first and soon we were all following them. Landon was sobbing when we got up there, sitting on the edge of the bath with his blood dripping on the floor. The bathroom mirror had been smashed into little pieces.

"Everyone," Phoenix said, taking charge and blocking the door. "It's best if you don't crowd him, I'll talk to him."

We nodded in understanding and after sending a few more worried looks into the bathroom, we left.

"I'll go and get Phoenix the medical bag," I said to Walter. "He'll need it."

"Okay," Walter nodded, still mad about Melody's mother.

Going into the kitchen, I went to get the bag and returned to the bathroom. Knocking on the door gently, I waited until Phoenix grunted for me to come in. Landon was still crying and Phoenix was sitting next to him, holding and inspecting Landon's injured hand. When he saw what I was holding, he nodded and thanked me. I stayed there after Phoenix took the bag and started getting out what he needed.

"I'm sorry Landon," I said, wanting to do anything to lessen his pain.

Landon looked up at me, his brown eyes swimming. He couldn't say anything, but chewed on his lip ring to stop his bottom lip trembling. Before I could stop myself, I bent over and hugged him. I knew he needed it. He lifted his good hand and laid it on my back.

"I miss her," Landon murmured, sniffing loudly.

"I miss her too," Phoenix said, and I suddenly got the idea that they weren't just talking about Melody anymore.

It made sense now why the boys had been acting solemn recently. Eli and his breakdown after his date with Hayley, Phoenix and his quiet response after Walter and I had been careless when watching Melody, Walter and the sombre way he'd been after we'd had our little falling out, Severn in the middle of the night and Landon now. They were thinking about their sister.

If I didn't know any better, I would say that the anniversary of her death was upon us.

35

It was Sunday morning and when Walter woke up with a long sigh, I knew today was the day his sister Eunice had died all those years ago.

"Today's the anniversary isn't it?" I asked Walter softly, rubbing his chest.

Walter nodded, looking up at the ceiling, "Third day in December."

I sighed quietly and lay my head on his shoulder, wrapping my arm around his slender waist.

"We're going Central today," Walter said, rubbing my back gently.

"To her grave?" I murmured, remembering that Walter had been brought up in Central London.

"Yeah," he nodded with another heartfelt sigh, "to her resting place."

There was a knock at the door and Giovanni stood in the doorway looking solemn.

"Just checking you were up," he said. "We're leaving at eleven."

Walter looked at him, "What time is it now?"

"Nine something," Gio responded.

"Okay," Walter nodded.

After Gio left, he sat up and set his feet on the other side of the bed, rubbing his bruised face. I went to hug Walter from behind, feeling his smooth skin under my chin as I rested it on his shoulder.

"If you want me to be there, I will," I told him.

"It's your choice," he replied. "I don't want you to feel like I'm forcing you."

"You wouldn't be," I said sharply. "I want to come, I just didn't know if I'd be welcome."

Walter frowned, "You are."

I kissed his neck softly, "I love you."

Walter smiled, "I love you more."

I went to use the bathroom first and when I came back I saw Walter laying out a clean black shirt on his bed and a very nice coat I'd never seen him wear before.

"I don't know if I have any formal dresses," I started to feel self-conscious.

"It doesn't have to be formal," Walter said to me. "She wouldn't mind what you wore really."

"Okay," I said, trying to think of what I could put on.

Walter went to use the bathroom and I started going through my clothes. I found a simple black dress which I had only worn a couple times before. Although it wasn't fancy, I decided it would do and I took it downstairs to iron.

In the kitchen, Severn was sitting over a bowl of soggy cereal and Landon was topless and ironing a shirt. His right hand was bandaged but it didn't seem to bother him. He didn't look as sad as he had yesterday, but that didn't mean he didn't feel like it on the inside. He wasn't the only one missing the mischievous two year old, we all were. It was so quiet without Melody.

"Pass it Coral," Landon said, holding his hand out. "I'll iron it."

"No Landon, your hand," I said, clutching my dress to my chest out of politeness. "I'll do it."

Landon shook his head and pulled the fabric out of my grip, "Thanks."

I smiled, "Thank you, Landon."

"No problem."

Sitting down next to Severn I poured myself some cereal. Severn was already dressed in black trousers and a white shirt.

"You look very chic," I said to him with a small smile.

Severn smiled back, "Thanks, I always try my best."

Landon laughed, "I was the one who ironed it for you. I don't think I've ever seen you iron anything in your life, Severn."

Severn didn't even have to think about it, "Yeah, you're probably right."

Eli came down dressed in a neat white shirt and dark blue trousers, his eyes were rimmed red and I could tell he was hurting badly.

"Where's Phoenix?" he muttered. "We need to go soon."

"Relax," Landon said to Eli as he started ironing my dress. "Eat something. Gomez and Gio are still getting ready."

Eli sat and started to eat, well eat as much as he could muster. After finishing my cereal, I went up to change and looked at myself in the black dress that came to rest just below my knees.

"You look really good," Walter came in after his shower.

"Thank you," I turned to face him, glancing at the tattoo of Eunice's initials on his hip.

He came to kiss me on the cheek, "Thank you for deciding to come."

"Walter," I held his face before he could move away. "You don't need to thank me. I'm there for you as much as you're there for me."

He smiled sweetly and kissed me on the lips this time. I didn't want the kiss to end, it was so heartfelt and passionate. I ran my hands down his muscular chest, feeling Walter's tongue stroke mine, making me moan quietly in his mouth. Walter gripped my waist, allowing his hands to slide down the smooth material of my dress and grip my behind.

"Walter," I murmured, pulling away from his lips.

"Sorry," he said, taking his hands off me immediately.

"No," I said with a shy smile. "It's not that. I just wanted to say that we're going to be late if you don't get dressed. I don't want to delay the journey."

He nodded, turning away to get his clothes off his bed. I knew he was about to strip before he did it.

329

"Bye Walter," I waved at him, heading for the door. "I'll be downstairs."

He laughed quietly as I shut his door on my way out. I was glad I had made him smile a bit more. Eventually, all the boys came down to eat and my stomach fluttered at the sight of Walter. He was drenched in black, from head to toe, and looking the smartest I'd ever seen him. He was gorgeous.

"Has everyone eaten?" Phoenix asked, stepping into the kitchen in similar dark attire.

"Yes," Giovanni answered, putting the last of the bowls in the dishwasher.

"Where's Landon?" Phoenix looked around. "It's time to go."

"Gone to get dressed," Walter replied. "He won't be long."

Phoenix sighed, "Okay."

"Aren't you going to eat?" Gomez asked his eldest brother.

"I'm not hungry," Phoenix only muttered.

Landon came down in smart navy blue trousers and a shirt with his coat on top. He had his hair all gelled back and had taken out his lip piercing, making him look quite different. Who knew how much of a change a small piece of metal could make to one's face?

"Let's go," Landon said pointing to the door with both hands.

"Flowers?" Severn asked him.

"We're getting them on the way," Phoenix said.

Both cars stopped off at a florist on the way to Central London and we all bought roses, red ones and white ones, to lay for Eunice. Phoenix went ahead a bought a whole bouquet of them and then we were back on the road.

The journey was quiet and it was gloomy outside, looking like it might rain at any moment. We arrived within the hour at a large cemetery and walked up a gravelled path, being whipped by the wind as rows and rows of gravestones passed us on either side. All I could hear was the sound of our feet crunching against the ground and the cawing of crows that perched on marble memorials and flapped from one tombstone to the next.

The boys knew exactly where they were going and I followed them, holding Walter's hand, feeling the gang scars along his little finger. We turned onto the grass, weaving through the cemetery until we came to stop at one spot.

The boys fanned out around a headstone that read:

'EUNICE SIMPSON 1999 – 2007 Forever Loved.'

The simple words, so bitterly sweet, immediately made the hair on my arms stand. She had only been eight years old, too young to leave the world and her brothers behind.

Giovanni was crying quietly and Walter put his other arm around his shoulders, pulling him in for side hug. Severn bent down to place his white rose in front of Eunice's grave and was unable to stand. Instead, he remained kneeling as he broke into sobs, knotting his fingers in the damp grass and shoulders shaking as he bowed his head.

"Eunice..." Severn wept, pulling out a piece of paper he'd folded in his pocket and he began to read. "I miss you so m-much. Even though we fought, we were close. I looked up to you. You taught me how to get away with faking sick and how to nick sweets from the kitchen without Mum or Dad noticing. You're always in my heart sis, I love you."

Gomez put a hand down on Severn's shaking shoulder and put his rose beside his brother's. I took deep breaths, trying to be strong for the boys, for Walter, even though I was close to tears myself. It was hard.

"I miss you sis," Gomez murmured, looking down at the grave with a sorrowful expression and reading from his own message that he'd written. "I just....I just miss you so much, I wish you were here. I wish you'd had the chance to grow up and be in the gang, to go on dates, to have Phoenix shout at you for staying out too late – " he smiled. "I love you and I know you're okay. Rest peacefully."

"She's proud of you guys," Walter said quietly to the triplets. "You've been strong and you'll always be her little brothers."

Severn only cried harder, leaning over so that he was in a balled position on the ground and Giovanni rubbed his eyes, stepping forwards to lay his rose down. He knelt in front of the headstone, whispering to his sister as he tried not to cry again. I heard him say 'I love you' when he was finished.

Landon was looking upwards at the harsh grey skies, blinking back his tears and Phoenix had his straight and reserved face on, with a hint of pain in his eyes.

"Next year will be ten years," Walter sighed sadly. "I can't believe it. It's gone so fast, so much time without her."

"I know," Eli nodded, wrapping his arms around his slender frame and holding himself together. His green eyes were shining and when he blinked, tears slid down his face. He placed his flowers down and knelt next to Severn, swallowing as he started to read from his pre-written letter.

"You were more than a best friend to me," Eli said with difficulty. "There was so much more we didn't get to do and share together...I miss you. You were so cheeky Eunice, you always made me laugh. I know it's not your fault you're not here anymore...but I also know you're happy where you are now. I love you Eunice and...I always...I always...will...I-love you."

Eli's words stopped as he was overcome with tears and he covered his face, crying hard into his hands. Landon went and draped an arm around him, putting down his red rose onto the grass and unfolding a piece of paper from his breast pocket.

"I love you sis," Landon read in a hoarse, pain filled voice. He smiled as his eyes brimmed with tears. "I miss how I used to tease you, including that one time when I cut all your dolls' hair off. You'd always get so angry with me and then give me your payback. I still remember the time you cut all the shoelaces on all my shoes and Mum and Dad got so mad they didn't buy me new ones, so I had to go to school with your pink light up shoes with the Velcro straps. I wasn't laughing at the time, but you were. You were so proud of that one, I have to give you credit for being so creative."

We all smiled at the memory, Severn rubbing his eyes and Giovanni blowing his nose.

"You'll always be in my heart," Landon got to his feet, "my sweet little sister."

Walter let go of my hand after a few moments and he stepped forwards to lay his rose down on the growing pile. He bent his head as he pulled out his letter and sighed, tugging his hand through his dark hair.

"Eunice," Walter said softly. "It makes me laugh every time I think of the time I told you that your reflection was just an evil

332

version of yourself, and if you stayed alone in the bathroom too long, she'd come out and pull you back into the mirror with her."

The boys chuckled quietly and Walter continued after a tearful laugh.

"When Phoenix found out and told you that I was lying, I'll always remember when I came to find that you'd poured shower gel all over my bed and well, like Landon said, it wasn't funny at the time but I'm laughing now," Walter read with a smile. "I wished that we could have made more memories like that, but life isn't always fair. My life has never been the same since you passed. I just want you to know that I love you Eunice and that will never change."

Putting the letter back into his pocket, Walter got up again, his whole body trembling as he came to grip my hand in his again. It took me a couple of seconds to realise the boys were looking at me, waiting for me to talk to their sister.

"Uh...um...isn't Phoenix going to go before me?" I stammered, shocked that I was even being allowed this opportunity. I hadn't written anything.

"After," Phoenix said and I nodded.

Walking on quaking legs and feeling all eyes on me, I went to lay my rose on Eunice's grave.

"I never got to meet you Eunice," I said, my voice just above a whisper. "But I've gotten to know each of your brothers and I feel like I've gotten to know a little bit more about you through what they've told me. You seemed like a lovely girl and I wish I'd had the honour of introducing myself properly. Rest in peace, you'll always be loved."

I tried to swallow the massive lump in my throat as I went to stand back next to Walter and he looked down at me with a proud expression, making me feel a little warmer inside. Phoenix laid his bouquet by Eunice's grave and Landon motioned for us to start heading back as Phoenix said his words.

I looked back to see Phoenix rubbing his eyes with the back of his sleeve, seeing that he had a heart and he missed his sister just as much as the rest of the boys did. He was human, he just didn't want us to see it.

***

We went to have lunch in a restaurant afterwards and we all started to breathe again, allowing ourselves to smile a little more.

"I feel good," Giovanni said, rolling his shoulders. "I feel like me and Eunice just had a good catch-up."

"Same," Landon half-smiled. "Even though it was kind of a one-sided conversation."

"Not to me," Eli murmured. "I feel like she heard me and she was telling me she's okay. One day we'll meet again."

We were silent for a little while, thinking about Eli's words.

"Well," Walter was first to speak again. "What are we going to order?"

"I'm surprised Gio hasn't already read through the menu like three times already," Gomez said with a smirk, leaning back in his seat.

Giovanni quickly snatched up a menu and we chuckled.

We ordered our meals and soon the jokes started to flow again. It wasn't as crazy and loud as usual, but more like a dampened version, which felt just right. The boys were still remembering their sister and it wasn't as if they'd switch back to their usual selves thirty minutes after visiting Eunice's grave.

"I once told her that her dolls were really alive and they watched her every night when she was asleep, then they would stuff her with cotton and make her a doll for revenge," Walter said with a cheeky smile on her face.

I widened my eyes and the boys started to laugh in disbelief.

"She actually told me about that," Eli smiled. "Then you and me had a fight over it."

"Yeah," Walter nodded, smiling even more widely. "I remember. You bit me, you bitch."

"Walter you're like the grim reaper," Landon cried with laughter. "What a mean kid."

"It *was* pretty mean," Walter admitted with a nod. "With the mirror I just wanted her to stop taking ages in the bathroom, but the one about the dolls, well there was no reason really."

I laughed at him, imagining how much of a bully little Walter was, but how he and his sister loved each other really.

"Should we order dessert?" Giovanni was already looking at the back page of the menu.

"To be honest, I feel like sleeping," Severn said tiredly, trying to lean on Phoenix's arm, who shrugged him off.

"When do you not?" Landon grinned, earning a few chuckles.

I felt my phone vibrating in my pocket and something told me to just check it. I pulled it out and saw with shock, that Ario had texted me.

"What is it?" Walter turned to look at me when I gripped his thigh.

I showed him my phone and Walter frowned, "Open it."

I opened the text and instantly felt like bringing up the food I'd just eaten. The text was only three words long:

We have Hayley.

36

Eli was silent with fury.

"We have to go back," Severn was wide awake now, looking around at us with round eyes.

I myself was struggling to keep my food down and I squeezed Walter's hand as my stomach tightened uncomfortably. He was holding my hand just as tight.

"They could be bluffing," Phoenix said with consideration. "It could be an ambush they want us to walk into."

"It's not a bloody bluff," Eli burst angrily. "They have her, otherwise they wouldn't know her name. Yeah, they've probably seen me and her around, or her and Coral, but that doesn't mean they know who she is. Seeing her with us only confirms that they can use her as hostage. They got her to tell them her name, meaning they have her."

"Eli's right," I said reluctantly, wishing so much that he hadn't been. "Hayley's never introduced herself to the Santiagos and neither have I or Eli. She must have told them herself, meaning she's with them right now."

Eli bent his head, gripping his hair with both his hands so tight that it must have hurt. He was trying not to fall apart. The Santiagos couldn't have had better timing, a massive blow to the

Simpsons when they were already down over the date of their sister's death.

"Why are they doing this? What do they want?" I raised the question.

"It's payback for our ambush after they tried to take Melody," Walter explained.

"But this seems a little extreme," I creased my brows.

From as far as I knew, the gangs counteracted each move with an equally similar one. Kidnapping Hayley was *not* the same as a fight outside the pub. It didn't make sense.

"I can't fight in this," Gomez said, trying to fully rotate his arms in his slim fitting white shirt.

"Neither," Giovanni agreed, attempting to flex his arm.

"We have to go home first anyway," Landon said with a frown. "We don't have weapons."

"Shit yeah," Gomez realised in annoyance. "Okay we change when we get home."

"This is going to take too long," Eli was shaking his head, his eyes full of worry.

"Should we try texting back?" I asked. "Maybe he'll tell us where they are, where Hayley is."

"Leave them in the dark," Giovanni muttered. "So they don't expect a thing."

"But saying nothing might cause them to hurt her," Eli looked at him sharply.

If they hadn't already...

"Let's ask for proof that they have her first of all," Walter said lowly. "If they give the phone to her, we could tell her what to do."

"I doubt they'd be that dumb," Landon said.

"They've played dumb before," Phoenix said with a scowl. "Pretending they didn't know the Dartfish was working for us, or that Coral was with us either. They'd probably use whatever we tell her against us."

"That's when we decide to be smarter than them," Landon put his hand down on the table. "We tell her some phony shit that they might take as credible. It would throw them off what we will really be planning."

"Which is?" Eli demanded. "We're wasting time."

337

"No," Phoenix argued. "Running in there blind will make things worse. We need to plan properly. They won't hurt her in the meantime."

"When did you receive the text?" Eli fixed me with his green eyes.

I quickly unlocked my phone again with shaking hands and widened my eyes when I saw Ario had sent me another text.

"The first one was seven minutes ago. He sent another one just three minutes ago," I said, my heart pounding loudly in my chest. "It says that...their boss is back."

I had to leave the table then, rushing to the toilet to throw up. Everything tasted like acid and hot tears sprang to my eyes as I retched again and again until I was empty. Sitting back I tried to breathe slowly, to not let my feelings cloud my mind. I needed to help Hayley. She didn't deserve to be taken by the Santiagos. She had nothing to do with any of the rivalry between the gangs, I felt like I was responsible.

"Coral," Walter was knocking on the door. "Let me in, please."

"Coming," I said weakly, climbing to my feet and washing my face and hands in the sink before opening the door.

Walter cupped my face, searching my eyes, "Do you want me to take you to the hospital? You could stay there until this is all over. I promise you we'll get Hayley back safe."

I shook my head, "I can't wait this out alone. Please Walter, don't make me."

"I don't want you hurt," he creased his brows. "You're already so pale and weak Coral, you won't get any better if you come with us."

"Walter," I leaned my forehead against his chest. "I have to be there. Waiting alone in the hospital would be hell, not knowing what's going on or if any of you are okay."

"Okay," Walter sighed and then he kissed my head. "But you stay by my side, alright?"

I nodded, "Alright."

We went to join the boys who had already paid the bill and were getting up to leave the restaurant. Outside, the sun was setting and we needed to get a move on.

"Do we have a proper plan then?" Gomez was the first to ask as we walked to where we'd parked the cars.

"Well their boss is back," Gio said. "This is probably something they've been planning for a while."

"So?" Severn scowled. "That shouldn't put us off. They wanted our attention so bad that they had to abduct a human being? Then we'll give it to them, full force."

"That's it Severn," Walter nodded in agreement. "We don't give a damn about their boss, we'll fight to the death if we have to."

"Don't say that," I said immediately.

"Too soon man," Gio murmured, rubbing his hair.

"Listen," Phoenix said as we came to stop by the cars. "This is what Carlos was talking about, the end of the small fights and the start to the Santiagos taking over our territory. It's not going to happen. When we get back, we'll have Coral call the police from a phone box and report threatening gang activity in the location Ario gives us. That'll probably set them in a panic and Hayley will manage to get away. The police take her in and she's fine. Maybe a couple of the splinters will get arrested, that would be a bonus. In the eyes of the police, we were never involved and so they get nothing on us."

We thought about Phoenix's idea. It could definitely work, all without a proper fight. That sounded like the best option.

"Let's do that," I said, leaning against Walter.

"Yeah," the triplets nodded.

"What if they don't give us a location?" Eli asked.

"Of course they will," Landon said. "Otherwise it would all be pointless."

"Text him," Phoenix said to me.

I took my phone out and opened up Ario's messages. My hands were shaking so much that Walter texted him for me.

"'Where are you?'" he asked the group. "That okay?"

We nodded and Walter typed it in and sent it.

"Let's hurry and go already," Giovanni opened Landon's car door.

We were five minutes into our journey home when Ario replied.

"Do you know Fountain Skate Park?" I asked Walter.

"Yeah," Walter nodded. "It's in their territory, East side."

339

"Great," I sighed. "Of course they'd pick unfamiliar place."

"We know they turf just as much as they know ours," Walter told me. "It won't be a problem. Tell him we'll be there."

"Okay," I texted Ario back.

***

Arriving home a painful forty minutes later, we ran into the house, the boys stripping as they went to get changed into comfortable, warm wear. The boys also stocked up on weapons, including various knives, guns and aluminium bats. Walter gave me his smallest knife, which was a three inch switch blade. He taught me how to reveal the sharp metal by turning the safety switch off and pressing the button on the hilt. I didn't want to have to use it, but at least I knew how to.

I couldn't stop thinking about Hayley. She had been in the hands of the Santiagos for more than an hour and from her side, she hadn't heard back from us at all. She must have been so scared.

"Come on," Phoenix barked, from downstairs. "We're going."

Driving through the night, we came to a stop in neutral territory. It was my turn to help, to play my part as an accomplice to the Simpson gang.

"Coral," Phoenix said to me, his eyes boring into mine. "You tell the police that you were on your way back from the shopping complex and you've just seen a gang heading East from there, they were talking about a fight in a skate park and shouting threats. They were very intimidating and were carrying weapons. They won't ask your name or anything like that. They know gangs are a problem and it's rare to get a tip. They can't trace the call to us either."

I was nodding, trying to take in all that Phoenix was telling me. I was shaking, partly from the cold and partly from the nerves. Walter gave my shoulder an encouraging squeeze and I walked into the phone box, picking up the phone and holding it to my ear as I dialled 999.

The dial only rang for a few seconds before it was answered with, "Hello, 999 what is your emergency?"

340

I didn't even need to act scared. I was terrified. My voice caught in my throat before I managed to get my first words out, and after that, they just kept tumbling. At one point I even started crying, thinking about what Hayley could possibly be going through. The operator told me to calm down and take deep breaths, to describe the situation and how many gang members there were. I said about six or seven and described them all as aged between fifteen to early twenties, dark haired and dark eyed. They were making all sorts of horrible threats in both English and Spanish, and I'd seen them holding knives and maybe guns too. She told me that the police was on their way and thanked me for the tip, saying that my call may prevent the fight and even save some lives.

"That was good," Walter hugged me when I put the phone down.

I clung onto him, sniffing.

"I'm glad I could help," I replied after a couple deep breaths.

Landon gave my arm a rub. "You're doing well."

"Thanks," I said. "Let's go."

Back in the cars again, we drove eastwards, searching for a place where we could observe the outcome without being spotted by the Santiagos or by the police themselves. The Simpsons could easily fit the same description I gave of the Santiagos. It wasn't impossible for people to pretend they couldn't speak Spanish.

We parked in a residential area a short walk away from the skate park. The boys said that there was a block of flats that overlooked the park that we could hopefully get into. Walking in the bitter cold we soon arrived at a large, plain grey, story building that rose high into the sky.

"The skate park is on the other side," Landon explained in a low voice. "We wait for someone to come out the back door, I'll slip in and hold the door open for all of you."

Nodding in agreement, we stayed in the shadows in an alley across the road whilst Landon went and leant against the wall near the back door. Time passed agonisingly slowly and my heart rate picked up when someone finally left the building through the back entrance. Landon slipped his foot in before the door closed and motioned for us to come over as soon as the street was quiet again.

It was dark and dingy inside the building, smelling faintly of urine. The lights were either blown or flickering and we climbed quietly to the fourth or fifth floor, where we looked out a window in the stairway. From the window, we could see the concrete skate park across the road at the front of the building.

"It's empty," Gomez whispered.

"Damn splinters," Walter hissed under his breath.

"Shh," Phoenix quietened them, if any of the residents saw us crowded in the building with visible baseball bats, I'm sure they wouldn't hesitate to call the police unless the boys threatened them to keep their mouths shut.

The police themselves showed up within seconds as we were stood watching from above, and they got out of their cars with torches to search the scene. After a couple of minutes, the officers were on their walky-talkies and probably deciding to move on.

"They're leaving," my shoulders sank in disappointment; there went our chance to end this without a confrontation.

"Of course they wouldn't have showed," Landon muttered in anger.

Phoenix cursed with a sigh, "We wait until the police has left the area, then we go out there. They're probably hiding somewhere close by."

Ten minutes later, when we were sure the police had left, we descended the stairs and left the building through the front. Across the road I saw a few figures sitting on a concrete block in the corner of the park.

"The blockheads," Severn recognised them.

Eli shook his head in anger, growling out curses. I searched for Hayley, but I didn't see her.

The twins, Miguel and Manuel got to their feet when they saw us coming. They grinned and I felt like hitting them, anything to knock those stupid smug looks off their faces.

"Where is she?" Eli demanded, marching up to them with a knife in his hand.

"Ask nicely and we might tell you," Miguel smirked, not even flinching.

"Cut the bull," Phoenix snapped, walking up to them. "Take us to wherever you lot are hiding out."

"You called the police," Manuel said. "Do you think we're going to forgive that?"

"I don't give a damn," Phoenix replied. "You're worth nothing to me."

Eli lost patience and held his knife right up to Miguel's throat, causing Manuel to whip out his own knife and point it towards Eli's gut.

"Cut him and you die," Manuel said in a low voice and then he looked at Phoenix. "If you move, your brother dies."

"You forgot," Landon said, appearing from the dark behind Manuel with a gun aimed at the base of his spine. "You're outnumbered over here."

The twins shared a look and then Manuel put his knife away before raising his hands. Phoenix lowered Eli's hand, freeing Miguel's throat.

"Take us," Landon said, prodding Manuel in the back with his gun. "Now."

The boys scowled and muttered insults in Spanish before turning and leading us out the back of the skate park and into the darker, back alleys of their territory.

"Carlos it's us," Miguel called when we reached one large looking alley between a closed antique shop and a dry cleaners.

Walking into the darkness, my eyes took a couple seconds to adjust and Walter held onto my hand so as not to lose me in the gloom.

The first person I saw was Hayley.

Her hands and feet were tied with thick layers of duck tape and her mouth had also been taped over. She looked so pale and her hair was tangled. I wanted to crush all the Santiagos, take all that stuff off of her and get her home, safe and warm. Phoenix was holding the back of Eli's hoodie, stopping him from doing the exact same, it seemed.

Carlos was standing next to Hayley, who wouldn't have been able to run without falling to the ground. Diego was near Carlos, looking at us in disgust. I dreaded to think that he'd tried to mess around with Hayley. It made me furious knowing that it could have been very possible.

"Miguel, come over here," Ario said, standing to the side with Paulo.

Miguel gave Manuel a glance and walked over to join the rest of his gang. Landon held onto Manuel with his arm around the boy's neck and the gun pressed against his side.

"Give her back and I won't shoot him," Landon said.

Diegos seized Hayley roughly and held her in the same position but with a gun to her head.

"Hand him over and I won't kill the bitch," he growled mercilessly.

"Landon," Eli said lowly.

Landon sighed and clenched his jaw, releasing Manuel and pushing him forwards so that he went to join his side, casting us a dark look.

"Good," Diego said, smiling as he let go of Hayley who was shaking in fear and fright.

"Now let's get to business," Carlos smirked, his cheekbones looking very prominent.

"What do you want?" Phoenix said calmly.

"It's not for me to say," Carlos said, turning his head to look at a person I hadn't noticed, hanging back in the dark. "Meet our true leader and my father..."

A dark haired man walked into view and as soon as he did so, a foul, familiar scent worked its way into my nose. I inched closer into Walter's side, my eyes wide with the fear of something simply impossible happening right before me.

"...Pedro," Carlos spoke.

Pedro's sinister eyes looked right at me and he smiled. My legs gave out and Walter grabbed me, holding me tight with a frightened face.

"Coral," he searched my face with wide eyes.

I couldn't speak. He...he...

"Nice to see you again," my father spoke.

Carlos frowned sharply, abruptly looking at Pedro, "You already know her?"

By their facial expressions, all the Santiagos were thinking the same thing, and my guess was that the Simpsons were thinking that too.

Pedro smirked, his eyes never leaving mine.

"She's my daughter."

Everyone's eyes were round with shock and I felt Walter stiffen with absolute rage. I didn't expect anything different after finding out that this was the man who had abused me from the age of seven to ten.

"No," I tried to deny it even though I knew it was pointless. "My father's name was Paul Sanger. Not...not Pedro Santiago. He didn't even speak Spanish."

"Anyone can make fake documents," the man only laughed.

"Papa...what?" Carlos murmured, looking between Pedro and me with disbelief.

"If that was really true," Diego was shaking his head to himself. "Then why haven't we heard about it until now?"

"*Muchachos*," Pedro said to his gang. "There are a lot of things I don't tell you. She was one of them. I didn't know I had a daughter, not until she was about seven or eight I believe. I was with her for three years..."

"We thought you were up North," Ario interrupted with a stunned look.

"I lied," my father smirked without a single care. "I was being a dad to my *gringa* daughter right here in London up until I got eight years for armed robbery and assault. Today is my third day out and I didn't think she'd still be in the area, what a sweet reunion. I guess this means a change of plans *muchachos*."

Walter launched himself at him and it was Phoenix who grabbed him last minute before he could do anything rash without thinking.

"I'll kill you!" Walter was shouting and swearing. "I swear, I'll kill you!"

Landon had to grab a hold of Walter too, or Walter would have surely gotten the gun out his pocket. Walter stopped struggling and stood there, his chest rising and falling quickly as he looked at my father with hatred. Landon held onto his arms.

"We will trade Hayley for Coral," Pedro said with amusement in his features, making Hayley flinch when he put his hands down on her shoulders.

I could tell by the faces of Carlos, Diego, Ario, the twins and Paulo, that that was not the original plan, but they had to go along with their boss' wants...and he didn't want the Simpsons' turf or businesses anymore, he wanted me.

345

"Never," Walter spat on the floor and raised his middle finger at him. "You give Hayley back, and we won't kill you all."

Pedro's words struck pure fear in my heart, "She's a Santiago by blood and we want her back."

37

I wasn't going with them.

Blood or no blood, I was with the Simpsons and no one else.

I looked at my...family. Carlos and Diego, my half-brothers. Ario, my cousin. He looked like he felt sick, I know I did too.

"Come here," Pedro held his hand out to me. "Cupcake."

Before I could even utter a word, there were lights coming from behind us and the sound of voices and we all froze. The police. I'd forgotten they were still searching.

Eli was the first to move, running right at the Santiagos and hitting Diego in the ribs with his bat to get to Hayley, who got pushed and fell to the floor. Unable to grab Hayley fast enough, Carlos put a gun to the back of Eli's neck as he tried to pull his girlfriend to her feet. The Santiagos started running further down the alley way taking Eli with them by force.

Having no other direction to go in, we ran with the Santiagos, hoping the alley would lead us away from the police. Walter roared in anger and raced past me, going after Ario and hitting him in the back of the head so hard that Ario stumbled. Walter held onto him, pressing a weapon into his back and we kept running. I didn't know who was where in the panic and confusion of things, but I was aware that Landon was gripping my hand, making sure I didn't get left behind.

The Santiagos, knowing the area well, had already vanished down the various backstreets, leaving us behind. I was so relieved when I saw that Walter hadn't been kidding when he'd said they knew East side well. We had somehow doubled back on ourselves and were back in the area where the cars were parked, without the police tracing us.

Leaving no time to waste, we jumped into the cars and started driving at an inconspicuous pace out of East Side. My whole body was shaking uncontrollably and Landon looked back at me in concern.

"I know it's a stupid question Coral, but are you managing okay?" he asked me gently.

"I'm managing," is all I said.

Walter was in the back next to me, his arm around Ario's neck and a gun jabbing Ario's stomach. Ario was quiet, taking shallow breaths and looking out the window, trying to memorise where we were taking him.

"Here," Landon tossed an empty backpack at Walter. "Put it over his head."

Walter did so and I looked away, trying not to feel too much concern for Ario. They had probably treated Hayley the same way. Oh shit, Hayley. She had been left behind, probably in the hands of the authorities now. She was safe, hopefully being taken to the hospital. She was okay now, but this was far from over.

"They took Eli," Walter muttered in a dark voice. "I'm so close to killing this shit right now."

"Walter," Landon warned. "They have Eli, which is exactly why we can't kill him."

All the while, Ario said nothing and my feelings were going all over the place. I was meant to be angry with him, but seeing him in such a vulnerable position made me soften, I couldn't help it – it was in my nature.

When we pulled up in a dark destination, I frowned in confusion. For some silly reason, I had assumed we were driving home, not here, wherever here was. Getting out of the car I saw that we were in a large, abandoned plot. Weeds sprung out between the gravel everywhere and there were a couple old looking shacks too. I assumed it used to be a building site of some sort, but had long time been discarded. We must have been out of West Side because I didn't even know this area existed.

Phoenix was parked close and he and the triplets got out of his car.

My blood froze in my veins when I only counted two of the triplets.

"Where's Severn?" Landon's eyes widened when he too noticed.

Gio stared at us, "We thought he was with you."

Walter swore and punched Ario in the stomach, making him grunt and double over in pain, the bag still over his head.

"So they have Eli and Severn?" Gomez asked in a low voice.

"Maybe Severn got away," I tried. "He might even be with the police."

"Maybe," Phoenix muttered, but I could tell he didn't think so.

He started walking towards one of the shacks and we followed. Using a key, Phoenix opened the wooden door and turned on a light that was hanging in the middle of the small, dusty room.

"What is this place?" I whispered, looking at the ancient cans of paint on the wooden shelves, and rusting tools left discarded on a table in the corner.

"A front," Phoenix said and walked a couple strides to the left before bending down and pulling up the floorboards.

I watched with wide eyes as he revealed a trap door which led to underground. I felt like I was dreaming. Phoenix pulled up the door and he started doing down the steps, Landon holding my hand and helping me down into the gloom.

"This is massive," I said with wide eyes as I looked at the underground drug lab that Phoenix had constructed.

There were rows upon rows of tables with lamps hanging above them. I pictured people wearing overalls and cutting the product that the Simpsons received from their supplier, into smaller batches.

"This is where all the shit takes place," Landon said.

Behind us, I whipped my head round when I heard the sound of someone falling down the stairs and widened my eyes when I saw

349

Ario groaning on the floor, the bag now fallen off his face. Walter had shoved him and he wasn't stopping there.

"Stupid splinter," Walter was growling as he stomped on Ario's body.

Ario tried to shield himself as best as he could, but Walter knelt down and wrapped his hands around Ario's neck, choking him. The boys weren't doing anything, they only watched silently and I felt that if I didn't act, Walter might go too far and I didn't want anyone dead.

"Stop," I rushed at Walter and clung onto the back of his hoodie, trying to hold him back. "Walter please, stop."

Walter kicked Ario in the stomach one more time before he took several steps back and turned away from him, trying to calm down. Ario was bleeding and I didn't like the way he was breathing. It was so weak and laboured.

"Are you done now?" Phoenix asked Walter.

Walter nodded, swallowing down his anger.

"First of all, nobody touch anything," Phoenix addressed all of us. "If the police do happen take us in, we can't have any traces of the product ourselves."

We nodded, taking care to stay away from the tables, chairs and even the walls.

"So," Gomez said, looking at us. "Are we just gonna pretend we didn't just hear all that stuff about Coral...and her dad...and the rest of the damn Santiagos?"

I felt their eyes on me and I dropped my gaze. I still couldn't believe it myself.

"So that's your cousin," Gio stated, looking down at Ario who had his blue eyes closed.

"I guess so," I answered.

My father was Ario's uncle, making Ario, Miguel, Manuel and Paulo my cousins.

"But you don't look Hispanic," Gomez commented.

"My mum was blonde with blue eyes and my...dad has brown hair and brown eyes. I have both blonde hair and brown eyes," I mumbled, not sure if that even answered the question.

"And she's slightly tanned," Landon was looking at me closely. "Just a little bit."

His words took me all the way back to when Diego...my...brother, had tried to molest me in town one afternoon and how he'd said I was looking tanned for this time of year. Thinking back about it now, made me feel sicker than I had felt previously. I told myself that he hadn't known, neither of us had known.

Phoenix walked over to Ario who cracked an eye open as he approached and looked up at him. Crouching down, he half lifted Ario up by the front of his jacket.

"Call Carlos and give me your phone," Phoenix demanded.

Ario remained unresponsive and I was hoping for his sake that he would cooperate. I didn't doubt that Phoenix would lose his cool and beat the crap out of him, like Walter had just done.

"Are you deaf?" Phoenix tightened his fist in Ario's jacket.

Ario looked at him blankly and then he shifted his gaze to me. He must have seen the concern in my eyes because he fished his phone out of his pocket and gave it to Phoenix.

"Call him," Phoenix pushed it back into his hand.

"I can't with you holding me like that," Ario muttered.

Phoenix shoved him against the wall so that Ario was in a sitting position and the he called Carlos.

"Speaker. Now," Phoenix demanded.

Ario did as told and Carlos picked up on the third ring.

"Hola, Ario?" Carlos' voice was husky and low.

"Si," Ario answered and then started speaking in Spanish, saying things he didn't want us to hear.

"English," Phoenix growled, getting out a small knife and jabbing it in and yanking it quickly out of Ario's arm.

"Ahh," Ario cried out, squeezing his eyes shut and Carlos' tone changed immediately.

"Phoenix," Carlos snarled through the phone. "Every cut, bruise, stab you give to my boy...I'll give to the both of yours."

"So they *do* have Severn," Giovanni's shoulders sank.

"We are prepared to trade Ario for Eli and Severn," Phoenix said to Carlos.

"Since when did one equal two?" Carlos replied in a dull tone.

"Since I said so," Phoenix frowned.

351

There was some shuffling on the other end and then the voice of my father came through. I gripped Walter's hand, trembling even though I was nowhere near him.

"We'll take Ario and Coral for Eli and Severn," Pedro said.

"Coral isn't going anywhere," Phoenix said, making me feel a little warmer inside.

"Then you only get one brother," Pedro said with a hint of anger in his voice. "Simple."

Phoenix cut the call and almost crushed Ario's phone in his hand as he gripped it angrily. He looked at us, wanting our input.

"Say we trade Ario for Severn," Landon suggested to Phoenix. "Eli will find a way to get out."

"He's sly like that," Gomez nodded in agreement.

"What if he doesn't?" Gio frowned.

"Then we fight," Walter said.

Phoenix nodded, thinking it through.

"Call back," he said to Ario, shoving his phone in his hand again.

Ario had to use his left arm to take the phone as his right one was still bleeding from Phoenix's cut.

"Who is it?" Phoenix asked as soon as the call was picked up.

"Carlos."

"We'll take Severn for Ario," Phoenix said.

There was a small pause, "You're going to leave your other brother Eli?"

I could tell Phoenix wasn't happy, but he wasn't going to give me up.

"Yes," he snapped. "Where are we meeting?"

Carlos gave him a location and Phoenix nodded.

"No weapons," Phoenix said. "A quick swap and that's it."

"What?" Gomez hissed quietly.

Walter gave Phoenix an incredulous look and even Landon frowned at him in confusion.

"Are you serious?" Carlos muttered.

"I'm serious," Phoenix replied. "If we're gonna fight, it's gonna be fist on flesh."

"Why?"

"I don't want any more of my boys getting badly hurt," Phoenix said, making Gio and Gomez share a dubious look.

"Wait," Carlos demanded and then the other side went quiet.

Whilst Carlos went to discuss things with the gang, Phoenix covered the receiver and turned to us.

"I'm confident the police are still looking around for us and if they do catch any of us with weapons, that's four years max for a knife – let alone a gun," Phoenix explained to us.

The boys nodded in realisation.

"That's a big gamble," Landon said. "They might decide to bring their weapons and cut us to pieces."

"I'd rather have a couple more scars than a couple more years in jail," Phoenix said. "And trust me, you would too."

No one could argue with that.

"Phoenix," Carlos' voice was back on the call.

Before Phoenix could say anything, Ario started speaking fast in Spanish, most likely explaining everything that Phoenix had just said about the risk of carrying weapons at the moment.

"Little shit," Phoenix growled and grabbed Ario's hand, running the edge of his blade along his knuckles.

Ario cried out sharply and then clutched his wounded hand to his chest, sobbing tearlessly. Carlos and now Diego too were yelling down the line and then all of a sudden we could hear Eli's voice too.

"Let them hear you," Diego was snarling and then Eli shouted in pain, making my stomach lurch.

Whatever Diego was doing, he didn't stop and Eli kept shouting, making Phoenix and the boys grit their teeth in fury.

"Stop it!" Walter took the phone from Phoenix and roared down the line. "If you don't stop it right now, Ario is dead."

He cut the line with Eli still howling in pain in the background. Walter's hands were shaking so hard when he threw Ario's phone which smashed into pieces on the concrete ground.

"That's it. Let's go," Gomez was already heading for the stairs, determined to get his brothers back

Landon put the bag back over Ario's head and we left the drug lab just as hidden as we'd found it.

***

353

Driving to the new destination, I kept stealing glances at Ario who was shaking and shuddering as he held his bleeding arm to his chest with his injured hand. The bag over his head was making it harder for him to draw air also.

I sighed quietly and looked out the window. Ario would be fine. He'd been shot before and survived, this was no big deal I told myself. I'm sure Phoenix knew how to give a lethal cut and he wouldn't have been silly enough to do that if the Santiagos had both Eli and Severn. I chose to spend the rest of the journey trying to tell myself I could face seeing that man again. I wasn't ten anymore, I was stronger now.

Stepping out into the cold again, my stomach started to turn as I wondered what condition we would find the boys in. We walked in silence, none of us carrying a single weapon and feeling slightly vulnerable. Hopefully the Santiagos had stayed true to their word.

We met in another secluded back alley in East Side and on arrival I saw that they had tied both the Simpson's hands behind their backs with the same duck tape they'd used to secure Hayley.

Eli looked wrecked. He had gashes on both sides of his slender face and a swollen, busted lip. There were blood stains on his jumper, most likely from fresh wounds the Santiagos had inflicted on him, but even in his weakened condition, he stood as close to Severn as Diego would let him, trying to support Severn as he swayed. Severn too had been beaten and he looked like he was about to keel over, either from pain or fatigue. Probably both. Paulo kept him straight, steadying his shoulders each time Severn tipped to one side.

"Severn first," Phoenix called over to the Santiagos as he held Ario in front of him. "Untie his hands."

Paulo had to unwind the tape from Severn's wrists the long way, confirming that that they weren't carrying any weapons that he could have used to cut through it. Whilst they watched Paulo free Severn's hands, Eli ripped himself out of Diego's grip and started running to our side.

"Send over Coral," Pedro commanded furiously, stopping Diego from running after him.

"She's not part of the deal," Phoenix said, trying not to smirk.

354

Now Eli was with us, all we needed to do was trade Ario for Severn. That was until Pedro shattered that illusion of mine.

"Send her over, now!" Pedro yelled, grabbing Severn and tightening his hands around his neck.

My muscles locked, not wanting to be even an inch closer to that man, but not wanting Severn hurt at all.

"He's going to kill him," I said, balling my shaking hands into fists.

"Coral," Walter held my arm. "You don't need to listen to him. He's not going to kill Severn."

"He can't breathe Walter," I said in a panic, glancing back at Severn who was struggling. "I don't care what it takes, I have to help him."

Walter shook his head, knowing what I was saying.

"I'll try to bluff it," I said quietly. "When I get close enough for them to let go of him, I'll run."

Walter didn't buy it and I knew it was going to be unlikely, but Severn was really being strangled and I had to do something fast. I didn't want anyone dead, especially if I knew I could have prevented it. I started walking towards the Santiagos before Walter had time to say anything and he grabbed my arm, stopping me.

"Trust me Walter," I said, looking back at him and the other Simpson brothers.

They all looked wary.

"Please Walter," I gave him a desperate look.

Walter let go.

I made my way towards the Santiagos, towards my father's sickening smile. He let go of Severn's throat, making him cough as he fought to breathe again.

"Start walking Severn," I called out to him.

That's when Pedro decided to hold Severn back. Realising with dread that I'd been caught out, the Simpsons raced to grab me before the Santiagos could and both sides started to fight. It was fist on flesh, like Phoenix had wanted, and I was caught in the middle of it. At some point, I felt myself being seized by no one else but my father.

Immediately my legs crumpled beneath me and I felt myself fall to the ground.

"Get up," he shook me. "You've grown, my cupcake."

Shutting my eyes tight, I thrashed around, starting to cry. My worst nightmares were coming to life and I couldn't handle it. I needed Walter. I needed him now.

I opened my eyes when I heard Pedro grunt. It had been Carlos who'd pushed him off me. Pedro fixed Carlos with a mad look of disbelief and I before he could react, there was shouting.

"Hands in the air!"

I scrambled to my feet and felt Walter engulfing me in a tight embrace, pulling me far away from Pedro as possible.

"I'm sorry," he said to me again and again. "I'm sorry I wasn't there to stop him putting his hands on you."

"Hands in the air, now!"

"It's okay," I whispered, raising my hands in the air.

We were surrounded. The police had backed us up against the wall with their guns and torches aimed at us. Thank God Phoenix had been right. They had no reason to shoot because we weren't carrying anything threatening.

Both gangs had separated themselves and I noticed that Severn was still on the other side. Risking a look in Pedro's direction, I saw him glaring at Walter and me. He had missed his chance to do whatever he had wanted with me and he knew he wouldn't be getting another opportunity again. The degree of his anger frightened me, even though he wasn't near me anymore.

Severn stumbled towards us when Pedro got out his gun. We both looked at Severn at the same time and I watched in horror, knowing what Pedro was about to do.

"Stand down!" an officer ordered but the look in his eyes showed that Pedro was about to do no such thing.

A single gunshot rang out.

Severn fell forwards.

Time seemed to run double the speed then, and I stood stunned as the police opened fire at Pedro Santiago. Each shot echoed painfully loud and his body was jerked violently as he was riddled with lead. My father seemed to be looking at me as he fell to his knees, thick blood spilling from his mouth. Then his eyes went blank and he tipped forwards and landed on the pavement, dead.

"Send down the paramedics," an officer was saying but I felt like someone was rapidly turning down the volume.

Everything went dark and it was peaceful, at last.

38

Hayley's voice sounded through my sleep and I felt so relieved to hear that she seemed okay. I wanted to see her but was unable to open my eyes.

"Coral, can you hear me?"

My eyelids wouldn't open and I felt myself shift in the bed. Yes, I was lying down in a bed.

"I think she's waking up," Hayley said to someone.

There was a short silence and then I could hear Walter.

"Coral," he said softly, kissing my forehead.

I finally managed to pry open my eyes and blinked a couple times before my vision cleared enough to see Walter and Hayley sitting by my bed. Hayley looked a lot better and all the colour had been returned to her face.

"I'm in the hospital?" I croaked at them.

"Yes sweetheart," Walter said, taking my hand in his.

Fragments of what happened before found their way back to me. I remembered Severn being shot in the back by Pedro, Gomez and Giovanni running to his side as the police shouted for them to stay back, Landon's voice raw and pain filled as he cried for his brother when they took Severn into the ambulance. Pedro, my father, was dead. Memories of Carlos sobbing and shaking Pedro's blood soaked body as he lay on the ground. Diego's ashen face as he watched wordlessly, Ario so weak that he had already collapsed to the ground.

"How long have I been sleeping?" I frowned, not liking the idea that important things had been happening while I was out and unaware. "Severn, is he okay?"

"Almost a day," Walter told me, avoiding my second question. "How are you feeling?"

I raised a hand to my warm cheek, feeling a layer of dressing on it. It was hurting, but it was a muted kind of pain, as if I had a lot of drugs in my system that were relieving it.

"You got hit by some ricochet," Walter said. "Bullet bounced off the wall and grazed your cheek."

I raised my brows, "I don't remember that."

Walter rubbed my hair. "You needed a couple stitches."

I half smiled, touching the scar on his own cheek, "I guess that makes us even."

Hayley smiled too, "I'm glad you're okay Coral, you had us scared for a second."

"I was worried about you Hayley," I said to her. "I hope the Santiagos weren't too rough."

She shook her head, "They weren't. Carlos and Ario would always stop the twins or Diego from harassing me. But to be honest, I wasn't really their main interest, they wanted to make arrangements for the Simpsons to give them part of their territory. At least, that's what I gathered. They were speaking Spanish mostly."

Walter scowled, "As if that would ever happen."

"Yeah," Hayley murmured. "And then when you showed up and Pedro saw you...he changed his mind. You were all he wanted."

I shivered involuntarily just thinking about that man.

"I can't believe he was your father Coral," Hayley sent me such a sympathetic look. "I heard about what happened to him."

"Yeah," I replied. "Well he shot Severn. I hope...I hope Severn isn't dead, is he?"

Hayley glanced at Walter who looked at the sheets. I realised how exhausted he was, I knew he hadn't slept at all.

"Walter," my lips started to tremble. "Severn?"

358

"He's had surgery, but he's still in critical condition," Walter finally said. "The bullet got one of his kidneys and they had to remove it but the other kidney isn't able to function sufficiently on its own, I don't know why. They put him on the waiting list for kidney transplant, but we all know that won't be very useful. We asked for an honest opinion and the doctor said his body is losing the fight..."

"Can't they take mine, or yours or anyone's?" I asked desperately.

Walter sighed, running a hand down his face, "We've tried but none of us are compatible. His body will reject it because of our blood types. Typical isn't it? Just so damn typical. You'd think with there being so many of us in the family, you'd get at least one person who matched him."

Walter had his jaw clenched in anger and I put my hand over his, trying to calm him even though I wasn't exactly calm myself.

"What about mine?" I gripped onto his hand. "Maybe my blood type will be okay for him."

"You're too weak and dehydrated Coral," Walter shook his head. "They would never go ahead with it, hell I would never go ahead with it. It would put too much strain on your body."

I shook my head, "There has to be some way."

"I tried too," Hayley said. "I'm still seventeen so they won't even consider me for a donation."

An utter of pain had me looking around to see where it had come from. Hayley turned also and went over to another bed which was placed next to mine, which I hadn't even noticed.

"Eli, honey, are you okay?" Hayley bent down and rubbed Eli's hair before cupping his bashed up face in her hands.

Eli's wounds had been treated and dressed and I saw that both his hands were rolled in bandage.

"No," he swallowed. "I need to get out. I don't want to be here."

"He doesn't like hospitals," Walter said warily, "at all."

I started to sit up and Walter helped me move so that my legs hung over the edge of the bed.

"Not dizzy or anything?" Walter made sure.

I shook my head, "I'm okay."

Walking over to Eli's bedside, Hayley drew me a seat and I tried to calm Eli down.

"Eli, everything is under control here," I told him even if it wasn't exactly true.

Eli shook his head and squeezed his green eyes shut, "Please. I need to leave."

He tried to get up out of the bed but Walter gently pushed him down, making Eli more determined to get out.

"You need rest," Walter said but Eli kept struggling.

"Walter, stop," Eli cried as Walter pinned him down by his wrists. "You don't understand – "

"I do understand," Walter interrupted him. "A lot of bad things have happened to us in hospitals like this one. I know you're scared...so am I. We all are, but you need to calm down now or I'll call a nurse or someone."

Eli's eyes widened and he slowly stopped fighting, allowing Walter to release his grip on him and stand back.

"You're doing really well," Hayley said to Eli, kissing his battered cheek softly.

Eli nodded, sadness in his eyes as he undoubtedly thought about his sister.

"What happened to your hands," I lightly touched one of his bandaged ones.

Eli frowned looking at his injuries, "Diego did it. He pierced both my hands with his knife, almost all the way through for whatever you guys were doing to Ario."

Walter scowled in anger, "I told that piece of shit to stop."

"Well he didn't," Eli said blankly and then his face creased. "How's Severn?"

Walter mirrored his expression and explained to Eli that Severn needed the right donor and fast. Doctors said they doubted he would survive the night, which was almost upon us and Eli's face fell and he let out a long sigh.

"I don't know what I'd do if we lost him a day after we lost Eunice all those years ago," Eli mumbled.

"Don't say that," Walter hardened his face and Hayley rubbed Eli's hair out of his face.

"You're not going to lose anyone," Hayley told him.

Eli said nothing, he just looked down.

360

"Can I go and see Severn?" I asked Walter.

Walter swallowed hard and I realised that he had chosen to stay here with me and Eli not just because he was concerned for us, but because he was afraid of seeing Severn get any worse. I held his hand firmly.

"It's okay Walter," I said quietly. "You are such a strong person."

He looked down at me with passion in his eyes, "So are you Coral. I've said it once before and I'm saying it again. You're stronger than you think, I love you."

"Me too," I stroked his bruised face.

"I'll see you later," Hayley said as I got up to leave. "I'm gonna stay here with Eli for a bit. Hopefully Severn is managing well."

"Hopefully," Walter said.

Walter and I walked down the hospital to the critical care unit where Severn was being kept. For the first time since waking up, I thought about how Ario was doing. He had been badly hurt, mostly courtesy of Walter, but I didn't know what kind of condition he was in at the moment.

"What are they doing here?" Walter tensed when he saw Carlos, Diego and Paulo sitting on a row of seats in the corridor just outside the area Severn was being held.

Walter and I walked right past them and I hadn't even been able to look any of my relatives in the eye. All I hoped was that Ario wasn't in critical condition also.

"Is Ario in here?" I asked Walter quietly as we entered the special wing, walking past occupied rooms.

"I don't think so," Walter muttered. "But I don't really care."

"I was just wondering why the Santiagos were outside," I said, a hint of fear noticeable in my voice.

Walter paused, looking down at me.

"Pedro is dead Coral," he said to me. "That one I know for sure. I saw them take his body away in a bag."

I nodded, remembering all of a sudden how it had been Carlos who had pushed my father off of me in the heat of the fight. I wanted to thank him, but didn't know how.

361

Walter took me to a room where Severn was lying peacefully asleep with all sorts of monitors beeping around him. Phoenix, Landon, Gomez and Giovanni were all in there with Severn.

"Hey Coral," Landon sent me a shattered smile. "Good to see you up and about."

"Glad you're okay," Gio nodded at me.

"Thank you," I murmured, turning to look at Severn who looked so helpless lying there.

"I can't believe this," Phoenix muttered. "We're expected to just wait here for our brother to die?"

Gomez sighed shakily, "If he dies, I'll die too."

"Don't say that," Landon winced. "They're trying as hard as they can to help him."

Giovanni, who was sitting right next to Severn, touched his brother's blond hair.

"I can't imagine life without him," Gio mumbled, rubbing his eyes.

"There has to be a way," I tried and Landon nodded, attempting to stay hopeful.

"Maybe he'll get a donor by tonight," Landon said.

"Yeah," Walter muttered lowly. "And who says that he would be compatible with that donor? It's unlikely."

"Have hope," I said to him and Walter only rubbed his face, trying not to break.

Phoenix sighed and stood up, "I'm going to get some food. What do you guys want?"

"I'm not hungry," Gio muttered, touching Severn's hand.

The rest of us raised our brows and shared looks.

"Come Giovanni," Landon held his hand out to him. "You need to eat something."

"I don't want to," Gio shook his head, looking down at his brother. "I'm staying with him."

Gomez hardened his jaw and looked down, "We'll be back later."

Giovanni nodded and we filed out of Severn's private room, leaving the cacophony of sounding machines behind us. Severn was hanging between life and death and I hoped with all my heart that he'd pull through somehow.

"Please God," I whispered a quiet prayer. "Please."

We were walking out of the critical care unit when Paulo suddenly sprung to his feet and walked up to us. Phoenix looked down at the youngest Santiago with a frown, waiting to hear whatever he had to say.

"I want to donate my kidney," Paulo said, his warm brown eyes solemn.

Phoenix blinked at him, we all did.

"Paulo, what?" Diego stood up, giving his cousin a crazed look. "That's not what you said you wanted to tell them. What happened to saying sorry for your loss?"

"Well I lied, he's not dead yet," Paulo looked at him and then turned to look at all of us. "What I wanted to tell you is that I want to give one of my kidneys to Severn. I heard you guys talking before. I know he's not gonna make it without a transplant."

"But, why?" Phoenix looked at him with a stone cold face, showing no emotion at all.

Paulo sighed, "I lost my uncle...and I don't want to lose anyone else, good or bad."

"Look kid," Phoenix said, giving him a very brief pat on the shoulder. "I appreciate the thought, but don't waste our time."

"I'm serious," Paulo frowned, again making Diego and Carlos give him astonished looks.

"Well," Landon said when Phoenix wouldn't speak. "We can call the doctor and see if he can test to see whether you'd be compatible with him."

So that's what he did, Landon went off and came back ten minutes later with Severn's doctor. The doctor took one look at Paulo and smiled sympathetically.

"How old are you son?" he asked, knowing that in the light of the moment, we'd all forgotten Paulo had to be over eighteen to donate.

"F-fifteen," Paulo replied, realising the truth also.

"I'm afraid you can't donate if you're under eighte – "

"I'll do it," Carlos cut him off, getting to his feet and putting an arm around Paulo's shoulders. "My blood type is universal, I already know that. It won't get rejected."

Diego stared at his older brother as if he'd lost his mind and then he sat down heavily, putting his head in his hands, too grief stricken to deal with his brothers choices.

"Are you serious?" Gomez muttered to him.

"I'm serious," Carlos said, standing up straighter.

He wasn't exactly up to scratch both physically and emotionally, but he was doing this. He was saving Severn's life. The life of the rival gang member his father had tried to kill and ultimately paid the price of death for. At that moment I felt so grateful.

"Alright," the doctor said, giving Carlos' arm a pat. "Let me take you to my office and we'll talk about the procedure and give you a little test to make sure your kidney isn't rejected."

"Will you be able to do it today?" Phoenix asked as they turned to leave.

"We'll try our hardest to get it done as soon as possible," the doctor replied. "We're aware of your brother's critical condition and he will be given priority."

"Thank you," Phoenix said, and although he was looking at the doctor, I knew he was also thanking Carlos Santiago, his so-called archenemy.

39

"How are you feeling Severn?" Giovanni and Gomez had their faces just inches away from their brother's.

Severn had the side of his face against his pillow and he blinked slowly, frowning at them.

"Like shit," he rasped.

The boys cheered, so happy just to hear Severn's voice again and I grinned so wide. I was thrilled. After another 3 hour surgery last night, Severn had slept through the night-time and we had returned early the next morning to see him finally awake.

"I missed you man," Landon ruffled Severn's hair ever so lightly.

Phoenix pushed all the boys away from him, "Give him room. Let him recover."

Walter smiled, standing at the foot of Severn's bed with his arm around my shoulder.

"But he only just woke up," Gomez pulled a face.

"I don't care," Phoenix said, giving Severn's back a rub. "Let him sleep."

"Get better soon you lazy shit," Eli grunted to Severn. "You sleep too much anyway."

Severn sent his brothers a weak smile, "Sleep is good."

"Enough," Phoenix said to Severn softly. "Don't talk, just rest."

"Come on guys," Landon hooked his arms around Gomez and Gio's necks playfully. "Let's leave the sleeping beauty."

"Hey," Severn called in a weak voice.

We laughed and then left Severn to sleep in peace.

"I'm going to see Carlos," Phoenix said to the group. "I have to thank him for what he did."

The boys nodded.

"I still didn't see that coming," Gomez said.

"Especially after his dad was killed," Landon added.

"I know," Phoenix muttered and started to leave. "Don't wake him up again."

"We won't," Gio smiled.

Phoenix half-smiled back and was about to walk away when I stopped him.

"Uh, Phoenix can I, by any chance, come with you?" I asked politely after lightly touching his back.

He turned and looked down at me with a questionable glance.

"I just...I just want to talk to Carlos too and I don't know where he's recovering, I thought I could just go with someone," I quickly added.

What I didn't mention, was how I didn't want to walk in there alone in case Diego and the twins were also with Carlos. I wouldn't be bold enough to thank Carlos for what he did for me if that was the case.

"Come on then," Phoenix said after a little pause.

"See you in a bit," I said to Walter and the boys.

I hadn't told Walter my plans and he looked at me with an expression I didn't understand. He looked sad.

"See you," Walter said to me and Landon threw me a childish wave.

Following Phoenix's fast pace, we soon arrived in another ward where Carlos was being placed. Like Severn, he had his own room and Diego was sitting in one of the chairs by Carlos' bed.

"Look who is it," Diego said, looking up at Phoenix with a sour expression.

"Don't get excited," Phoenix cast him a glance. "I didn't come to see you."

"Well I'm not leaving you alone with my brother," Diego crossed his arms over his chest.

"I didn't ask for that either," Phoenix cut his eyes at him and then looked at Carlos who was lying in the bed with the sheets drawn halfway up his bare torso.

"Is it comfortable for you to be lying on your back?" Phoenix asked him.

Carlos smirked, "Since when did you care if I was comfortable or not?"

"You're right," Phoenix snapped. "I don't."

Carlos smiled and looked at Phoenix expectantly.

Phoenix sighed, "I want to thank you. Properly. I know you didn't have to help Severn and I still don't really understand why you did, but he would have died if you didn't donate at the time that you did."

Carlos had his thick brows raised as he witnessed Phoenix lowering his pride for once.

"I did it because even though Severn is as much a rival as you are to me, he's still a fifteen year old kid," Carlos said. "Paulo was right, I don't want any more death."

"Well," Phoenix paused. "My condolences."

"Damn," Carlos grinned. "You don't have to say anything if you don't mean it."

Phoenix said nothing, making Carlos laugh a little bit before Diego ordered him not to strain himself too much.

"*Si hermano*," Carlos gave his brother a smile.

"So," Phoenix said. "I'm going to leave you now. We can talk about where the gangs stand later."

"Bye," Carlos said.

Phoenix gave my back a small pat and with that he left me alone with my half-brothers.

My stomach clenched and I immediately dropped my gaze, "I uh...I..."

"Sit down if you like," Carlos said, motioning to the chair on the opposite side of the bed to where Diego was sitting.

I went to sit stiffly by his bed and looked down at my hands.

"Diego," Carlos said. "You're making her nervous."

"I don't blame her," he grumbled under his breath and then he sighed.

"Call me a coward or whatever," Diego said, looking across the bed at me, "but I can't do this in English."

I had no idea what Diego was talking about, but then he started to speak in Spanish, looking me right in the eye, honestly and earnestly. Although I knew nothing he was saying, I could tell how heartfelt he was being. I recognised 'lo siento' and 'hermana' as meaning 'sorry sister'. I didn't know what to say, but it seemed Diego wasn't interested in hearing anything from me anyway and with a respectful nod, he left the room.

"He said he's sorry," Carlos said to me, "for being so inappropriate to you. He said it's okay if you never forgive him, he understands. He wants to be a brother to you, if you'll let him. Again, he understands if you don't want that."

My eyebrows went sky high. I had very mixed emotions about what had just happened, but it felt good to know we were on better terms and that he probably wasn't going to be horrible to me anymore.

"Wow," I stared at the floor. "I didn't know he could be so...nice. Sorry."

"Nah it's okay," Carlos smiled. "I'm not offended. He's got his problems but he's got his good sides too."

Even though Carlos looked so relaxed and content, I knew he was hurting. I could see it, and it was understandable. He had known the good sides to our father too, the sides I had never experienced during my time with him.

"I just want to thank you," I said. "For helping me get away from Pedro that night. Why...why did you do it?"

Carlos sighed, his pain showing through for a second.

"It was the way he looked at you," he said, lifting his gaze to meet mine again. "It wasn't right."

"Yeah," I nodded. "I didn't have the best of times with him as a child."

"And I believe you," Carlos said, looking off into space. "He was capable of horrible stuff and had done bad things that I knew about, and bad things that I didn't know about."

"Yeah," I murmured, glancing at the tattoo across his oblique muscles that read S.S. most likely standing for Santiago Splinters.

"But at the same time I know he wasn't all bad...not to you and the others."

"True, but it's no excuse," Carlos muttered and then he sighed and ran a hand down his face.

"Still, I'm sorry for the loss," I told him, because it was true.

Although my father's death brought me relief, it wasn't the same for Carlos and the gang, and I respected that.

Carlos surprised me by reaching out and taking a hold of my hand.

"I'm sorry on his behalf for the shit he put you through," Carlos said to me. "I want to be a big brother to you, but like Diego said, only if you want me to be."

"Yes," I smiled widely. "I'd like that."

Carlos squeezed my hand before letting go with a grin, "First of all we need to teach you Spanish."

"Of course," I laughed and then my face became more sombre. "How is Ario doing?"

"Ario," Carlos rubbed his chest. "I heard he's doing fine. I haven't seen him since before my surgery last night, but I'll see him soon."

"Can I ask you something a little more off topic?" I blurted as a question popped into my mind.

"Okay," Carlos looked amused.

"Phoenix once said you two tried to work together to form a gang, but it hadn't worked out," I said. "What happened?"

Carlos' amused smile widened, "Well you know Phoenix. He thinks he's the best and even though now he's better at listening to people's opinions, he wasn't like that in the past."

"I can picture that," I said, imagining a younger version of Phoenix.

"He just couldn't work with an associate on the same level as him," Carlos explained. "He wanted to be the sole leader, so we split before we even properly began and well that's when we ended up forming two separate gangs. My father took over from the moment I suggested it, and that's how it's been. I was the leader on the outside and Pedro was the true one behind the scenes."

"Well it makes a lot more sense now," I said with a nod. "Would you ever consider putting all this rivalry behind you and just getting on with the Simpsons, which I'm sure you, at least, are very capable of."

Carlos breathed out a big breath, "That's what Phoenix and I will discuss when we get the time. Right now it's too busy to make any important decisions."

"I get it," I said and then got up. "Thank you Carlos for your time and I guess for everything too. I know you're still recovering, so get better soon."

"Thank you *hermana*," Carlos replied. "Ario's room is literally just down the corridor from here. I don't remember the number, but his door should be open anyway."

"Okay," I said. "Thanks again."

I sent my brother a wave and left his room, heading towards Ario's to see how he was recovering and to attempt to talk things over.

I knocked on Ario's open door and Miguel and Manuel Santiago looked up at me sharply. Ario himself was in the bed and his facial expression froze when he saw me standing there.

"Hi," I said shyly.

"Guys, can you leave us alone?" Ario said to his brothers.

Miguel and Manuel, for once, did not scowl at me. They didn't smile either, they simply stood up and walked out past me without a word. I took that as an improvement.

"Come in," Ario arched an eyebrow at me. "Why are you still standing out there?"

I smiled, "Sorry I wasn't thinking."

I went and sat down on one of the bedside chairs and looked at Ario properly. His face was black and blue and so was the rest of his body for that matter. He too was topless like Carlos had been, and I could tell his ribs were damaged by the shallow breaths Ario took.

"Let's lay it all out on the table," I said after a breath.

Ario nodded, "I agree."

"So..." I looked down. "You first?"

I glanced up to see him smile, "Fine, I'll go first. I'm sure it was pretty obvious, you know, from the kiss that I liked you. I had no idea we were cousins. It's so messed up things turned out this way and to be honest, now we know the truth...I'm glad you stuck with Walter...even though I hate the guy with the passion."

"Yeah," I said in agreement. "I didn't see it coming either and it makes life much simpler knowing that we never went any further."

I shuddered, thinking about how horrible that would have been. Ario shivered too and then he groaned, covering his face with his hands.

"Uhh I just remembered I told you about the damn mango lube," he grumbled.

I started to laugh, actually forgetting all about that moment up until now. Ario joined in with the laughter too until he winced in pain, scrunching up his face and taking short gasps.

"I'm sorry," I said worriedly, wishing I could relieve just a little bit of the pain Walter had caused him.

"It's not your fault," he mumbled, trying to give me a smile. "This is so weird Coral."

"I know," I said, smiling back. "But in all honesty, although I...um...you know, I was attracted you initially, as we got to know each other, I started to see you as a brother."

"Really?" Ario raised his brows. "Is this before or after you started doing Walter's dirty work?"

I winced and bit my bottom lip, "I'm sorry about that. Really. I felt so bad throughout it all Ario and I wasn't pretending to get along with you, I honestly enjoyed hanging out."

He nodded, "It doesn't matter to me anymore anyway. I'm sorry about what we did to your flat."

I tried not to burst into a massive grin.

"What?" my cousin gave me a weirded out look.

"We sound like five year olds," I chuckled.

"True true," Ario smiled, closing his eyes briefly.

"Are you tired?" I asked him.

"*Si*," he answered, opening his eyes. "You should start speaking Spanish Coral."

"I know," I said with a bright beam. "That's what Carlos told me too. What's the word for cousin?"

"It's *primo* for a boy, *prima* for a girl," Ario explained. "But we don't do cousins in our family. Its brothers and sisters. So that's *hermanos* and *hermanas*."

"Okay *hermano*," I said.

"*Bueno hermano*," Ario corrected.

"*Bueno hermano*," I repeated. "Thanks."

"Mate, you've learnt nothing, don't thank me," Ario laughed weakly.

"Hey," I pushed his shoulder lightly. "I'm trying."

"Sure," Ario closed his eyes again.

I stood up and paused before giving his hair a ruffle.

"Get better soon," I said to him.

"*Gracias*," Ario opened one blue eye. "You too, with your cheek."

"Thanks," I smiled.

I left Ario's room and saw Paulo coming in my direction. I started grinning at him and he smiled back.

"Hi Paulo," I said, already in a good mood after spending time with Ario.

"Hey," he greeted me.

"I really want to tell you how much I appreciated your actions yesterday," I told him. "It took a lot to want to do something for your rival, especially after a member of your own gang lost their life. I give you a lot of respect for that."

Paulo rubbed his slim arm, "It's not that big a thing. I know we're on opposite sides and all, but if Severn had died I wouldn't have any one to compete with, you know?"

I smiled warmly at him, "I understand."

"We aren't friends. I don't like him, but at the same time I guess I do like him too," Paulo shrugged. "He only seems to feel the first towards me, but I don't mind. I beat him up whenever I get the chance and he does the same to me."

I laughed and pulled him into an unexpected hug, "*Gracias, hermano*."

Paulo chuckled as we pulled away, "For what?"

"Just thank you," I said patting his shoulder. "See you around."

Paulo looked a little confused but he smiled all the same, "See you."

I made my way back to Severn's room and walked in on all the boys with sad expressions, looking like something bad had happened again.

"Is Severn okay?" my eyes instantly darted to his bed, where he slept calmly.

"He's fine," Landon said, shadows under his brown eyes.

"What's the matter with everyone then?" I frowned in concern, they were happy when I had left.

Walter, who was sitting on the floor with his chin propped on his knees, lifted his face to look at me with a devastated appearance.

"Are you joining the Santiagos then?" he asked me in a quiet voice.

All the brothers waited silently for my response, all as serious as anything. Even Phoenix looked like he remotely cared about my answer. So that was what had gotten them all feeling down? They thought I was going to leave and join the other gang?

"Of course not," I cried and then lowered my voice when I remembered Severn. "How could I just leave you guys?"

"Well we weren't sure," Gomez said glumly. "They *are* your family after all."

"That may be technically true," I nodded. "But it's been you guys who have been there for me these past couple months. Not them. I've gotten to know you all and there's still more to get to know. You're family to me and there's no way I could ignore all that and waltz out of here without a second glance. I mean, really? Walter, how could you honestly think that? You should know me. When I say I love you, I mean it."

"I know that," he said with a sigh. "But you have the total right at the same time to get to know them too, to spend more time with them and all that. I wasn't sure if you'd just eventually want to go and join them instead, even if you were with me."

"Well that's silly," I said the plain truth, "because I may be a Santiago by blood, but I'm a Simpson by heart."

"Awww," Landon pressed a hand to his chest dramatically and got up to embrace me in a massive hug. "That's actually the most touching thing I've ever heard Coral."

I laughed into his chest, "They aren't just words either, I meant it."

"I know you did," Walter had gotten up and replaced Landon's hug with his.

I held him back and smiled into his warmth.

"I shouldn't have doubted you," Walter said to me. "I'm sorry."

"That's okay," I told him and when he pulled away, I held my arms out to the others. "Anyone else?"

The triplets, Gomez and Giovanni threw themselves at me, jostling me like a piece of paper and I laughed even though it did hurt my healing cheek a little bit. Eli came and gave me a hug too, to my surprise.

"I'm glad you're staying," he said, rubbing my back.

"Same here," I replied, "for as long as Phoenix let's me anyway."

Phoenix, who was sitting in the corner of the room, let out a smile and even though it was a small one, it really made me finally feel accepted by all of the brothers.

And that was a feeling that couldn't be replaced.

Epilogue

Severn was discharged from the hospital five days later and we went home in high spirits.

The boys were laying low for a couple of months, knowing that the police were probably keeping tags on them, and Phoenix had even considered dropping the drugs altogether and starting fresh somewhere else. Landon had stared at him for a full minute, waiting for Phoenix to say he was kidding, even though we all knew that Phoenix didn't joke.

In the end, Phoenix had shrugged it off and said we would see what happened after things had cooled off.

The Simpsons were still rivals with the Santiagos, but there hadn't been any fights or even much interaction with them for the rest of the month of December. Phoenix said he and Carlos had agreed it was best not to attract attention from the police so soon after what had happened.

I however, had met up with Ario and Paulo on the weekends a couple of times and I'd even spent time with Carlos one afternoon in The Dartfish. They had told me about Pedro's burial coming up just before Christmas and they were wise not to even ask if I wanted to come. I had wished them all the best about it anyway and hadn't seen them until Christmas Eve, when I went round with presents for them all.

I had never had to shop for males before, but I'd ended up getting Paulo a world map to extend his already broad geographical knowledge, scarves for Miguel and Manuel and a Christmas jumper for Ario as well as a *Dora The Explorer* backpack just for the fun of it. For Diego I got him a snow hat – to cover that messy hair of his, and I got Carlos nice leather gloves.

I was well received by them all and I made them promise not to open my presents until Christmas Day. Miguel and Manuel actually apologised for being so aggressive and rude to me in the past and they gave me shoulder pats which Ario laughed at them for, making them crack identical smiles. I wasn't expecting anything back from them but widened my eyes when Ario handed me a bag full of presents.

"From all of us," he had told me with a chilled out smile.

"Thank you, I mean *Gracias*," I had grinned at him before giving him a tight squeeze.

Carlos had laughed and given me a side hug whilst Diego had smiled, keeping his distance. I had left their home still grinning and Paulo and Ario had walked me out of East territory safely.

Christmas day had been reserved for the Simpson brothers only and we'd spent the whole day indoors, eating, laughing, sleeping and then eating some more. It was relaxing and actually the first Christmas where I had truly enjoyed myself. Walter had bought me a beautiful gold necklace which I knew had cost a lot of money. He'd also written me a very touching note and I had coincidentally written him one too. I had bought Walter a nice watch, Landon a new lip piercing, Eli, Gomez, Gio and Severn different types of aftershave and Phoenix a ring which Walter and I both paid for. For Hayley I had gotten her a cute makeup bag and she'd bought me great smelling bath bombs. I had received all sorts of things from the Santiagos and the Simpsons also, including a brand new laptop from Carlos, a random fruit juicer from Landon, a lovely leather bracelet from Phoenix and a pretty Spanish fan from Ario.

Hayley had come round in the evening and we'd watched movies all together until her parents called her to come home. Eli had given her a goodnight kiss and dropped her at her house whilst the rest of us went to bed with swollen stomachs and foolish grins.

***

Now, it was the evening of New Year's Day and the Simpsons had something in store for me.

"Are you comfortable?" Landon grinned at me.

"Yeah," I nodded, placing my hand on the table in front of me.

Phoenix looked over at me from the other side, heating up his knife in a lighter so that it almost burned red hot. I felt my stomach squeeze. This was going to hurt.

"I'm here," Walter was sitting on the chair next to me, stroking my hair soothingly.

I held his hand with my free one in my lap. I had chosen to get this done, to get the gang marks that Phoenix had actually allowed me to have when I'd asked him. A few months ago, and that would never have been the case.

"I'm getting nervous just watching," Giovanni said, sitting on the counter gorging on a packet of cookies.

"Not helping Gio," Gomez gave his leg a push. "You'll be fine Coral."

"Okay," I swallowed, staring at the heated knife edge.

"You *do* know it's going to hurt even after he's finished?" Severn mumbled to me.

"Yes Severn, I know."

"You clearly don't know when to be quiet, do you?" Eli gave him a look. "No wonder you cried when you got yours done."

"I didn't cry," Severn laughed as he ran his finger along his gang marks, making Giovanni and Gomez grin.

"Jeez Phoenix," Walter gave him a pained look. "Isn't it hot enough now?"

Phoenix looked over at him, "Almost. If it's not just right, it won't leave a good enough scar."

"Is it too late to back out?" I sent them a nervous grin.

Landon came behind me and massaged my shoulders, "It's not too bad, don't listen to cry baby Severn. He's the last born for a reason."

377

I sent Severn a smile and he shook his head at Landon.

"But it does hurt," Landon added in a lower voice. "Not gonna lie."

"Landon," I cried just as Phoenix turned off the lighter.

My stomach flipped over and Phoenix took hold of my hand delicately, turning it so that he could see the outside of my little finger.

"Ready?" Phoenix asked me, his eyes boring into mine.

Thoughts suddenly ran through my mind like a whirlwind and in the midst of it, it came to me that I wouldn't have been where I was now if Walter and I hadn't crossed paths that one night. I wouldn't have known the Simpsons and I wouldn't have discovered that the Santiagos were my relatives. All in all, I started with nothing and ended up with a bigger family than I could have ever prayed for. I looked forwards to what the future would bring, starting with becoming part of this family, the Simpson gang.

"Coral?" Walter murmured, his lips near my neck ready to try and distract me from the oncoming pain. "You ready?"

"Yes," I nodded. "I'm ready."

Liked the first story? The sequel to The Seven Deadly Simpson Brothers is now out! Look for Snakes and Splinters on the Amazon Kindle store!

ADJOA SARFO-BONSU

THE

SEVEN

DEADLY

Simpson Brothers
Memoirs

Want more of the Simpson Brothers? Their short book of memoirs is now available on the Amazon Kindle store!

Adjoa Sarfo-Bonsu (Jojo B) is a young adult who started this book on the day of her last A-Level exam and went on to complete it during her gap year. She loves travelling, starry skies, playing her ukulele and reading YA fiction.. She started writing aged five and hasn't stopped since (apart from during those grueling public exams).

For more of her works, including those of paranormal and teen fiction genres, visit her Wattpad page: wattpad.com/user/Jojo_B

To keep up to date with her current work, follow her Facebook page: https://www.facebook.com/Jojo-B-985895238114642/

Printed in Great Britain
by Amazon

7R00220